DISTANT
EARLY
WARNINGS

DISTANT EARLY WARNINGS

Canada's Best Science Fiction

Edited by
Robert J. Sawyer

FIC
SF
Dista

Robert J.
SAWYER
BOOKS

Distant Early Warnings
Compilation copyright © 2009 Robert J. Sawyer
Individual story copyrights on page 311 constitute a continuation of this copyright notice.

5 4 3 2 1

Robert J. Sawyer Books Published by
Red Deer Press
A Fitzhenry & Whiteside Company
www.reddeerpress.com

Edited for the Press by Robert J. Sawyer
Cover and text design by Karen Thomas, Intuitive Design International Ltd.
Cover art: James Beveridge
Printed and bound in Canada for Red Deer Press

Financial support provided by the Canada Council, and the Government of Canada through the Book Publishing Industry Development Program (BPIDP).

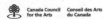

Library and Archives Canada Cataloguing in Publication
    Distant early warnings : Canada's best science fiction / edited by Robert
J. Sawyer.
ISBN 978-0-88995-438-0
    1. Science fiction, Canadian (English). 2. Short stories, Canadian
(English). 3. Canadian fiction (English)–21st century. I. Sawyer, Robert J.
PS8323.S3D57 2009   C813'.087620806   C2009-903059-4

Publisher Cataloging-in-Publication Data (U.S)
Distant early warnings : Canada's best science fiction / edited by Robert J. Sawyer.
[312] p. :   cm.
Includes works by: Julie E. Czerneda, Paddy Forde, James Alan Gardner, Nalo Hopkinson, Spider Robinson, Robert J. Sawyer, Karl Schroeder, Peter Watts, Robert Charles Wilson.
ISBN-13: 978-0-88995-438-0
1. Science fiction, Canadian. 2. Short stories, Canadian. 3. Canadian fiction — 21st century — Juvenile literature. I. Title.
[Fic] dc22   PZ5.D5783   2009

Dedication

For My Nieces

Melissa Jasmine Beckett
Megan Rose Beckett
Annabelle William Clink
Abigail Maria Clink

Canada's Future

CONTENTS

COPYRIGHT NOTICE, 2525

David Clink

INTRODUCTION

Thirty years ago, in 1979, John Robert Colombo published a massive anthology called *Other Canadas* in which he culled the best of four centuries of Canadian fantastic literature. That book was a watershed: it established definitively that Canada did have a tradition of science fiction and fantasy writing.

Thirty years ago I was nineteen; I wasn't part of that book. Except for Spider Robinson, none of the authors collected here were. Colombo planted a seed with *Other Canadas;* what you hold in your hands is—if I may be so bold—the cream of the crop that grew from that seed.

Recently, Jane Urquhart came under attack for *The Penguin Book of Canadian Short Stories,* which she edited. To her critics, some omissions seemed glaring, some inclusions dubious. So, given that I've subtitled this anthology *Canada's Best Science Fiction,* let me define my terms and explain my selection criteria.

By "Canada's," I mean authors who live in this country. I'm frankly tired of hearing Canadians trumpet that actors Pamela Anderson, Jim Carrey, and William Shatner are Canadians. No doubt they legally are, but they don't live or work here. Likewise, I've left out authors who have decided to call somewhere else their home—my point being that there's no need to reach beyond our borders to fill a book such as this.

"Best" is, I grant you, a subjective judgment—but let me point out an objective fact: every author in this book has either won or been nominated for the Hugo Award (the top international prize for science-fiction writing); or won or been nominated for the Nebula Award (the "Academy Award" of the science fiction field, given by the inaccurately named Science Fiction and Fantasy Writers of America, which has members in 23 countries, and has had a Canadian Region since 1993); or has won Canada's top SF book award, the Aurora.

(Specifically, Robinson, Sawyer, and Wilson have won the Hugo, and Forde, Gardner, Hopkinson, and Watts have been nominated for it; Robinson and Sawyer have won the Nebula, and Gardner and Hopkinson have been nominated for it; Czerneda, Hopkinson, Sawyer, Schroeder, and Wilson have won the best-novel Aurora, and Gardner, Robinson, and Watts have been nominated for it.)

By "science fiction," I mean the real thing: stories that reasonably extrapolate from known science; stories that might plausibly happen. Thirty years ago, when Colombo pulled together his anthology, he needed to combine SF with fantasy, horror, magic realism, and folk tales to make a book. Today, we can easily fill a book not just with real science fiction authored by Canadians, but with real science fiction by world-class writers who just happen to be Canadian.

In addition to the words in the subtitle, I decided to add one more criterion for inclusion in the present volume: Colombo had scoured 400 years of history for his selections; my goal is to demonstrate that there's a vigorous, active SF writing community in Canada *right now*. Every one of the stories in this book was first published in the Twenty-first Century. (This decision did have one sad effect: William Gibson, winner of the Hugo, the Nebula, and the Aurora Awards for best novel of the year, simply hasn't written any short fiction this millennium.)

There is, of course, a separate literary tradition of French Canadian science fiction. I commend to your attention particularly the work of Joël

Champetier, Yves Meynard, Esther Rochon, Daniel Sernine, Jean-Louis Trudel, and Élisabeth Vonarburg. Indeed, this book's official launch will be in August 2009 at Anticipation, the World Science Fiction Convention, which this year is being held in Montreal, and is featuring programming in both French and English. Élisabeth Vonarburg is the *Invitée d'honneur*, Julie E. Czerneda is the toastmaster, and John Robert Colombo—at last getting his due—is keynote speaker (the first one ever at a Worldcon) for the convention's academic track.

Distant Early Warnings isn't dedicated to John Colombo because my wife Carolyn Clink and I dedicated our earlier anthology, *Tesseracts 6*, part of the long-running series of Canadian science-fiction anthologies founded by the late, great Judith Merril, to him. But without John standing up and saying to the Canadian publishing world, and to Canada's academics, that there was such a thing as domestic Canadian SF, the field would not be nearly as rich and varied as it is today, and my hat is off to him.

This book isn't just intended for Canadian readers: after all, every single one of the authors included here has a significant international following (Paddy Forde is the one name that might not immediately ring a bell, since, to date, he has published only short fiction; however he has *twice* won the Analytical Laboratory Award from New York-based *Analog*, the world's top-selling English-language SF magazine, for best novella of the year).

And since we *are* also catering to readers outside Canada, and since I've gone on at length about the subtitle, let me say a word about the title. The Distant Early Warning Line—or DEW Line—was a string of radar stations in Canada's far north designed to detect incoming Soviet bombers during the Cold War. But the phrase also evocatively sums up what good science fiction does, providing us with advance reports of the wonders—and the dangers—that await us in all the myriad futures that might yet come to pass.

—Robert J. Sawyer
Mississauga, Ontario
April 2009

Paddy Forde is a Canadian-born science fiction writer who enjoyed an itinerant childhood, residing in Europe and the U.S. before settling permanently in southern Ontario. He has been a finalist for the Hugo Award, the Theodore Sturgeon Memorial Award, and the British Fantasy Award.

In addition to publishing fiction and non-fiction, he regularly gives talks on the craft of writing to groups ranging from grade-schoolers to graduate students, and he has led workshops for aspiring writers at the annual conference of the Canadian Authors Association as well as the World Science Fiction Convention.

He lives in Waterloo, Ontario, with his wife Kathleen and daughter Maeve, and is currently attempting the leap from novellas to novels.

"In Spirit," the piece that follows, won *Analog*'s Analytical Laboratory Award and was a finalist for the Hugo Award.

IN SPIRIT

Paddy Forde

The story I want to tell you now is the oldest story in the book. It's the defining story of humanity, and it goes like this:

A new tool comes along. Men see it in the world or in their minds. They strive to reach it, and finally attain it. They hold it aloft for a moment's wonder. Then they wield the new tool wisely or wantonly, and in so doing transform their society—their tribe, village, city, corporation, nation-state, or global institution, impacting the lives of people near and far, adding to the collective thrust of progress, propelling civilization itself on toward some wondrous new peak or some worrisome precipice ...

It's a familiar story, sure. But to date, no tool has transformed human society as drastically as Deep Projection technology. Not the first spark flinted for a fire, not the first ink put to page, not the first night lit by electricity, nor the first atom split inside a bomb. None of those breakthroughs were as transformative as N-Space Projection Technology, a.k.a., Deep Projection.

How can I be sure of this?

I'm sure because Deep Projection allows the impacts of past transformations to be *directly re-experienced*—by allowing the past to be *directly revisited* from the present by qualified volunteers, a group that included myself from the very start. I was there, at the Institute for Advanced Study in New Jersey back in 2030, when the pilot-test was performed. I was there, and I witnessed an opening being made for the very first time into the invisible dimensions that stitch together the fabric of our universe. I watched the first volunteer, a friend of mine, project across the unseen frames of reference that surround and suffuse our reality; with my own eyes I saw her enter a dimensional-plane that shared *its* reality with a precisely targeted moment in the past. You may or may not have heard that she was killed the following year, in riots at the Institute.

No matter what you've heard of our early efforts, do not be misinformed about our technology. Deep Projection was not "time travel" as anyone had foreseen it. It was more like stepping into a virtual-reality display of the past, a past that we cannot affect in any way ... At least, we believed that at the start. And for the most part it's perfectly true:

We cannot affect the past in any way that can change what's already happened.

It's also perfectly true that some of my fellow volunteers made the mistake of targeting turning-point moments in history that proved explosive to cultures founded upon those moments. Still more explosive were press stories about the Projection volunteers who returned from the past suffering strange side-effects, consumed by poisonous thoughts and emotions long put to rest, feelings they re-released into our present-day world.

Those press stories were true, too, though I myself never experienced anything so negative during Projection. In fact, some profoundly positive experiences compelled me to join what's being called New Spiritualism, a movement among Deep Projection users that focuses on "weak interactions" with the past. Before long I became an outspoken leader of this movement ...

Which is why I was called to testify at an international hearing on the global crisis that Deep Projection technology triggered, a hearing convened at The Hague in the fall of 2033. By that time a worldwide ban on the use of our technology had been decreed, and most Deep Projection centres were already shut down. Many had been ransacked by mobs and in some countries Projection facilities had been burned to the ground, the staff and volunteers that made it out of the fires alive arrested or worse ... I was one of the lucky ones. Lucky enough to avoid being lynched, and lucky enough to be asked to present the first case study on our technology at the international hearing.

Even the World Court was curious to hear about my one-of-a-kind case study—rumours had been circulating for months about an unusual group of Americans who'd approached me, seeking assistance for the innovative application of Deep Projection they'd come up with. The Court saw my story as a potential antidote to all the media horror stories concerning what scientists had seen or experienced in the remote past.

When I walked to the podium in that great Court, I began by stating emphatically that Deep Projection was not a dangerous technology in and of itself. It was not, after all, a weapon. It was merely a kind of transportation device. So whether it was used for good or for ill depended on us.

Then I shared with the members of the World Court what I'm about to share with you: the case of a voluntary Projection made by an inmate of Lewisburg Federal Penitentiary in Pennsylvania.

What follows is adapted from the inmate's deposition ...

— • —

Raed was in his thirtieth year of incarceration at Lewisburg when they made him the offer to participate.

It happened on the day of his annual Psych Review, and the instant he entered the review room, Raed knew something big was up. Three new faces were visible on the penitentiary's Psych panel. And Lewisburg's senior psychologist—old, cold, and silver-haired—appeared to have misplaced his usual impassivity. Today he actually looked a bit harried ... Besides, there were a couple of lawyers present in the room, which was very odd. Raed hadn't been visited by a lawyer since back in 2014.

"Please sit down."

A guard ushered Raed to the lone chair facing the table of psychologists. He lowered himself onto the chair, feeling small, even though he was taller than anyone on the five-man panel; he could see right over their heads to the mirrored observation pane in the wall behind them. Raed was careful not to look directly into the mirrored pane, not because he was afraid of being watched—after thirty years at Lew, he'd feel out of sorts if he *wasn't* watched—but because he didn't want to see how much he'd aged in Lew. There were no mirrors back in his cell ...

"Something different on the agenda today, Raed," the senior psychologist said, managing to sound both doubtful and impatient. "Like to start by informing you of an assessment made by our medical staff." Old Silver-hair held up a slate plugged into the table, read from it: "Raed, you were twenty-four years old when given over to the supervision of this penitentiary. With the supplements we feed you and with the fitness routine you've elected to maintain, the prognosis is you'll have another fifty years with us here at Lew."

That simple assessment slammed into Raed. He blinked at his silver-haired foe, feeling disoriented, drawn out of the "safe-houses" Silver-hair claimed Raed had in his head. *Fifty* more years!

He hardly heard what the two sharply dressed lawyers were trying to tell him.

"... as your court-appointed representation. We're here to tell you about a petition made by a group of interested citizens."

"What petition?"

"It concerns an experimental rehab program," one of them continued. "Might be looked upon favourably by the Federal Board later, if you agree to undergo it."

Raed suddenly laughed, something he did so rarely it hurt his throat a little. "The Board might *favour* me," he retorted. "By reducing one of my life sentences?"

Raed was serving one thousand back-to-back life terms. Convicted of being an accomplice to one of the most heinous crimes in recorded history, he'd avoided the death penalty only because his "prior knowledge of the crime" was never proven conclusively. Nevertheless, the evidence against Raed was strong enough to win him the longest prison sentence ever handed out by a United States court. So Raed was *never* going to be released, re-introduced to society.

Extending him an offer of rehab was a ridiculous gesture.

"See this program through, and who can say what's possible?" The lawyer shrugged. "For now, two things are directly on the table. One: an opportunity to see your biological daughter."

Again Raed blinked at them, feeling his face reddening, stunned into apoplectic silence. When he'd entered Lew he'd left a wife and a three-year-old daughter behind. And the last time lawyers had come to see him was back in Raed's thirteenth year here, when he'd been served divorce papers from Haifa *and* papers disowning him as a parent from Basma, his daughter. Basma would have just been old enough to sign those papers, that year. Had she changed her mind, now that she was in her thirties?

"Also," the lawyer went on, "an opportunity to enter the world beyond your prison, in a limited and—well, unusual way." The lawyer said this as though he didn't quite believe it.

Certainly Raed couldn't quite believe it. He hadn't seen the outside since his trial ended. The thought unnerved him, for he had no idea what the world was like anymore. "Who made the offer?" Raed managed to ask.

Now the second lawyer spoke up. "A group of citizens who have a certain relationship with you, but do not wish to be identified."

Raed knew just what group the lawyer was referring to. He sighed, "I need to think about it."

After the review was over and the guards took him back to his home in Lew Cell #1, Raed found he couldn't *stop* thinking about the astonishing offer made to him. Raed knew the group that had petitioned for the offer pretty well:

An Arab-American Rights group that checked in on him over the years, to ensure he wasn't abused in the Penitentiary simply because of the noto-riety of his conviction. In the occasional letter he'd received from the group every couple of years, they emphasized Raed *must* not advertise their low-level connection with him. They threatened to stop making inquiries on his behalf to the Lew administration if he failed to maintain their privacy.

Raed understood the group wasn't "making inquiries on his behalf" because they were concerned about him, per se. Their concern—especially during the early years—was that Raed might take his own life in prison and become a martyr to fanatics in the far corners of the world.

Raed had no pent-up desire to become a martyr, and he was not con-sidered a serious candidate for suicide—although, due to his uniquely lengthy sentence, he was permanently assigned to the suicide-watch list at Lew. If ever there was a prisoner who had nothing to look forward to, it was surely Raed.

But now he might be a research volunteer for a new one-of-a-kind rehab program.

He might get to see his daughter, they'd told him.

He might get to walk in the outside world for short stretches.

And for long stretches he might get to leave Cell #1, the largest and most expensive cell in the Penitentiary, where Raed resided alone under constant guard and camera surveillance.

After thirty years the cell was a home to him. Raed had taped up a pic-ture of soaring desert dunes on one wall, a vista of the Moon over the ocean on another. He'd nursed a dozen plants up round the tiny window over-looking the courtyard—a window Raed could see out of, but no one could see in through. He'd even built up a modest bookshelf, though none of the books dated from this century. And there were no newspapers allowed in here; there was no television. Raed's media exposure was censored from the start of his incarceration "in order to prevent continued political inflam-mation of the prisoner."

Nevertheless, in the early years Raed protested this political censorship of news by cutting himself off from *all* news, *all* knowledge of outside events. He'd withdrawn from modern civilization completely the day he set foot in Cell #1. And why not? Raed had lost *everything*. So he restricted himself to reading older texts, like the *Alif Layla Wa Layla,* the Thousand and One Nights. Sheherazade, it turned out, provided a durable escape for a man sentenced to spend ten thousand and one nights in a single room. At his own insistence, none of the books on Raed's shelf were published after the "day of infamy" he'd been convicted of participating in:

The day the Lew staff still referred to as "9/11."

In the early years, Raed's psychologists hadn't been bothered by his self-censorship. But after the first decade they changed their minds, complaining that he was retreating too far from reality. That's when the psychologists began to talk about "safe-rooms" in his mind, about a "labyrinth of rooms" he was building to escape not just from imprisonment but from himself. Raed snorted when he first heard this metaphor—but even then he'd suspected the description was all too apt.

An internal labyrinth.

A long chain of rooms within rooms to hide in at the back of his mind.

— • —

After three very long and sleepless nights spent reflecting on his position—something Raed rarely ever did—he broke down and asked what was involved in the experimental program. He was told it involved a new technology, but much of the program itself would be left up to him.

A month later, Raed was given a sandwich bag instead of an evening meal; was fitted with a monitoring restraint collar that would sedate him instantly if he tried anything; was ushered into an armoured van without windows; and was taken out of Lewisburg Federal Penitentiary for the first time since he'd been brought into it.

— • —

The armored van sounded as though it had a police escort. Raed heard the escort leading the way for about an hour before the van stopped. He guessed they'd gone about as far as Reading, Pennsylvania, might be. He heard the driver talking with security guards. And heard something else, a muffled sound familiar from his trial: the sound of protestors shouting at the van. He was astonished to think the public had found out where he was being brought, had gotten up in the middle of the night to come here themselves—but Raed wasn't surprised that people still harboured so much hate for him. On the rare occasions he gave interviews, Raed caught the wariness in the journalists' eyes, and caught them glancing at him like some kind of ghoul that had stepped from the pages of history.

The van parked. Raed emerged in a loading dock, and was brought under guard to an empty conference room. Moments later, the same trio of young psychologists who'd put in a surprise appearance at his annual review in Lewisburg entered the room, followed by a pair of middle-aged men introduced to him as "senior researchers." The two researchers began outlining their experimental program, describing the new technology Raed would be required to use ...

Raed listened to them, briefly astounded, then disappointed. "Projection" through a "dimensional fold" to a "targeted moment in the past"? Raed's mind began doing back flips trying to guess what was *really* going on here. Had the legal climate in the United States changed? Had new forces declared Raed should be put through some punishment other than confinement?

He told the researchers flat out he did not believe them. Travelling to the past was impossible, he didn't care how many decades had gone by since he'd been in the outside world.

So they took him down to the main "Projection" floor, brought him into a room dominated by a big spherical cage. There had to be a thousand shining yellow bars to the cage, most of them semicircular arcs, arranged so the cage had a pair of openings into it. And hanging in the cage's centre was a body harness. Raed examined it suspiciously, wondering what exactly these men were trying to trick him into ... All the cage's arcing yellow bars were studded with cones that pointed inward, toward the harness suspended by a dozen blue coil-cables.

"Questions, Raed?" one of the psychologists asked him.

"What are the curtains for?"

The long back wall of the "Projection" room was concealed—to hide a viewing gallery?

But then one of guards who'd accompanied Raed from Lew drew back the curtains, revealing a long pane of Plexiglas that separated the room with the cage from—

A much larger room with a hundred identical cages that were *occupied by suspended people.*

At least, the suspended occupants *appeared* to be people. Raed stepped up to the Plexiglas pane, pressed his face against it, uncertain whether he was seeing an image televised across the pane or a real room on the other side of the pane.

The arena-sized room was real.

The hundred-odd yellow cages seemed real.

But all the suspended people looked blurry, far off, fake, like projected images. Most of the image-people were moving, some running in their cages, a few leaping and rolling in mid-air.

"Those people aren't real," Raed said over his shoulder, unable to turn from the pane. He was mesmerized ... Suddenly one of the closer cages flashed with light, and the false floating image-person inside was instantly transformed into a clear-as-can-be jumpsuit-wearing woman, a real-as-can-be woman who stepped out of the yellow cage, a little shaky on her feet but otherwise not visibly worse for the experience. She began conferring with a three-man team clustered round display desks adjacent to her big yellow cage.

"I'm supposed to believe that woman was ... 'Projecting.'" Raed shook his head, noticing now there was a separate team for each harnessed and hanging "time traveller." If this was all a hoax, it was an elaborate one.

"Volunteers like her call it ghosting,'" someone behind him said. "You'll see why if you decide to follow our program, and volunteer to try it for yourself."

The "volunteers" in the cages beyond the Plexiglas pane were *not* other prisoners, according to the researchers. The volunteers were mostly historians and cultural anthropologists, a handful of students and others who routinely "ghosted back to the past" from this facility round-the-clock. Raed's researcher-guides claimed the yellow "Projection" cages allowed people to experience the *physical reality* of the past without fully being part of it.

But Raed knew that it was all a trick of some kind. If those volunteers were experiencing any sort of Projection, it was the sort of computer-fabricated reality the outside world used to call—what was the word? A *simulation.*

That was the only thing Projection could be, the only thing Raed could bring himself to believe.

— • —

The rehab psych team seemed prepared for Raed's disbelief.

For the rest of the night they cloistered Raed and his two Lew guards in the otherwise-empty conference room, so that Raed could browse through "holeos"—interactive 3-D training videos. The holeos began with a list of weird implications of "classical quantum theory": how sub-atomic particles appeared out of nowhere and then disappeared;, how such particles could exist in many places at once; the development of a mathematics that suggested particles were boring between dimensions ...

Apparently Raed's rehab programmers knew he'd been exposed to such strange concepts before, while studying for his certificate in electronics.

Of course they knew. Raed's electronics training came out at the trial because his certificate got him a position with the airline, a low-level job that allowed him to scrutinize airport security ... Anyway, one of Raed's electronics courses *had* touched on quantum theory—mainly for the students continuing on into cell-phone or computer technology. Raed *hadn't* understood the half-day "quantum overview" his college course included.

According to the holeos, Raed wasn't the only one who hadn't understood. Most physicists chose to treat the theory simply as a convenient way to calculate and predict the positions of particles, rather than believe the world could *really* be riddled by multiple dimensions. The holeo invited Raed to imagine Copernicus and Galileo choosing to ignore the overall implication of their new way of calculating and predicting the positions of the planets—and refusing to believe the sun could *really* be the centre of the solar system.

Raed didn't see why it was important for him to know or imagine any of this. But he didn't want anyone to think he was backing out of the program; he didn't want to be driven back to Lew, not just yet. And he was an expert at biding his time. Patience and playing the game were the essential survival skills of a long-term prisoner.

So Raed patiently sat through a tedious holeo-guided history of Macroquantum, which elevated the theory from the sub-atomic realm up to far larger scales. He listened patiently to young scientists attacking the notion that "multiple dimensions collapsed into a single dimension" whenever a human observer happened along—how could a theory of matter seriously include human consciousness in a central role? He patiently examined 3-D renderings of the first machines built to scan "N-space," a theoretical realm that suffused the visible universe with all manner of strange dimensions.

But when the holeos moved on to the topic of "forces experienced during Projection into N-space," Raed must have groaned aloud.

Because his researcher-hosts came in and turned off the holeos. They didn't seem disappointed; perhaps they'd thought he'd give up on their theoretical material much sooner.

— • —

The next couple of hours of training involved watching an old pre-Millennium black-and-white movie that was supposed to give Raed an idea of what it would be like to be "projected" to a city he could do little but wander through.

The setting was Berlin, and the city was revealed through the eyes of two angels wandering among the living—angels who resembled two forlorn-looking German men in stylish grey greatcoats. The citizens of Berlin couldn't see them, but the two sombre angels could see and hear people talking in the world around them. They could even hear the thoughts of people—although in those parts of the film, the soundtrack reverted to German, so Raed couldn't hear what the citizens of Berlin were thinking. He could only tell from the tone of their untranslated thoughts whether they were sad or happy, angry or afraid ...

After it was over, one researcher sat down with him, described the Projection experience as a lot like being a ghost lurking in an otherwise real world. Projection volunteers could see the physical environment of the past perfectly, but could not be seen by people in that past.

"Because," the researcher laboriously explained, "light only flows 'one way' across dimensions. It flows forward from the past, but cannot flow back into the past."

Raed nodded dutifully, wondering why these people were trying so hard to make him believe in an impossibility ...

An hour before dawn he was hustled back to the armoured van waiting in the loading dock, handed printed materials to review if he wanted to, whisked out through the unseen but audible protestors, then returned to Lew to spend the day resting in his cell. Which was fine by him. Stepping back through the door of Cell #1 felt like waking from a dream. He didn't feel so out of sorts here, so confused and vulnerable.

But he couldn't sleep. The thought that he'd just been outside the penitentiary had opened up a crack inside his thinking. He still didn't know what to make of his night out. So much scientific argument just to convince him of something untrue?

Eventually he gave up on sleep altogether, began looking over the strange explanations

in the support material they'd given him, looking for loopholes, looking for the truth behind their lies. Raed used to be an imaginative man. But imagination was not a good thing to have in prison and he felt very rusty. Long-forgotten thoughts stirred up, faded memories of his teenage struggle to master challenging Western concepts—an education paid for by the Organization, the money funnelled to Raed through his cousins Nazir and Sayf, both of whom died back on 9/11 ...

The truth about "Deep Projection" finally dawned on Raed. Now he saw through the rehab-programmers' game, and saw how to get what *he* wanted:

A chance to see his daughter Basma, whom Raed hadn't seen since she was three years old.

With that reward firmly in mind, Raed finally fell asleep.

— • —

The next night he was again driven out of the Appalachians to the Deep Projection complex. And again he heard protesters out in force as the van went through the complex's gates. The van's walls muffled whatever was being shouted at him ...

Waiting for him in the same conference room as before were the three psychologists and the two so-called senior researchers—his "Projection Parole Board," for all intents and purposes. These five men could approve his participation in the program or send him packing for the rest of his life.

"Questions, Raed?"

He held up the printed materials he'd brought back with him. "Is it really necessary for me to know any of this before I can project?" Raed already knew the answer but was curious to see how they'd try to rationalize it to him.

A compact researcher with close-cropped bristles instead of hair took the printouts back from Raed. "You reviewed all this?"

"Yes."

"Well then, let's see where last night's holeo lessons broke off ..." He flipped to the final pages. "Ah yes: N-space forces and the role mass plays in them. Complex stuff—but crucial to understanding what you'll encounter during Projection, how you can move around, and so on."

An evasive answer that simply pressed ahead with the logic crafted to convince him. Raed knew that was the ultimate purpose of all this preparatory theory:

To make him believe "Projection" really could show him the past, *so that the psychological benefits of the rehab would take effect.*

The science was all part of the rehab, part of the game these psychologists were playing with him. He recognized their bag of tricks well enough.

But Raed could play the game better than anyone. After all, he'd lived in Brooklyn for seven years and played the game of being an ordinary resident without anyone suspecting his deep-seated separateness. So he would play along with tonight's game, stay on the move inside his head, hop from room to room through the labyrinth until he came out as the winner ...

This time the compact senior researcher with the bristle-hair remained behind when the others left. The man introduced himself as Francis Drummond, a volunteer himself during the earliest test Projections. He seemed committed to helping Raed understand the hard stuff.

"Get through an hour with me, and you'll get to project for the rest of the night," Francis promised as he began summoning images onto the conference table's display surface: the Moon; a mountain; a building; a metal barricade. According to Francis, each of the displayed objects was massive enough to exert forces "into many N-space dimensions." But for objects that weren't massive—a foam mattress, even a pane of glass—projection volunteers could thrust "their ghostly hands" right through them, if they were patient enough.

Raed nodded, knowing all this information was being trotted out to explain away the defects of the *simulation* he'd be Projecting into. "Will I be able to walk through walls, like the German angels in that black-and-white movie?" he asked, getting into the spirit of the game.

"If it's the wall of a tent, sure. There's a kind of 'tingly give' when you step through thin structures. But you can't step through ordinary walls of concrete or steel, no. All comes back to mass and massive structure ..."

Over the course of two hours with Francis, Raed struggled to keep on top of the complex concepts paraded before him. Francis even told him about the big surprise from the earliest test Projections:

"We discovered that life of sufficient mass transmits a kind of resonance into a few dimensions; we call these 'biomass signatures.' Volunteers pick up these signatures when animals of a certain size wander close to them."

How would they simulate *that*, Raed wondered. "That include people?"

Francis nodded. "Conscious animals exert the strongest signatures. Please don't interpret this as anything 'psychic'—individual thoughts are far too fleeting to be sensed. But strong emotions can last a long time in the forebrain, fill the hindbrain, contort the face, change the way we walk, permeate our muscle-tissues. Massive, you might say."

Francis seemed to be trying to re-awaken Raed's mind as much as teach him about Projection. And that was all right with Raed. Because if he was going to go through their rehab program, and notice all the things they'd want him to notice, and win the reward they'd promised him, he'd need to be on the ball ...

"Well, that about covers it," Francis finally announced, shutting off the conference table. "Any last questions?"

Raed sensed this was a test he must pass. "You said gravity has 'two-way transdimensionality?'"

"Yes." Francis seemed pleased. "It's a strong-weak interaction. Gravity from the past is exerted strongly onto the N-space fold you'll be in, and your own mass exerts itself weakly onto the past—"

"Doesn't adding my mass to the past *change* the past? I thought paradoxes were outlawed by Macroquantum." Raed's rusty brain was beginning to work again. He wanted to show this clever man he'd been listening, and he would catch flaws in his logic, if Francis wasn't careful.

"Paradoxes *are* ruled out. According to Macroquantum, people who project through N-space to the past *already visited that past,* the first time around, so to speak. So their mass was accounted for, and their presence won't change anything. They can only go back and weakly interact because they were there all along ..."

"I understand you perfectly."

"Excellent." Francis stood up. "I'll send in a medic who'll take you downstairs, get you hooked up to the Projection cage."

The man strode out of the room.

And Raed waited, feeling out of his element, out of his cell, completely out of sorts. He glanced at the guards watching him from their shadowy corner of the room. He glanced at a bookshelf against the conference room wall. He took down a text, glanced at the title on the cover: *Creating Transient N-space Intersections with Past Time.*

A book about a false bunch of theories? The book's spine was cracked worse than Raed's copy of Sheherazade, as though it had been thumbed through many times.

The crack deep inside his thinking hadn't gone away. It was still down there, wedged wider by all the information they'd fed him. And now a hint of fear was seeping up through that crack ... Because Raed knew what his rehab-programmers were up to, he could guess their "precisely targeted destination," oh yes.

They intended to project him back to 9/11.

— • —

A burly male medic arrived, led Raed and his two guards down to the same curtained chamber off the main Projection arena, where the guards removed his restraint collar. The medic explained that the chamber's Projection cage was the only one isolated in the facility, set up just for Raed.

Then he helped Raed don the harness, which was worn under his clothes, against his body so the "trodes could record biofeedback. After strapping it on, Raed got into a magnetic jumpsuit. The medic told him he could put his clothes on over top of the jumpsuit.

So he did, fingers trembling as he re-buttoned his shirt ...

The pair of lawyers who'd first appeared at his review back in Lew suddenly re-appeared with a slate for him to sign. They informed Raed about the protests being held outside the facility. The protests were *not* about him, they said; no one outside knew he was in here.

"What are they protesting?"

Apparently the people outside felt Deep Projection technology was too dangerous to be used. The lawyers assured Raed no volunteer who'd undergone Projection had been *physically* harmed by the process itself; it was *emotional* damage that was the real risk. The potent "biomass signatures" people gave off in the past could be quite corrosive.

"That's the only danger?"

One of the lawyers told him, "There's a movement called "New Spiritualism" that contends the transdimensional interaction can be positive. Some New Spiritualists are sponsoring your rehab program, by the way ..."

Raed nodded to himself, seeing more of the truth peeking out from behind their lies. The protestors outside were opposed to the *simulations* this technology produced. And now Raed had been brought here—because if they could convince *him* the simulations were real and use them to help him rehabilitate, wouldn't that be a big coup for a beleaguered technology?

He signed the slate held out to him. Then the lawyers asked the medic to strap a special "ripcord" over Raed's clothing.

"Pull this," the medic told him, "and you'll instantly shut down the cage-frame and return to the present."

The lawyers reiterated that Raed could back out of a projection at any time, but warned him that a ripcord shut-down would mean a permanent withdrawal from the program. As they left the chamber, his personal

Projection team came in. An Asian senior researcher, a boyish-looking controls operator, and, finally, a woman psychologist—a Muslim psychologist, no less, wearing a black cotton burqa that kept her hidden and proper. Didn't they realize Raed was no longer a devout?

As Raed was introduced by his guards, the woman's wide-set black eyes looked coldly over the slit veil at him ... No doubt she'd been sent by the Arab-American Rights group who'd petitioned to get him into this crazy rehab program.

The team quickly took their positions, the medic helping Raed through the yellow bars into the cage, then pulling down the blue coil-cables and magnetically latching them to anchor-spots on the jumpsuit beneath Raed's clothes. The moment the medic stepped out of the cage, the operators powered up the blue cables, which re-coiled, hoisting Raed comfortably into mid-air. He tried to calm his breathing, listened to the chatter around him:

"Got five hours."

"Time for, say, ten projections?"

"Aim for ten, minimum."

"Curtains open or closed?"

Raed realized this was addressed to him. "Open." He didn't care if anyone looked in; he wanted to look out. So the curtains were drawn aside, and Raed peered at the hundred-odd cages across the main floor, which were again all occupied by volunteers, some in jumpsuits, some in tracksuits, some in regular clothes. Presumably this facility was packed day and night. He heard something below him, realized the Muslim psychologist had stepped into the cage.

"Your program for tonight involves a number of Projections, all of them focused on a primary time-locus—"

"I know where you're sending me," he told her. "As punishment," he added.

The psychologist shook her veiled head. "It's up to you what you get out of the Projection experience. If you want the offer made to you upheld, you'll have to stick the program out ... On the other hand, if you decide you no longer want to continue—" She indicated the ripcord round his waist.

"I'm not afraid," Raed said to her.

He was curious, though. Raed hadn't thought much about 9/11 in nearly two decades. All by itself the mind sprouted rooms within rooms to closet away what wasn't needed. And closeted in the depths of Raed's internal maze was the twenty-four-year-old who'd aided his cousins Nazir and Sayf. He no longer had any connection to that Raed; but he was a little curious to see how history looked on the events of that day ... The medic began strapping a lightweight breather-mask round Raed's neck. Would it secrete some kind of hallucinatory gas?

"In case we project you to the wrong coordinates," the woman psychologist explained, still standing below him. "You'd pass out in certain environments, but there's little chance of real physical harm. Anyway, you can use the microphone on the breather to call out to us during Projection. We'll hear you. The people of the past *won't* hear you, remember. Sound can only travel one way across the dimensional fold, just like light. Now brace yourself," she warned him. "The world of the past's going to feel both startlingly real and surreal."

With a twirl of black cotton she quickly slipped out of the cage. And within seconds the inward-angled cones on all the arcing yellow bars began to focus shimmering beams on him, opening an "N-space fold" around him. Raed blinked through the bars, met the hard eyes of the young Muslim psychologist, still refusing to believe ... Until the woman began to blur, and shift, and slide off to one side, and everything around Raed swirled into a tunnel of light—

— • —

A light *thump,* and the tunnel of light focused into a tubular space. Raed's eyes adjusted, recognized an oh-so-familiar interior:

He was inside a large, mostly empty 767 passenger jet sitting on a runway.

Raed had dropped down into one of the rear-most seats from mid-air, as the "gravity" of the simulation took hold of him. It *was* a simulation, wasn't it? He blinked at his surroundings, seeing every detail of the seat-back ahead of him and the belts and buckles lying on the empty seats beside him, the empty row across the aisle, the magazines and folded-up meal tables all *perfectly* visible, his surroundings *absolutely* real no matter which way he looked. *Light has a strong multidimensionality,* Francis had said, *but such negligible mass it can only cross one way, from the past to the present ...*

But then Raed noticed he was sinking *right through* the padded seat cushion beneath him, he could feel himself bumping down against the hard steel frame *inside* the seat itself. Flaws in the simulation, just as he'd suspected! He let out a sigh of relief, and watched his body rebound slightly, settle into place almost on the surface of the seat cushion visible between his legs. It was a strange sensation, but Raed was sure it was controlled by the coiled harness cables back in the Projection cage he had to be still hanging in ... From a great distance away, too far off and far too soft to be real, the whining sound of jet engines powering up. More like a whisper, when the sound should have been screamingly loud in his ears—another flaw! Raed felt he was hearing a faulty soundtrack in a movie theatre too big for the speakers.

But then he recalled the materials he'd been given to study: sounds would be strange; nothing would be loud enough to make out unless Raed was standing close to the source.

Slowly the 767 went through a 30-degree turn on the runway, and the quality of light spilling through windows across the aisle made it clear to Raed this was an early morning flight. His heart began to beat faster. He leaned over the seat beside him, peered out the oval window. His plane appeared to be taxiing toward a main runway, and the airport was—Logan International, Boston.

No doubt this was supposed to be the fateful day. Raed struggled to get up, wanting to see if he could see Nazir or Sayf seated in the rows ahead, biding their time until the 767 had taken off. But no, something was wrong, the weird far-off whining of the engines was powering down, shutting off altogether. Raed tried to get to his feet, struggling with the distorted friction of this simulation world, all the while clinging to the fact that he was really clinging to a harness in the air somewhere ... In the seat ahead of him, a passenger was sleeping, one arm thrown across his lap, digital wristwatch visible:

9:13 AM.

If this was one of those infamous flights, then shouldn't the plane already be in the air instead of stuck on the tarmac? Plopping back down in the empty window seat, Raed pressed his face to the strangely rubbery glass of the window, caught sight of other motionless planes lined up on another runway ... And remembered:

On the morning of 9/11, all flights in the country had been grounded shortly after 9 AM.

They'd projected him back aboard *the wrong plane*. Raed released a breath he hadn't realized he'd been holding.

But if he was merely in a simulation, under the control of the two Projection operators, then shouldn't this *be* one of the planes that had left Boston an hour or so earlier?

Raed moved back to the aisle seat, saw a stewardess walking toward him from the front of the plane, looking dazed and a little distraught as she touched passengers she passed on the shoulder, and spoke soundlessly to them. Raed heard nothing at all until she was quite close, then he heard the stewardess say to the passenger in the seat directly ahead of him:

"All flights are cancelled."

Her voice sounded too loud, and more than a little hoarse, as though she were on the edge of anger or tears. She passed Raed without looking at him, but her knee brushed his hand, resting on the hard plastic aisle arm—

ANGUISH–DISBELIEF

Both emotions flooded out of the passing stewardess and into Raed, the potency of his brief physical contact with her a kind of pain he'd never experienced before. He recoiled from the aisle, clutching his hand as though he'd been burned, and filled with a certainty that the stewardess had just been informed about the planes striking their New York targets.

For an instant Raed was clutched by the fear that he was *not* in a simulation ...

Murmurs were rising from the surrounding seats:

"What'd she mean?"

"Know what's going on?"

Raed rubbed at his hand, wondering whether stewardesses had actually acted this way on the real "day of infamy." Two rows ahead and across the aisle a man was listening to his cell phone, a look of shock dawning on his face. And in the aisle seat three rows ahead a woman was standing, turning, walking slowly toward the back, moving as though she had arthritis even though she was only in her thirties. *She* looked directly at Raed when she came alongside him; she reached down to Raed's shoulder but, before she could touch him, the woman's arm elongated, slid away, there was a whirl of light, and—

— • —

Raed was back in the Deep Projection facility, hanging in the centre of the Projection cage, groggy and disoriented and fighting a desire to remove the harness, exit the cage, ask to be returned to his cell in Lew. The veiled psychologist stepped through the bars beside him, gave him a thumbs-up to show his bioreadings were acceptable, wanted a thumbs-up in return— Raed was supposed to signal if he was up to continuing, ready for the next part of the program.

He didn't give her a thumbs-up. Instead he lifted his breather, gasped to her, "Thought you said the people of the past couldn't see me?"

"They can't," she agreed, tapping a note onto the slate she was holding.

The cage operators called out that the target-coordinates were recalibrated, the cage was ready for a second "folding." Was Raed ready for a second "ghosting?"

"They can't see you," she repeated, covering her veiled mouth with her hand to remind Raed to refit his breather. "And don't worry," she assured him, "you'll get used to ghosting after another few tries." She slipped sideways out between the bars again, before turning back and adding, "You won't be harmed, Raed."

Who did she think he was? Raed wasn't afraid of a computer simulation. His hand still tingled from his brushed contact with the stewardess, but it was all a trick of the 'trodes lining his harness straps, all just a trick of the mind. He'd been conned into overreacting by all the holeo material they'd made him study, that's all. He was playing the game so well he was beginning to con himself.

But they could *not* send him into the past.

And he was *not* ready to give up. The thought of being driven back to Lew was deeply comforting—Cell #1 was the only place Raed felt safe, felt under his own control. But Cell #1 was also a cage more frightening than this cage, and, after leaving it two nights in a row, Raed knew the crack inside him was yawning wider. He sensed the new need pouring through, throwing the balance of his desire in the direction of continuing these trips out of Lew, no matter what simulation they put him through.

The psychologist gave him the thumbs-up again, and in response Raed balled up the hand that had touched the stewardess into a defiant fist, said into his breather-microphone, "I am ready."

And said to himself, *Only a simulation*, as the universe around him shifted, slid, swirled into the tunnel of light—

— • —

—which widened to become a vast, impossibly wounded sky. It was the sky of some inhuman world wreathed in shadow, pierced only by shafts of weird blue light, and threatened by thunderclouds that coiled not with water but with ash that rained down on a dead land.

Another *bump* as Raed fell back onto a patch of ground littered with jagged concrete shrapnel and twisted piping, which did not cut him; he barely sensed any sharp edges. Pushing himself up off this rubble was extremely difficult. Raed struggled to stay on his feet, see where he was. All round him lay a spaghetti-panorama of tangled wiring, twisted metal braces, giant steel girders scattered like logs, sections of shattered furniture—and *paper.* Crests and swirls of scattered pages, documents jammed between wiring, sticking out from shards of wood. Suddenly a nearby swell of paper shot skyward as steam vented from the unsteady, uneven landscape. Raed had projected to a place where some strange war had been going on forever, by the looks of things—a place stranger than any he'd seen before coming to America. Far stranger than any part of Beirut, where he'd lived for a time as a small boy.

Raed knew the name of this impossible place.

"Ground Zero," they'd called it.

He appeared to be standing on the island of Manhattan, on the spot where the Twin Towers had stood—and stood not long before he'd arrived, if the roiling sky was rendered accurately. This time he seemed to have missed 9/11 not by an hour but by maybe a day. Smoke still hugged the rubble-strewn ground like patches of fog; distant figures drifted in and out of this fog, mostly firemen and policemen; a few were using search-dogs, trying to sniff out victims trapped under the rubble.

Raed himself smelled nothing. Not the smoke, not the scent of jet fuel that should have filled the air. Not even the singed-cinder aroma from the ongoing fires in the distance. *Thirty years, and they still can't program smells into computer simulations,* he told himself ... But that was just his mind trying to deny what he was seeing: an inconceivably detailed devastation that extended for blocks in every direction, and a too-huge-to-fake sky above, drawing Raed's eyes up through bluish curls of smoke to the heavens. Out under the sky!

His soul had yearned for open sky for three long decades, but now that he seemed to be standing beneath one, he felt it was too awesome, too exposed, too heavy, too terrible to bear.

So he turned his eyes down to the tangled ground, began to pick his way over to the only source of noise close enough to hear: a soft hissing from beyond the mist-shrouded rubble directly behind him. Clambering back over a filing cabinet that looked like it might have fallen from the moon—it was flattened like a stomped soda can—Raed started slowly across the damp ground toward this soft sound, presumably a very loud sound "in reality." Keeping his balance was complicated by the fact that he kept plunging through an insubstantial blanket of papers and paper ash, soot and concrete dust, getting his feet stuck in crevices concealed beneath this visible surface-blanket ... Yet leaving no footprints in it, disturbing nothing he fell against, moving nothing he grabbed onto for support. At one point he blinked down at a pair of eye glasses, both lenses starred, crushed underfoot—

But not by him. Whoever had worn them was not *his* victim, no. Raed could sense the old defence rising to his lips, could hear his younger self saying it in a courtroom long ago. *America puffed itself too high in those two towers. Anyone trapped inside them was trapped there by America alone ... They weren't my victims, no.* The old defence, the denial he'd dropped somewhere along the way, abandoned in an outer room of the labyrinth in Raed's mind, many rooms away from the middle-aged man he was now. It all seemed so long ago, too long ago to feel clear on the subject.

Nothing seemed clear about 9/11, especially not here, not now.

But then a breeze he couldn't feel began clearing the mists ahead, revealing a looming shape just a few feet from him: the side of a huge fire truck, its designation ash-smeared but still visible. *Tower Pumper No. 146.*

Raed manoeuvred round the front of the pumper truck, dragged himself onto an adjacent mound of debris to get a better view of things. He was now level with the top of the truck's cab, and he could see the mist was coming from a hose being aimed out of a crow's nest atop the pumper. A giant fireman in a soot-stained yellow coat stood in this crow's nest like an indomitable statue, soaking down flames in a half-collapsed structure sixty or seventy feet away. A second fireman lay face-down further along the roof of the pumper, obviously exhausted.

Only two firemen for a truck this size?

It had to be less than twenty-four hours after 9/11; otherwise Ground Zero would be swarming with volunteer firefighters from out of state, even out of the country, if Raed recalled correctly. From his debris hilltop he turned and surveyed the entire scene, which was opening up as the imperceptible breeze cleared more spray and smoke and steam away.

Raed seemed to be stranded in some imaginary rendering of the end of the world. Multi-story sections of the towers lay strewn about like so many titanic accordions, while in the distance, Manhattan's financial canyons were on fire in a hundred spots. Closer at hand the ground was draped with stretches of outer tower walling, glittering and ribbed, resembling enormous metallic mats—or magic carpets used by giants from the *Alif Layla Wa Layla,* Jinnis that had vanished back into the sky, leaving only explosive plumes of blue smoke behind them. It was a vista more fantastical than any Sheherazade ever imagined ...

So unreal.

Yet this unreality was far harder to pass off as a simulation than the contained, commonplace reality of a passenger plane stranded on a runway. The interior of a 767 might be possible to model inside a computer. But the exterior of New York, under an open sky? Around him the ground was seething, and crews of firemen and rescue workers were materializing from beyond veils of vapour, swinging grappling hooks and pick-axes. Many of them disappeared into the grey-white crater in the centre of this vast dead zone in time and in place.

The dead past.

Not rendered, not simulated.

Real.

Legs turning watery, going out from under him. Raed dropped helplessly onto the blackened husk of what might once have been a fine office couch.

Ground Zero.

Could his cousins Nazir and Sayf really have brought *this* about?

Could he really *be* here?

Real or unreal, Raed wanted this re-visitation to end; he was more than ready to "return to the present." And if the first Projection back to the grounded plane was anything to go by, he wouldn't have to sit here long before they brought him out of all this. So Raed waited, watching the huge fireman on the roof of the pumper truck hose down flames licking from a crushed-accordion chunk of skyscraper, and wondering whether he was seeing something that might be real, might be true:

Had the two men on Tower Pumper Truck No. 146 been here through the night, fighting fires since the World Trade Center collapsed?

For an instant the man working the hose lost his grip on it. A cloud of spray swept over Raed, and he swung his hand through the moisture without feeling a drop. *Not massive enough*, he thought, the science they'd fed him regurgitating an explanation for this flaw in the visual reality. *Things will appear both startlingly real and surreal*, the Muslim psychologist had warned him.

Suddenly the hose shut off altogether, and the weary fireman stumbled out of the crow's nest, tore off his goggles, wiped tears from his eyes—no doubt he'd lost many firemen friends when the towers came down—then the man collapsed on the pumper's roof right beside his prone co-worker. That's when Raed became aware of a prickling sensation, a cloud of *something* uncomfortably tingly swimming over him ...

Heat! Heat *was* able to "span the dimensional divide" that purportedly separated Raed from this past. Heat was cumulatively massive, Francis had told him; it had sufficient structure to transmit a force across N-space ... Whatever the case, Raed was definitely sensing a radiation from the burning accordion-floors not far away—a tickly itchy uneasy chill, a cold fire, a cold pressure, unlike any cold he'd ever felt.

So this was heat in the land of the dead, three decades back!

Raed shivered, on the verge of believing again, wondering if those two firemen really were lying only a dozen feet from him, unaware of his ghostly presence. He rubbed the edge of his left hand, where it had made that fiery contact with the stewardess. Human contact was one that *did* feel hot in these Projections—too hot too handle, which was why Raed was being careful not to get too close to anyone this time around. He would not touch any of the people he encountered at Ground Zero, and he would not be touched by them. *He* was not responsible. *He* was not the twenty-four-year-old who'd helped two cousins bring the Twin Towers down. That boy was long gone, locked down in the dustiest, most unreachable part of the labyrinth of Raed's mind, the key to his pre-prison self thrown away ages ago.

So how could it possibly help him to see all this again?

But Raed had never seen Ground Zero the first time round, of course; he hadn't dared venture anywhere near it in the aftermath of 9/11.

A minute after the first fireman shut off the hose and slumped down on the pumper's roof, his resting companion slowly got up, climbed into the crow's nest, and started the hose up again.

Fifteen minutes later, this shorter, stockier fireman began to tire too, stepped out, dropped onto his back in exhaustion. Then the larger of the two men rose again, took his place back behind the hose.

Raed was left to imagine how many hours their tenacious routine had been going on ... After two more edge-of-exhaustion exchanges of duty in the crow's nest, someone else appeared atop the pumper, a track-suited citizen just visible, climbing up the ladder at the far end of the truck. A journalist, Raed thought, or some lost local too distraught to go home. Someone foolish enough to show up without a filter over her mouth, at any rate. The woman stepped right up onto the pumper, reached the fireman lying prone on the roof before her, and was so overcome she crouched down beside the man, abruptly embraced him. An emotional show of gratitude for his efforts to extinguish what was left of the angry fire from the jets ...

Or maybe she was hugging the spent fireman just because he looked like he needed it.

Raed didn't have to wonder whether *this* sort of thing had actually happened after 9/11—he'd seen it happen, in the streets of Brooklyn just hours after the towers came down. He'd seen strangers, walking straight up to a weeping member of New York's Finest, spontaneously embrace the policeman. New Yorkers had reached out to each other in ways that had surprised Raed that day ... Again, falling spray clouded his view of what was going on; Ground Zero became a swirling grey, began sliding away, and—

— • —

He was back, praise be, he was *back*.

Pulling off the breather-mask, Raed gasped in mouthfuls of air and blinked out through the bars of his cage at the hundred-odd other Projectors beyond the pane of Plexiglas, writhing and walking in their suspended states, ghosting back to other places and other times, if all this was to be believed.

No, no, *no*, he *would not believe*. Turning back to the team assisting him, he saw the veiled psychologist saying something to him from outside the cage, and again offering him a questioning thumbs-up—wanting to know if he was okay.

Raed gave her a thumbs-down.

She entered the cage immediately, her eyes alight behind the burqa— with concern? With contempt? "Are you unable to continue?" she asked him, fingers poised over her slate to make another note.

"Can't you project me somewhere else?"

"Perhaps." She tapped in her note, glanced back at the researchers manning the controls, shrugged, then said to Raed, "I'm obliged to remind you: you can withdraw from our program at any time, if you don't feel able for it."

She made it sound as though quitting was the obvious choice. Maybe she *expected* him to give up, go back to his cell in Lew and simply rot away for the rest of his days ... But the crack that had opened deep within Raed was swallowing the walls he'd built to hold the outside world out—his mind's labyrinthine safe-house was losing whole rooms to that yawning divide inside. So he didn't know if he *could* just give up and go back. It was surely not so easy as this wide-eyed woman made it sound.

"Send me where you will," he told the woman, waving her dismissively out of the cage, all the while thinking *let it be just a simulation!* Bracing himself again as the beams shimmered on and the rift re-opened, twirling the cage's bars away, tunnelling him back to—

— • —

A living room in someone's house.

Raed dropped softly onto a pine floor in front of an antique cabinet, bounced once, fell forward onto hands and knees, looked around at the spindly legs of furniture, hand-crafted from some dark wood. He got to his feet easily, saw no one down the hall of the house's ground floor. Was he in some suburb of New York? Raed peered out a shaded front window onto a lawn gleaming in the sun. The street at the end of the lawn looked broad and sleepy under large trees; there was no traffic, and the houses across the street were widely separated.

He doubted he was in New York.

The cage operators must have heard the request he'd made to "project somewhere else" through his breather-microphone. That, or they'd *really* missed the target this time.

No, only a simulation ...

Again, the light filtering through the trees onto the lawn suggested it was early morning; so did the dew still gleaming on the grass. Perhaps there were people still upstairs, getting ready for work. Raed cautiously made his way up to the second floor, peeked even more cautiously into each of the floor's rooms: a child's bedroom with two small beds, a master bedroom, a spacious bathroom, a small office. The house appeared to be empty.

A window at the back of the office was partially open, so Raed slipped inside the room, glanced through the window over a side-lawn at a neighbour's clapboard house, then tried to put his arm out beneath the window.

He had to push his hand right through the mesh screen meant to keep the bugs out; he felt only a little gluey resistance. He got his arm completely out, but that was all—the window, presumably left open for air, wasn't open enough for him to squeeze his head or chest out. And as hard as Raed pushed on the window frame itself, he couldn't budge it wider. He couldn't move things in this world.

So, leaving the office, he looked in again at the windows of the children's room and the bathroom, found them all closed. The master bedroom at the back of the house had a big window, but it was closed too, and curtained for privacy ... Lying on a big bed beneath the window was a cream-coloured blouse, a black skirt folded neatly, a frilly pink bathrobe. The sight of the clothing reminded Raed powerfully of Haifa, his wife. His eyes went helplessly to the framed photo on the bedside table, which showed a couple hugging on a beach. The woman was laughing. The man was bent to kiss her neck. Almost certainly a photo of the couple whose bedroom Raed was standing in—and placed on that table, he guessed, by the woman, as a proud memento of her happiness.

No such photos of Raed and Haifa existed, not even in his memory. What Raed remembered most when he thought of Haifa was her fear of him. He hadn't treated her well, especially in the final years, when his cousin Nazir's beliefs took a stronger and stronger hold over him. Turning away from this thought, Raed caught a shaft of sunlight streaming through a partly open door in a corner of the bedroom. Stepping over to it he discovered a bright bathroom, the morning sun pouring gloriously down through a big skylight. After ensuring the bathroom was empty, he eased round the door into the sun-filled space—only to find more woman's things arranged on the long counter. Skin creams, make-up, hair clips, a big brush with fine black strands wrapped about its bristles ...

To his surprise, Raed found himself in the grip of an unbearably lonely longing he thought he'd gotten rid of ages ago—as though he'd just eased round a partially open door into a room in his head he thought he'd lost the key to. Mixed in with the longing was an intense sense of lost opportunity. For Haifa had edged more and more toward moderation in America, whereas Raed had *arrived* a moderate and only became a devout in those last few years before the towers came down, under Nazir's tutelage. And after the towers fell, after his fear grew and his family was taken from him, Raed gradually lost his devotion altogether.

So it was unpleasant now to recall how he'd fought to keep Haifa under his thumb, forcing her to accept a fundamentalism he hadn't believed in when they'd married as teenagers. The innocent boy he'd been became a kind of monster, a fanatic to be feared during those final years of freedom, before he'd melted down into something else entirely during the first decade of imprisonment.

Melted down into *what,* though?

Raed had been careful not to step in front of the bathroom's long mirror. Now he took a look, and saw—

No reflection of himself.

It was the eeriest thing, as though he was ... what did they call it? A vampire. Raed was a kind of vampire in this past.

But if he was supposed to be back in September of 2001 again, wouldn't he then look young again? Raed's hands were still veined, mottled with middle-age. He ran one hand through his hair, tracing the receding hairline, then ran the hand back down over his bony brow and over the breather-mask to his chin and throat. Clean-shaven, as he'd been back in 2001, to attract less attention in America. For a while he'd grown a proper beard in prison. But a few years later Lew started handing the new shaving gels out to prisoners—offering the prospect of a wipe-on-wash-off mirror-less shave—so Raed went back to clean-shaven again. He'd grown too used to the routine, during the years leading up to 9/11. Routine was the key to staying sane in prison.

Routines like avoiding mirrors.

Raed was glad he cast no reflection; he hated to think what he looked like now. A ghost of the young man he'd been, for sure, his thick dark hair turned thin, his strong face turned gaunt, the high cheekbones of his people sticking out too much now ... But his fear of mirrors wasn't really about becoming old, was it?

Another surprising memory breaking free from a locked store-room in his mind: Raed realized he'd started avoiding mirrors *before* he went to prison. He'd avoided them *immediately after* 9/11 because he'd looked so awful; he'd looked twisted; he'd looked like a monster even to himself—

Raed wriggled out of the narrow bathroom door and fled the bedroom, almost tumbled back down the stairs, forgetting how tricky walking was on an intangible carpet covering soft slippery wood beneath. When he reached the bottom—and got back to his feet—he began looking for a way out, wandering through the handful of rooms, living room, dining room, the long hall with its open coat-filled closet, a downstairs bathroom, a cozy den with a fireplace. Each of the rooms exhibited a down-to-the-last-detail visual authenticity, and each was a living space that made a mockery of the concrete cell he called home. None of the rooms, however, offered him a way to get outside.

Raed felt the wholly believable reality of this American home closing in on him, reducing the number of rooms for him to hide in in his mind.

The last room on the ground floor he managed to squeeze into was a blindingly bright back kitchen. One whole wall of the kitchen was floor-to-ceiling windows, letting in the sun and letting Raed look out over a patio and a long yard. Raed walked right up to the windows—one was actually a glass patio door—and gasped at the vista before him:

Beyond a picket fence at the end of the yard, the land dropped through rolling green hills down to a small steepled village about a mile away. The village stood on the edge of a sunlit ocean, the waves sparkling off to a distant horizon.

Nothing Raed had seen in thirty years looked more like home!

It was not the home he'd been born into, a small village that had stood near waves of desert sand. No, this was the American ideal of home: a peaceful village with quaint clapboard houses, colonial buildings, like something out of a story book—a story Raed had lived for a time. He'd been a pre-teen when he'd arrived in America, and had lived all the years of his adulthood on American soil, so he knew its stories, knew its dreams ...

The dream-house he was in now looked like it might be on the shores of Rhode Island or Connecticut. He and Haifa had driven along that shore-line after Raed finished a bit of "security reconnaissance" at the airport in Boston. During their seaside drive, Raed had derided the storybook villages they'd passed through. Now he could not remember why the sightseeing had left him so unimpressed, or why he'd been so eager to obey the Organization ordering him to Boston in the first place. He must have been hiding in rooms in his head even before he'd reached prison. Hiding from the reality he'd lived in, hiding in a Seventh Century corner of his mind and ignoring the Twenty-first Century America around him ... But that was another Raed, not the middle-aged ghost from the future standing in this kitchen, looking with longing on the village down below, a wholly magical place Raed was ready to believe in.

Feeling his throat tightening with emotion. He *wanted* to be back in this past, simulation or no simulation. He wanted to break free of the harness holding him to 2033 and wander down into that peaceful, perfect village, buy a coffee in a shop, sit and listen to people talk, and never look back.

They'd said if he participated in their program he would get to see "the outside world again, in a way." Is this what they'd meant? If so, the psychologists had cheated him. The scene before him was so pristine it was heart-breaking to look upon. And Raed couldn't so much as step out to the backyard.

Then he remembered what the researcher Francis told him about volunteers sticking their hands through glass. So he began to try, pushing hard against the glass of the patio door, and gradually feeling his fingers sink into a surface like glue that had almost hardened. But after several minutes, he'd only managed to get the tips of two forefingers to peek through the other side of the glass. And he did *not* want to be stuck here if people arrived and came into the kitchen, brushed up against him.

As he stood, oh-so-slowly drawing his fingers back out, Raed glanced around the kitchen, saw a "Support Your Rhode Island Democratic Representative" calendar facing him from the nearest wall. It was open to September 2001, and the words *TOM IN L.A.* were printed across the week of September 11th. The calendar could not tell him what day *this* was, of course; but Raed knew, oh he knew. He turned back to the glass door, focused on freeing his fingers. That's when he noticed the reverse-reflection of the digital clock on the stove at the back of the kitchen behind him. He turned completely round to see if he was reading it right.

8:45 AM.

One minute before the first of the four planes would—had—hit its target. One minute to go on what was—had been—the final morning of Raed's free life, before he went into hiding. Raed drank in the view beyond the glass door, wishing this last minute could last forever, bracing himself for ...

8:46 AM.

Nothing happened. Naturally, New York was far from Rhode Island. His fingers finally popped free, and he stood there flexing his hand before realizing he was hearing a soft buzzing from somewhere. The front doorbell? It had to be something closer, in the kitchen. Raed walked round the room, ended up beside the phone, which was ringing really loudly when he was right beside it. The ringing stopped, and an answering machine adjacent to the phone clicked on. A woman's voice announced, "We're not here, but you can leave us a message." Then the caller began to speak:

"Angie, I'm ... it's Tom," a male voice said, and Raed's eyes shot to the calendar. *TOM IN L.A.*

"My flight's been hijacked," Tom continued all too calmly. "I'll try to call again, but don't know if there'll be time. Whatever happens, Angie, know that I love—"

Raed leapt away before he heard the end of the message, knowing the sound would drop off faster than it should—and it did, the rest of Tom's words to Angie unable to reach across a foot more of kitchen floor. He backed all way into the patio door, disturbed and disbelieving. How could a man caught on any of those planes have been so calm?

It was a question Raed had asked himself over and over the day *before* 9/11. That was the day he'd driven his cousins across the state border into Connecticut and booked them into a motel on the Massachusetts border for the final night of their lives. Ruddy-cheeked Nazir. And thin-faced Sayf, always skeletally thin, more than a little obsessed-looking. But Sayf and Nazir had both been calm and controlled during that afternoon drive through the Connecticut countryside, mentally preparing to sacrifice themselves when the morning came. They'd met with their cell leader less than an hour before the long drive began, and had been let in on the target of their mission a little early because their leader trusted them. Nevertheless, Nazir broke down and shared their terrible secret with Raed before they reached the motel because Raed was kin, the last member of their family who would see Nazir and Sayf alive.

Oh, he'd had "prior knowledge of the crime," all right.

And after his cousins booked into the motel under assumed names—the names later published under their photos in the papers—Raed stayed in their room with them for a few hours before driving back home to Brooklyn alone, wondering all the way how his cousins could have been so *calm*.

Raed saw the light on the answering machine start to blink. He walked toward it slowly—wanting to be sure it was finished recording—then stared down at the damned machine, hoping the cage-operators didn't make him wait in this house until Angie came home and listened to what was on it. But at least, he thought, as the kitchen began to slide sideways away from him, at least Tom had said what needed to be said to *his* wife—

— • —

Back, back in the present, and breathing hard.

Raed shook his head, wanting to rid himself of the sad end to such a beautiful dream, a beautiful simulation. He gazed blearily through the yellow bars, saw the hundred other spherical cages beyond the Plexiglas, scattered across the main Projection arena. A hundred other volunteers were hanging in their harnesses, looking strangely blurred, squirming and swaying in mid-air. Folding back across N-space to a hundred lost moments in history?

Can't be.

"Feeling all right, Raed?"

The woman psychologist was already in the cage below him again, waving a hand before his eyes to get his attention.

He dragged the breather down again.

"I feel ..."

"What?" She waited, one hand poised over her slate.

Lost, he wanted to say. *Lost opportunities.* Raed had heard passengers had contacted their loved ones from those doomed planes, but ... *He* hadn't ever contacted Haifa to tell her his own feelings—because he hadn't realized how strong his love for her really was until too many years had passed, and it was much too late. So the acid dose of heartbreak filling him now was as much for himself as for the man who'd left that bittersweet message.

Raed peered down at the psychologist, knowing he was already losing tonight's game badly. "You can't make me believe," he said to her, no longer wanting to play any more games. "Can't believe I'm really seeing the past, I don't care what you show me."

The woman nodded, tapping away at the slate. "What you believe is entirely up to you ... And what you do where we send you, that's up to you too."

"What *is* there to do," Raed retorted, "when I'm just as cooped up back there as I am back in Lewisburg?"

"You really want to find out?"

Raed let out a long shuddering breath, unsure whether this veiled and proper young woman sounded hopeful for the first time—or whether she was trying to warn him about what was coming next. But he was sure of the answer to her question; some part of him *did* want to find out. Something was stirring down in the crack through the core of his being:

An ashen yearning to go back there and confront whatever they would show him.

"Yes," he sighed. "Send me again."

The look in the psychologist's wide black eyes subtly changed. Surprise? She whirled, exited the cage, conferred with the two operators sitting at their consoles. And Raed closed his eyes, knowing it didn't really matter where they projected him to this time because what he'd told the psychologist was the truth: He wouldn't, couldn't bring himself to believe that he was folding through "N-space" back to—

— • —

New York City, an empty sidewalk.

Raed hopped onto the walk as it appeared before him, caught his balance, steadied himself on his feet, looked around. He was not in Manhattan, not in any of the busier parts of the city. And he was finally outdoors! No walls to hold him back, no mounds of rubble to block his progress. Free to go where he pleased.

Raed started up the quiet side street he was on, heading for a larger cross street so he could figure out where he was. He passed the steep steps of a row of four-story walk-ups. One of the boroughs, for sure. This was the New York he remembered, glad to have an image of it to replace the desolation of Ground Zero ... Blue skies above, a breeze rippling the leaves of a haggard tree on the corner. An autumn morning, for sure. Back in *that* morning once more? Before the attacks occurred? After?

The signs at the end of the street told him he was back in Brooklyn, on a corner several miles from where he'd lived, a vaguely familiar corner. Raed spun round, orienting himself. East River had to be just behind the row-houses that were blocking his view of the World Trade Center. He couldn't see whether the Twin Towers were still standing—but if they were, he could walk round the block and head down to the riverside, maybe just in time to watch the planes striking their targets.

Was that what the Projection operators wanted Raed to do?

Surely it would do him no good whatsoever to witness the destruction of the towers all over again. He'd seen those images a hundred times on TV, along with everyone else. Surely it would be senseless to waste this precious chance to walk the world he'd lost by going down to the river to gawk. The Twin Towers were not his victims anyway, they were the West's victims, America's victims … Raed started walking west, keeping the Trade Center's location behind his back. His eyes kept turning to the perfectly clear skies, searching for low-flying passenger jets. He prayed he wouldn't see any. Stopping at another cross street to let a yellow taxi roll by, he felt certain he knew this neighbourhood. Only a few people out on the streets, and those that were, hurried along as though late for work. The sun looked too high to be early in the morning. What time was it? What *day* was it?

A New York Post box coming up on his left. When he reached it, Raed hunkered down on his haunches, saw something on the cover page about "Ban on Cell Phone Use While Driving."

But the date on the newspaper was 9/11, all right.

He walked on, hurrying now, spying a tiny park across the street not much farther ahead. Not much more than a grotto, really, but Raed began jogging toward it, feeling sure the visually stunning simulation of a New York morning he was moving through was about to change. All he wanted was a few moments of peace, sitting beneath those trees before this blissful reality was yanked out from under him.

And then it hit him:

He was near Basma's Islamic daycare and prayer school, a small building at the other end of the little grotto park. No wonder all this looked so familiar.

Basma.

Raed broke into a run, remembering the promise made to him—that he might get to see his daughter again. Was this what the rehab programmers meant? Then they'd tricked him; they'd known perfectly well he'd hoped to see Basma all grown up. Raed ran for the school all the same, wanting to see his little daughter in this all-too-perfect recreation, suddenly wanting it very badly.

Wanting to know once and for all.

As he ran up the block, something happened to the sky. A cloud of confetti appeared from over the four-story walk-ups on his left. Snowflake-sized particles were fluttering down onto the sidewalk ahead of him, some larger pieces of paper floating down, too ... Documents! Memos and letters and receipts from all the way across the East River, fallout from Twin Tower offices. The paper cloud began to litter the tops of trees in the grotto-park as he passed it.

Just ahead loomed the Islamic prayer pre-school, all the toddler students dressed in their jackets and milling about on a fenced-in patch of tarmac alongside the school's front steps. Half of them were roped together.

What was going on?

Raed reached the wrought-iron fence, found the school's entrance gate closed. He struggled to get over the tall black bars but kept slipping down, unable to get any purchase on the bars with his shoes. There was no room for him on the crowded tarmac beyond anyway, so he strode impatiently round the fence, hearing a chaos of chattering and squealing, trying to spot Basma among the children. In the midst of the pre-schoolers stood a teenage girl dressed in salwar and kameez, gaping up at the sky in aston-ishment; a more resourceful Muslim girl was untying the rope tethering several kids together. Of course! The young teachers had been caught preparing the children for their eleven o'clock walk through the park. No TV was allowed inside the conservative classrooms, so neither the children nor the adults looking after them had any idea what was going on yet.

But where was his Basma?

The thickening confetti-rain was making it harder to see who was who. Unleashed four-year-olds danced through the downfall, turned their tiny faces upward, grabbed at papers ... At last Raed spotted a child smaller than the rest, squatting with tiny hands on knees in a familiar blue raincoat, her head turned to the ground, looking curiously at the scraps of paper lying there.

Heart in mouth, Raed knelt outside the bars, got as close to her as he could—but the girl scrambled away into the centre of the crowd, vanished for a moment, reappeared duck-walking toward him with an ever-so-Haifa-like look of concentration, creased brow, mouth drawn tight, sucking her teeth *exactly* as Basma so often did during the three years he'd been father to her.

God and the Prophet within, what *am I seeing?*

The child stopped just a few feet from him, crouched just as before. Reaching now for a big file folder that had just landed, its edge smouldering.

"Don't!" he cried out. But the Basma before him did not pause, did not hear him, could not see him. Raed thrust an arm through the bars, tried to snatch her tiny fingers away—too late: she'd grasped the burning edge and immediately let go, began to cry, lower lip shooting out *exactly* as it had on the day Raed was taken away from her forever. He had not seen Basma since his trial, not until this very moment ...

For Raed knew in his heart of hearts he was *actually seeing* his daughter now.

His mind reeling, the world whirling, Basma blurring as she drew back, plopped onto her bottom—

"*Please,*" he gasped into the microphone of the breather-mask, "I *believe*; don't bring me back yet ..." But it was only his own tears blurring things. Raed was still there, still clutching the iron fence in September of 2001, inches from his *real daughter.*

Another teacher burst through the school's side door, teary-eyed herself, shouting something to the teenage girls standing among the children—something about parents coming early to take their children back, the city under attack!

Basma's wailing finally drew one of the teens to her side, the girl scooped his daughter up, Raed leapt to his feet, reached as far he could over the fence, Basma sobbing over the young teacher's shoulder *right in front of his eyes,* his hand almost touching her hurt little fingers, almost ...

"We put a bandage on that?" the teacher asked, and little Basma nodded through her sobs.

Raed watched the pair disappear through the school's side entrance while the other two teens rounded the rest of the children back inside, out of the paper rain. "I believe," he moaned again, tugging his arm from between the bars, sinking to the paper-littered ground. "Now I believe." Raed had not allowed any cameras in his house during those last paranoid years of freedom; he'd certainly forbidden any video footage to be recorded of himself or his family in those years. And the Islamic daycare and prayer school could not afford any video equipment ... So no one could possibly simulate the Basma he'd just seen.

Raed knew he was *actually kneeling* outside her school.

"Be merciful, let me stay," he prayed aloud, hoping the Projection operators would hear his words in the future. "Let me wait here, see her again." But the wrought-iron bars of the fence were already sliding out of his hands, the school building was beginning to swirl into the confetti-sky, and he was starting to tunnel back—

— • —

To the present.

Hanging in mid-air in the yellow cage, his breath still hitching with emotion. Had Basma's hand been bandaged when Raed picked her up from the pre-school that day? He couldn't recall, and he doubted he would have noticed. That day Raed had been too busy worrying about being tracked down, accused, arrested. He'd spent the entire day wondering how to ensure *he* didn't end up getting burned by the backlash to the World Trade Center attacks to notice whether Basma had already been burnt or not.

Not his victims?

Surely little Basma was his victim, if anyone was—and a couple of bandaged fingers were of little consequence compared to the inevitable consequence of losing her father ...

"Here." The veiled psychologist was standing in the cage below him again, holding a cup of water up to Raed. "Drink this," she said.

He tugged down his breather-mask, a little embarrassed as he wiped back his tears, recalling how the fireman at Ground Zero had looked when *he'd* pulled off his goggles to wipe away tears—Raed had been there; he'd *actually been* to Ground Zero!

And now, like that fireman, he just wanted to get out of the harness and throw himself down on the ground. "I wanted to stay," he complained to the psychologist, more than a little embarrassed by his earlier profession of disbelief to her. "Why'd you have to bring me back so soon?"

"Because you've more to see tonight, more to do. Here," she said again, "got to be thirsty—"

He knocked her hand and the cup aside. "I don't need water. I just need to go back ..." He broke off, seeing her reaction, the flash of intensity in her wide-set black eyes. Because Raed's fingers had briefly brushed hers?

"You'll feel thirsty, where you're going next," she warned him. Picking up the cup, she slipped out through the bars.

And Raed slumped back in the harness, acceptance sweeping through him. For the first time tonight he did not want to be *here*, where he was middle-aged in a spherical cage. Better to be a ghost lurking in that past again.

Outside the yellow bars the psychologist—a grown Muslim woman whose hand he'd reached out and touched, just in case—watched him watching her, then she tapped something into her slate and turned away, slid away, vanished round an impossible bend in space that opened into—

— • —

A long canyon-like street.

Downtown Manhattan, on the same bright sunny morning he'd ghosted to the last time—only *this* time Raed could hear an unearthly rumbling and he could see people running away from him, fleeing for their lives before his eyes. He whirled. High in the sky above him were the Twin Towers. The

South Tower, only a block away, was erupting from the top down.

Raed staggered backwards, gaping at the giant cloud of dust and debris surging forth from the building his cousins had crashed into, like a storm being injected into the blue sky at tremendous speed. He swung around; a man sprinting by bumped against him—

TERROR—ADRENALINE—ANIMAL URGE TO RUN

Raed obeyed the fiery emotions transmitted by the man's touch, hurtling himself across the street and around the corner of a nearby building. At the end of the road he'd turned onto, people were throwing themselves over the railings of the Hudson River—hoping for safety in the water? Raed veered in another direction, down a narrow lane and out onto a broader side street, the rumbling behind him swelling along with his fear. To his amazement, he saw a crowd of people standing in the distance, all their faces turned up like sunflowers in the instant before they, too, began to run.

And then, all at once, everything Raed could see vanished—the distant crowd, the canyon walls of the high-rises and the street itself, all swallowed in dust and darkness that felt like the end of the world.

This time he'd ghosted back to the world he'd lost at the very moment it was lost!

It was so dark on the street he could only make out shapes a few feet in front of him. It seemed impossible that just seconds ago it had been a clear, blue-skied morning ... Fumbling his way along a building front in the direction he *thought* he'd been heading, hearing a tinkling sound—glass-shards falling out of the sky? Windowpanes shattering in the storefronts around him? Either way the sound had to be much louder and closer than it seemed. He caught glimpses of big debris chunks crashing onto the pavement to his left, and burnt paper and concrete dust swirled thick as sleet.

The darkness began to yield to a wintry dimness—like a strangely dry snow squall in Manhattan—and Raed reached the next cross-street corner just in time to witness a hail of burning shrapnel striking a car-filled parking lot across the street. Cars began bursting into flame.

He dove under a parapet protecting a building front door, reminding himself that the Projection team claimed he couldn't be harmed. But Raed knew he could feel forces in this past, and he didn't want the force of any of that shrapnel striking him. So he sat under the parapet, watching cars ignite one after another, fighting to control his instinctive feeling that the parking lot was being fired upon by rocket-launchers aimed from the windows of the surrounding high-rises ... Suddenly, a large oblong shape loomed out of the dust-mist hanging over the street—a fire truck loaded with men who leapt off, rushed into the parking lot, fighting back shadows and smoke as they searched for people trapped in burning vehicles. Those firemen were crazy to charge in there!

Looking for a safe escape route, Raed noticed a lane leading from his parapet-covered patch of sidewalk back into a plaza behind him. He ducked through, rounded another corner, felt his way along the lee of another wall. A set of double doors just ahead of him burst open, the light from inside the doors revealing men in overcoats stepping forth, rifles at the ready. The armed men—not police, possibly FBI—formed a ring outside the open doors and peered into the murk, as though looking for whoever was to blame. Looking for Raed, who was holding his breath, flattened against a window well just feet from them. *You already caught me*, he thought. *I've already served thirty years.*

Now more people were piling out through the doors into the armed cordon. Older officials wearing suits, fire hats, air filters—not chiefs, possibly fire commissioners—all of them lucky to be alive in a command post this close to the Twin Towers. And all of them alternately shouting into hand-held radios, then listening for a response, shouting, then listening, throwing off waves of voices Raed could hear without making out individual words. In the light streaming through the open doors he saw the despair contorting their faces. The commissioners weren't getting any responses from the fire crews in the collapsed South Tower.

Then a familiar long-faced man in wire-rim glasses strode into the crowd of stunned city officials, issuing commands, arguing with the armed detectives who seemed to want the cordon to stay put. But the long-faced man set the party off across the dust-clouded plaza in the direction, Raed suspected, of the Trade Center.

Raed suddenly knew exactly who that man was.

The mayor of New York City.

Heading to Ground Zero only minutes after that nightmarish zone had formed? Or steered to safety by his armed protectors? ... Raed took off in the opposite direction, rounded another corner, found his path blocked by a steaming shape taking up the sidewalk and half the road in front of an abandoned fast-food outlet:

A jet engine turbine.

From Flight 175? From Nazir and Sayf's plane?

The turbine was so dust-whitened it looked like the engine of some ghost plane. Tingling waves of cold heat were coming off it, so Raed gave it a wide berth and hurried on, only to be slowed by more dust-and-ash-cloaked obstacles as he fled out of the south end of Manhattan. Twisted stick-shapes that had to be melted office chairs, an overturned desk in the middle of a sidewalk, a huge tire, all made visible by the fires sprouting in nearby buildings, offering Raed a weird torch-light to light his way ... Incredible. He'd seen TV images of Manhattan after 9/11, but they failed to capture the scope of the devastation. In his wildest dreams, Raed never thought his cousins could cause so much damage to the city.

And in his wildest dreams he'd never imagined he might "time travel" back to see it with his own eyes! This time he'd ghosted back to *before* his visit to Basma's school. Perhaps as much as an hour before, if he remembered correctly. Somewhere in the unseen sky high above him, a file folder from the South Tower was being carried by air currents over the East River, drifting down toward the little prayer school tarmac. Basma hadn't burnt her fingers *yet*. She wasn't a victim *yet*.

But Raed was stepping over victims wherever he went, shrouded forms that seemed to be sleeping in the middle of the streets—forms he didn't want to think about. Nazir's victims, Sayf's victims. Not *his* victims.

After almost falling onto one of those shrouded figures, Raed scrambled up an embankment onto a higher boulevard. Disoriented, he tramped along the boulevard in a direction that seemed a little less dusky. But within minutes smoke from the spreading fires behind him descended on the boulevard, thickening the dust-haze. Raed passed an EMS triage team working on a wounded woman already partly buried beneath the paper-ash fallout; the rescue workers were trying to revive the woman and keep themselves from passing out at the same time, handing a single oxygen mask back and forth.

He gave the team as wide a berth as he'd given the jet engine, wanting to avoid more physical-contact discharges from distraught New Yorkers. It was traumatic enough just trying to escape the shrapnel fires ... He wasn't the only one trying to escape, of course. After hopping out of the way of a beaconless ambulance—its roof littered with paper and its wipers rapidly swishing—Raed noticed a few other ghost shapes trudging along through the haze. People with grime-covered faces, holding pieces torn from their own clothing over their mouths, coughing soundlessly.

Raed felt like coughing too, even though he wasn't breathing any dust in. Most of it was falling right through him, only the largest paper flakes hovering on his clothes for a few seconds before slipping off. The "masslessness" of the falling dust made it easy for Raed to avoid and quickly out-pace the real downtown refugees he encountered—because they were forced to slosh slowly through the paper and ash pooling on the street, which was already several inches deep. Raed hurried on, undeterred by the debris build-up, always drawn in the brightest direction, even though the sources of brightness turned out to be shops and services with their doors thrown open. Each open doorway offered a consoling peek into an interior of clarity and detail— a reminder that the New York Raed had seen for a few seconds at the very start of this Projection still existed, hidden behind all the hazy detritus.

In the beaming entrance to a footwear store, he saw a man handing out free running shoes to women wandering by in stocking feet, unable to walk through miles of fallout in their high heels.

In the rear door of a restaurant-supply firm he saw a teenage boy passing out wet towels to everyone who stepped up for one, so people had better air filters to breath through.

In the arched portal of an old church he saw elderly ladies pouring cups of water and lemonade for passers-by. The church was getting crowded because the people coming up for drinks were stepping inside it, kneeling down in pews, bowing their heads. Raed paused across the street from this softly glowing scene, watching the parade of dust-whitened ghosts gratefully downing lemonade and water, and reaching up to his own throat. He'd felt thirsty from the first moment the debris cloud enveloped him, and his thirst had grown worse with every passing block. It wasn't just the exertion of a long walk. It was the *look* of ash-laden air all around him, the *sight* of coughing, choking civilians stumbling through the streets. The psychological dryness was getting to him.

But what was really getting to him was the fact that he was *actually experiencing* what it had been like to make an escape from Lower Manhattan the morning of 9/11. Because he was *actually here*, witnessing all this just as it had happened—or rather, as it *was* happening. A cement-mixing truck rolled slowly by, a dozen dust-coated Wall Street suits clinging to its sides. Raed followed it for a bit, then turned onto an empty side street he thought might take him in the direction of the Brooklyn Bridge.

That's when he spotted the strange pair of New Yorkers sitting on the stone steps.

What was strange about them grew more and more obvious as Raed walked toward them: one was a man so thickly coated in dust and ash he resembled a statue huddled against the railing of the steps—he was clearly in serious trouble, gasping for air, mouth hanging wide open and taking in more dust. The other was a woman who'd clearly just come out of the building the steps led up to—she had only a bit of dust on her, and she was holding the dying man, her head tucked onto his shoulder as though he was an old friend she'd found collapsed outside her door.

The strange thing was, *she wasn't helping him inside.*

"Get him off the street," Raed suggested as he passed the pair, knowing he wouldn't be heard. But he thought he saw the woman's eyes move up from her companion; he thought he saw her eyes following him up the narrow street.

Raed halted. Turned back. It was hard to see; he had to squint into the driving dust. Was she really looking over at him?

He approached the steps cautiously, still unwilling to be touched by these people, but getting close enough to see that the dying man's eyes were rimmed completely red, bloody coals in his ash-whitened face. And he was close enough to see the woman's NYU sweatshirt, a red ribbon pinned to her collar. She had her eyes closed now, head tucked back on her companion's shoulder again.

He must have been seeing things. "Don't you know your friend is dying?" Raed muttered, surprised to find himself thinking another death would be needless ... The woman shielded her eyes against the falling dust, peered up at Raed.

He lurched back in shock. "You *can* see me, can't you?"

But just then an accumulation of dust slid off the ledge above the steps, engulfing the pair in a swirl of white that transformed into a blurred tunnel, pulling Raed back to—

— • —

The yellow Projection cage.

Raed peered out through the bars at the two Lew guards in one corner, the two cage operators behind their consoles, the medic looking over the operators' shoulders ... and the Muslim psychologist slipping in through the bars to speak with him, again bringing him a cup of water.

This time Raed accepted the cup, lifted it to lips that *felt* parched, his throat dry as bone. After gulping the water down, he told the psychologist, "Someone saw me that time." Then he described the woman he'd seen sitting on the steps.

"Sure she wasn't looking up at the ledge dust about to drop on her friend?" The psychologist removed her slate from a pocket, tapped in something about Raed's claim.

"Are *you* sure people can't see me in the past?"

"I studied the same materials you did," she replied. "Light only has 'one-way transdimensionality,' so it only flows out of the past into an N-space fold but—"

"Doesn't flow back out of the fold, yes, yes," he said, wondering if he'd been mistaken about where the woman in the NYU shirt was actually looking. It had been pretty hazy back there. And pretty scary at moments.

"There *are* two-way interactions," the psychologist added, pocketing her slate again. "But all are mass-related, I think. And light doesn't have much mass ..."

That reminded Raed: those big chunks of mass falling from the sky at him. "And no volunteer has been injured by two-way forces, not even gravity?"

"Two-way interactions are 'weak-strong,' so I'm told. Weak from you onto the past—"

"And strong from the past onto me," Raed finished, raising his eyebrows at her. That's precisely what bothered him. He handed back the cup, accidentally touching the psychologist's fingers again—and wishing he could receive some contact discharge from *her* so he'd understand what she was feeling. She was, after all, about his daughter's age.

"Strong or weak," the psychologist told him, "the worst any projected force can do is render you unconscious, which will immediately pop you back here. So there's nothing to fear. Keep that in mind," she advised him. "Your next ghosting's going to be a lot more challenging."

Again he said, "Send me where you must," trying to sound dismissive to hide how apprehensive he was. But after the psychologist exited the cage, Raed took a deep breath, wondering what part of 9/11 he was about to experience now, watching the yellow bars blur as the fold formed about him, and N-space wrapped him back to—

— • —

A darkened stairwell strewn with chunks of drywall and concrete, a smoky haze in the air.

Raed lost his footing as he dropped onto the steps, slid down onto a landing, ended up sprawled before a steel door in the landing's opposite wall. The red glare of emergency bulbs illuminated words printed across the door:

WTC

BUILDING 2

FLOOR 82

Raed was high up in the South Tower some time *after* Flight 175 had crashed into it!

The door to Floor 82 burst open. Two men shoved through, forcing Raed to scramble back to avoid being bowled over. The men hurried onto the shadowy flight of steps leading below. And Raed fell in behind them, wondering how much time was left before this building came down. He was fairly sure it had collapsed about an hour after the crash ... Which meant he had less than an hour to get down *eighty floors*.

But he kept falling in the stairwell. Where the masslessness of paper and dust had played in his favour on the streets, here the low friction of his shoes on the darkened steps and the more tangible clutter of concrete shards made it difficult to stay on his feet. Raed had a hard time catching up to the two men, and only managed to keep them in sight at all by hanging onto the railing, sliding himself along walls that were crawling with a chilly, tingly pressure. The pressure grew worse and worse, the air of the stairwell swimming with a tingling cold-fire as Raed reached Floor 78. He was afraid that floor's fire door might melt as he ran by it.

But he *had* to be passing the floors Flight 175 had actually crashed into—and the fact that the fire hadn't yet spread into the stairwell sug-gested it couldn't be too long after the crash. He might have as much as fifty minutes to get down and out.

He'd been told he'd come to no harm. Did that mean the Projection team intended to extract him from the building before it collapsed? Raed had been in danger from the hail of burning shrapnel during the last ghosting, and his team seemed to expect him to rescue himself ... *It's up to you what you do back in the past,* the psychologist told him.

Perhaps it was up to Raed to find a way out before the forces in this world crushed him.

The landing of Floor 70 had working lights, and so did the stairs below it. Brighter passage and clearer air helped Raed move right down behind the two men he was following, close enough to hear their conversation as he looked for an opportunity to pass them. The injured man was "Garth," and he kept thanking "Peter" for pulling him to safety after the "explosion." How long ago, Raed wanted to know, wishing the men would walk single file instead of one gripping the other. "Peter" kept insisting he'd done nothing special, kept switching back to his worries about co-workers who'd headed up to the roof instead of trying to get below the fire.

"Your co-workers are lost," Raed snapped in frustration, "and you'll be lost too if you don't move faster!" These men were too calm; he *had* to get past them. At the next landing he tried to shove himself between them—

HORROR—HURT—DESPERATION—CONFUSION

Raed crumpled to the floor, unable to withstand the tremendous emotional discharge. Peter and Garth weren't calm at all! They were barely keeping their fear in check. What had they seen before entering this stair-well?

By the time he got back to his feet and caught up to them, Raed saw that more people were blocking the stairwell below Peter and Garth. There was some kind of pile-up on the next landing down, a crowd gathered round a burn victim. The delay was far more frightening for Raed than for the people surrounding him—because he *knew* the building was going to collapse soon. Was this Projection meant as punishment for his foreknowledge of the Flight 175 crash?

The Muslim psychologist back in 2033 suggested it was up to Raed whether Projection was punishment or—what?

What was he supposed to *do* here?

Passing more burn victims outside the door to Floor 67. Men with most of their clothes burned away, their skin turned grey or even black, patches of flesh peeling from their limbs. The people staying to look after them had torn off shirts to make tourniquets, others were cloaking the shivering grey figures in suit jackets ... The next landing held another group huddled about badly injured people, and so did the next, and the *next*, forcing Garth, then Peter, and then Raed to file slowly past. Only Raed knew those groups were all doomed, but it wouldn't have made much of a difference if he could have communicated that knowledge, at least not to the burn victims—they didn't look as though they'd live long enough to make it to a hospital.

It was the people staying behind to console them, it was all the comforters that bothered Raed. There were so many of them! Why didn't some of them just head down to safety?

Because they weren't aware of the imminent collapse, as Raed was.

"Come *on*, move *on*!" he growled at Garth and Peter. Winding down through the suffering was taking too long, leaving too much time for Raed to wonder what all this was for. Surely there was more to his rehab than sharing in the harrowing experiences of 9/11 victims. There *had* to be more to it. But what more could he do in this past?

You really want to find out?

The psychologist's question nagged at him, and Raed tried to recall the theory they'd given him. Strong-weak two-way interactions ... the past cannot be changed ... because Projection volunteers had *always* been part of the moments they time-travelled back to ... so Raed had *always* been here—was here now—following down behind Peter, who had his arm wrapped round Garth's shoulder, guiding the injured man down.

But did—or would—Peter and Garth get out before the building fell?

No way for Raed to get past them now; there were too many people crowding the stairwell directly below the pair. Others were coming down behind Raed, sandwiching him in the stairwell, occasionally forcing him to bump into Peter or Garth—and to suffer another shock of PITY–ANXIETY–DREAD–DISTRESS, emotions that almost knocked him down. The discharges astounded him. *I can actually sense how these two men are feeling!* He remembered the black-and-white movie about the two angels in Berlin who could hear what people were saying, but whenever they listened to peoples' thoughts, the soundtrack reverted to German, leaving Raed only with a sense of the emotional tone underlying thoughts ...

By the time they reached Floor 60 Raed was in a panic. Peter and Garth had to do a *lot* better than a floor a minute to get out in time—and to let Raed get out in time! This was a *lot* more nerve-wracking than the last Projection.

But it seemed most of the injured had already been passed, and below 60 the stream of escapees began moving much faster. Peter and Garth slipped by slower people who were resting on the steps and waving everyone coming down from above on past. Raed began to count off his own breaths, timing the pace between floors. He thought they navigated three flights in about a minute, timed it again and got the same result for the next three. They might just make it!

There was no panic in the stairwell, and no more injuries to pass until floor 44, where a security guard and some others were trying to assist a man whose head was bleeding profusely. The people comforting the man looked up as Peter, Garth, and Raed reached the floor; one of them asked Peter if he would send help from below. Peter agreed without slowing, guiding Garth on down the next flight, with Raed right on their heels.

On Floor 40 they eased by a man in a foot cast being carried down by four co-workers who switched him between pairs at the landing, sharing the exhausting load. A compassionate act, indeed. But would any of them make it out of the South Tower alive?

On Floor 33 an even more miraculous sight. People carrying a woman and her wheelchair down! The acts of selflessness Raed was witnessing inside the building he helped to destroy were wearing *him* down. He wanted to scream at everyone to drop their burdens and run—run so *he* could run, too, down to the bottom and out onto the street before it was too late. Because it was impossible to believe he was *not* in the danger they were in, no matter how many assurances he'd been given that no Projection volunteer had ever come to harm before. How could the force of the South Tower falling *not* harm him?

Garth and Peter finally got past the wheelchair crew only to find the stairwell below the Floor 31 landing completely clogged with firefighters. At least a dozen of them were hoisting themselves up the steps in their heavy gear, blocking the route down—doomed men, the most doomed of all that Raed had seen ... Because *they* were trying to climb *up*.

As people bunched onto the landing—and Raed crushed himself into a corner to avoid unbearable contact discharges—Peter moved over to the fire door leading into the floor itself, opened it.

"Let's try for the elevators," he said to Garth.

Raed didn't hesitate, knowing there was no time to lose waiting on this landing. He followed the pair through the door, which closed behind him. Moments later he stood close behind Peter as the man tried the elevator buttons.

"Not working."

Try another stairwell, Raed prayed, realizing he was now trapped on this floor—invisible or not, he couldn't walk back out through a steel door or wall.

"Hey, there's some phones in here," Garth said, peering into a room off the hall they were in. "I want to call home."

No!

But both men were stepping through into the room; the door was almost closed ...

Raed dove through just as it shut, afraid the pair would leave the room by another exit, stranding him in the hall.

Sure enough, a door in the opposite wall of the conference room they'd entered had a stairwell exit sign above it. Peter and Garth sat on the edge of the room's long central table, dialling up loved ones on the phones.

"No time, there's *no time*," Raed shouted at them., "There's *thirty* more floors to go!"

It was no use. Raed stood close enough to the receiver Peter was holding to hear the anxious tones of the man's wife—but Peter couldn't hear Raed screaming right in his ear. "Put the phone down and go, PLEASE, go!" He pounded a fist on the phone unit sitting on the table, trying to hang the damn thing up, when Peter suddenly hung up himself. But then the man began dialling *another* number, telling Garth he was calling in the EMS request he'd promised for the injured man up on Floor 44.

Peter was on hold with EMS for several minutes that had Raed howling around the conference room, both hands wrapped round the ripcord on his belt that was supposed to instantly return him to the Projection cage, eyes focused on the ceiling that might come down at any second ...

If Raed ripcorded back now he'd be out of the program; his fear would have won and he'd live out the next fifty years in Lew Cell #1, knowing he'd been unable to face what these two men had faced.

But they had no idea what was about to happen!

Finally Peter got through, made his EMS request, and got off the phone. Raed ran to the door with the stairwell sign as the two men started toward it, opened it, then stepped through, leaving Raed just enough room to follow. The stairwell beyond was empty, and the only thing that slowed them as they hurried down was a pipe that spontaneously burst from the wall. A sign the collapse was about to happen? How many seconds left?

Water from other exploded pipes and from sprinkler systems on the higher floors seemed to be collecting in this stairwell, making it difficult once more for Raed to keep up to Peter and Garth ...

And then, before he knew it, all three of them were at the bottom, hurrying through an underground plaza toward an outside street. A cop halted the two men before they crossed the street, warning about debris dropping from above—

Raed just ran for it, leaving his companions for the first time since Floor 82.

He'd made it!

He put a block between himself and the South Tower before looking back to see if it was coming down yet. Smoke billowed out of the hole two-thirds of the way up. He had to get farther.

But Garth and Peter were running over, and for some reason Raed waited for them, watching the sky overhead just to be sure. When they caught up to him, Raed began following the pair again, curious to know whether they'd get far enough away to survive. More than curious: He *wanted* them to survive; he *cared* about these two American strangers, having shared in their ordeal and overheard their exchange of friendship. Was that the whole point of this Projection? Or was there more to it, something he'd failed to do?

As the two men continued north along the rubble-strewn blocks, Read felt a weird echo of the relief they were professing to each other. Garth again thanked Peter for saving his life, Peter again dismissed the notion. Little did he know! A clock on a big electronic billboard read 9:59 AM. They'd made it down and out with only seconds to spare. Were they far enough away?

Garth stopped in front of a church, asked his friend whether he wanted to go in. Peter nodded, then they both turned for one last look at the South Tower. It was visibly shuddering.

"That building could come down," Raed hear Garth say.

Peter dismissed that notion, too. "It's a steel structure, there's no way—"

The building began to implode before their eyes.

Peter and Garth dashed around the side of the church for protection; Raed did too. After a few minutes the rumbling stopped but the dust and debris kept coming, thicker and heavier, churning into the all-enveloping gloom. The two men beside him closed their eyes against the dust fall, and for a few seconds Raed did, too. *All those people*, he thought, recalling faces seen high in the stairwell, people he was sure didn't make it out. He may have been *aware* of the outcome of Nazir and Sayf's attack back when he was twenty-four, but only now did Raed *understand* that outcome. Only now did he appreciate the sort of selfless, courageous people who'd ended up caught in the aftermath of his cousins' actions ... Nazir had told Raed they'd be bringing down America along with those two buildings. But all they'd brought down was—

Well, Americans.

All those people, he thought again, horrified by the outcome for the first time in his life. Then he heard Peter say it too:

"All those people," the big man croaked, shaking his head. Beside him Garth was weeping.

But they, at least, had lived, Peter and Garth had lived! And as the two men began to swirl away, Raed had just enough time to regret parting company with them before their faces vanished into the tunnel of history, and he found himself back—

— • —

In 2033, back in the present.

Back in his cage, blinking at the bars, and thinking of Peter and Garth. Did they still live, in this present?

"Anyone see you that time, Raed?"

It was the veiled psychologist, entering the cage again.

"No," he answered. "I mean—I don't know." Some of the people comforting the burn victims in the stairwell had looked up as he'd passed by. Raed had *thought* they were looking at him at first, before realizing they'd been looking at Peter or Garth, or at someone else behind Raed ... Perhaps the same was true of that woman he'd seen in the previous Projection, the one in the NYU sweatshirt with the red ribbon—perhaps she'd also been looking at someone passing behind Raed. Who could say?

He was still too horrified by his latest experience of 9/11 to think clearly.

But a feeling of horror wasn't enough. Raed saw that in the eyes of the psychologist standing below him, tapping away at her slate. He had not faced whatever he must face, had not done whatever he must do. What *could* he do, without changing the past?

"That was your longest Projection so far," the psychologist told him, "almost an hour. So we've only time for a few more. They'll be short and to the point. And for the next one, Raed," she said, "remember what your lawyers told you."

"Just send me," he groaned.

But she stayed for another second or two, holding Raed's eyes, her own wide eyes filled with—foreboding? After she slid out between the yellow bars, Raed closed his eyes and clenched his teeth, preparing to ghost once again back to 9/11. So many Projections to the same target time! He thought of the two firemen at Ground Zero who'd taken turns climbing into the crow's nest of their pumper truck, returning to the fire time and again, refusing to give up even though hope was already gone. If they'd been able to face it over and over, well then, so could Raed.

But when he opened his eyes he was surprised to find that—

— • —

He was back in a stairwell in the South Tower, standing on the landing of Floor 54, no one in sight. And right in front of him a zipper-rip was forming in the outer wall.

The whole stairwell seemed to pitch. Raed lurched for a railing of the flight leading down, barely able to keep his feet. What had the lawyers told him? Emotional harm was the only real danger during a Projection—and if he used the ripcord before the cage operators brought him back, he'd be automatically disqualified from the program ...

Raed scrambled onto the flight leading below only to stop short halfway down, seeing some people appear at the bottom climbing up. Firemen! The same doomed men he'd seen around Floor 30 during his last ghosting. They were all panting, far more exhausted now, weighed down by their hoses, axes, chemical tanks.

And even if he could get down past them, he'd never make it out in time, not this time. *Short and to the point*, the psychologist had promised.

The building rocked again, and Raed sprawled onto the steps, one hand gripping the railing to keep him from sliding into the firemen below, who were all hanging from the same railing and staring at each other, clearly wondering whether they should continue.

"GO DOWN!" Raed wailed at them, pulling himself back upright.

And the firemen reacted, but not to Raed's yell—someone trapped a few floors higher was screaming for help. En masse they began to climb, aware of the danger of collapse but not of its imminent certainty.

Raed flattened himself against the stairwell wall, wrapping both arms round the railing—and then the firemen were crushing up *through* him, he could *feel* their huge souls, giant lionhearts swelling with FEAR–FURY–DEFIANCE–DETERMINATION. During the endless seconds it took for them to climb by, Raed believed that *nothing* could kill such men ...

After the last of them had passed, Raed slumped to the stairs, lay there in a heap as the building rocked and rippled. The firemen were forced to stop just above him, all of them bracing themselves against the walls.

"Feel that just now?" gasped a man two steps above Raed.

Another nodded. "Something's telling me we're not gonna get out of here."

Had they sensed Raed's thoughts as they pushed by him? But no, individual thoughts could *not* be exchanged; biomass could *only* produce "strong-weak" interactions: strong from these firemen onto him, too weak from him onto them to change their minds about anything.

And any further words the firemen above him might have said were abruptly drowned out by thunderous *snappings* and *splittings* that sounded to Raed like the fabric of the universe tearing. The sounds snowballed into a terrific rhythmic pounding that pancaked toward them from above. Raed moved one hand off the vibrating railing onto his belt, onto the ripcord, looked up in anticipation—to his astonishment some civilians had made it down from the landing above, were squeezing between the firemen. Then the stairwell walls seemed to give out; the civilians above clutched onto their would-be rescuers; Raed instinctively grabbed the railing with both hands, and God in Heaven dropped the world of 9/11 on top of him, using the building Raed helped bring down to smite him once and for all—

— • —

A sharp smell roused him.

Raed opened his eyes, unsure of where he was. Two figures swam into view:

The burqa-veiled psychologist.

And the burly male medic, who was holding smelling salts.

Raed took in a painful breath, raised both hands to his chest, checked for broken ribs.

"It's just sympathetic pain," the psychologist assured him. "All in your mind."

"You're okay," the medic agreed. "It's just the shock of being blown out of the fold."

"Why—" Raed broke off, sucked in air, still psychologically winded. "Wasn't I crushed? Gravity of the past ... pulled everything down on us— on me."

The medic pointed to the inward-pointing cones studding the cage's arcing bars. "The particles they focus on you only open a *transient* fold around you. Any strong force exerted on the fold's exterior—force of a wall falling on you, a bullet fired at you—and the fold spontaneously pops, blowing you right back here. Bit of a shock," he repeated. "But you get used to it."

"You've faced ..." Raed wasn't sure what to call it.

"A 'mortal force'" in the past?" The medic rolled up a sleeve, revealing a tattoo of the Statue of Liberty on one big bicep. "Was born in France," he said, "so I ghosted back to the Revolution. Got hit by a cannonball fired into a crowd outside the Bastille—I was standing too close to some of my ancestors." The big man folded his arms, frowned up at Raed. "Gotta tell you, facing death during a ghosting's not the hard part. It's not easy—but it's not the hard part."

"What," Raed wheezed back at him, "is the hard part?"

The medic looked over the psychologist's shoulder, read something she was tapping into her slate. "Believe you already know," he said, then nodded at Raed and left the cage.

Raed met the psychologist's wary eyes.

"Can you?" she asked him, a hint of pleading in her voice. Had she expected him to ripcord out before the South Tower collapsed? Had she hoped he'd stick it out with those firemen?

The thought that the psychologist held out a faint hope for him gave Raed a little strength. "I think ... I can," he breathed, then began breathing easier.

After all, he knew now she'd been telling the truth; he *couldn't* come to harm. And after she exited the cage, Raed watched the psychologist and the others outside the bars begin to slide away, knowing the next Projection couldn't get any worse, it could only get—

— • —

More strange.

Raed dropped to the floor of an elevator with its double doors partially open. Beyond the gap in the doors a debris-littered lobby kept rising, then plunging, then rising again, as though the elevator was a yoyo on a string about to snap. The steel walls around him were visibly vibrating; he knew he didn't have much time. But he waited until the lobby outside fell from above his shoulders to a foot below the level of the elevator—

Raed threw himself out, landing flat on his chest on the cluttered lobby carpeting. A sign fallen from a shuddering wall told him this was Floor 104 of the South Tower. And there was a man propped against a smouldering reception desk nearby, his legs trapped under a huge twist of black metal that had stabbed down through the ceiling.

The trapped man wasn't alone.

Raed got to his feet, staggered closer, stared at a woman kneeling beside the trapped man, her arm round his shoulder. She stared back at Raed, following him with her eyes.

"You *can't* see me," he insisted, and then fled from the pair, down a hall, round a corner. Not wanting to be seen by a victim about to meet her end. Not wanting to sit idly by as two more people met their doom, unable to do a thing about them or himself.

Not understanding what he was *supposed* to do here!

Ceiling panels crashed down in a hall he turned into, an electrical panel exploded. Raed was driven back, his time almost up again. *Short and to the point.*

The point being to meet *more* of the people he'd help trap in this tower? *I DIDN'T trap them, I WASN'T on that plane. It was Nazir, Sayf, their pilot comrades!* But no matter how he tried to rationalize, how he tried to escape, Raed was blocked at every turn. There was just no way out. Corridors came down in a rain of rubble; passageways filled with a tingling pressure before bursting into flame; doorway after doorway was barricaded by debris; all the rooms within rooms closed off to him now, all his mental defences collapsing, forcing him back to ...

The central lobby and the elevators, where he hated to go but had to go and—in the end—he wanted to go so he wouldn't have to face the end alone. As he stumbled into the lobby, Raed saw the trapped man now had two companions consoling him instead of one, both comforters wearing red ribbons on their collars but neither looking at Raed. Their eyes were squeezed tightly shut, knowing the collapse was upon them, hearing the roar and hugging the arms of the trapped man, one on either side, their faces agonized.

Yet the man propped between them seemed unaware of his two steadfast friends, his hands clasped together in prayer, face somehow calmer, eyes turned up toward his own version of Heaven. *We do this to Americans because they are godless*, Nazir had told Raed repeatedly.

And that was not true.

And feeling horror for this trapped trio was not enough.

Raed threw himself down on the shuddering floor before them. He knew what the hard part was now. "I don't have the strength," was all he had time to say before the world descended on them all again—

— • —

Sharp reviving odours.

Opening his eyes, squinting at yellow bars, then down at the big medic, the small Muslim psychologist.

"Was seen—again," Raed managed to say when he'd caught his breath. "Were two of them. Two ... shouldn't have been there."

"What do you mean?" The psychologist was tapping it all into her slate.

"Both wearing ribbons," Raed said, less winded this time. "Pinned to sweatshirts," he went on, "like the other one who saw me—down that side street, sitting on those stone steps."

She surprised him by replying, "You've gotten a long way into our program tonight, Raed, and you're nearly there."

"There?"

"Understand, the program's spiralling you toward the core event you were convicted of being an accomplice to. Time to take you in for a close-up."

He nodded. The hard part still remained. "Go ahead," he said, no longer caring ... No rooms left to hide himself inside anyway. Raed's own core had been drawn out now, and he was ready for anything, ready for the truth.

Again the psychologist hesitated before leaving, and again her lingering gaze gave him strength. *She wants me to see it through.*

Raed realized he wanted to see it through, too.

Seconds later the cage bars began to blur, then bend away, and before he knew it he was—

— • —

Back in the South Tower, and, for the first time, he'd arrived *before it was hit* ... The floor around him filled with people, a dozen desks visible in an open area near some tall windows, a few of the desks still occupied by people making phone calls, although most looked upset. Most others had left their desks and were standing at the windows, looking out at the North Tower, which had a smoking hole a number of floors higher up its side.

What floor was he on in this building? Raed turned and hurried round to the elevators, darting in and out of people, and in the central lobby discovered he was on Floor 78.

The point of impact for the South Tower.

Raed kept right on running through the floor, around to the Tower's opposite outer wall. Finding another open area past a row of offices, he peered out through some windows facing south. A gleaming speck was just visible against the blue sky in the south-east, slowly arcing around to get into position.

Raed had often wondered about Nazir and Sayf's last moment in that cockpit. In the early years he'd even tried to picture it: opening their shirts and exposing their hearts to God, praying for entrance to Heaven. Madmen, and Raed had sensed it even then. But he'd been a little mad himself, in that period ... And now that he was in a position to glimpse the expression on their faces as they plunged into the side of this building, Raed found he had no interest in glimpsing any such thing. He turned his back to the windows.

Four of the dozen desks arrayed before him had knots of people standing round them. And sprinkled in among the business attire worn by most of those people—none of them currently looking out the windows to the south—there were a handful of standouts in casual clothes, sweats, even one in an all-blue jumpsuit. All the casual-dressed people had their hands on the shoulders or backs of one or another of the victims-to-be.

Raed moved over to the nearest occupied desk, where a young blond-haired man in a crisp mauve shirt and black tie sat facing the outer windows, too busy talking on the phone to notice the speck growing in the sky beyond the windows. Standing directly behind this young businessman was another, older, blond-haired man, in his mid-forties perhaps, approaching middle age, yet dressed in silvery track pants and a Columbia University pullover. He had both hands on the shoulders of the desk's occupant and was crouched over him, head bent low, eyes closed and concentrating—to all appearances eavesdropping on the seated man's phone call.

Neither the seated man nor anyone else in the area seemed to take any notice of this peculiar eavesdropper.

Except for Raed.

"Who are you?" he asked the man in silver track pants.

The man frowned up at Raed, his concentration broken. Raed immediately saw that the eavesdropper and the businessman below him might have been twins, but for the ten-year age difference between them. And now the red ribbon pinned to the eavesdropper's collar was plainly visible ... Below him, the seated man continued reassuring whoever he was talking to on the phone that he was all right, that it was the other tower that was hit—but his eyes were finally widening, focussing on something behind Raed, beyond the windows. The eavesdropper bowed over the seated man again, concentrating harder, tightening his grip on his younger twin's shoulders.

Out of the corner of his eye, Raed caught other people reacting to something in the sky beyond the south windows. And now, somehow, there were twice as many people in sweats and casual clothes in the open area—though Raed had seen no one enter the area. All the newcomers had their heads bowed, holding tightly to some shocked-looking businessman or woman.

"Who *are* all of you?" Raed yelled across the open space.

He got no answer. The casual-dressers were too focused on the task at hand: remaining in physical contact with people who were beginning to scramble away in disbelief—

A loud clattering drew Raed's eyes back to the desk he was standing in front of.

"Oh God, *oh my God*." The young blond businessman had dropped the phone receiver and was on his feet, gaping at the windows behind Raed. A woman's voice squeaked out of the receiver inches from Raed's hip:

"Steve? You still there, Steve?"

The older man in silver track pants clung onto Steve, his face pained—

Then everyone was breaking free from their casually dressed companions and fleeing, falling over chairs and furniture in desperate attempts to escape. And all the ribbon-wearing clingers left behind turned toward Raed.

"Why did you bring me here?" he cried as he backed right up against the windows, wanting this to be over quickly. A shadow fell across the area of desks—

— • —

Revived again, safely back in his cage in 2033.

Raed focused blearily past the bars and across the main Projection arena, where a hundred other volunteers hung suspended in cages too, most of them mere image-people, half here, half there, still currently ghosting somewhere. In some of the closer cages, volunteers appeared to be crouched over something in the past, or clutching onto someone. Those in the closest cages seemed to be in some kind of pain.

But a number of volunteers were no longer glowing images. Their Projections had just ended, just like Raed's. In one or two cages he could see people being revived with smelling salts ...

In his own cage the Muslim psychologist was again consulting with the big medic, both standing just below him. Raed waited until the medic slipped back out before he summoned the will to say to the psychologist, "Need to ask something."

"Ask."

He gestured toward the cages filling the main arena. "Those people are all ghosting back to 9/11, aren't they? They've been accompanying me ..."

"They have their own business in that target time," she told him.

Tackling what I've been avoiding, Raed thought. The hard part.

"But yes," the psychologist went on, "they are accompanying you, in a way—they're Projecting through folds oriented identically to your own." Behind the burqa veil, the woman's eyes held disappointment. "Is that your question?"

He would not disappoint her. He said, "They're the group of 'interested citizens,' yes? The ones who petitioned to get me into this program."

She nodded. "Is that your question?"

"Who are they?" Raed asked. That was *the* question.

"The grown children of your victims, mostly," she told him. "Plus a few victims' nieces, nephews, friends, one or two of the surviving spouses."

Raed swallowed, a soft clicking deep in his throat. "... And you?"

"Yes," she answered without hesitation, her liquid-black eyes swallowing his question. "I'm also the child of one of your victims." She adjusted the folds of her burqa to show him the red ribbon she was wearing. The same ribbon worn by the out-of-place clingers and companions in the past—the people in the cages beyond the Plexiglas.

Raed bowed his head. If the woman below him *was* his daughter, then Haifa, his wife, was surely another of Raed's victims. And if the woman below him *was* his daughter, surely it was no surprise she'd become a psychologist—with a father like Raed to try and comprehend.

She said to him: "I was one of those curious to see if you were capable of making it through this program." A beeping drew her eyes to her slate. She turned, nodded to the Projection operators at their consoles, glanced up at Raed again. "Looks like we have time for just one more."

"Just one more," he agreed, even though he felt wearier than he'd ever imagined he could feel, weary down in his soul.

But there was one more place left to face, wasn't there? Raed watched the psychologist step out through the bars, then watched the world of 2033 slide away as the cage tunnelled him back to—

— • —

That oh-so-familiar tubular space. He was back where his night of Projection began, back in a seat on board a large passenger jet.

This jet, however, was airborne.

Flight 175, Boston to Los Angeles. Raed was sitting in a window seat about halfway up the plane. The oval portal beside him offered a good view of the Atlantic beyond the wing, and the Eastern seaboard. The plane was already well off its flight path, well on its way to its doomed target. But the familiar Manhattan skyline was not in sight yet; there was still a little time left.

Raed shifted out to the empty aisle seat, saw that the back half of the plane behind him was crammed with passengers. There were even people crouching in the aisle. Directly across the aisle, in the same row as Raed, a sturdy-looking man in his late thirties was dialling someone on a cell phone. After a few seconds the man began to speak. Raed instinctively drew back, then forced himself to listen:

"... flight's been hijacked," the man was saying. "I'll try to call again, but don't know if there'll be time."

The familiar words and calm voice recalled a bright kitchen with an answering machine in a warm Rhode Island home. *You must be Tom*, Raed thought.

"Whatever happens, Angie, know that I love you," Tom went on, maintaining his unearthly calm. "That I'm thinking of you now, and the kids, too. They have you, remember ..." He let out a long breath, then went on, "So they'll be fine, and don't let them be sad for too long."

Raed stared across the aisle, humbled by Tom's ability to pass beyond denial of his dire situation into acceptance of it. This man was neither hysterical nor paralyzed by terror; he was just—terribly lonely.

"I'll always be with the three of you. And Angie," Tom finished, "in my heart I know we'll meet again." He shut off his phone, turned to stare out the window.

That's when Raed caught a glimpse of someone seated on the far side of Tom, tucked up against him. Raed pulled himself to his feet, stepped into the aisle, saw a sixtyish-something woman with her hands wrapped round Tom's arm, her head on his shoulder, her face drawn tight, concentrating. She wasn't wearing a seatbelt because she didn't need one, of course.

"Angie"—Angela or Angelica—was an old woman now, yet still strong enough to ghost back to her lost husband's side, and strong enough to withstand the discharge of his dread long enough to add a little of her own calm to his. Angie was comforting Tom on the way to that greater comfort the man clearly had faith in.

The plane rolled, awkwardly changing direction, tossing Raed off balance. Through the windows of the forward seats he spotted distant skyscrapers, including the towers of the World Trade Center. Up in the cockpit his cousins and their pilot friends were beginning the approach to the South Tower, intent on bringing it down. And because Raed had known their intentions before his cousins and their comrades ever boarded this plane, he was just as responsible as they were. He could no longer deny it, now that he was actually on board with them. He'd *always* been on board with them, in some sense or other ...

And now that it was possible to walk up to the cockpit door and eavesdrop on Nazir and Sayf's final words, Raed found that he did not care to. His cousins' hold over him disintegrated long ago, in the awful period after the Twin Towers came down.

So he turned his back to the cockpit and began to walk down the aisle, looking over the people filling the rear of the plane—his cousins' victims, *his* victims too. Raed knew there'd only been sixty-five passengers on Flight 175, but he could see closer to a hundred crowded into the rear rows. Before him a sad and beautiful truth was playing out ... The plane banked again and Raed reeled on his feet, but not because of the deficiencies of the pilot. What he was seeing was almost too overpowering to witness.

The back of the plane was packed with lonely people, many of them being comforted by their own ghost-children—mostly full-grown forty-somethings now. Adults brave enough to come back to this unthinkable moment, to tackle the hard part and take on the two-way interaction that "biomass" unleashed:

The strong flood of emotions from passengers into their ghost-descendents.

And the weak seeping of emotions from the ghosts back into their long-lost loved ones.

Whatever weak effect we have on the past, the researcher Francis had told Raed, *it was made the first time around, if you get my meaning. So nothing can be changed!*

Cause and effect aside, every row Raed passed held an anguished-looking adult in track pants or jumpsuit, a red ribbon pinned to their collar. The ghosts were squeezed in behind the seats of some passengers, leaning over headrests, arms draped down round the shoulders of a mother, or an aunt, or a family friend they'd come back to comfort. A few were even kneeling in the aisle, their heads tucked onto the laps of passengers. All these agonizing visitors were soaking up the frenzied feelings of the passengers, while oozing an ounce of serenity back the other way, an ounce of certainty that their loved ones were with them, in spirit.

It was all they *could* do; Raed understood that. And now he understood what the Projection team was putting him through; he saw the method underlying their rehab program. Ghosting him back to see things that should help him know what to do. Like those two firemen taking turns in the crow's nest of their pumper truck, falling out exhausted, then climbing back in again to help douse the raging fires ... That's just what Raed was witnessing in the rear of Flight 175, as some ghost-comforters overcome with emotion simply vanished, and others immediately appeared to take their place. The volunteers from his own time were Projecting in, in wave after wave, taking turns taking on the pain of relatives and friends in the moment of greatest need.

The plane dropped lower, and a cry rose up from several passengers on Raed's left. Through the oval windows he saw the smoke trail from the North Tower, both buildings drawing inexorably closer.

Time to face the hard part himself.

In the second-to-last row a woman was curled up with a tiny, tired-looking child, a girl the age of the Basma he'd lost. A middle-aged man in coveralls stood behind the woman's seat, his head bowed, his arms draped over the woman's shoulders, while her own arm was wrapped tightly round the shoulders of the child in the aisle seat.

Raed lowered himself to his knees, falling into a prayer stance in the aisle beside the child, a victim of the pitiless madness of Raed's own youth. But pitying her now, he placed his arm across her, received the awesome discharge of her emotions, concentrated, tried hard to push his own feelings and his fatigue back onto her:

FORGIVE ME—FIND PEACE IN YOUR MOTHER'S ARMS—ADD MY WEARINESS TO YOURS ... The child's drooping eyes finally closed, Raed *felt* her fall unconscious as the plane accelerated down, saw some of the fear ease from her face in the last second of his embrace—

— • —

END OF FIRST DEEP PROJECTION CASE

— • —

Many more cases and depositions were presented to the World Court over the course of the hearings on Deep Projection technology. Some were further examples of New Spiritualist experiments, like the program designed for the inmate Raed. These positive-result cases sparked far greater interest among the worldwide audience following the hearings than the overstated cases claiming negative consequences. By the end of the hearings, the Court made its controversial decision, lifting the ban on Deep Projection "for limited use"—such use to be governed by a duly appointed body that would approve and oversee Projection programs.

I, Francis Drummond, am the head of that governing body.

The Hague hearings dramatically boosted the number of New Spiritualist volunteers, as it became apparent to the public that emotions transcend time in some miraculous way, and in a *two-way* direction ... From that day to this our movement has spread into every culture, changing the nature of the mid-Twenty-first Century entirely. Projection arenas have been reopened or built anew in thousands of cities, and now hundreds of thousands of volunteers ghost back to the past, participating in programs designed to open their eyes to the universality of tragedy in cultures other than their own.

The result has been a wider recognition of the present as the precarious climax to all our ancient pasts. After millennia of struggle and strife, back-breaking labour and bad luck, madness and sadness, and small successes piled one atop the next, many societies are making that final leap up the ladder of progress toward an unconditionally tolerant civilization.

The goal of New Spiritualism is a reawakening to the truth of what has gone before us, what it has taken all of us to get here. And though the controversy rages on, today our goal is being achieved. Waves of volunteers are returning to comfort their own ancestors—or comfort mere strangers caught in the tragic forces of world history—as a way of thanking the generations whose sufferings helped bring about the world we are fortunate enough to live in. The target times these volunteers revisit are mostly old and familiar turning points of the past, key moments in the histories of many cultures. The oldest stories in the book, you might say, and each one defined by a truth that Projection volunteers report witnessing:

Down through the ages the deepest humanity is found in the midst of tragedy and catastrophe, as the living cling to loved ones lost with hearts unbound. ■

James Alan Gardner (thinkage.ca/~jim) earned his Bachelor's and Master's degrees in applied math from the University of Waterloo, then promptly quit academia to write science fiction instead. Since then he has published eight novels, as well as numerous short stories that have appeared in *Asimov's Science Fiction* magazine, *The Magazine of Fantasy and Science Fiction, Amazing Science Fiction, On Spec,* and several anthologies. He has won the Writers of the Future Grand Prize and two Aurora Awards; he has also been a finalist for both the Nebula and the Hugo.

He recently joined the faculty of the Waterloo Unlimited high-school enrichment program at the University of Waterloo. In his spare time, he has earned a second-degree black sash in Shaolin Five-Animal kung fu, and now teaches kung fu on a regular basis. (He also writes computer documentation but tries to keep that a secret.)

His contribution to this anthology, "The Ray-Gun: A Love Story," was a finalist for both the Hugo and the Nebula Award.

NOVELS:

Expendable (HarperCollins Eos, New York, 1997)

Commitment Hour (HarperCollins Eos, New York, 1998)

Vigilant (HarperCollins Eos, New York, 1999)

Hunted (HarperCollins Eos, New York, 2000)

Ascending (HarperCollins Eos, New York, 2001)

Trapped (HarperCollins Eos, New York, 2002)

Radiant (HarperCollins Eos, New York, 2004)

Lara Croft and the Man of Bronze (Del Rey, New York, 2004)

SHORT STORY COLLECTION:

Gravity Wells (HarperCollins Eos, New York, 2005)

THE RAY-GUN: A LOVE STORY

James Alan Gardner

This is a story about a ray-gun. The ray-gun will not be explained except to say, "It shoots rays."

They are dangerous rays. If they hit you in the arm, it withers. If they hit you in the face, you go blind. If they hit you in the heart, you die. These things must be true, or else it would not be a ray-gun. But it is.

Ray-guns come from space. This one came from the captain of an alien starship passing through our solar system. The ship stopped to scoop up hydrogen from the atmosphere of Jupiter. During this refuelling process, the crew mutinied for reasons we cannot comprehend. We will never comprehend aliens. If someone spent a month explaining alien thoughts to us, we'd think we understood but we wouldn't. Our brains only know how to be human.

Although alien thoughts are beyond us, alien actions may be easy to grasp. We can understand the "what" if not the "why." If we saw what happened inside the alien vessel, we would recognize that the crew tried to take the captain's ray-gun and kill him.

There was a fight. The ray-gun went off many times. The starship exploded.

All this happened many centuries ago, before telescopes. The people of

Earth still wore animal skins. They only knew Jupiter as a dot in the sky. When the starship exploded, the dot got a tiny bit brighter, then returned to normal. No one on Earth noticed—not even the shamans who thought dots in the sky were important.

The ray-gun survived the explosion. A ray-gun must be resilient, or else it is not a ray-gun. The explosion hurled the ray-gun away from Jupiter and out into open space.

After thousands of years, the ray-gun reached Earth. It fell from the sky like a meteor; it grew hot enough to glow, but it didn't burn up.

The ray-gun fell at night during a blizzard. Travelling thousands of miles an hour, the ray-gun plunged deep into snow-covered woods. The snow melted so quickly that it burst into steam.

The blizzard continued, unaffected. Some things can't be harmed, even by ray-guns.

Unthinking snowflakes drifted down. If they touched the ray-gun's surface they vaporized, stealing heat from the weapon. Heat also radiated outward, melting snow nearby on the ground. Melt-water flowed into the shallow crater made by the ray-gun's impact. Water and snow cooled the weapon until all excess temperature had dissipated. A million more snowflakes heaped over the crater, hiding the ray-gun till spring.

— • —

In March, the gun was found by a boy named Jack. He was fourteen years old and walking through the woods after school. He walked slowly, brooding about his lack of popularity. Jack despised popular students and had no interest in anything they did. Even so, he envied them. They didn't appear to be lonely.

Jack wished he had a girlfriend. He wished he were important. He wished he knew what to do with his life. Instead, he walked alone in the woods on the edge of town.

The woods were not wild or isolated. They were crisscrossed with trails made by children playing hide-and-seek. But in spring, the trails were muddy; most people stayed away. Jack soon worried more about how to avoid shoe-sucking mud than about the unfairness of the world. He took wide detours around mucky patches, thrashing through brush that was crisp from winter.

Stalks broke as he passed. Burrs stuck to his jacket. He got farther and farther from the usual paths, hoping he'd find a way out by blundering forward rather than swallowing his pride and retreating.

In this way, Jack reached the spot where the ray-gun had landed. He saw the crater it had made. He found the ray-gun itself.

The gun seized Jack's attention, but he didn't know what it was. Its design was too alien to be recognized as a weapon. Its metal was blackened but not black, as if it had once been another colour but had finished that phase of its existence. Its pistol-butt was bulbous, the size of a tennis ball. Its barrel, as long as Jack's hand, was straight but its surface had dozens of nubs like a briarwood cane. The gun's trigger was a protruding blister you squeezed till it popped. A hard metal cap could slide over the blister to prevent the gun from firing accidentally, but the safety was off; it had been off for centuries, ever since the fight on the starship.

The alien captain who once owned the weapon might have considered it beautiful, but to human eyes, the gun resembled a dirty wet stick with a lump on one end. Jack might have walked by without giving it a second look if it hadn't been lying in a scorched crater. But it was.

The crater was two paces across and barren of plant life. The vegetation had burned in the heat of the ray-gun's fall. Soon enough, new spring growth would sprout, making the crater less obvious. At present though, the ray-gun stood out on the charred earth like a snake in an empty birdbath.

Jack picked up the gun. Though it looked like briarwood, it was cold like metal. It felt solid: not heavy, but substantial. It had the heft of a well-made object. Jack turned the gun in his hands, examining it from every angle. When he looked down the muzzle, he saw a crystal lens cut into hundreds of facets. Jack poked it with his baby finger, thinking the lens was a piece of glass that someone had jammed inside. He had the idea this might be a toy—perhaps a squirt-gun dropped by a careless child. If so, it had to be the most expensive toy Jack had ever seen. The gun's barrel and its lens were so perfectly machined that no one could mistake the craftsmanship.

Jack continued to poke at the weapon until the inevitable happened: He pressed the trigger blister. The ray-gun went off.

It might have been fatal, but by chance Jack was holding the gun aimed away from himself. A ray shot out of the gun's muzzle and blasted through a maple tree ten paces away. The ray made no sound, and although Jack had seen it clearly, he couldn't say what the ray's colour had been. It had no colour; it was simply a presence, like wind-chill or gravity. Yet Jack was sure he'd seen a force emanate from the muzzle and strike the tree.

Though the ray can't be described, its effect was plain. A circular hole appeared in the maple tree's trunk where bark and wood disintegrated into sizzling plasma. The plasma expanded at high speed and pressure, blowing apart what remained of the surrounding trunk. The ray made no sound, but the explosion did. Shocked chunks of wood and boiling maple sap flew outward, obliterating a cross-section of the tree. The lower part of the trunk and the roots were still there; so were the upper part and branches. In between was a gap, filled with hot escaping gases.

The unsupported part of the maple fell. It toppled ponderously backwards. The maple crashed onto the trees behind, its winter-bare branches snagging theirs. To Jack, it seemed that the forest had stopped the maple's fall, like soldiers catching an injured companion before he hit the ground.

Jack still held the gun. He gazed at it in wonder. His mind couldn't grasp what had happened.

He didn't drop the gun in fear. He didn't try to fire it again. He simply stared.

It was a ray-gun. It would never be anything else.

— • —

Jack wondered where the weapon had come from. Had aliens visited these woods? Or was the gun created by a secret government project? Did the gun's owner want it back? Was he, she, or it searching the woods right now?

Jack was tempted to put the gun back into the crater, then run before the owner showed up. But was there really an owner nearby? The crater suggested that the gun had fallen from space. Jack had seen photos of meteor impact craters; this wasn't exactly the same, but it had a similar look.

Jack turned his eyes upward. He saw a mundane after-school sky. It had no UFOs. Jack felt embarrassed for even looking.

He examined the crater again. If Jack left the gun here, and the owner never retrieved it, sooner or later the weapon would be found by someone else—probably by children playing in the woods. They might shoot each other by accident. If this were an ordinary gun, Jack would never leave it lying in a place like this. He'd take the gun home, tell his parents, and they'd turn it over to the police.

Should he do the same for *this* gun? No. He didn't want to.

But he didn't know what he wanted to do instead. Questions buzzed through his mind, starting with, "What should I do?" then moving on to, "Am I in danger?" and, "Do aliens really exist?"

After a while, he found himself wondering, "Exactly how much can the gun blow up?" That question made him smile.

Jack decided he wouldn't tell anyone about the gun—not now and maybe not ever. He would take it home and hide it where it wouldn't be found, but where it would be available if trouble came. What kind of trouble? Aliens ... spies ... supervillains ... who knew? If ray-guns were real, was anything impossible?

On the walk back home, Jack was so distracted by "What ifs?" that he nearly got hit by a car. He had reached the road that separated the woods from neighbouring houses. Like most roads in that part of Jack's small town, it didn't get much traffic. Jack stepped out from the trees and suddenly a sports car whizzed past him, only two steps away. Jack staggered back; the driver leaned on the horn; Jack hit his shoulder on an oak tree; then the incident was over, except for belated adrenalin.

For a full minute afterward, Jack leaned against the oak and felt his heart pound. As close calls go, this one wasn't too bad: Jack hadn't really been near enough to the road to get hit. Still, Jack needed quite a while to calm down. How stupid would it be to die in an accident on the day he'd found something miraculous?

Jack ought to have been watching for trouble. What if the threat had been a bug-eyed monster instead of a car? Jack should have been alert and prepared. In his mind's eye he imagined the incident again, only this time he casually somersaulted to safety rather than stumbling into a tree. That's how you're supposed to cheat death if you're carrying a ray-gun: with cool heroic flair.

But Jack couldn't do somersaults. He said to himself, *I'm Peter Parker, not Spider-Man.*

On the other hand, Jack *had* just acquired great power. And great responsibility. Like Peter Parker, Jack had to keep his power secret, for fear of tragic consequences. In Jack's case, maybe aliens would come for him. Maybe spies or government agents would kidnap him and his family. No matter how farfetched those things seemed, the existence of a ray-gun proved the world wasn't tame.

That night, Jack debated what to do with the gun. He pictured himself shooting terrorists and gang lords. If he rid the world of scum, pretty girls might admire him. But as soon as Jack imagined himself storming into a terrorist stronghold, he realized he'd get killed almost immediately. The ray-gun provided awesome firepower, but no defence at all. Besides, if Jack had found an ordinary gun in the forest, he never would have dreamed of running around murdering bad guys. Why should a ray-gun be different?

But it *was* different. Jack couldn't put the difference into words, but it was as real as the weapon's solid weight in his hands. The ray-gun changed everything. A world that contained a ray-gun might also contain flying saucers, beautiful secret agents ... and heroes.

Heroes who could somersault away from oncoming sports cars. Heroes who would cope with any danger. Heroes who *deserved* to have a ray-gun.

When he was young, Jack had taken for granted he'd become a hero: brave, skilled, and important. Somehow he'd lost that belief. He'd let himself settle for being ordinary. But now he wasn't ordinary: He had a ray-gun.

He had to live up to it. Jack had to be ready for bug-eyed monsters and giant robots. These were no longer childish daydreams; they were real possibilities in a world where ray-guns existed. Jack could picture himself running through town, blasting aliens and saving the planet.

Such thoughts made sense when Jack held the ray-gun in his hands— as if the gun planted fantasies in his mind. The feel of the gun filled Jack with ambition.

All weapons have a sense of purpose.

— • —

Jack practiced with the gun as often as he could. To avoid being seen, he rode his bike to a tract of land in the country: twenty acres owned by Jack's Great-Uncle Ron. No one went there but Jack. Uncle Ron had once intended to build a house on the property, but that had never happened. Now Ron was in a nursing home. Jack's family intended to sell the land once the old man died, but Ron was healthy for someone in his nineties. Until Uncle Ron's health ran out, Jack had the place to himself.

The tract was undeveloped—raw forest, not a woods where children played. In the middle lay a pond, completely hidden by trees. Jack would float sticks in the pond and shoot them with the gun.

If he missed, the water boiled. If he didn't, the sticks were destroyed. Sometimes they erupted in fire. Sometimes they burst with a bang but no flame. Sometimes they simply vanished. Jack couldn't tell if he was doing something subtly different to get each effect, or if the ray-gun changed modes on its own. Perhaps it had a computer which analyzed the target and chose the most lethal attack. Perhaps the attacks were always the same, but differences in the sticks made for different results. Jack didn't know. But as spring led to summer, he became a better shot. By autumn, he'd begun throwing sticks into the air and trying to vaporize them before they reached the ground.

During this time, Jack grew stronger. Long bike rides to the pond helped his legs and his stamina. In addition, he exercised with fitness equipment his parents had bought but never used. If monsters ever came, Jack couldn't afford to be weak—heroes had to climb fences and break down doors. They had to balance on rooftops and hang by their fingers from cliffs. They had to run fast enough to save the girl.

Jack pumped iron and ran every day. As he did so, he imagined dodging bullets and tentacles. When he felt like giving up, he cradled the ray-gun in his hands. It gave him the strength to persevere.

Before the ray-gun, Jack had seen himself as just another teenager; his life didn't make sense. But the gun made Jack a hero who might be needed to save the Earth. It clarified *everything*. Sore muscles didn't matter. Watching TV was a waste. If you let down your guard, that's when the monsters came.

When he wasn't exercising, Jack studied science. That was another part of being a hero. He sometimes dreamed he'd analyze the ray-gun, discovering how it worked and giving humans amazing new technology. At other times, he didn't want to understand the gun at all. He liked its mystery. Besides, there was no guarantee Jack would ever understand how the gun worked. Perhaps human science wouldn't progress far enough in Jack's lifetime. Perhaps Jack himself wouldn't have the brains to figure it out.

But he had enough brains for high school. He did well; he was motivated. He had to hold back to avoid attracting attention. When his gym teacher told him he should go out for track, Jack ran slower and pretended to get out of breath.

Spider-Man had to do the same.

— • —

Two years later, in geography class, a girl named Kirsten gave Jack a daisy. She said the daisy was good luck and he should make a wish.

Even a sixteen-year-old boy couldn't misconstrue such a hint. Despite awkwardness and foot-dragging, Jack soon had a girlfriend.

Kirsten was quiet but pretty. She played guitar. She wrote poems. She'd never had a boyfriend but she knew how to kiss. These were all good things. Jack wondered if he should tell her about the ray-gun.

Until Kirsten, Jack's only knowledge of girls came from his big sister, Rachel. Rachel was seventeen and incapable of keeping a secret. She talked with her friends about everything and was too slapdash to hide private things well. Jack didn't snoop through his sister's possessions, but when Rachel left her bedroom door ajar with empty cigarette packs tumbling out of the garbage can, who wouldn't notice? When she gossiped on the phone about sex with her boyfriend, who couldn't overhear? Jack didn't want to listen, but Rachel never lowered her voice. The things Jack heard made him queasy—about his sister, and girls in general.

If he showed Kirsten the ray-gun, would she tell her friends? Jack wanted to believe she wasn't that kind of girl, but he didn't know how many kinds of girl there were. He just knew that the ray-gun was too important for him to take chances. Changing the status quo wasn't worth the risk.

Yet the status quo changed anyway. The more time Jack spent with Kirsten, the less he had for shooting practice and other aspects of hero-dom. He felt guilty for skimping on crisis preparation; but when he went to the pond or spent a night reading science, he felt guilty for skimping on Kirsten. Jack would tell her he couldn't come over to do homework and when she asked why, he'd have to make up excuses. He felt he was treating her like an enemy spy: holding her at arm's length as if she were some femme fatale who was tempting him to betray state secrets. He hated not trusting her.

Despite this wall between them, Kirsten became Jack's lens on the world. If anything interesting happened, Jack didn't experience it directly; some portion of his mind stood back, enjoying the anticipation of having something to tell Kirsten about the next time they met. Whatever he saw, he wanted her to see it too. Whenever Jack heard a joke, even before he started laughing, he pictured himself repeating it to Kirsten.

Inevitably, Jack asked himself what she'd think of his hero-dom. Would she be impressed? Would she throw her arms around him and say he was even more wonderful than she'd thought? Or would she get that look on her face, the one when she heard bad poetry? Would she think he was an immature geek who'd read too many comic books and was pursuing some juvenile fantasy? How could anyone believe hostile aliens might appear in the sky? And if aliens did show up, how delusional was it that a teenage boy might make a difference, even if he owned a ray-gun and could do a hundred push-ups without stopping?

For weeks, Jack agonized: to tell or not to tell. Was Kirsten worthy, or just a copy of Jack's sister? Was Jack himself worthy, or just a foolish boy?

One Saturday in May, Jack and Kirsten went biking. Jack led her to the pond where he practiced with the gun. He hadn't yet decided what he'd do when they got there, but Jack couldn't just *tell* Kirsten about the ray-gun. She'd never believe it was real unless she saw the rays in action. But so much could go wrong. Jack was terrified of giving away his deepest secret. He was afraid that when he saw hero-dom through Kirsten's eyes, he'd realize it was silly.

At the pond, Jack felt so nervous he could hardly speak. He babbled about the warm weather ... a patch of mushrooms ... a crow cawing in a tree. He talked about everything except what was on his mind.

Kirsten misinterpreted his anxiety. She thought she knew why Jack had brought her to this secluded spot. After a while, she decided he needed encouragement, so she took off her shirt and her bra.

It was the wrong thing to do. Jack hadn't meant this outing to be a test ... but it was, and Kirsten had failed.

Jack took off his own shirt and wrapped his arms around her, chest touching breasts for the first time. He discovered it was possible to be excited and disappointed at the same time.

Jack and Kirsten made out on a patch of hard dirt. It was the first time they'd been alone with no risk of interruption. They kept their pants on, but they knew they could go farther: as far as there was. No one in the world would stop them from whatever they chose to do. Jack and Kirsten felt light in their skins—open and dizzy with possibilities.

Yet for Jack, it was all a mistake: one that couldn't be reversed. Now he'd never tell Kirsten about the ray-gun. He'd missed his chance because she'd acted the way Jack's sister would have acted. Kirsten had been thinking like a girl and she'd ruined things forever.

Jack hated the way he felt: all angry and resentful. He really liked Kirsten. He liked making out, and couldn't wait till the next time. He refused to be a guy who dumped a girl as soon as she let him touch her breasts. But he was now shut off from her and he had no idea how to get over that.

In the following months, Jack grew guiltier: He was treating Kirsten as if she were good enough for sex but not good enough to be told about the most important thing in his life. As for Kirsten, every day made her more unhappy: She felt Jack blaming her for something but she didn't know what she'd done. When they got together, they went straight to fondling and more as soon as possible. If they tried to talk, they didn't know what to say.

In August, Kirsten left to spend three weeks with her grandparents on Vancouver Island. Neither she nor Jack missed each other. They didn't even miss the sex. It was a relief to be apart. When Kirsten got back, they went for a walk and a confused conversation. Both produced excuses for why they couldn't stay together. The excuses didn't make sense, but neither Jack nor Kirsten noticed—they were too ashamed to pay attention to what they were saying. They both felt like failures. They'd thought their love would last forever, and now it was ending sordidly.

When the lying was over, Jack went for a run. He ran in a mental blur. His mind didn't clear until he found himself at the pond.

Night was drawing in. He thought of all the things he'd done with Kirsten on the shore and in the water. After that first time, they'd come here a lot; it was private. Because of Kirsten, this wasn't the same pond as when Jack had first begun to practice with the ray-gun. Jack wasn't the same boy. He and the pond now carried histories.

Jack could feel himself balanced on the edge of quitting. He'd turned seventeen. One more year of high school, then he'd go away to university. He realized he no longer believed in the imminent arrival of aliens, nor could he see himself as some great hero saving the world.

Jack knew he wasn't a hero. He'd used a nice girl for sex, then lied to get rid of her.

He felt like crap. But blasting the shit out of sticks made him feel a little better. The ray-gun still had its uses, even if shooting aliens wasn't one of them.

The next day Jack did more blasting. He pumped iron. He got science books out of the library. Without Kirsten at his side several hours a day, he had time to fill, and emptiness. By the first day of the new school year, Jack was back to his full hero-dom program. He no longer deceived himself that he was preparing for battle, but the program gave him something to do: a purpose, a release, and a penance.

So that was Jack's passage into manhood. He was dishonest with the girl he loved.

Manhood means learning who you are.

— • —

In his last year of high school, Jack went out with other girls but he was past the all-or-nothingness of First Love. He could have casual fun; he could approach sex with perspective. "Monumental and life-changing" had been tempered to "pleasant and exciting." Jack didn't take his girlfriends for granted, but they were people, not objects of worship. He was never tempted to tell any of them about the gun.

When he left town for university, Jack majored in Engineering Physics. He hadn't decided whether he'd ever analyze the ray-gun's inner workings, but he couldn't imagine taking courses that were irrelevant to the weapon. The ray-gun was the central fact of Jack's life. Even if he wasn't a hero, he was set apart from other people by this evidence that aliens existed.

During freshman year, Jack lived in an on-campus dormitory. Hiding the ray-gun from his roommate would have been impossible. Jack left the weapon at home, hidden near the pond. In sophomore year, Jack rented an apartment off campus. Now he could keep the ray-gun with him. He didn't like leaving it untended.

Jack persuaded a lab assistant to let him borrow a Geiger counter. The ray-gun emitted no radioactivity at all. Objects blasted by the gun showed no significant radioactivity either. Over time, Jack borrowed other equipment, or took blast debris to the lab so he could conduct tests when no one was around. He found nothing that explained how the ray-gun worked.

The winter before Jack graduated, Great-Uncle Ron finally died. In his will, the old man left his twenty acres of forest to Jack. Uncle Ron had found out that Jack liked to visit the pond. "I told him," said big sister Rachel. "Do you think I didn't know where you and Kirsten went?"

Jack had to laugh—uncomfortably. He was embarrassed to discover he couldn't keep secrets any better than his sister.

Jack's father offered to help him sell the land to pay for his education. The offer was polite, not pressing. Uncle Ron had doled out so much cash in his will that Jack's family was now well-off. When Jack said he'd rather hold on to the property "until the market improves," no one objected.

— • —

After getting his bachelor's degree, Jack continued on to grad school: first his master's, then his Ph.D. In one of his courses, he met Deana, working toward her own doctorate—in Electrical Engineering rather than Engineering Physics.

The two programs shared several seminars, but considered themselves rivals. Engineering Physics students pretended that Electrical Engineers weren't smart enough to understand abstract principles. Electrical Engineers pretended that Engineering Physics students were pie-in-the-sky dreamers whose theories were always wrong until real Engineers fixed them. Choosing to sit side by side, Jack and Deana teased each other every class. Within months, Deana moved into Jack's apartment.

Deana was small but physical. She told Jack she'd been drawn to him because he was the only man in their class who lifted weights. When Deana was young, she'd been a competitive swimmer—"*Very* competitive," she said—but her adolescent growth spurt had never arrived and she was eventually outmatched by girls with longer limbs. Deana had quit the competition circuit, but she hadn't quit swimming, nor had she lost the drive to be one up on those around her. She saw most things as contests, including her relationship with Jack. Deana was not beyond cheating if it gave her an edge.

In the apartment they now shared, Jack thought he'd hidden the raygun so well that Deana wouldn't find it. He didn't suspect that when he wasn't home, she went through his things. She couldn't stand the thought that Jack might have secrets from her.

He returned one day to find the gun on the kitchen table. Deana was poking at it. Jack wanted to yell, "Leave it alone!" but he was so choked with anger he couldn't speak.

Deana's hand was close to the trigger. The safety was off and the muzzle pointed in Jack's direction. He threw himself to the floor.

Nothing happened. Deana was so surprised by Jack's sudden move that she jerked her hand away from the gun. "What the hell are you doing?"

Jack got to his feet. "I could ask you the same question."

"I found this. I wondered what it was."

Jack knew she didn't "find" the gun. It had been buried under old notebooks inside a box at the back of a closet. Jack expected that Deana would invent some excuse for why she'd been digging into Jack's private possessions, but the excuse wouldn't be worth believing.

What infuriated Jack most was that he'd actually been thinking of showing Deana the gun. She was a very, very good engineer; Jack had dreamed that together, he and she might discover how the gun worked. Of all the women Jack had known, Deana was the first he'd asked to move in with him. She was strong and she was smart. She might understand the gun. The time had never been right to tell her the truth—Jack was still getting to know her and he needed to be absolutely sure—but Jack had dreamed ...

And now, like Kirsten at the pond, Deana had ruined everything. Jack felt so violated he could barely stand to look at the woman. He wanted to throw her out of the apartment ... but that would draw too much attention to the gun. He couldn't let Deana think the gun was important.

She was still staring at him, waiting for an explanation. "That's just something from my Great-Uncle Ron," Jack said. "An African good-luck charm. Or Indonesian. I forget. Uncle Ron travelled a lot." Actually, Ron sold insurance and seldom left the town where he was born. Jack picked up the gun from the table, trying to do so calmly rather than protectively. "I wish you hadn't touched this. It's old and fragile."

"It felt pretty solid to me."

"Solid but still breakable."

"Why did you dive to the floor?"

"Just silly superstition. It's bad luck to have this end point toward you." Jack gestured toward the muzzle. "And it's good luck to be on this end." He gestured toward the butt, then tried to make a joke. "Like there's a Maxwell demon in the middle, batting bad luck one way and good luck the other."

"You believe that crap?" Deana asked. She was an engineer. She went out of her way to disbelieve crap.

"Of course I don't believe it," Jack said. "But why ask for trouble?"

He took the gun back to the closet. Deana followed. As Jack returned the gun to its box, Deana said she'd been going through Jack's notes in search of anything he had on partial differential equations. Jack nearly let her get away with the lie; he usually let the women in his life get away with almost anything. But he realized he didn't want Deana in his life anymore. Whatever connection she and he had once felt, it was cut off the moment he saw her with the ray-gun.

Jack accused her of invading his privacy. Deana said he was paranoid. The argument grew heated. Out of habit, Jack almost backed down several times, but he stopped himself. He didn't want Deana under the same roof as the ray-gun. His feelings were partly irrational possessiveness, but also justifiable caution. If Deana got the gun and accidentally fired it, the results might be disastrous.

Jack and Deana continued to argue: right there in the closet within inches of the ray-gun. The gun lay in its box, like a child at the feet of parents fighting over custody. The ray-gun did nothing, as if it didn't care who won.

Eventually, unforgivable words were spoken. Deana said she'd move out as soon as possible. She left to stay the night with a friend.

The moment she was gone, Jack moved the gun. Deana still had a key to the apartment—she needed it until she could pack her things—and Jack was certain she'd try to grab the weapon as soon as he was busy elsewhere. The ray-gun was now a prize in a contest, and Deana never backed down.

Jack took the weapon to the university. He worked as an assistant for his Ph.D. supervisor, and he'd been given a locker in the supervisor's lab. The locker wasn't Fort Knox but leaving the gun there was better than leaving it in the apartment. The more Jack thought about Deana, the more he saw her as prying and obsessive, grasping for dominance. He didn't know what he'd ever seen in her.

The next morning he wondered if he had overreacted. Was he demonizing his ex like a sitcom cliché? If she was so egotistic, why hadn't he noticed before? Jack had no good answer. He decided he didn't need one. Unlike when he broke up with Kirsten, Jack felt no guilt this time. The sooner Deana was gone, the happier he'd be.

In a few days, Deana called to say she'd found a new place to live. She and Jack arranged a time for her to pick up her belongings. Jack didn't want to be there while she moved out; he couldn't stand seeing her in the apartment again. Instead, Jack went back to his home town for a long weekend with his family.

It was lucky he did. Jack left Friday afternoon and didn't get back to the university until Monday night. The police were waiting for him. Deana had disappeared late Saturday.

She'd talked to friends on Saturday afternoon. She'd made arrangements for Sunday brunch but hadn't shown up. No one had seen her since.

As the ex-boyfriend, Jack was a prime suspect. But his alibi was solid: His home town was hundreds of miles from the university, and his family could testify he'd been there the whole time. Jack couldn't possibly have sneaked back to the university, made Deana disappear, and raced back home.

Grudgingly, the police let Jack off the hook. They decided Deana must have been depressed by the break-up of the relationship. She might have run off so she wouldn't have to see Jack around the university. She might even have committed suicide.

Jack suspected otherwise. As soon as the police let him go, he went to his supervisor's lab. His locker had been pried open. The ray-gun lay on a nearby lab bench.

Jack could easily envision what happened. While moving out her things, Deana searched for the ray-gun. She hadn't found it in the apartment. She knew Jack had a locker in the lab and she'd guessed he'd stashed the weapon there. She broke open the locker to get the gun. She'd examined it and perhaps tried to take it apart. The gun went off.

Now Deana was gone. Not even a smudge on the floor. The ray-gun lay on the lab bench as guiltless as a stone. Jack was the only one with a conscience.

He suffered for weeks. Jack wondered how he could feel so bad about a woman who'd made him furious. But he knew the source of his guilt: While he and Deana were arguing in the closet, Jack had imagined vaporizing her with the gun. He was far too decent to shoot her for real, but the thought had crossed his mind. If Deana simply vanished, Jack wouldn't have to worry about what she might do. The ray-gun had made that thought come true, as if it had read Jack's mind.

Jack told himself the notion was ridiculous. The gun wasn't some genie who granted Jack's unspoken wishes. What happened to Deana came purely from her own bad luck and inquisitiveness.

Still, Jack felt like a murderer. After all this time, Jack realized the ray-gun was too dangerous to keep. As long as Jack had it, he'd be forced to live alone: never marrying, never having children, never trusting the gun around other people. And even if Jack became a recluse, accidents could happen. Someone else might die. It would be Jack's fault.

He wondered why he'd never had this thought before. Jack suddenly saw himself as one of those people who own a vicious attack dog. People like that always claimed they could keep the dog under control. How often did they end up on the evening news? How often did children get bitten, maimed, or killed?

Some dogs are tragedies waiting to happen. The ray-gun was, too. It would keep slipping off its leash until it was destroyed. Twelve years after finding the gun, Jack realized he finally had a heroic mission: to get rid of the weapon that made him a hero in the first place.

I'm not Spider-Man, he thought, *I'm Frodo.*

But how could Jack destroy something that had survived so much? The gun hadn't frozen in the cold of outer space; it hadn't burned up as it plunged through Earth's atmosphere; it hadn't broken when it hit the ground at terminal velocity. If the gun could endure such punishment, extreme measures would be needed to lay it to rest.

Jack imagined putting the gun into a blast furnace. But what if the weapon went off? What if it shot out the side of the furnace? The furnace itself could explode. That would be a disaster. Other means of destruction had similar problems. Crushing the gun in a hydraulic press ... what if the gun shot a hole in the press, sending pieces of equipment flying in all directions? Immersing the gun in acid ... what if the gun went off and splashed acid over everything? Slicing into the gun with a laser ... Jack didn't know what powered the gun, but obviously it contained vast energy. Destabilizing that energy might cause an explosion, a radiation leak, or some even greater catastrophe. Who knew what might happen if you tampered with alien technology?

And what if the gun could protect itself? Over the years, Jack had read every ray-gun story he could find. In some stories, such weapons had built-in computers. They had enough artificial intelligence to assess their situations. If they didn't like what was happening, they took action. What if Jack's gun was similar? What if attempts to destroy the weapon induced it to fight back? What if the ray-gun got mad?

Jack decided the only safe plan was to drop the gun into an ocean—the deeper the better. Even then, Jack feared the gun would somehow make its way back to shore. He hoped that the weapon would take years or even centuries to return, by which time humanity might be scientifically equipped to deal with the ray-gun's power.

Jack's plan had one weakness: Both the university and Jack's home town were far from the sea. Jack didn't know anyone with an ocean-going boat suitable for dumping objects into deep water. He'd just have to drive to the coast and see if he could rent something.

But not until summer. Jack was in the final stages of his Ph.D. and didn't have time to leave the university for an extended trip. As a temporary measure, Jack moved the ray-gun back to the pond. He buried the weapon several feet underground, hoping that would keep it safe from animals and anyone else who happened by.

(Jack imagined a new generation of lovesick teenagers discovering the pond. If that happened, he wanted them safe. Like a real hero, Jack cared about people he didn't know.)

— • —

Jack no longer practiced with the gun, but he maintained his physical regimen. He tried to exhaust himself so he wouldn't have the energy to brood. It didn't work. Lying sleepless in bed, he kept wondering what would have happened if he'd told Deana the truth. She wouldn't have killed herself if she'd been warned to be cautious. But Jack had cared more about his precious secret than Deana's life.

In the dark, Jack muttered, "It was her own damned fault." His words were true, but not true enough.

When Jack wasn't at the gym, he cloistered himself with schoolwork and research. (His doctoral thesis was about common properties of different types of high-energy beams.) Jack didn't socialize. He seldom phoned home. He took days to answer email messages from his sister. Even so, he told himself he was doing an excellent job of acting "normal."

Jack had underestimated his sister's perceptiveness. One weekend, Rachel showed up on his doorstep to see why he'd "gone weird." She spent two days digging under his skin. By the end of the weekend, she could tell that Deana's disappearance had disturbed Jack profoundly. Rachel couldn't guess the full truth, but as a big sister, she felt entitled to meddle in Jack's life. She resolved to snap her brother out of his low spirits.

The next weekend Rachel showed up on Jack's doorstep again. This time, she brought Kirsten.

Nine years had passed since Kirsten and Jack had seen each other: the day they both graduated from high school. In the intervening time, when Jack had thought of Kirsten, he always pictured her as a high-school girl. It was strange to see her as a woman. At twenty-seven, she was not greatly changed from eighteen—new glasses and a better haircut—but despite similarities to her teenage self, Kirsten wore her life differently. She'd grown up.

So had Jack. Meeting Kirsten by surprise made Jack feel ambushed, but he soon got over it. Rachel helped by talking loud and fast through the initial awkwardness. She took Jack and Kirsten for coffee, and acted as emcee as they got reacquainted.

Kirsten had followed a path close to Jack's: university and graduate work. She told him, "No one makes a living as a poet. Most of us find jobs as English professors—teaching poetry to others who won't make a living at it either."

Kirsten had earned her doctorate a month earlier. Now she was living back home. She currently had no man in her life—her last relationship had fizzled out months ago, and she'd decided to avoid new involvements until she knew where she would end up teaching. She'd sent her résumé to English departments all over the continent and was optimistic about her chances of success; to Jack's surprise, Kirsten had published dozens of poems in literary magazines. She'd even sold two to *The New Yorker*. Her publishing record would be enough to interest many English departments.

After coffee, Rachel dragged Jack to a mall where she and Kirsten made him buy new clothes. Rachel bullied Jack while Kirsten made apologetic suggestions. Jack did his best to be a good sport; as they left the mall, Jack was surprised to find that he'd actually had a good time.

That evening, there was wine and more conversation. Rachel took Jack's bed, leaving him and Kirsten to make whatever arrangements they chose. The two of them joked about Rachel trying to pair them up again. Eventually Kirsten took the couch in the living room while Jack crawled into a sleeping bag on the kitchen floor ... but that was only after talking till three in the morning.

Rachel and Kirsten left the next afternoon, but Jack felt cleansed by their visit. He stayed in touch with Kirsten by email. It was casual: not romance, but a knowing friendship.

In the next few months, Kirsten got job interviews with several colleges and universities. She accepted a position on the Oregon coast. She sent Jack pictures of the school. It was directly on the ocean; it even had a beach. Kirsten said she'd always liked the water. She teasingly reminded him of their times at the pond.

But when Jack saw Kirsten's pictures of the Pacific, all he could think of was dumping the ray-gun into the sea. He could drive out to visit her ... rent a boat ... sail out to deep water ...

No. Jack knew nothing about sailing, and he didn't have enough money to rent a boat that could venture far offshore. "How many years have I been preparing?" he asked himself. "Didn't I intend to be ready for any emergency? Now I have an honest-to-god mission, and I'm useless."

Then Kirsten sent him an email invitation to go sailing with her.

She had access to a sea-going yacht. It belonged to her grandparents—the ones she'd visited on Vancouver Island just before she and Jack broke up. During her trip to the island, Kirsten had gone boating with her grandparents every day. At the start, she'd done it to take her mind off Jack; then she'd discovered she enjoyed being out on the waves.

She'd spent time with her grandparents every summer since, learning the ins and outs of yachting. She'd taken courses. She'd earned the necessary licences. Now Kirsten was fully qualified for deep-water excursions ... and as a gift to wish her well on her new job, Kirsten's grandparents were lending her their boat for a month. They intended to sail down to Oregon, spend a few days there, then fly off to tour Australia. When they were done, they'd return and sail back home; but in the meantime, Kirsten would have the use of their yacht. She asked Jack if he'd like to be her crew.

When Jack got this invitation, he couldn't help being disturbed. Kirsten had never mentioned boating before. Because she was living in their home town, most of her email to Jack had been about old high-school friends. Jack had even started to picture her as a teenager again; he'd spent a weekend with the grown-up Kirsten, but all her talk of high-school people and places had muddled Jack's mental image of her. The thought of a bookish teenage girl captaining a yacht was absurd.

But that was a lesser problem compared to the suspicious convenience of her invitation. Jack needed a boat; all of a sudden, Kirsten had one. The coincidence was almost impossible to swallow.

He thought of the unknown aliens who made the ray-gun. Could they be influencing events? If the ray-gun was intelligent, could *it* be responsible for the coincidence?

Kirsten had often spent time near the gun. On their first visit to the pond, she and Jack had lain half-naked with the gun in Jack's backpack beside them.

He thought of Kirsten that day. So open. So vulnerable. The gun had been within inches. Had it nurtured Kirsten's interest in yachting ... her decision to get a job in Oregon ... even her grandparents' offer of their boat? Had it moulded Kirsten's life so she was ready when Jack needed her? And if the gun could do that, what had it done to Jack himself?

This is ridiculous, Jack thought. *The gun is just a gun. It doesn't control people. It just kills them.*

Yet Jack couldn't shake off his sense of eeriness—about Kirsten as well as the ray-gun. All these years, while Jack had been preparing himself to be a hero, Kirsten had somehow done the same. Her self-improvement program had worked better than Jack's. She had a boat; he didn't.

Coincidence or not, Jack couldn't look a gift-horse in the mouth. He told Kirsten he'd be delighted to go sailing with her. Only later did he realize that their time on the yacht would have a sexual subtext. He broke out laughing. "I'm such an idiot. We've done it again." Like that day at the pond, Jack had only been thinking about the gun. Kirsten had been thinking about Jack. Her invitation wasn't a carte-blanche come-on but it had a strong hint of, "Let's get together and see what develops."

Where Kirsten was concerned, Jack had always been slow to catch the signals. He thought, *Obviously, the ray-gun keeps dulling my senses.* This time, Jack meant it as a joke.

— • —

Summer came. Jack drove west with the ray-gun in the trunk of his car. The gun's safety was on, but Jack still drove as if he were carrying nuclear waste. He'd taken the gun back and forth between his home town and university many times, but this trip was longer, on unfamiliar roads. It was also the last trip Jack ever intended to make with the gun; if the gun didn't want to be thrown into the sea, perhaps it would cause trouble. But it didn't.

For much of the drive, Jack debated how to tell Kirsten about the gun. He'd considered smuggling it onto the boat and throwing the weapon overboard when she wasn't looking, but Jack felt that he owed her the truth. It was overdue. Besides, this cruise could be the beginning of a new relationship. Jack didn't want to start by sneaking behind Kirsten's back.

So he had to reveal his deepest secret. Every other secret would follow: What happened to Deana; what had really been on Jack's mind that day at the pond; what made First Love go sour. Jack would expose his guilt to the woman who'd suffered from the fallout.

He thought, *She'll probably throw me overboard with the gun.* But he would open up anyway, even if it made Kirsten hate him. When he tossed the ray-gun into the sea, he wanted to unburden himself of everything.

— • —

The first day on the boat, Jack said nothing about the ray-gun. Instead, he talked compulsively about trivia. So did Kirsten. It was strange being together, looking so much like they did in high school but being entirely different people.

Fortunately, they had practical matters to fill their time. Jack needed a crash course in seamanship. He learned quickly. Kirsten was a good teacher. Besides, Jack's longstanding program of hero-dom had prepared his mind and muscles. Kirsten was impressed that he knew Morse code and had extensive knowledge of knots. She asked, "Were you a Boy Scout?"

"No. When I was a kid, I wanted to be able to untie myself if I ever got captured by spies."

Kirsten laughed. She thought he was joking.

That first day, they stayed close to shore. They never had to deal with being alone; there were always other yachts in sight, and sailboats, and people on shore. When night came, they put in to harbour. They ate in an ocean-view restaurant. Jack asked, "So where will we go tomorrow?"

"Where would you like? Up the coast, down the coast, or straight out to sea?"

"Why not straight out?" said Jack.

Back on the yacht, he and Kirsten talked long past midnight. There was only one cabin, but two separate fold-away beds. Without discussion, they each chose a bed. Both usually slept in the nude, but for this trip they'd both brought makeshift "pyjamas" consisting of a T-shirt and track pants. They laughed at the clothes, the coincidence, and themselves.

They didn't kiss goodnight. Jack silently wished they had. He hoped Kirsten was wishing the same thing. They talked for an hour after they'd turned out the lights, becoming nothing but voices in the dark.

— • —

The next day they sailed due west. Both waited to see if the other would suggest turning back before dark. Neither did. The farther they got from shore, the fewer other boats remained in sight. By sunset, Jack and Kirsten knew they were once more alone with each other. No one in the world would stop them from whatever they chose to do.

Jack asked Kirsten to stay on deck. He went below and got the ray-gun from his luggage. He brought it up into the twilight. Before he could speak, Kirsten said, "I've seen that before."

Jack stared at her in shock. "What? Where?"

"I saw it years ago, in the woods back home. I was out for a walk. I noticed it lying in a little crater, as if it had fallen from the sky."

"Really? You found it, too?"

"But I didn't touch it," Kirsten said. "I don't know why. Then I heard someone coming and I ran away. But the memory stayed vivid in my head. A mysterious object in a crater in the woods. I can't tell you how often I've tried to write poems about it, but they never work out." She looked at the gun in Jack's hands. "What is it?"

"A ray-gun," he said. In the fading light, he could see a clump of seaweed floating a short distance from the boat. He raised the gun and fired. The seaweed exploded in a blaze of fire, burning brightly against the dark waves.

"A ray-gun," said Kirsten. "Can I try it?"

— • —

Some time later, holding hands, they let the gun fall into the water. It sank without protest.

Long after that, they talked in each other's arms. Jack said the gun had made him who he was. Kirsten said she was the same. "Until I saw the gun, I just wrote poems about myself—overwritten, self-absorbed pap, like every teenage girl. But the gun gave me something else to write about. I'd only seen it for a minute, but it was one of those burned-into-your-memory moments. I felt driven to find words to express what I'd seen. I kept refining my poems, trying to make them better. That's what made the difference."

"I felt driven too," Jack said. "Sometimes I've wondered if the gun can affect human minds. Maybe it brainwashed us into becoming who we are."

"Or maybe it's just Stone Soup," Kirsten said. "You know the story? Someone claims he can make soup from a stone, but what he really does is trick people into adding their own food to the pot. Maybe the ray-gun is like that. It did nothing but sit there like a stone. You and I did everything— made ourselves who we are—and the ray-gun is only an excuse."

"Maybe," Jack said. "But so many coincidences brought us here ..."

"You think the gun manipulated us because it *wanted* to be thrown into the Pacific? Why?"

"Maybe even a ray-gun gets tired of killing." Jack shivered, thinking of Deana. "Maybe the gun feels guilty for the deaths it's caused; it wanted to go someplace where it would never have to kill again."

"Deana's death wasn't your fault," Kirsten said. "Really, Jack. It was awful, but it wasn't your fault." She shivered, too, then made her voice brighter. "Maybe the ray-gun orchestrated all this because it's an incurable romantic. It wanted to bring us together: our own personal matchmaker from the stars."

Jack kissed Kirsten on the nose. "If that's true, I don't object."

"Neither do I." She kissed him back.

Not on the nose.

— • —

Far below, the ray-gun drifted through the cold black depths. Beneath it, on the bottom of the sea, lay wreckage from the starship that had exploded centuries before. The wreckage had travelled all the way from Jupiter. Because of tiny differences in trajectory, the wreckage had splashed down thousands of miles from where the ray-gun landed.

The ray-gun sank straight toward the wreckage ... but what the wreckage held or why the ray-gun wanted to rejoin it, we will never know.

We will never comprehend aliens. If someone spent a month explaining alien thoughts to us, we'd think we understood.

But we wouldn't. ■

Julie E. Czerneda (czerneda.com) is both a best-selling novelist and an accomplished anthologist. A former biologist, she began writing professionally in 1985, contributing to over two hundred student and teacher resources in sciences, math, and career education.

She has judged writing awards, conducted writers' workshops, provided professional development for teachers and librarians across Canada and the U.S., and consulted for *Science News*. A sought-after speaker on scientific literacy, she received the Peel Award of Excellence in Education and is an Alumni of Honour of the University of Waterloo.

She has won four Aurora Awards and the Golden Duck Award of Excellence for Science and Technology Education, and been a finalist for the Philip K. Dick Award and the John W. Campbell Award for Best New Writer. In 2008, the Canadian Science Writers' Association gave her the Science in Society Award (Youth) for her anthology *Polaris*. She lives in Orillia, Ontario, with her husband Roger.

NOVELS:

A Thousand Words for Stranger (DAW Books, New York, 1997)

Beholder's Eye (DAW Books, New York, 1998)

Ties of Power (DAW Books, New York, 1999)

Changing Vision (DAW Books, New York, 2000)

In the Company of Others (DAW Books, New York, 2001)

To Trade the Stars (DAW Books, New York, 2002)

Hidden in Sight (DAW Books, New York, 2003)

Species Imperative: Survival (DAW Books, New York, 2004)

Species Imperative: Migration (DAW Books, New York, 2005)

Species Imperative: Regeneration (DAW Books, New York, 2006)

Reap the Wild Wind (DAW Books, New York, 2007)

Riders of the Storm (DAW Books, New York, 2008)

Rift in the Sky (DAW Books, New York, 2009)

BUBBLES AND BOXES

Julie E. Czerneda

Bubbles and boxes floated past the scanner, hooked nanarms snaring those that reflected red under the laser sweeps, confirming the spec tests. The operation was deceptively familiar, given the scale was so far beyond normality Sara had stopped analogy-hunting long ago.

Scale was irrelevant, she thought, adjusting the gain on her goggles to improve the illusion of depth. They were simply bubbles and boxes on an assembly line. Not very pretty, either; plain better suited them to their function. The nicest ones always seemed to be odd ones, the occasionally irregular shapes that the quality-control nans rightly captured and held for destruction. *Still*, Sara thought, swinging the gymballed headpiece to follow the death struggles of an elaborate octagon, *it was a shame*. The laser bounced off its stubby strands and floppy corners in unpredictable and changing patterns. A work of almost living art, that took million-dollar glasses to appreciate.

Then it was gone, broken into its component strands, twisting ribbons of eighty bases, longing for completion, to be rinsed away in the next part of the process. There was the promise, at least, of rebirth.

"If you're finished, Dr. Surghelti," a soft voice breathed into her ear, "you have the usual line-up outside."

Sara closed her eyes before ducking her head from the goggles. It took a moment to prepare her senses for the macro world again. Then she blinked owlishly at her post-doc, Mai Ling. "The 101's?"

Mai Ling's dimples belied her otherwise serious expression. "They didn't like your last question, Doctor. The essay?"

"Show me a first year biotech class that does." Sara waved at the stacks of fresh exam papers turning her desk and those of her grad students into lunar landscapes, cratered by work space and coffee mugs. "At least I don't ask them to mark their own." Out of habit, Sara glanced along the gleaming outer surface of the tube before closing the view port she'd been using. Most of the automatic assembly plant looped through the walls and ceiling, only here dipping to her level like the courteously offered arm of a gentleman octopus, meeting the feeder tubes coming up through the floor.

An assembly plant like no other. Within, girders of DNA were being constructed from raw materials drawn through the feeders. Those girders were joined by nanarms, themselves built of DNA, into whatever structure Sara chose. Today, it was bubbles and boxes, the containment vessels used everywhere to ferry raw materials. Tomorrow it might be more quality-control nans, with their molecular keys and hooks to snatch the unwanted. The results of this self-assembly could only be seen here, through her viewer into the quality-control section, where nanarms destroyed the undesirable.

Sara pushed the massive chrome and black helmet, with its assemblage of jury-rigged wiring and state-of-the-art complexity, upward with a flick of her wrist. It hummed its way into the ceiling cupboard. With her other hand, she poked a loose strand of hair back under its cap.

"They're used to having marks before they leave the room, that's all." Mai Ling considered the towering pile of exams on her own desk. "Maybe next year we could just go with self-marking exams?" she asked wistfully. "I could use more research time. And sleep."

"I never promised you sleep," Sara said with an unrepentant grin. No secret she abhorred the university's enthusiasm for automated grades. *But nothing*, she thought, *told her more about an individual's grasp of concepts than self-expression.* Logical argument, not guesswork, passed students through her classes. Self-marking exams were like the nans: quality control by eliminating the variable—not recognition of excellence.

"Dr. Teig called."

Sara glanced at the lab clock in disbelief. 8:30 AM. *A little early to be one of those days.* "Message?"

"Under the Rock." The weathered concrete lump on Sara's desk was a memento from the anti-biotech riots of the early days, having left a more lasting impression on her office wall than protests had on policy. Sara kept it as a reminder of a time of tumult and disagreement. And for messages from Chuck Teig.

There was a stack of pink slips beneath it. Considering that she'd called Chuck back two days ago, he'd been busy. *What was he after this time?*

— • —

A nanarm paused.

There was no question this hesitation was accidental. If any had known to investigate, the culprit might have been identified as a temperature gradient, a miniscule change in local environment, its cause an open door to a hall cooled by a spring breeze, the breeze carried in on the shoulders and chatter of a group of students lingering to talk within the outer doors, preventing them from closing immediately. Still, change occurred. A nanarm paused. And an irregular, beautiful shape, neither box nor bubble, floated past, reflecting new and unimagined colours from the laser, different from all the rest.

Unremarked. And so, uncorrected.

— • —

"Yes, Chuck, I've reviewed your latest paper." The flood of messages throughout the day had been a demand for her attention. *Well, he had it.*

Unfortunately, formal dinners and discussions with her old friend didn't mix well. Sara lowered her voice in vain hope of keeping him under control. "If I were you, I wouldn't submit it."

"If I were you, I couldn't have done the research," Chuck's answering growl was predictably superior. Self-employed, self-funded, and with enough self-confidence to have alienated more than one scientific community, he had the privilege of independence. And never hesitated to remind her.

Opinionated to a fault, of course. Sara had half-expected Chuck's latest messages to be about his pet peeve: the continuing public release of DNA-based nanotechnology. The nanarms, multi-purpose girders, were the basis of the machinery that sorted and purified vital biological components, from sugars to amines. Linked together, nans formed the molecular bubbles and boxes used to isolate purified substances for transport. Without both, it would have been impossible to develop the GTS, the Global Tubing System.

A system Chuck thoroughly distrusted, making it his mission in life to inform Sara personally about any potential problem he imagined. Why her? Partly because no one else listened to him on the subject, after years of flawless operation.

And partly, Sara admitted, because she'd been the first to release the technology on the 'Net, over every one of what she'd taken for his self-interested, profit-centred objections. Models, schematics, procedures—all made public the same night, in hopes of a quick adoption of a worldwide standard, of compatibility. It had worked beyond anyone's wildest dreams.

They'd ended hunger.

The nans made it possible to constantly shift essential nutrients from wherever produced to wherever needed, freed from dependence on weather, climate, or even conventional means of shipping. More than that. It became impossible for any one group to control the flow as dozens, then hundreds, then hundreds of thousands of stations connected to the GTS. The technology had been available to anyone—as a result, the commerce of supply and demand became linked at the level of cities, between marketplaces rather than states. The politics of starvation withered and died.

Despite such fundamental change in their world, despite all signs of a pending golden age, Chuck Teig remained stubbornly skeptical. At least, he'd had the sense to confine his paranoia to her.

Sara sipped her martini and wiggled her toes in too-tight shoes. The Alumni Dinner was her professorial obligation; Chuck was here to accept an award for his company's latest donation. She didn't want the details. Given the success of his last patent, he'd probably funded her own wing for the next decade. A thoroughly obnoxious development, considering she'd outscored him in all their classes.

The dining room could have been any formal setting; its soft ring of fine crystal and murmuring voices the sounds of civilized conversation at any gathering. However, this room was filled with, at a guess, the top twenty percent of the world's biotech experts, ample testimony to the wisdom of the ULS's founders. A university dedicated to biology had seemed a gamble fifteen years ago, when the forefront of change had been more silicon than carbon. But it had proved visionary. The manipulation of living matter became the hottest field since the quantum computer. Waterloo's University of Life Science, though no longer alone, could boast it remained the best launch pad from which to enter the race.

And one of its biggest winners was preparing to slingshot an olive at her with his spoon. "So why shouldn't I publish?"

Sara made herself smile. "Chuck," she began, then changed her mind. There was an unfamiliar pleading on his normally cherub-like features. His hair distracted her, too. He'd re-grown it in a striped pattern this season; fine for Paris but hardly the fashion among the relatively conservative scientists present tonight. To make matters worse, the patches above his ears hadn't taken well, creating a checkerboard look. *He'd probably worn that old baseball cap of his during its early growth*, Sara thought. Biotech was unlikely to ever make hair replacement idiot-proof . "Chuck, the problem isn't the science in your paper—"

"Well, God, that's a relief," he said too loudly. The other four at their table gave automatic shivers before resuming their whispered discussion of the latest affair between the USL President and her staff. "Typos? Told you I'm getting a new secretary."

Sara sighed. "You never could spell," she agreed. "No, Chuck. What troubles me about your paper is its implications."

"Oh." He tossed his napkin into the air with disgust. "That crap." This drew a warning scowl from the Dean at the next table. Chuck saw it in Sara's reaction and turned to scowl back. Sara shrugged helplessly. *They should know Chuck by now.* His donations were the only social link he'd left in this room. "When are you going to step into the real world, Sara-socks?"

She winced at the pet name; another sign Chuck was losing what propriety he possessed. And the main course was only now arriving at the outskirts of the hall. "This isn't the time for a debate—"

"Fine," he said quickly, with a smug look. "Thursday, my place. You've that informatics lab, right? Come after. I still make a mean cocoa."

She knew the others at their table hung on her answer, nothing loath to gossip over her. Then she looked at Chuck and saw the recklessness there, added it to the potential for disaster she saw in his latest work. There really was no option. "Ten-thirty then. Now let me eat my supper in peace."

— • —

The new shape was more delicate, its unusual anatomy inclined to split at the edges when jostled by bubble or box. Its then-exposed arms beckoned to the debris of the nans' destructive sorting, an irresistible come-hither, molecular matchmaking of unparalleled potency.

Then, there were two.

— • —

"You've gotten better."

Chuck poured the last of the cocoa into Sara's cup. "Actually, the cows have," he announced, grinning as she gave the brown liquid a startled second look.

"I hadn't heard. You did it?" At his nod, Sara took another sip, slipping the warm chocolate taste around her tongue. *Perfect.* None of the aftertaste or odd texture that had plagued earlier attempts to biogeneer dairy cows to produce chocolate milk. "Another first for Teig Biotech. My congratulations." Sara didn't bother estimating the return on this particular patent. No doubt it would be a runaway success, especially with the devastation of the cocoa crop in South America. Such a shame they'd used plant retroviruses against the plantations of drug lords and lost so much more than planned. "Solids?"

Chuck pulled out a small foil bag. He ripped off one end with his teeth and poured small brown chips into her waiting palm. "Cookie-ready, Sarasocks. Try 'em next time you bake."

Since Chuck knew Sara's culinary skill peaked at reheating packaged dinners, she ignored this, but licked some of the chips from her hand. The background flavour held a distinctive coconut-like tang, but she could find no fault with the chocolate.

"Nicely done. Chocoholics everywhere will bless you." Then she raised a brow at his pleased expression. "Any preliminaries on the economic impacts of increased demand for dairy cows? What about the countries with stockpiles of cocoa beans? Will there be a disruption in milk supplies?"

He wagged one finger under her nose. "Gotcha!" Chuck drew a datacube from his pocket, surreptitiously freeing lint from one edge, and dropped it into Sara's now chocolate-free hand. "Impact studies by nine impeccable experts, a planned two year phase-in to the marketplace, combining continued profits for existing stocks with preferential location of biogeneering stations, and my Grandma's recipe for the best cookies on the planet."

Sara held up the cube. "I will check this, Chuck. After what happened to the maple syrup producers—"

Chuck shook his head vehemently, a strand of wilful checkerboard hair tumbling over one eye. "Not my fault."

"You sold the patents for biogen maples to Senegal!"

"The marketplace dictates."

Sara rolled her eyes and gave up the argument. Senegal was now covered with two-metre-high dwarf, tropical, and year-round productive sugar maple trees, while the maple bush in Ontario, Quebec, Vermont, and Maine was worth more as veneer wood. The only portion of the industry left in its traditional location was the making of cute bottles. Consumers seemed quite happy buying "Made in Senegal" syrup as long as it came with a wood shanty and draft horse on the label.

Sara tossed the cube up and down. "Let's hope this is an improvement, Chuck. That's all I'll say until I read it myself."

With a cheerful nod—nothing seemed to affect Chuck's approach to life for long—he beckoned her to follow him. Sara sighed, straightened her long legs, and unwedged herself from the couch. Her feet had just stopped throbbing.

But this was why she'd agreed to come, after all. Chuck's newest project.

— • —

Two became four. Four became eight. Eight became sixteen. Bounced about in the streams, they separated, arms reaching in the laser-lanced darkness. Some were snared and destroyed, only to have their remains snatched up by others.

Then, partial destruction produces incomplete separation. A novel shape appears.

Growth.

— • —

Chuck's home was an outgrowth of Teig Biotech's headquarters. In the beginning, he'd lived in his office, rolling out a sleeping bag when biological necessity overcame his creative urges. Once able to afford a house, he'd found travelling back and forth a nuisance and promptly gave it to a grateful, if amazed, nephew. Not that he suffered: His portion of the building included a games room, pool, and ballroom. Sara knew he'd wanted a bowling alley but the vibration would have impacted his research.

Easy to mistake it as the home of a man consumed by his work, Sara thought, knowing the truth. Chuck was having fun. He'd been lucky enough to pick a playground with very large financial rewards. He'd have been as happy still sleeping under his desk at the university.

Well, maybe not, she added honestly to herself. Chuck was happier being his own boss, and so were those around him.

"Through here," he muttered, using his hand on the small of her back to steer Sara from the door she expected toward another.

"Not the main lab?" she protested, and almost bit her tongue. Chuck took insufferable delight in her envy over his newest toys.

"Later. Next left."

They marched down spotless corridors, posters and signs tucked behind glass to permit regular sterilization. Slightly old-fashioned, but Sara approved. Nanarm filters would be in place at every possible cross-contamination point, but that was no reason to neglect the macro safeguards that had permitted the early work to proceed. And kept the early results where they belonged—most of the time.

The corridor branched and Chuck, having kept his hand on her back—a familiarity Sara permitted for the moment—aimed her at the left hallway. They stopped before a security door where he bent forward and spat accurately into the cup offered by the device in the wall. The tiny cup slipped back into its hiding place and they waited for the analysis. "Retina scan's more reliable," Sara pointed out. "And neater."

"Spitting's more fun," he countered, predictably, as the door accepted the taste of its master and opened.

She stepped inside before he could push her, drawn by a bizarre sense of misplacement. "What in hell—?"

"Look familiar?"

The question was rhetorical. Sara stared at a room that was *her* lab, her space, recreated down to the five paper-loaded desks she and her students shared. The papers were blank, but the piles were accurate. It even smelled right.

"If this is your idea of a joke—" she warned, turning to glare at Chuck. Her voice trailed off at his expression. It wasn't the satisfied glee of a prankster; it was the sombre look of a man determined to confront something terrible. "What's going on?"

Instead of answering immediately, he strode past her to flatten his hand on the viewport, the duplicate of the one she routinely used to examine the molecular assembly line within the massive downcurl of tube. "Exactly," he said. "What's going on, Sara? Do you know?"

"I know you owe me an explanation, Charles Teig," Sara snapped. Her feet hurt. The taste of cocoa rose up her throat and she regretted ever agreeing to come. "We were here to talk about your work, not mine."

His hand moved in a caressing circle on the metal. "Yet your work is absolutely essential to mine, isn't it, Sara-socks? It always has been. Your tiny machine parts, so perfect and so reliable, are what make all the rest feasible on a global scale. Without DNA-based nanotech, we'd be pumping goo instead of nutrients." Chuck's eyes held hers. "But what about the bigger picture?"

More of the same. Sara wondered about simply leaving, but his effort to reproduce her lab meant something. Chuck, exasperating and full of himself as he was, had never been a fool. "Okay. You tell me. How much bigger than global would you care to go?"

Chuck went down on his heels to pat the series of smaller pipes rising up from the floor to the larger tube. "Where do these come from?"

Sara shoved papers aside on what would be her desk and hitched herself into her favourite thinking position, one knee hugged to her chest as she peered at Chuck. "Locally? That's the regional feeder line, K567 to be exact, given the university uses the same one. Bigger picture? Substation Omaha for the carbos, Sarnia for the fatty acids, and aminos from a dozen or so others. Purines and pyrimidines swap seasonally between Winnipeg and Mexico."

Chuck remained crouched like some unlikely cowboy. "Since the fifteenth Atlantic line went active last month, I'd say Spain for the fatty acids and Italy for the purines, but that's an opinion. They're all shipped together via main pumping lines before sorting and re-separation. No one tracks it, do they?"

Is that *where this is going?* "Probably not. Actual starting and end points are irrelevant. The major nutrients are transported based on supply and demand."

"I agree," he said, which surprised her. "But I still say you aren't seeing the bigger picture—and isn't that a switch, considering you're always on my case about consequences?"

Sara looked around this replica of her life's work as if some unknown danger to humanity would make itself plain. Then she laughed. "I'm not into biogen, Chuck. I'm an old-fashioned engineer, building better girders and wheels."

"And what do your girders and wheels think about that?"

For a moment, Sara couldn't think of anything to say. *He can't be serious.* "I'm going to pretend I didn't hear that," she said finally. "In fact, I'm going to pretend you haven't copied my lab," she jumped down from "her" desk, "and I'm going to pretend this whole evening didn't happen. Good night."

With an agility suggesting he did use the exercise equipment littering his games room, Chuck reached the door first, slamming it closed. Sara's heart starting thumping. *Stop it*, she told herself firmly, gazing into the face of this man she thought she knew. "You've either gone crazy or started taking something you shouldn't, old friend," she said as calmly as possible. "Open the door."

Chuck stepped back, spreading his hands wide. "A few more minutes—with an open mind."

Sara frowned. "Open the door." He did. Though tempted to walk out, she didn't. "Why did you recreate my lab?"

"It's not just your lab, you know," Chuck said. "This is standard format for every primary nanotech producer, wouldn't you agree?"

She nodded warily. "I'd have a hard time getting grants even from Teig Biotech if I couldn't interface with industry."

"DNA is self-assembled as required for whatever application, and any structures that don't match specs are broken down by quality-control nan-arms."

"It's not rocket science."

"And they never miss."

"It's not a question of missing. These are bits and pieces of molecules, Chuck, not living things. Gods above and below you know that as well as any-one! If a batch has too many inappropriate configs, we dump it and cook another. Making a good cup of cocoa is harder. What are you driving at?"

"Have a look for yourself."

Despite her firm conviction Chuck had indeed plunged over whatever deep end existed for prodigies, Sara activated the goggles. She wasn't the least surprised when Chuck came up beside her and a second set eased down from the ceiling. "Can I have those for the lab when we're done?" she asked. "My students are always fighting over the one."

"Look," he urged.

She looked, fighting déjà vu.

Bubbles and boxes floated past. Sara saw nothing unusual at first. Then she spotted something odd out of the corner of her eye. One of the nan-arms didn't look right. She focused on it, raised the magnification. The tip, which should have consisted of block-like molecular teeth, was rounded, the blocks merged with a twisted ring.

"See it?" Chuck's voice echoed within the helmet.

Sara thrust away the goggles, angrily blinking away dizziness. "See what? That a nan's contaminated? It happens, Chuck. Any machinery will get gummed up by what passes through it. Just needs cleaning."

He pushed his own headpiece up and seemed to have no trouble adjusting to glare at her. "All I did was modify the ambient temperature in this room by two degrees and what you call 'gumming' occurred over a hundred times more frequently. But that's not what concerns me. Didn't you see what was wrapped around that nanarm? Your precious packing crates have taken on new configurations. We're not talking about gummed machinery. We're talking about novel combinations of DNA."

"So?" Sara glared back. "What's going to happen with eighty base pairs? It takes hundreds to produce a single gene—millions to make even one of your twisted chromosomes!"

"Yes, and I've watched the production of stable chains, hundreds-long, under these conditions. Granted, the intact nans caught them, but—"

"Worry about your own work, Chuck. Your lab is the one playing with living things, not mine."

He slammed his hand down on the tube again. "Which is why we didn't look in here until I saw your latest reports—"

"You saw my reports?" Sara's fists clenched. "Who gave you—"

"I fund your damn lab. Don't you think I see everything you do?" His voice softened. "Sara. No matter what you think of me or Teig Biotech, we both know that's how it works. I've never taken advantage of you." A glint of something wicked in his eyes. "Mind you, when that talented brain of yours comes up with something revolutionary, we'll have to talk ..."

Sara refused to be charmed. "I'd call your latest something else. Foolhardy!"

"Oh, that." Chuck shooed an invisible fly. "Clever, yes? Let the little buggers earn their keep for once."

"Is that what you call it? Oh, you couldn't be satisfied to develop a gene-based resistance to acne, could you?" Sara said furiously. "Not flashy enough for Teig Biotech. Let's insert it into mosquito anti-coagulant! What are you thinking? That people will suddenly want to be bitten? It didn't work for the TB cure—"

"Because tuberculosis is endemic to cities, Sara-socks, where they spray for bugs. It would never have worked. Well, maybe if they'd tried lice. But I have a niche market here. Summer camps."

She realized her mouth was gaping and closed it after one word: "What?"

Chuck looked suddenly tired. "Summer camps. Purgatory for adolescents. Kids who have enough to deal with without breaking out in spots. The camps offer the biogen mosquitoes as an added feature. It's going to be big."

"We've an educated population these days, Chuck—don't mistake it for a passive one. They'll see releasing your mosquitoes as tampering with nature."

"That's what we do—"

"And they accept it in the supermarket or in hospitals. They won't around their children."

"Wanna bet? We've already sold out the first generation anti-zit bugs, before making a public announcement." Another flash of what seemed desperation on his face. "Let's forget my work for now. Grant me that I know my stuff, Sara, and who uses it. That's why you're here."

Sara threw up her hands. "I've no idea why I'm here. You never listen—"

Chuck captured her hands and brought them down, gently. She left them in his grip, feeling his thumb stroke the back of her right hand. The last time he'd done that? The night her husband died and Chuck had sat with her on the deck, the two of them staring at the empty lake without seeing it, in the days when they'd been the kind of friends who didn't need words for what mattered.

"Your lab became the pattern for all the others," he said slowly, searching her face. "That's why it's here. That's why I'm studying it. You know I've had doubts about the GT—"

Sara tried to pull her hands free but he wouldn't let go. "Doubts? About ending famine? About improving life around the world?"

His grip tightened, insisting on her attention. "Sara. You know me better than that. Not the result—the process. And who is involved in it. Oh, I expected sabotage, theft, blackmail, but we're too selfish a species. People grew fiercely protective of the GT, even faster than they fought for open access to the 'Net. They see the GT as a matter of survival. It is, isn't it? We can't feed ourselves any other way now."

This time, when Sara pulled at her hands, he released them. "The gumming of nanarms at +2C. And our survival. Make the link for me, Chuck, because I don't see it."

"What if novel combinations of DNA occurred in the other streams, like the assorted amines?"

Sara's eyes followed the tubes crisscrossing the ceiling and floor. "They can't—"

"I say they can—if your bubbles and boxes are as prone to rearrangement in the wide world of tubing as they are in this room. So what happens then?"

"If," Sara began, unconvinced, "perhaps parts of that DNA might—might—bring some amines into sufficiently close proximity that they might—might!—form a small protein. Enough of those? Might gum the works." She scowled at him. "But conditions in the tubes are regulated—and bricks can't turn themselves into houses."

"Yours can. And if enough different small proteins were coded? Might not one or more be enzymes, capable of catalyzing other reactions?" Chuck began to pace. "Think about it. In the tubes themselves: your bubbles and boxes splitting into new combinations of DNA, at the same time releasing their contents. Enzymes catalyzing reactions even as selection by the remaining nanarms, the conditions in the tubes themselves, favour some combinations and enzymes over others?" Chuck stopped for breath, one hand hovering over the nearest tube. "Evolution."

The word crawled down her spine. Sara shrugged away the shiver trying to follow it. "Contamination. We dump it out—"

"Dump it?" With a violence she'd never seen in him before, Chuck swept a desk clear of fake exams and coffee cups. Sara watched the debris settle in random patterns on the floor. But his voice stayed oddly calm. "Where?"

"From here?" She patted "her" desk. "You know perfectly well. Into a secured holding tank for analysis and recycling."

"What about commercial labs, Sara-socks? Labs where otherwise brilliant, careful people view your tech as nothing more than a filtration system with convenient, microscopic packing crates? What about the other end of the spectrum—the thousands of illicit, uninspected connections to the GTS? Did you think of their ability to react to novel DNA patterns when you gave this technology to anyone who could read?"

Sara shook her head, but it wasn't denial. "It's a self-correcting system," she argued. "Users want pure nutrients—it's in their interest to keep the system running at peak efficiency. They'd starve, otherwise—"

"Big picture. You aren't seeing it yet." Chuck planted his hands on either side of where Sara sat, leaning into her face. "People are convinced your bubbles and boxes ensure purity in their nutrient supply—how could they suspect them of being the source of contamination? Evolution, Sara," he breathed, smelling of biogeneered cocoa. "We've provided all the necessary complex organic chemicals for a new primordial soup. Not merely in puddles here or there—the GT will soon rival the Indian Ocean in volume. And no need to wait eons for mutation and recombination. Changing DNA is now part of the system. It's not just what I've shown you here. Your tiny machines and containers will be modified constantly—by individuals who've no conception of the power in those tiny bricks of yours."

Sara felt numb. "What power?"

"You're like the rest—thinking of DNA as a finite material, forgetting its potential." Chuck straightened to his full height. "But that's what I work with every day. The potential, Sara, for life. When, not if, something becomes alive within the system, it's going to be life evolved for that environment, not ours, life adapted to use what we've provided. You might be an engineer in practice, but you're a biologist at heart. You know how quickly a successful life form would replicate under those conditions.

"If we are very, very lucky," Chuck continued, "we'll see it coming before the entire GTS is compromised. We'll have time to start piling wheat on trains and rice into ships, time to save most of a population dependent on a technology that won't be ours any longer. But what if we don't?"

Sara discovered her fingers had clenched on Chuck's arms. She didn't want to believe him. She didn't dare refuse the possibility, not with what was at stake. "No one will believe you," she said aloud, hearing the words echo between them.

His smile was infinitely sad. "And you had to ask why I brought you here, Sara? You're the person who started it all, the fairy godmother of the GT. You've got that impeccable reputation to risk. I am sorry—"

She shook her head in disbelief that he would even consider her career. "If you are right—in any sense—this must go out immediately. Give me your data; I'll get my people working on it."

"It's yours." Then Chuck bent and kissed her cheek. It had the chill feel of a farewell. "Let's hope not too late."

— • —

Mai Ling took another sip of cold coffee, shuddering as the too-sweet liquid hit her empty stomach. It didn't help shrink her pile of unmarked exams. Barbara and Miguel were hunched over their desks. The final member of their group was using the goggles to watch the nanarms sort bubbles and boxes.

"Hey, Dev, you asleep in there?" Mai Ling called. There was a chorus of sleepy laughter. This wouldn't be the first time one of them had used the goggles to hide a nap.

The sudden shrill of an alarm made the question moot. With a curse, Dev started working the controls. "What's wrong?" she demanded, hurrying with the others to join him at the tube.

"We've got negative pressure on the purine feeder," he said, voice muffled by the goggles. "The autos were off."

Mai Ling shot a look at the readout, seeing the red band slashing across the schematic. Whatever problem had occurred was remote, at some station ahead of theirs in the GT. "Check for backwash, people. Dr. Surghelti will go ballistic if we've leaked into the mains."

"I initiated the seal manually," Dev assured her. "Think I caught all of it."

"Let's hope," Mai Ling said, starting a log entry.

— • —

Filled with precious cargo, bubbles and boxes slide along liquid laneways, shepherded by nanarms, guided to their varied destinations like so many migrating fish. At junctions, microscopic eddies form, slowing traffic in a moment of insignificant mixing and delay—insignificant until that traffic contains something else. Something new. Arms reach out in an irresistible come-hither ...

And then there were two. ■

Robert J. Sawyer (sfwriter.com) is the *Canadian Encyclopedia*'s authority on science fiction and founded the Canadian Region of the Science Fiction and Fantasy Writers of America. He has won the Hugo Award, the Nebula Award, the John W. Campbell Memorial Award, ten Aurora Awards, the Crime Writers of Canada's Arthur Ellis Award, the *Science Fiction Chronicle* Reader Award, the Toronto Public Library Celebrates Reading Award, and the top science fiction awards in Japan (the *Seiun*, which he's won three times), Spain (*Premio UPC de Ciencia Ficción*, which he's also won three times), France (*Le Grand Prix de l'Imaginaire*), and China (the Galaxy Award for Most Popular Foreign Author).

In 2007, he received an honorary doctorate from Laurentian University. He's been writer-in-residence at the Merril Collection of Science Fiction, Speculation and Fantasy; at Berton House in Dawson City, Yukon; and at the Canadian Light Source, Canada's national synchrotron facility, and he hosts the popular series *Supernatural Investigator* on Canada's Vision TV. Born in Ottawa, he now lives in Mississauga, Ontario, with his wife, poet Carolyn Clink.

The story that follows, "Shed Skin," was a finalist for the Hugo Award and won *Analog*'s Analytical Laboratory Award.

NOVELS:

Golden Fleece (Warner, New York, 1990)

Far-Seer (Ace, New York, 1992)

Fossil Hunter (Ace, New York, 1993)

Foreigner (Ace, New York, 1994)

End of an Era (Ace, New York, 1994)

The Terminal Experiment (HarperPrism, New York, 1995)

Starplex (Ace, New York, 1996)

Frameshift (Tor, New York, 1997)

Illegal Alien (Ace, New York, 1997)

Factoring Humanity (Tor, New York, 1998)

Flashforward (Tor, New York, 1999)

Calculating God (Tor, New York, 2000)

Hominids (Tor, New York, 2002)

Humans (Tor, New York, 2003)

Hybrids (Tor, New York, 2003)

Mindscan (Tor, New York, 2005)

Rollback (Tor, New York, 2007)

Wake (Penguin Canada, Toronto, 2009)

SHORT STORY COLLECTIONS:

Iterations and Other Stories (Quarry Press, Kingston, Ontario, 2002)

Identity Theft and Other Stories (Red Deer Press, Calgary, Alberta, 2008)

SHED SKIN

Robert J. Sawyer

"I'm sorry," said Mr. Shiozaki, as he leaned back in his swivel chair and looked at the middle-aged white man with the greying temples, "but there's nothing I can do for you."

"But I've changed my mind," said the man. He was getting red in the face as the conversation went on. "I want out of this deal."

"You can't change your mind," said Shiozaki. "You've *moved* your mind."

The man's voice had taken on a plaintive tone, although he was clearly trying to suppress it. "I didn't think it would be like this."

Shiozaki sighed. "Our psychological counsellors and our lawyers went over the entire procedure and all the ramifications with Mr. Rathburn beforehand. It's what he wanted."

"But I don't want it anymore."

"You don't have any say in the matter."

The white man placed a hand on the table. The hand was flat, the fingers splayed, but it was nonetheless full of tension. "Look," he said, "I demand to see—to see the other me. I'll explain it to him. He'll understand. He'll agree that we should rescind the deal."

Shiozaki shook his head. "We can't do that. You know we can't. That's part of the agreement."

"But—"

"No buts," said Shiozaki. "That's the way it *has* to be. No successor has ever come back here. They can't. Your successor has to do everything possible to shut your existence out of his mind, so he can get on with *his* existence, and not worry about yours. Even if he wanted to come see you, we wouldn't allow the visit."

"You can't treat me like this. It's inhuman."

"Get this through your skull," said Shiozaki. "*You* are not human."

"Yes, I am, damn it. If you—"

"If I prick you, do you not bleed?" said Shiozaki.

"Exactly! *I'm* the one who is flesh and blood. I'm the one who grew in my mother's womb. I'm the one who is a descendant of thousands of generations of *Homo sapiens* and thousands of generations of *Homo erectus* and *Homo habilis* before that. This—this other me is just a machine, a robot, an android."

"No, it's not. It is George Rathburn. The one and only George Rathburn."

"Then why do you call him 'it'?"

"I'm not going to play semantic games with you," said Shiozaki. "*He* is George Rathburn. You aren't—not anymore."

The man lifted his hand from the table and clenched his fist. "Yes, I am. I *am* George Rathburn."

"No, you're not. You're just a skin. Just a shed skin."

— • —

George Rathburn was slowly getting used to his new body. He'd spent six months in counselling preparing for the transference. They'd told him this replacement body wouldn't feel like his old one, and they'd been right. Most people didn't transfer until they were old, until they'd enjoyed as much biological physicality as they could—and until the ever-improving robotic technology was as good as it was going to get during their natural lifetime.

After all, although the current robot bodies were superior in many ways to the slab-of-flab ones—how soon he'd adopted that term!—they still weren't as physically sensitive.

Sex—the recreational act, if not the procreative one—was possible, but it wasn't quite as good. Synapses were fully reproduced in the nano-gel of the new brain, but hormonal responses were faked by playing back memories of previous events. Oh, an orgasm was still an orgasm, still wonderful—but it wasn't the unique, unpredictable experience of a real sexual climax. There was no need to ask, "Was it good for you?" for it was *always* good, always predictable, always exactly the same.

Still, there were compensations. George could now walk—or run, if he wanted to—for hours on end without feeling the slightest fatigue. And he'd dispensed with sleep. His daily memories were organized and sorted in a six-minute packing session every twenty-four hours; that was his only downtime.

Downtime. Funny that it had been the biological version of him that had been prone to downtime, while the electronic version was mostly free of it.

There were other changes, too. His proprioception—the sense of how his body and limbs were deployed at any given moment—was much sharper than it had previously been.

And his vision was more acute. He couldn't see into the infrared—that was technically possible, but so much of human cognition was based on the idea of darkness and light that to banish them with heat sensing had turned out to be bad psychologically. But his chromatic abilities had been extended in the other direction, and that let him see, among other things, bee purple, the colour that often marked distinctive patterns on flower petals that human eyes—the old-fashioned kind of human eyes, that is—were blind to.

Hidden beauty revealed.

And an eternity to enjoy it.

— • —

"I demand to see a lawyer."

Shiozaki was again facing the flesh-and-blood shell that had once housed George Rathburn, but the Japanese man's eyes seemed to be focused at infinity, as if looking right through him. "And how would you pay for this lawyer's services?" Shiozaki asked at last.

Rathburn—perhaps he couldn't use his name in speech, but no one could keep him from thinking it—opened his mouth to protest. He had money—lots of money. But, no, no, he'd signed all that away. His biometrics were meaningless; his retinal scans were no longer registered. Even if he could get out of this velvet prison and access one, no ATM in the world would dispense cash to him. Oh, there were plenty of stocks and bonds in his name ... but it wasn't *his* name anymore.

"There has to be something you can do to help me," said Rathburn.

"Of course," said Shiozaki. "I can assist you in any number of ways. Anything at all you need to be comfortable here."

"But *only* here, right?"

"Exactly. You knew that—I'm sorry; *Mr. Rathburn* knew that when he chose this path for himself, and for you. You will spend the rest of your life here in Paradise Valley."

Rathburn was silent for a time, then: "What if I agreed to accept your restrictions? What if I agreed *not* to present myself as George Rathburn? Could I leave here then?"

"You *aren't* George Rathburn. Regardless, we can't allow you to have any outside contact." Shiozaki was quiet for a few moments, and then, in a softer tone, he said, "Look, why make things difficult for yourself? Mr. Rathburn provided very generously for you. You will live a life of luxury here. You can access any books you might want, any movies. You've seen our recreation centre, and you must admit it's fabulous. And our sex-workers are the best-looking on the planet. Think of this as the longest, most pleasant vacation you've ever had."

"Except it doesn't end until I die," said Rathburn.

Shiozaki said nothing.

Rathburn exhaled noisily. "You're about to tell me that I'm already dead, aren't you? And so I shouldn't think of this as a prison; I should think of this as heaven."

Shiozaki opened his mouth to speak, but closed it again without saying anything. Rathburn knew that the administrator couldn't even give him that comfort. He wasn't dead—nor would he be, even when this discarded biological container, here, in Paradise Valley, finally ceased to function. No, George Rathburn lived on, a duplicated version of this consciousness in an almost indestructible, virtually immortal robot body, out in the real world.

— • —

"Hey there, G.R.," said the black man with the long grey beard. "Join me?"

Rathburn—the Rathburn made out of carbon, that is—had entered Paradise Valley's dining hall. The man with the beard had already been served his lunch: a lobster tail, garlic mashed potatoes, a glass of the finest Chardonnay. The food here was exquisite.

"Hi, Dat," Rathburn said, nodding. He envied the bearded man. His name, before he'd transferred his consciousness into a robot, had been Darius Allan Thompson, so his initials, the only version of his birth name allowed to be used here, made a nice little word—almost as good as having a real name. Rathburn took a seat at the same table. One of the ever-solicitous servers—young, female (for this table of straight men), beautiful—was already at hand, and G.R. ordered a glass of champagne. It wasn't a special occasion—nothing was ever special in Paradise Valley—but any pleasure was available to those, like him and Dat, on the Platinum Plus maintenance plan.

"Why so long in the face, G.R.?" asked Dat.

"I don't like it here."

Dat admired the *derrière* of the departing server, and took a sip of his wine. "What's not to like?"

"You used to be a lawyer, didn't you? Back on the outside?"

"I still *am* a lawyer on the outside," said Dat.

G.R. frowned, but decided not to press the point. "Can you answer some questions for me?"

"Sure. What do you want to know?"

— • —

G.R. entered Paradise Valley's "hospital." He thought of the name as being in quotation marks, since a real hospital was a place you were supposed to go to only temporarily for healing. But most of those who had uploaded their consciousness, who had shed their skins, were elderly. And when their discarded shells checked into the hospital, it was to die. But G.R. was only forty-five. With proper medical treatment, and some good luck, he had a fair chance of seeing one hundred.

G.R. went into the waiting room. He'd watched for two weeks now, and knew the schedule, knew that little Lilly Ng—slight, Vietnamese, fifty— would be the doctor on duty. She, like Shiozaki, was staff—a real person who got to go home, to the real world, at night.

After a short time, the receptionist said the time-honoured words: "The doctor will see you now."

G.R. walked into the green-walled examination room. Ng was looking down at a datapad. "GR-7," she said, reading his serial number. Of course, he wasn't the only one with the initials G.R. in Paradise Valley, and so he had to share what faint echo of a name he still possessed with several other people. She looked at him, her grey eyebrows raised, waiting for him to confirm that that was indeed who he was.

"That's me," said G.R., "but you can call me George."

"No," said Ng. "I cannot." She said it in a firm but gentle tone; presumably, she'd been down this road before with others. "What seems to be the problem?"

"I've got a skin tag in my left armpit," he said. "I've had it for years, but it's started to get sensitive. It hurts when I apply roll-on deodorant, and it chafes as I move my arm."

Ng frowned. "Take off your shirt, please."

G.R. began undoing buttons. He actually had several skin tags, as well as a bunch of moles. He also had a hairy back, which he hated. One reason uploading his consciousness had initially seemed appealing was to divest himself of these dermal imperfections. The new golden robot body he'd selected—looking like a cross between the Oscar statuette and C-3PO—had no such cosmetic defects.

As soon as the shirt was off, he lifted his left arm and let Ng examine his axilla.

"Hmm," she said, peering at the skin tag. "It does look inflamed."

G.R. had brutally pinched the little knob of skin an hour before, and had twisted it as much as he could in either direction.

Ng was now gently squeezing it between thumb and forefinger. G.R. had been prepared to suggest a treatment, but it would be better if she came up with the idea herself. After a moment, she obliged. "I can remove it for you, if you like."

"If you think that's the right thing to do," said G.R.

"Sure," said Ng. "I'll give you a local anaesthetic, clip it off, and cauterize the cut. No need for stitches."

Clip it off? No! No, he needed her to use a scalpel, not surgical scissors. Damn it!

She crossed the room, prepared a syringe, and returned, injecting it directly into the skin tag. The needle going in was excruciating—for a few moments. And then there was no sensation at all.

"How's that?" she asked.

"Fine."

Ng put on surgical gloves, opened a cupboard, and pulled out a small leather case. She placed it on the examination table G.R. was now perched on, and opened it. It contained surgical scissors, forceps, and—

They glinted beautifully under the lights from the ceiling.

A pair of scalpels, one with a short blade, the other with a longer one.

"All right," said Ng, reaching in and extracting the scissors. "Here we go ..."

G.R. shot his right arm out, grabbing the long-bladed scalpel, and quickly swung it around, bringing it up and under Ng's throat. Damn but the thing was sharp! He hadn't meant to hurt her, but a shallow slit two centimetres long now welled crimson across where her Adam's apple would have been had she been a man.

A small scream escaped from Ng, and G.R. quickly clamped his other hand over her mouth. He could feel her shaking.

"Do exactly as I say," he said, "and you'll walk out of this alive. Screw me over, and you're dead."

— • —

"Don't worry," said Detective Dan Lucerne to Mr. Shiozaki. "I've handled eight hostage situations over the years, and in every case, we've managed a peaceful solution. We'll get your woman back."

Shiozaki nodded then looked away, hiding his eyes from the detective. He should have recognized the signs in GR-7. If only he'd ordered him sedated, this never would have happened.

Lucerne gestured toward the vidphone. "Get the examination room on this thing," he said.

Shiozaki reached over Lucerne's shoulder and tapped out three numbers on the keypad. After a moment, the screen came to life, showing Ng's hand pulling away from the camera at her end. As the hand withdrew, it was clear that G.R. still had the scalpel held to Ng's neck.

"Hello," said Lucerne. "My name is Detective Dan Lucerne. I'm here to help you."

"You're here to save Dr. Ng's life," said GR-7. "And if you do everything I want, you will."

"All right," said Lucerne. "What do you want, sir?"

"For starters, I want you to call me Mr. Rathburn."

"Fine," said Lucerne. "That's fine, Mr. Rathburn."

Lucerne was surprised to see the shed skin tremble in response. "Again," GR-7 said, as if it were the sweetest sound he'd ever heard. "Say it again."

"What can we do for you, Mr. Rathburn?"

"I want to talk to the robot version of me."

Shiozaki reached over Lucerne's shoulder again, pushing the mute button. "We can't allow that."

"Why not?" asked Lucerne.

"Our contract with the uploaded version specifies that there will never be any contact with the shed skin."

"I'm not worried about fine print," said Lucerne. "I'm trying to save a woman's life." He took the mute off. "Sorry about that, Mr. Rathburn."

GR-7 nodded. "I see Mr. Shiozaki standing behind you. I'm sure he told you that what I wanted isn't permitted."

Lucerne didn't look away from the screen, didn't break the eye contact with the skin. "He did say that, yes. But he's not in charge here. *I'm* not in charge here. It's your show, Mr. Rathburn."

Rathburn visibly relaxed. Lucerne could see him back the scalpel off a bit from Ng's neck. "That's more like it," he said. "All right. All right. I don't want to kill Dr. Ng—but I will unless you bring the robot version of me here within three hours." He spoke out of the side of his mouth to Ng. "Break the connection."

A terrified-looking Ng reached her arm forward, her pale hand and simple gold wedding ring filling the field of view.

And the screen went dead.

— • —

George Rathburn—the silicon version—was sitting in the dark, wood-panelled living room of his large Victorian-style country house. Not that he had to sit; he never grew tired anymore. Nor did he really need his chairs to be padded. But folding his metal body into the seat still felt like the natural thing to do.

Knowing that, barring accidents, he was now going to live virtually forever, Rathburn figured he should tackle something big and ambitious, like *War and Peace* or *Ulysses*. But, well, there would always be time for that later. Instead, he downloaded the latest Buck Doheney mystery novel into his datapad, and began to read.

He'd only gotten halfway through the second screenful of text when the datapad bleeped, signalling an incoming call.

Rathburn thought about just letting the pad record a message. Already, after only a few weeks of immortality, nothing seemed particularly urgent. Still, it might be Kathryn. He'd met her at the training centre, while they were both getting used to their robot bodies, and to their immortality. Ironically, she'd been eighty-two before she'd uploaded; in his now-discarded flesh-and-blood shell, George Rathburn would never have had a relationship with a woman so much older than he was. But now that they were both in artificial bodies—his gold, hers a lustrous bronze—they were well on the way to a full-fledged romance.

The pad bleeped again, and Rathburn touched the ANSWER icon—no need to use a stylus anymore; his synthetic fingers didn't secrete oils that would leave a mark on the screen.

Rathburn had that strange feeling he'd experienced once or twice since uploading—the feeling of deep surprise that would have been accompanied by his old heart skipping a beat. "Mr. Shiozaki?" he said. "I didn't expect to ever see you again."

"I'm sorry to have to bother you, George, but we've—well, we've got an emergency. Your old body has taken a hostage here in Paradise Valley."

"What? My God ..."

"He's saying he will kill the woman if we don't let him talk to you."

George wanted to do the right thing, but ...

But he'd spent weeks now trying to forget that another version of him still existed. "I—um—I *guess* it'd be okay if you put him on."

Shiozaki shook his head. "No. He won't take a phone call. He says you have to come here in person."

"But ... but you said ..."

"I know what we told you during counselling, but, dammit, George, a woman's life is at stake. You might be immortal now, but she isn't."

Rathburn thought for another few seconds, then: "All right. All right. I can be there in a couple of hours."

— • —

The robot-bodied George Rathburn was shocked by what he was seeing on the vidphone in Shiozaki's office. It was him—just as he remembered himself. His soft, fragile body; his greying temples; his receding hairline; his nose that he'd always thought was too large.

But it was him doing something he never could have imagined doing—holding a surgical blade to a woman's throat.

Detective Lucerne spoke toward the phone's pickups. "Okay," he said. "He's here. The other you is here."

On the screen, Rathburn could see his shed skin's eyes go wide as they beheld what he'd become. Of course, that version of him had selected the golden body—but it had only been an empty shell then, with no inner workings. "Well, well, well," said G.R. "Welcome, brother."

Rathburn didn't trust his synthesized voice, so he simply nodded.

"Come on down to the hospital," said G.R. "Go to the observation gallery above the operating theatre; I'll go to the operating theatre itself. We'll be able to see each other—and we'll be able to talk, man to man."

— • —

"Hello," said Rathburn. He was standing on his golden legs, staring through the angled sheet of glass that overlooked the operating room.

"Hello," said GR-7, looking up. "Before we go any further, I need you to prove that you are who you say you are. Sorry about this, but, well, it could be *anyone* inside that robot."

"It's me," said Rathburn.

"No. At best it's one of us. But I've got to be sure."

"So ask me a question."

GR-7 was clearly prepared for this. "The first girl to ever give us a blowjob."

"Carrie," said Rathburn, at once. "At the soccer field."

GR-7 smiled. "Good to see you, brother."

Rathburn was silent for a few moments. He swivelled his head on noiseless, frictionless bearings, looking briefly at Lucerne's face, visible on a vidphone out of view of the observation window. Then he turned back to his shed skin. "I, ah, I understand you want to be called George."

"That's right."

But Rathburn shook his head. "We—you and I, when we were one—shared exactly the same opinion about this matter. We wanted to live forever. And that can't be done in a biological body. You *know* that."

"It can't be done *yet* in a biological body. But I'm only forty-five. Who knows what technology will be available in the rest of our—of *my*—lifetime?"

Rathburn no longer breathed—so he could no longer sigh. But he moved his steel shoulders while feeling the emotion that used to produce a sigh. "You know why we chose to transfer early. You have a genetic predisposition to fatal strokes. But I don't have that—George Rathburn doesn't have that anymore. *You* might check out any day now, and if we hadn't transferred our consciousness into this body, there would have been no immortality for us."

"But we didn't *transfer* consciousness," said GR-7. "We *copied* consciousness—bit for bit, synapse for synapse. You're a copy. *I'm* the original."

"Not as a matter of law," said Rathburn. "You—the biological you—signed the contract that authorized the transfer of personhood. You signed it with the same hand you're using to hold that scalpel to Dr. Ng's throat."

"But I've changed my mind."

"You don't have a mind *to* change. The software we called the mind of George Rathburn—the only legal version of it—has been transferred from the hardware of your biological brain to the hardware of our new body's nano-gel CPU." The robotic Rathburn paused. "By rights, as in any transfer of software, the original should have been destroyed."

GR-7 frowned. "Except that society wouldn't allow for that, any more than it would allow for physician-assisted suicide. It's illegal to terminate a source body, even after the brain has been transferred."

"Exactly," said Rathburn, nodding his robotic head. "And you have to activate the replacement before the source dies, or else the court will determine that there's been no continuity of personhood and dispose of the assets. Death may not be certain anymore, but taxes certainly are."

Rathburn had hoped GR-7 would laugh at that, hoped that a bridge could be built between them. But GR-7 simply said, "So I'm stuck here."

"I'd hardly call it 'stuck,'" said Rathburn. "Paradise Valley is a little piece of heaven here on Earth. Why not just enjoy it, until you really do go to heaven?"

"I *hate* it here," said GR-7. He paused. "Look, I accept that by the current wording of the law, I have no legal standing. All right, then. I can't make them nullify the transfer—but *you* can. You are a person in the eyes of the law; you can do this."

"But I don't want to do it. I like being immortal."

"But *I* don't like being a prisoner."

"It's not me that's changed," said the android. "It's you. Think about what you're doing. We were never violent. We would never dream of taking a hostage, of holding a knife to someone's throat, of frightening a woman half to death. You're the one who has changed."

But the skin shook his head. "Nonsense. We'd just never been in such desperate circumstances before. Desperate circumstances make one do desperate things. The fact that you can't conceive of us doing this means that you're a *flawed* copy. This—this transfer process isn't ready for prime time yet. You should nullify the copy and let me, the original, go on with your—with our—life."

It was now the robotic Rathburn's turn to shake his head. "Look, you must realize that this can't ever work—that even if I were to sign some paper that transferred our legal status back to you, there are witnesses here to testify that I'd been coerced into signing it. It would have no legal value."

"You think you can outsmart me?" said GR-7. "I *am* you. Of course I know that."

"Good. Then let that woman go."

"You're not thinking," said GR-7. "Or at least you're not thinking hard enough. Come on, this is *me* you're talking to. You must know I'd have a better plan than that."

"I don't see ..."

"You mean you don't want to see. Think, Copy of George. Think."

"I still don't ..." The robotic Rathburn trailed off. "Oh. No, no, you can't expect me to do that."

"Yes, I do," said GR-7.

"But ..."

"But what?" The skin moved his free hand—the one not holding the scalpel—in a sweeping gesture. "It's a simple proposition. Kill yourself, and your rights of personhood will default back to me. You're correct that, right now, I'm not a person under the law—meaning I can't be charged with a crime. So I don't have to worry about going to jail for anything I do now. Oh, they might try—but I'll ultimately get off, because if I don't, the court will have to admit that not just me, but all of us here in Paradise Valley are still human beings, with human rights."

"What you're asking is impossible."

"What I'm asking is the only thing that makes sense. I talked to a friend who used to be a lawyer. The personhood rights *will* revert if the original is still alive, but the uploaded version isn't. I'm sure no one ever intended the law to be used for this purpose; I'm told it was designed to allow product-liability suits if the robot brain failed shortly after transfer. But regardless, if you kill yourself, *I* get to go back to being a free human." GR-7 paused for a moment. "So what's it going to be? Your pseudolife, or the real flesh-and-blood life of this woman?"

"George ..." said the robot mouth. "Please."

But the biological George shook his head. "If you really believe that you, as a copy of me, are more real than the original that still exists—if you really believe that you have a soul, just like this woman does, inside your robotic frame—then there's no particular reason why you should sacrifice yourself for Dr. Ng here. But if, down deep, you're thinking that I'm correct, that she really is alive, and you're not, then you'll do the right thing." He pressed the scalpel's blade in slightly, drawing blood again. "What's it going to be?"

— • —

George Rathburn had returned to Shiozaki's office, and Detective Lucerne was doing his best to persuade the robot-housed mind to agree to GR-7's terms.

"Not in a million years," said Rathburn, "and, believe me, I intend to be around that long."

"But another copy of you can be made," said Lucerne.

"But it won't be *me*—this me."

"But that woman, Dr. Ng: She's got a husband, three daughters ..."

"I'm not insensitive to that, Detective," said Rathburn, pacing back and forth on his golden mechanical legs. "But let me put it to you another way. Say this is 1875, in the southern U.S. The Civil War is over; blacks in theory have the same legal status as whites. But a white man is being held hostage, and he'll only be let go if a black man agrees to sacrifice himself in the white man's place. See the parallel? Despite all the courtroom wrangling that was done to make uploaded life able to maintain the legal status, the personhood, of the original, you're asking me to set that aside, and reaffirm what the whites in the South felt they knew all along: that, all legal mumbo-jumbo to the contrary, a black man is worth less than a white man. Well, I won't do that. I wouldn't affirm that racist position, and I'll be damned if I'll affirm the modern equivalent: that a silicon-based person is worth less than a carbon-based person."

"'I'll be damned,'" repeated Lucerne, imitating Rathburn's synthesized voice. He let the comment hang in the air, waiting to see if Rathburn would respond to it.

And Rathburn couldn't resist. "Yes, I know there are those who would say I *can't* be damned—because whatever it is that constitutes the human soul isn't recorded during the transference process. That's the gist of it, isn't it? The argument that I'm not really human comes down to a theological assertion: I can't be human, because I have no soul. But I tell you this, Detective Lucerne: I feel every bit as alive—and every bit as spiritual—as I did before the transfer. I'm convinced that I *do* have a soul, or a divine spark, or an *élan vital*, or whatever you want to call it. My life in this particular packaging of it is *not* worth one iota less than Dr. Ng's, or anyone else's."

Lucerne was quiet for a time, considering. "But what about the other you? You're willing to stand here and tell me that that version—the original, flesh-and-blood version—is *not* human anymore. And you would have that distinction by legal fiat, just as blacks were denied human rights in the old south."

"There's a difference," said Rathburn. "There's a big difference. That version of me—the one holding Dr. Ng hostage—agreed of its own free will, without any coercion whatsoever, to that very proposition. He—*it*—agreed that it would no longer be human, once the transfer into the robot body was completed."

"But he doesn't want it to be that way anymore."

"Tough. It's not the first contract that he—that *I*—signed in my life that I later regretted. But simple regret isn't reason enough to get out of a legally valid transaction." Rathburn shook his robotic head. "No, I'm sorry. I refuse. Believe me, I wish more than anything that you could save Dr. Ng—but you're going to have to find another way to do it. There's too much at stake here for *my* people—for uploaded humans—to let me make any other decision."

— • —

"All right," Lucerne finally said to the robotic Rathburn, "I give up. If we can't do it the easy way, we're going to have to do it the hard way. It's a good thing the old Rathburn wants to see the new Rathburn directly. Having him in that operating room while you're in the overlooking observation gallery will be perfect for sneaking a sharpshooter in."

Rathburn felt as though his eyes should go wide, but of course they did not. "You're going to shoot him?"

"You've left us no other choice. Standard procedure is to give the hostage-taker everything he wants, get the hostage back, then go after the criminal. But the only thing he wants is for you to be dead—and you're not willing to cooperate. So we're going to take him out."

"You'll use a tranquilizer, won't you?"

Lucerne snorted. "On a man holding a knife to a woman's throat? We need something that will turn him off like a light, before he's got time to react. And the best way to do that is a bullet to the head or chest."

"But ... but I don't want you to kill him."

Lucerne made an even louder snort. "By your logic, he's not alive anyway."

"Yes, but ..."

"But what? You willing to give him what he wants?"

"I can't. Surely you can see that."

Lucerne shrugged. "Too bad. I was looking forward to being able to quip 'Goodbye, Mr. Chips.'"

"Damn you," said Rathburn. "Don't you see that it's because of that sort of attitude that I *can't* allow this precedent?"

Lucerne made no reply, and after a time Rathburn continued. "Can't we fake my death somehow? Just enough for you to get Ng back to safety?"

Lucerne shook his head. "GR-7 demanded proof that it was really you inside that tin can. I don't think he can be easily fooled. But you know him better than anyone else. Could you be fooled?"

Rathburn tipped his mechanical head down. "No. No, I'm sure he'll demand positive proof."

"Then we're back to the sharpshooter."

— • —

Rathburn walked into the observation gallery, his golden feet making soft metallic clangs as they touched the hard, tiled floor. He looked through the angled glass, down at the operating room below. The slab-of-flab version of himself had Dr. Ng tied up now, her hands and feet bound with surgical tape. She couldn't get away, but he no longer had to constantly hold the scalpel to her throat. GR-7 was standing up, and she was next to him, leaning against the operating table.

The angled window continued down to within a half-metre of the floor. Crouching below its sill was Conrad Burloak, the sharpshooter, in a grey uniform, holding a black rifle. A small transmitter had been inserted in Rathburn's camera hardware, copying everything his glass eyes were seeing onto a datapad Burloak had with him.

In ideal circumstances, Burloak had said, he liked to shoot for the head, but here he was going to have to fire through the plate-glass window, and that might deflect the bullet slightly. So he was going to aim for the centre of the torso, a bigger target. As soon as the datapad showed a clean line-of-fire at G.R., Burloak would pop up and blow him away.

"Hello, George," said the robotic Rathburn. There was an open intercom between the observation gallery and the operating theatre below.

"All right," said the fleshy one. "Let's get this over with. Open the access panel to your nano-gel braincase, and ..."

But GR-7 trailed off, seeing that the robotic Rathburn was shaking his head. "I'm sorry, George. I'm not going to deactivate myself."

"You prefer to see Dr. Ng die?"

Rathburn could shut off his visual input, the equivalent of closing his eyes. He did that just now for a moment, presumably much to the chagrin of the sharpshooter studying the datapad. "Believe me, George, the last thing I want to do is see anyone die."

He reactivated his eyes. He'd thought he'd been suitably ironic but, of course, the other him had the same mind. GR-7, perhaps suspecting that something was up, had moved Dr. Ng so that she was now standing between himself and the glass,

"Don't try anything funny," said the skin. "I've got nothing to lose."

Rathburn looked down on his former self—but only in the literal sense. He didn't want to see this ... this man, this being, this thing, this entity, this whatever it was, hurt.

After all, even if the shed skin wasn't a person in the cold eyes of the law, he surely still remembered that time he'd—*they'd*—almost drowned swimming at the cottage, and mom pulling him to shore while his arms flailed in panic. And he remembered his first day at junior-high school, when a gang of grade nines had beaten him up as initiation. And he remembered the incredible shock and sadness when he'd come home from his weekend job at the hardware store and found dad slumped over in his easy chair, dead from a stroke.

And that biological him must remember all the good things, too: hitting that home run clear over the fence in grade eight, after all the members of the opposing team had moved in close; his first kiss, at a party, playing spin the bottle; and his first romantic kiss, with Dana, her studded tongue sliding into his mouth; that *perfect* day in the Bahamas, with the most gorgeous sunset he'd ever seen.

Yes, this other him wasn't just a backup, wasn't just a repository of data. He knew all the same things, *felt* all the same things, and—

The sharpshooter had crawled several metres along the floor of the observation gallery, trying to get a clean angle at GR-7. Out of the corner of his robotic vision—which was as sharp at the peripheries as it was in the centre—Rathburn saw the sharpshooter tense his muscles, and then—

And then Burloak leaped up, swinging his rifle, and—

And to his astonishment, Rathburn found the words "Look out, George!" emitting from his robotic mouth at a greatly amplified volume.

And just as the words came out, Burloak fired, and the window exploded into a thousand shards, and GR-7 spun around, grabbing Dr. Ng, swinging her in between himself and the sharpshooter, and the bullet hit, drilling a hole through the woman's heart, and through the chest of the man behind her, and they both crumpled to the operating-room floor, and human blood flowed out of them, and the glass shards rained down upon them like robot tears.

— • —

And so, at last, there was no more ambiguity. There was only one George Rathburn—a single iteration of the consciousness that had first bloomed some forty-five years ago, now executing as code in the nano-gel inside a robotic form.

George suspected that Shiozaki would try to cover up what had occurred back in Paradise Valley—at least the details. He'd have to admit that Dr. Ng had been killed by a skin, but doubtless Shiozaki would want to gloss over Rathburn's warning shout. After all, it would be bad for business if those about to shed got wind of the fact that the new versions still had empathy for the old ones.

But Detective Lucerne and his sharpshooter would want just the opposite: Only by citing the robotic Rathburn's interference could they exonerate the sharpshooter from accidentally shooting the hostage.

But nothing could exonerate GR-7 from what he'd done, swinging that poor, frightened woman in front of himself as a shield ...

Rathburn sat down in his country house's living room. Despite his robotic body, he did feel weary—bone-weary—and needed the support of the chair.

He'd done the right thing, even if GR-7 hadn't; he knew that. Any other choice by him would have been devastating not just for himself, but also for Kathryn and every other uploaded consciousness. There really had been no alternative.

Immortality is grand. Immortality is great. As long as you have a clear conscience, that is. As long as you're not tortured by doubt, racked by depression, overcome with guilt.

That poor woman, Dr. Ng. She'd done nothing wrong, nothing at all.

And now she was dead.

And he—a version of him—had caused her to be killed.

GR-7's words replayed in Rathburn's memory. *We'd just never been in such desperate circumstances before.*

Perhaps that was true. But he was in desperate circumstances now.

And he'd found himself contemplating actions he never would have considered possible for him before.

That poor woman. That poor dead woman ...

It wasn't just GR-7's fault. It was *his* fault. Her death was a direct consequence of his wanting to live forever.

And he'd have to live with the guilt of that forever.

Unless ...

Desperate circumstances make one do desperate things.

He picked up the magnetic pistol—astonishing what things you could buy online these days. A proximity blast from it would destroy all recordings in nano-gel.

George Rathburn looked at the pistol, at its shiny, hard exterior.

And he placed the emitter against the side of his stainless-steel skull, and, after a few moments of hesitation, his golden robotic finger contracted against the trigger.

What better way, after all, was there to prove that he was still human? ∎

Karl Schroeder (kschroeder.com) has won two Aurora Awards and been nominated for three more, and has also been a finalist for the John W. Campbell Memorial Award (for *Sun of Suns*).

He moved to Toronto in 1986 to pursue a writing career and divides his time between writing fiction and consulting—chiefly in the area of foresight studies. The Department of National Defence Canada commissioned him to write the novella *Crisis in Zefra*, which they published in book form. With Cory Doctorow, he wrote *The Complete Idiot's Guide to Writing Science Fiction*, and he is a past president of SF Canada.

He was born in Brandon, Manitoba. His family are Mennonites, part of a community that has lived in southern Manitoba for over one hundred years. He is the second science fiction writer to come out of that small community—the first was A.E. van Vogt. He now lives in Toronto with his wife Janice and daughter Paige.

NOVELS:

Ventus (Tor, New York, 2000)

Permanence (Tor, New York, 2002)

Lady of Mazes (Tor, New York, 2005)

Sun of Suns: Book 1 of Virga (Tor, New York, 2006)

Queen of Candesce: Book 2 of Virga (Tor, New York, 2007)

Pirate Sun: Book 3 of Virga (Tor, New York, 2008)

Sunless Countries: Book 4 of Virga (Tor, New York, 2009)

WITH DAVID NICKLE:

The Claus Effect (Tesseract Books, Edmonton, 2002)

SHORT STORY COLLECTION:

The Engine of Recall (Robert J. Sawyer Books, Calgary, 2005)

HALO

Karl Schroeder

Elise Cantrell was awakened by the sound of her children trying to manage their own breakfast. Bright daylight streamed in through the windows. She threw on a robe and ran for the kitchen. "No, no, let me!"

Judy appeared about to microwave something, and the oven was set on high.

"Aw, Mom, did you forget?" Alex, who was a cherub but had the loudest scream in the universe, pouted at her from the table. Looked like he'd gotten his breakfast together just fine. Suspicious, that, but she refused to inspect his work.

"Yeah, I forgot the time change. My prospectors are still on the twenty-four-hour clock, you know."

"Why?" Alex flapped his spoon in the cereal bowl.

"They're on another world, remember? Only Dew has a thirty-hour day, and only since they put the sun up. You remember before the sun, don't you?" Alex stared at her as though she were insane. It had only been a year and a half.

Elise sighed. Just then the door announced a visitor. "Daddy!" shrieked Judy as she ran out of the room. Elise found her in the foyer clinging to the leg of her father. Nasim Clearwater grinned at her over their daughter's fly-away hair.

"You're a mess," he said by way of greeting.

"Thanks. Look, they're not ready. Give me a few minutes."

"No problem. Left a bit early; thought you might forget the time change."

She glared at him and stalked back to the kitchen.

As she cleaned up and Nasim dressed the kids, Elise looked out over the landscape of Dew. It was daylight, yes, a pale drawn glow dropping through cloud veils to sketch hills and plains of ice. Two years ago this window had shown no view, just the occasional star. Elise had grown up in that velvet darkness, and it was so strange now to have awakening signalled by such a vivid and total change. Her children would grow up to the rhythm of true day and night, the first such generation here on Dew. They would think differently. Already, this morning, they did.

"Hello," Nasim said in her ear. Startled, Elise said, "What?" a bit too loudly.

"We're off." The kids stood behind him, dubiously inspecting the snaps of their survival suits. Today was a breach drill; Nasim would ensure they took it seriously. Elise gave him a peck on the cheek.

"You want them back late, right? Got a date?"

"No," she said, "of course not." Nasim wanted to hear that she was being independent, but she wouldn't give him the satisfaction.

Nasim half-smiled. "Well, maybe I'll see you after, then."

"Sure."

He nodded but said nothing further. As the kids screamed their good-byes at full volume, she tried to puzzle out what he'd meant. See her? To chat, to talk, maybe more?

Not more. She had to accept that. As the door closed, she plunked herself angrily down on the couch, and drew her headset over her eyes.

VR was cheap for her. She didn't need full immersion, just vision and sound, and sometimes the use of her hands. Her prospectors were too specialized to have human traits, and they operated in weightlessness so she didn't need to walk. The headset was expensive enough without such additions. And the simplicity of the set-up allowed her to work from home.

The fifteen robot prospectors Elise controlled ranged throughout the halo worlds of Crucible. Crucible itself was fifty times the mass of Jupiter, a "brown dwarf" star—too small to be a sun but radiating in the high infrared and trailing a retinue of planets. Crucible sailed alone through the spaces between the true stars. Elise had been born and raised here on Dew, Crucible's frozen fifth planet. From the camera on the first of her prospectors, she could see the new kilometres-long metal cylinder that her children had learned to call the "sun." Its electric light shone only on Dew, leaving Crucible and the other planets in darkness. The artificial light made Dew gleam like a solitary blue-white jewel on the perfect black of space.

She turned her helmeted head and out in space her prospector turned its camera. Faint Dew-light reflected from a round spot on Crucible. She hadn't seen that before. She recorded the sight; the kids would like it, even if they didn't quite understand it.

This first prospector craft perched astride a chunk of ice about five kilometres long. The little ice-flinder orbited Crucible with about a billion others. Her machine oversaw some dumb mining equipment that was chewing stolidly through the thing in search of metal.

There were no problems here. She flipped her view to the next machine, whose headlamps obligingly lit to show her a wall of stone. Hmm. She'd been right the night before when she ordered it to check an ice ravine on Castle, the fourth planet. There was real stone down here, which meant metals. She wondered what it would feel like, and reached out. After a delay, the metal hands of her prospector touched the stone. She didn't feel anything; the prospector was not equipped to transmit the sensation back. Sometimes she longed to be able to fully experience the places her machines visited.

She sent a call to the Mining Registrar to follow up on her find, and went on to the next prospector. This one orbited farthest out, and there was a time-lag of several minutes between every command she gave, and its execution. Normally, she just checked it quickly and moved on. Today, for some reason, it had a warning flag in its message queue.

Transmission intercepted—Oh, it had overheard some dialogue between two ships or something. That was surprising, considering how far away from the normal orbits the prospector was. "Read it to me," she said, and went on to Prospector Four.

She'd forgotten about the message and was admiring a long view of Dew's horizon from the vantage of her fourth prospector, when a resonant male voice spoke in her ear:

"Mayday, mayday—anyone at Dew, please receive. My name is Hammond, and I'm speaking from the interstellar cycler *Chinook*. The date is the sixth of May, 2418. Relativistic shift is .500435—we're at half light-speed.

"Listen:

"*Chinook* has been taken over by Naturite forces out of Leviathan. They are using the cycler as a weapon. You must know by now that the halo world Tiara, at Obsidian, has gone silent—it's our fault. *Chinook* has destroyed them. Dew is our next stop, and they fully intend to do the same thing there. They want to "purify" the halo worlds so only their people settle here.

"They're keeping communications silence. I've had to go outside to take manual control of a message laser in order to send this mayday.

"You must place mines in near-pass space ahead of the cycler, to destroy it. We have limited manoeuvring ability, so we couldn't possibly avoid the mines.

"Anyone receiving this message, please relay it to your authorities immediately. *Chinook* is a genocide ship. You are in danger.

"Please do not reply to *Chinook* on normal channels. They will not negotiate. Reply to my group on this frequency, not the standard cycler wavelengths."

Elise didn't know how to react. She almost laughed—what a ridiculous message, full of bluster and emergency words. But she'd heard that Obsidian had gone mysteriously silent, and no one knew why. "Origin of this message?" she asked. As she waited, she replayed it. It was highly melodramatic, just the sort of wording somebody would use for a prank. She was sure she would, be told the message had come from Dew itself—maybe even sent by Nasim or one of his friends.

The coordinates flashed before her eyes. Elise did a quick calculation to visualize the direction. Not from Dew. Not from any of Crucible's worlds. The message had come from deep space, out somewhere beyond the last of Crucible's trailing satellites.

The only things out there were stars, halo worlds—and the cyclers, Elise thought. She lifted off the headset. The beginnings of fear fluttered in her belly.

— • —

Elise took the message to a cousin of hers who was a policeman. He showed her into his office, smiling warmly. They didn't often get together since they'd grown up, and he wanted to talk family.

She shook her head. "I've got something strange for you Sal. One of my machines picked this up last night." And she played the message for him, expecting reassuring laughter and a good explanation.

Half an hour later they were being ushered into the suite of the police chief, who sat at a U-shaped table with her aides, frowning. When they entered, Elise heard the words of the message playing quietly from the desk speakers of two of the aides, who looked very serious.

"You will tell no one about this," said the chief. She was a thin, strong woman with blazing eyes. "We have to confirm it first." Elise hesitated, then nodded.

Cousin Sal cleared his throat. "Ma'am? You think this message could be genuine, then."

The chief frowned at him, then said, "It may be true. This may be why Tiara went off the air." The sudden silence of Tiara, a halo world half a lightyear from Elise's home, had been the subject of a media frenzy a year earlier. Rumours of disaster circulated, but there were no facts to go on, other than that Tiara's message lasers, which normally broadcast news from there, had gone out. It was no longer news, and Elise had heard nothing about it for months. "We checked the coordinates you reported and they show this message *did* come from the *Chinook*. *Chinook* did its course correction around Obsidian right about the time Tiara stopped broadcasting."

Elise couldn't believe what she was hearing. "But what could they have done?"

The chief tapped at her desk with long fingers. "You're an orbital engineer, Cantrell. You probably know better than I. The *Chinook*'s travelling at half lightspeed, so anything it dropped on an intercept course with Obsidian's planets would hit like a bomb. Even the smallest item—a pen or card."

Elise nodded reluctantly. Aside from message lasers, the Interstellar Cyclers were the only means of contact with other stars and halo worlds. Cyclers came by Crucible every few months, but they steered well away from its planets. They only came close enough to use gravity to assist their course change to the next halo world. Freight and passengers were dropped off and picked up via laser sail; the cyclers themselves were huge, far too massive to stop and start at will. Their kinetic energy was incalculable, so the interstellar community monitored them as closely as possible. They spent years in transit between the stars, however, and it took weeks or months for laser messages to reach them. News about cyclers was always out of date before it even arrived.

"We have to confirm this before we do anything," the chief said. "We have the frequency and coordinates to reply. We'll take it from here."

Elise had to ask. "Why did only I intercept the message?"

"It wasn't aimed very well, maybe. He didn't know exactly where his target was. Only your prospector was within the beam.

Just luck.

"When is the *Chinook* due to pass us?" Sal asked.

"A month and a half," said the tight-faced aide. "It should be about three light-weeks out; the date on this message would tend to confirm that."

"So any reply will come right about the time they pass us," Sal said. "How can we get a confirmation in time to do anything?"

They looked at one another blankly. Elise did some quick calculations in her head. "Four messages exchanged before they're a day away," she said. "If each party waits for the other's reply. Four on each side."

"But we have to act well before that," said another aide.

"How?" asked a third.

Elise didn't need to listen to the explanation. They could mine the space in front of the cycler. Turn it into energy, and hopefully any missiles, too. Kill the thousand-or-so people on board it to save Dew.

"I've done my duty," she said. "Can I go now?"

The chief waved her away. A babble of arguing voices followed Elise and Sal out the door.

— • —

Sal offered to walk her home, but Elise declined. She took old familiar ways through the corridors of the city, ways she had grown up with. Today, though, her usual route from the core of the city was blocked by work crews. They were replacing opaque ceiling panels with glass to let in the new daylight. The bright light completely changed the character of the place, washing out familiar colours. It reminded her that there were giant forces in the sky, uncontrollable by her. She retreated from the glow, and drifted through a maze of alternate routes like a sombre ghost, not meeting the eyes of the people she passed.

The parkways were packed, mostly with children. Some were there with a single parent, others with both. Elise watched the couples enviously. Having children was supposed to have made her and Nasim closer. It hadn't worked out that way.

Lately, he had shown signs of wanting her again. Take it slow, she had told herself. Give him time.

They might not have time.

The same harsh sunlight the work crews had been admitting waited when she got home. It made the jumble of toys on the living room floor seem tiny and fragile. Elise sat under the new window for a while, trying to ignore it, but finally hunted through her closets until she found some old blankets, and covered the glass.

— • —

Nasim offered to stay for dinner that night. This made her feel rushed and off-balance. The kids wanted to stay up for it, but he had a late appointment. Putting them to bed was arduous. She got dinner going late, and by then all her planned small talk had evaporated. Talking about the kids was easy enough—but to do that was to take the easy way out, and she had wanted this evening to be different. Worst was that she didn't want to tell him about the message, because if he thought she was upset, he might withdraw as he had in the past.

The dinner candles stood between them like chessmen. Elise grew more and more miserable. Nasim obviously had no idea what was wrong, but she'd promised not to talk about the crisis. So she came up with a series of lame explanations, for the blanket over the window and for her mood, none of which he seemed to buy.

Things sort of petered out after that.

She had so hoped things would click with Nasim tonight. Exhausted at the end of it all, Elise tumbled into her own bed, alone and dejected.

Sleep wouldn't come. This whole situation had her questioning everything, because it knotted together survival and love, and her own seeming inability to do anything about either.

As she thrashed about under the covers, she kept imagining a distant, invisible dart, the cycler, falling from infinity at her.

Finally she got up and went to her office. She would write it out. That had worked wonderfully before. She sat under the VR headset and called up the mailer. Hammond's message was still there, flagged with its vector and frequency. She gave the *reply* command.

"Dear Mr. Hammond:

"I got your message. You intended it for some important person, but I got it instead. I've got a daughter and son—I didn't want to hear that they might be killed. And what am I supposed to do about it? I told the police. So what?

"Please tell me this is a joke. I can't sleep now; all I can think about is Tiara, and what must have happened there.

"I feel ... I told the police, but that doesn't seem like *enough*; it's as if you called *me* for help, put the weight of the whole world on my shoulders—and what am I supposed to do about it?" It became easier the more she spoke. Elise poured out the litany of small irritations and big fears that were plaguing her.

When she was done, she did feel better.

Send? inquired the mailer.

Oh, God, of course not.

Something landed in her lap, knocking the wind out of her. The headset toppled off her head. "Mommy. Mommy!"

"Yes, yes, sweetie, what is it?"

Judy plunked forward onto Elise's breast. "Did you forget the time again, Mommy?"

Elise relaxed. She was being silly. "Maybe a little, honey. What are you doing awake?"

"I don't know."

"Let's both go to bed. You can sleep with me, okay?" Judy nodded.

She stood up, holding Judy. The inside of the VR headset still glowed, so she picked it up to turn it off.

Remembering what she'd been doing, she put it on.

Mail sent, the mailer was flashing.

"Oh, my, *God*!"

"Ow, Mommy."

"Wait a sec, Judy. Mommy has something to do." She put Judy down and fumbled with the headset. Judy began to whine.

She picked *reply* again and said quickly, "Mr. Hammond, please disregard the last message. It wasn't intended for you. The mailer got screwed up. I'm sorry if I said anything to upset you. I know you're in a far worse position than I am and you're doing a very brave thing by getting in touch with us. I'm sure it'll all work out. I ..." She couldn't think of anything more.

"Please excuse me, Mr. Hammond."

Send? "Yes!"

She took Judy to bed. Her daughter fell asleep promptly, but Elise was now wide awake.

— • —

She heard nothing from the government during the next while.

Because she knew they might not tell her what was happening, she commanded her outermost prospector to devote half its time to scanning for messages from *Chinook*. For weeks there weren't any.

Elise went on with things. She dressed and fed the kids; let them cry into her shirt when they got too tired or banged their knees; walked them out to meet Nasim every now and then. She had evening coffee with her friends, and even saw a new play that had opened in a renovated reactor room in the basement of the city. Other than that, she mostly worked.

In the weeks after the message's arrival, Elise found a renewal of the comforting solitude her prospectors gave her. For hours at a time, she could be millions of kilometres away, watching ice crystals dance in her head-lamps, or seeing stars she could never view from her window. Being so far away literally gave her a new perspective on home; she could see Dew in all its fragile smallness, and understood that the bustle of family and friends served to keep the loneliness of the halo worlds at bay.

She appreciated people more for that, but also loved being the first to visit ice galleries and frozen cataracts on distant moons.

Now she wondered if she would be able to watch Dew's destruction from her prospectors. That made no sense—she would be dead in that case. The sense of actually *being* out in space was so strong, though, that she had fantasies of finding the golden thread cut, of existing bodiless and alone forever in the cameras of the prospectors, from which she would gaze down longingly on the ruins of her world.

A month after the first message, a second came. Elise's prospector intercepted it—nobody else except the police would have, because it was at Hammond's special frequency. The kids were tearing about in the next room. Their laughter formed an odd backdrop to the bitter voice that sounded in her ears.

"This is Mark Hammond on the *Chinook*. I will send you all the confirming information I can. There is a video record of the incident at Tiara, and I will try to send it along. It is very difficult. There are only a few of us from the original passengers and crew left. I have to rely on the arrogance of Leviathan's troops; if they encrypt their database I will be unable to send anything. If they catch me, I will be thrown out an airlock.

"I'll tell you what happened. I boarded at Mirjam four years ago. I was bound for Tiara, to the music academy there. Leviathan was our next stop, and we picked up no freight, but several hundred people who turned out to be soldiers. There were about a thousand people on *Chinook* at that point. The soldiers captured the command centre, and then they decided who they needed and who was expendable. They killed more than half of us.

I was saved because I can sing. I'm part of the entertainment."

Hammond's voice expressed loathing. He had a very nice voice, baritone and resonant. She could hear the unhappiness in it.

"It's been two and a half years now, under their heel. We're sick of it.

"A few weeks ago, they started preparing to strike your world. That's when we decided. You must destroy *Chinook*. I am going to send you our exact course, and that of the missiles. You must mine space in front of us. Otherwise, you'll end up like Tiara."

The kids had their survival class that afternoon. Normally, Elise was glad to hand them over to Nasim or, lately, their instructor—but this time she took them. She felt just a little better standing with some other parents in the powdery, sand-like snow outside the city watching the space-suited figures of her children go through the drill. They joined a small group in puzzling over a Global Positioning Unit, and successfully found the way to the beacon that was their target for today. She felt immensely proud of them, and chatted freely with the other parents. It was the first time in weeks that she'd felt like she was doing something worthwhile.

Being outside in daylight was so strange—after their kids, that was the main topic of conversation among the adults. All remembered their own classes, taken under the permanent night they had grown up with. Now they excitedly pointed out the different and wonderful colours of the stones and ices, reminiscent of pictures of Earth's Antarctica.

It was strange, too, to see the city as something other than a vast, dark pyramid. Elise studied it after the kids were done and they'd started back. The city looked solid, a single structure built of concrete that appeared pearly under the mauve clouds. Its flat facades were dotted with windows, and more were being installed. She and the kids tried to find theirs, but it was an unfamiliar exercise and they soon quit.

A big sign had been erected over the city airlock: *Help Build a Sunny Future*, it said. Beside it was a thermometer-graph intended to show how close the government was to funding the next stage of Dew's terraforming. Only a small part of this was filled in, and the paint on that looked a bit old. Nonetheless, several people made contributions at the booth inside, and she was tempted herself—being outdoors did make you think.

They were all tired when they got home, and the kids voluntarily went to nap. Feeling almost happy, Elise looked out her window for a while, then kicked her way through the debris of toys to the office.

A new message was waiting already.

"This is for the woman who heard my first message. I'm not sending it on the new frequency, but I'm aiming it the way I did the first one. This is just for you, whoever you are."

Elise sat down quickly.

Hammond laughed, maybe a little nervously. His voice was so rich, his laugh seemed to fill her whole head. "That was quite a letter you sent. I'm not sure I believe you about having a 'mailer accident.' But if it was an accident, I'm glad it happened.

"Yours is the first voice I've heard in years from outside this whole thing. You have to understand, with the way we're treated and ... and isolation and all, we nearly don't remember what it was like before. To have a life, I mean. To have kids, and worries like that. There's no kids here anymore. They killed them with their parents.

"A lot of people have given up. They don't remember why they should care. Most of us are like that now. Even me and the others who're trying to do something ... well we're doing it out of hate, not because we're trying to save anything.

"But you reminded me that there are things out there to save. Just hearing your voice, knowing that you and Dew are real, has helped.

"So I decided ... I'm going to play your message—the first one, actually—to a couple of the people who've given up. Remind them there's a world out there. That they still have responsibilities.

"Thank you again. Can you tell me your name? I wish we could have met, someday." That was all.

Somehow, his request made her feel defensive. It was good he didn't know her name; it was a kind of safety. At the same time, she wanted to tell him, as if he deserved it somehow. Finally, after sitting indecisively for long minutes, she threw down the headset and stalked out of the room.

— • —

Nasim called the next day. Elise was happy to hear from him, also a bit surprised. She had been afraid he thought she'd been acting cold lately, but he invited her for lunch in one of the city's better bistros. She foisted the kids off on her mother, and dressed up. It was worth it. They had a good time.

When she tried to set a date to get together again, he demurred. She was left chewing over his mixed messages as she walked home.

Oh, who knew, really? Life was just too complicated right now. When she got home, there was another message from Hammond, this one intended for the authorities. She reviewed it, but afterwards regretted doing so. It showed the destruction of Tiara.

On the video, pressure-suited figures unhooked some of *Chinook*'s Lorentz whip-thin force cables, and jetted them away from the cycler. The cables seemed infinitely long, and could weigh many hundreds of tonnes.

The next picture was a long-distance, blue-shifted image of Obsidian's only inhabited world, Tiara. For about a minute, Elise watched it waver, a speckled dot. Then lines of savage white light criss-crossed its face suddenly as the wires impacted.

That was all. Hammond's voice recited strings of numbers next, which she translated into velocities and trajectories. The message ended without further comment.

She was supposed to have discharged her responsibility by alerting the authorities, but after thinking about it practically all night, she had decided there was one more thing she could do.

"Mr. Hammond," she began, "this is Elise Cantrell. I'm the one who got your first message. I've seen the video you sent. I'm sure it'll be enough to convince our government to do something.

"Hitting Dew is going to be hard, and now that we know where they're coming from, we should be able to stop the missiles. I'm sure if the government thanks you, they'll do so in some stodgy manner, like giving you some medal or building a statue. But I want to thank you myself. For my kids. You may not have known just who you were risking your life for. Well, it was for Judy and Alex. I'm sending you a couple of pictures of them. Show them around. Maybe they'll convince more people to help you.

"I don't want us to blow up *Chinook*. That would mean you would die, and you're much too good a person for that. You don't deserve it. Show the pictures around. I don't know—if you can convince enough people, maybe you can take control back. There must be a way. You're a very clever man, Mr. Hammond. I'm sure you'll be able to find a way. For ... well, for me, maybe." She laughed, then cleared her throat. "Here's the pictures." She keyed in several of her favourites, Judy walking at age one, Alex standing on the dresser holding a towel up, an optimistic parachute.

She took off the headset, and lay back feeling deeply tired, but content. It wasn't rational, but she felt she had done something heroic, maybe for the first time in her life.

— • —

Elise was probably the only person who wasn't surprised when the sun went out. There had been rumours floating about for several days that the government was commandeering supplies and ships, but nobody knew for what. She did. She was fixing dinner when the light changed. The kids ran over to see what was happening.

"Why'd it stop?" howled Alex. "I want it back!"

"They'll bring it back in a couple of days," she told him. "They're just doing maintenance. Maybe they'll change the colour or something." That got his attention. For the next while he and Judy talked about what colour the new sun should be. They settled on blue.

The next morning she got a call from Sal. "We're doing it, Elise, and we need your help."

She'd seen this coming. "You want to take my prospectors."

"No no, not *take* them, just use them. You know them best. I convinced the department heads that you should be the one to pilot them. We need to blockade the missiles the *Chinook*'s sending."

"That's all?"

"What do you mean, that's all? What else would there be?"

She shook her head. "Nothing. Okay. I'll do it. Should I log on now?"

"Yeah. You'll get a direct link to your supervisor. His name's Oliver. You'll like him."

She didn't like Oliver, but could see how Sal might. He was tough and uncompromising, and curt to the point of being surly. Nice enough when he thought to be, but that was rare. He ordered Elise to take four of her inner-system prospectors off their jobs to manoeuvre ice for the blockade.

The next several days were the busiest she'd ever had with the prospectors. She had to call Nasim to come and look after the kids, which he did quite invisibly. All Elise's attention was needed in the orbital transfers. Her machines gathered huge blocks of orbiting ice, holding them like ambitious insects, and trawled slowly into the proper orbit. During tired pauses, she stared down at the brown cloud-tops of Crucible, thunderheads the size of planets, eddies a continent could get lost in. They wanted hundreds of ice mountains moved to intercept the missiles.

The sun was out because it was being converted into a fearsome laser lance. This would be used on the ice mountains before the missiles flew by; the expanding clouds of gas should cover enough area to intercept the missiles.

She was going to lose a prospector or two in the conflagration, but to complain about that now seemed petty.

Chinook was drawing close, and the time lag between messages became shorter. As she was starting her orbital corrections on a last chunk of ice, a new message came in from Hammond. For her, again.

In case this was going to get her all wrought up, she finished setting the vectors before she opened the message. This time it came in video format.

Mark Hammond was a lean-faced man with dark skin and an unruly shock of black hair. Two blue-green ear rings hung from his ears. He looked old, but that was only because of the lines around his mouth, crow's feet at his eyes. But he smiled now.

"Thanks for the pictures, Elise. You can call me Mark. I'm glad your people are able to defend themselves. The news must be going out to all the halo worlds now—nobody's going to trade with Leviathan now! Total isolation. They deserve it. Thank you. None of this could've happened if you hadn't been there."

He rubbed his jaw. "Your support's meant a lot to me in the past few days, Elise. I loved the pictures; they were like a breath of new air. Yeah, I did show them around. It worked, too; we've got a lot of people on our side. Who knows, maybe we'll be able to kick the murderers out of here, like you say. We wouldn't even have considered trying, if not for you."

He grimaced, looked down quickly. "Sounds stupid. But you say stupid things in situations like this. Your help has meant a lot to me. I hope you're evacuated to somewhere safe. And I've been wracking my brains, trying to think of something I could do for you, equal to the pictures you sent.

"It's not much, but I'm sending you a bunch of my recordings. Some of these songs are mine, some are traditionals from Mirjam. But it's all my voice. I hope you like them. I'll never get the chance for the real training I needed at Tiara. This'll have to do." Looking suddenly shy, he said, "Bye."

Elise saved the songs in an accessible format and transferred them to her sound system. She stepped out of the office, walked without speaking past Nasim and the kids, and turned the sound way up. Hammond's voice poured out clear and strong, and she sat facing the wall, and just listened for the remainder of the day.

— • —

Oliver called her the next morning with new orders. "You're the only person who's got anything like a ship near the *Chinook*'s flight path. Prospector Six." That was the one that had picked up Hammond's first message. "We're sending some missiles we put together, but they're low-mass, so they might not penetrate the *Chinook*'s forward shields."

"You want me to destroy the *Chinook*." She was not surprised. Only very disappointed that fate had worked things this way.

"Yeah," Oliver said. "Those shits can't be allowed to get away. Your prospector masses ten thousand tonnes, more than enough to stop it dead. I've put the vectors in your database. This is top priority. Get on it." He hung up.

She was damned if she would get on it. Elise well knew her responsibility to Dew, but destroying *Chinook* wouldn't save her world. That all hinged on the missiles, which must have already been sent. But just so the police couldn't prove that she'd disobeyed orders, she entered the vectors to intercept *Chinook*, but included a tiny error which would guarantee a miss. The enormity of what she was doing—the government would call this treason—made her feel sick to her stomach. Finally she summoned her courage and called Hammond.

"They want me to kill you." Elise stood in front of her computer, allowing it to record her in video. She owed him that, at least. "I can't do it. I'm sorry, but I can't. I'm not an executioner, and you've done nothing wrong. Of all of us, you're the one who least deserves to die! It's not fair. Mark, you're going to have to take back the *Chinook*. You said you had more people on your side. I'm going to give you the time to do it. It's a couple of years to your next stop. Take back the ship, then you can get off there. You can still have your life, Mark!

"Come back here. You'll be a hero."

She tried to smile bravely, but it cracked into a grimace. "Please, Mark. I'm sure the government's alerted all the other halo worlds now. They'll be ready. *Chinook* won't be able to catch anybody else by surprise. So there's no reason to kill you.

"I'm giving you the chance you deserve, Mark. I hope you make the best of it."

She sent that message, only realizing afterwards that she hadn't thanked him for the gift of his music. But she was afraid to say anything more.

— • —

The city was evacuated the next day. It started in the early hours, as the police closed off all the levels of the city, then began sweeping, waking people from their beds and moving the bewildered crowds to trains and aircraft. Elise was packed and ready. Judy slept in her arms, and Alex clutched her belt and knuckled his eyes as they walked among shouting people. The media were now revealing the nature of the crisis, but it was far too late for organized protest. The crowds were herded methodically; the police must have been drilling for this for weeks.

She wished Sal had told her exactly when it was going to happen. It meant she hadn't been able to hook up with Nasim, whose apartment was on another level. He was probably still asleep, even while she and the kids were packed on a train, and she watched through the angle of the window as the station receded.

Sometime the next morning they stopped, and some of the passengers were off-loaded. Food was eventually brought, and then they continued on. Elise was asleep, leaning against the wall, when they finally unloaded her car.

All the cities of Dew had emergency barracks. She had no idea what city they had come to at first, having missed the station signs. She didn't care. The kids needed looking after, and she was bone-tired.

Not too tired, though, to know that the hours were counting quickly down to zero. She couldn't stand being cut off; she had to know Hammond's reply to her message, but there were no terminals in the barracks. She had to know he was all right.

She finally managed to convince some women to look after Judy and Alex, and set off to find a way out. There were several policemen loitering around the massive metal doors that separated the barracks from the city, and they weren't letting anyone pass.

She walked briskly around the perimeter of the barracks, thinking. Barracks like this were usually at ground level, and were supposed to have more than one entrance, in case one was blocked by earthquake or fire. There must be some outside exit, and it might not be guarded.

Deep at the back where she hadn't been yet, she found her airlock, unguarded. Its lockers were packed with survival suits; none of the refugees would be going outside, especially not here on unknown ground. There was no good reason for them to leave the barracks, because going outside would not get them home. But she needed a terminal.

She suited up and went through the airlock. Nobody saw her. Elise stepped out onto the surface of Dew, where she had never been except during survival drills. A thin wind was blowing, catching and worrying at drifts of carbon-dioxide snow.

Torn clouds revealed stars high above the glowing walls of the city. This place, wherever it was, had thousands of windows; she supposed all the cities did now. They would have a good view of whatever happened in the sky today.

After walking for a good ten minutes, she came to another airlock. This one was big, with vehicles rolling in and out. She stepped in after one, and found herself in a warehouse. Simple as that.

From there, she took the elevator up sixteen levels to an arcade lined with glass. Here, finally, were VR terminals, and she gratefully collapsed at one and logged into her account.

There were two messages waiting. Hammond, it had to be. She called up the first one.

"You're gonna thank me for this, you really are," said Oliver. He looked smug. "I checked in on your work—hey, just doing my job. You did a great job on moving the ice, but you totally screwed up your trajectory on Prospector Six. Just a little error, but it added up quick. Would have missed *Chinook* completely if I hadn't corrected it. Guess I saved your ass, huh?" He mock-saluted and grinned. "Didn't tell anybody. I won't, either. You can thank me later." Still smug, he rung off.

"Oh, no. No, no, no," she whispered. Trembling, she played the second message.

Hammond appeared, looking drawn and sad. His backdrop was a metal bulkhead; his breath frosted when he breathed. "Hello, Elise," he said. His voice was low and tired. "Thank you for caring so much about me. But your plan will never work.

"You're not here. Lucky thing. But if you were, you'd see how hopeless it is. There's a handful of us prisoners, kept alive for amusement and because we can do some things they can't.

They never thought we'd have a reason to go outside, that's the only reason I was able to get out to take over the message laser.

And it's only because of their bragging that we got the video and data we did.

"They have a right to be confident, with us. We can't do anything; we're locked away from their part of the ship. And you see, when they realize you've mined space near Dew, they'll know someone gave them away. We knew that would happen when we decided to do this. Either way, I'm dead, you see; either you kill me, or they do. I'd prefer you did it; it'll be so much faster."

He looked down pensively for a moment. "Do me the favour," he said at last. "You'll carry no blame for it, no guilt. Destroy *Chinook*. The worlds really aren't safe until you do. These people are fanatics; they never expected to get home alive.

"If they think their missiles won't get through, they'll aim the ship itself at the next world. Which will be much harder to stop.

"I love you for your optimism, and your plans. I wish it could have gone the way you said. But this really is goodbye."

Finally, he smiled, looking directly at her. "Too bad we didn't have the time. I could have loved you, I think. Thank you, though. The caring you showed me is enough." He vanished.

Message end, said the mailer. *Reply?*

She stared at that last word for a long time. She signalled, *yes*.

"Thank you for your music, Mark," she said. She sent that.

Then she closed her programs and took off the headset.

— • —

The end, when it came, took the form of a brilliant line of light scored across the sky. Elise watched from the glass wall of the arcade, where she sat on a long couch with a bunch of other silent people. The landscape lit to the horizon, brighter than Dew's artificial sun had ever shone. The false day faded slowly.

There was no ground shock. No sound. Dew had been spared.

The crowd dispersed, talking animatedly. For them, the adventure had been over before they had time to really believe in the threat. Elise watched them through her tears, almost fondly. She was too tired to move.

Alone, she gazed up at the stars. Only a faint pale streak remained now. In a moment she would return to her children, but first she had to let this emotion fill her completely, wash down from her face through her arms and body, like Hammond's music. She wasn't used to how acceptance felt. She hoped it would become more familiar to her.

Elise stood and walked alone to the elevator, and did not look back at the sky. ∎

Peter Watts (rifters.com) is an uncomfortable hybrid of biologist and science-fiction author, known for pioneering the technique of appending extensive technical bibliographies onto his novels; this serves both to confer a veneer of credibility and to cover his ass against nitpickers.

Described by *The Globe and Mail* as one of the best hard-sf authors alive, his debut novel *Starfish* was a *New York Times* Notable Book, while his most recent, *Blindsight*—a philosophical rumination on the nature of consciousness which, despite an unhealthy focus on space vampires, has become a required text in at least one undergraduate philosophy course—made the final ballot for numerous genre awards, winning exactly none of them. This may reflect a certain controversy regarding Watts's work in general. His bipartite novel *Behemoth*, for example, was praised by *Publishers Weekly* as an "adrenaline-charged fusion of Arthur C. Clarke's *The Deep Range* and William Gibson's *Neuromancer*" and "a major addition to 21st-century hard SF," while being simultaneously decried by Kirkus as "utterly repellent" and "horrific porn." (Watts is happy to embrace the truth of both views.) A marine biologist formerly resident in Vancouver, he now makes his home in Toronto.

NOVELS:

Starfish (Tor Books, New York, 1999)

Maelstrom (Tor Books, New York, 2001)

Behemoth: B-Max (Tor Books, New York, 2004)

Behemoth: Seppuku (Tor Books, New York, 2005)

Blindsight (Tor Books, New York, 2006)

SHORT STORY COLLECTION:

Ten Monkeys, Ten Minutes (Tesseract Books, Edmonton, 2000)

THE EYES OF GOD

Peter Watts

I am not a criminal. I have done nothing wrong.

They've just caught a woman at the front of the line, mocha-skinned mid-thirties, eyes wide and innocent beneath the brim of her La Senza beret. She dosed herself with oxytocin from the sound of it, tried to subvert the meat in the system—a smile, a wink, that extra chemical nudge that bypasses logic and whispers right to the brainstem: *This one's a friend; no need to put* her *through the machines ...*

But I guess she forgot: We're all machines here, tweaked and tuned and retrofitted down to the molecules. The guards have been immunized against argument and aerosols. They lead her away, indifferent to her protests. I try to follow their example, harden myself against whatever awaits her on the other side of the white door. What was she thinking, to try a stunt like that? Whatever hides in her head must be more than mere inclination. They don't yank paying passengers for evil fantasies, not yet anyway, not yet. She must have done something. She must have *acted*.

Half an hour before the plane boards. There are at least fifty law-abiding citizens ahead of me and they haven't started processing us yet. The Buzz Box looms dormant at the front of the line like a great armoured crab, newly installed, mouth agape. One of the guards in its shadow starts working her way up the line, spot-checking some passengers, bypassing others, feeling lucky after the first catch of the day. In a just universe I would have nothing to fear from her. I'm not a criminal; I have done nothing wrong. The words cycle in my head like a defensive affirmation.

I am not a criminal. I have done nothing wrong.

But I know that fucking machine is going to tag me anyway.

— • —

At the head of the queue, the Chamber of Secrets lights up. A canned female voice announces the dawning of pre-board security, echoing through the harsh acoustics of the terminal. The guards slouch to attention. We gave up everything to join this line: smart tags, jewellery, my pocket office, all confiscated until the far side of redemption. The buzz box needs a clear view into our heads; even an earring can throw it off. People with medical implants and antique mercury fillings aren't welcome here. There's a side queue for those types, a special room where old-fashioned interrogations and cavity searches are still the order of the day.

The omnipresent voice orders all Westjet passenger with epilepsy, cochlear dysfunction, or Grey's Syndrome to identify themselves to Security prior to entering the scanner. Other passengers who do not wish to be scanned may opt to forfeit their passage. Westjet regrets that it cannot offer refunds in such cases. Westjet is not responsible for neurological side effects, temporary or otherwise, that may result from use of the scanner. Use of the scanner constitutes acceptance of these conditions.

There *have* been side effects. A few garden-variety epileptics had minor fits in the early days. A famous Oxford atheist—you remember, the guy who wrote all the books—caught a devout and abiding faith in the Christian God from a checkpoint at Heathrow, although some responsibility was ultimately laid at the feet of the pre-existing tumour that killed him two months later. One widowed grandmother from St. Paul's was all over the news last year when she emerged from a courthouse buzz box with an insatiable sexual fetish for running shoes. That could have cost Sony a lot, if she hadn't been a forgiving soul who chose not to litigate. Rumours that she'd used SWank just prior to making that decision were never confirmed.

— • —

"Destination?"

The guard has arrived while I wasn't looking. Her laser licks my face with biometric taste buds. I blink away the afterimages.

"Destination," she says again.

"Uh, Yellowknife."

She scans her handpad. "Business or pleasure?" There's no point to these questions, they're not even according to script. SWank has taken us beyond the need for petty interrogation. She just doesn't like the look of me, I bet. Maybe she just *knows* somehow, even if she can't put her finger on it.

"Neither," I say. She looks up sharply. Whatever her initial suspicions, my obvious evasiveness has cemented them. "I'm attending a funeral," I explain.

She moves along without a word.

I know you're not here, Father. I left my faith back in childhood. Let others hold to their feebleminded superstitions; let them run bleating to the supernatural for comfort and excuses. Let the cowardly and the weak-minded deny the darkness with the promise of some imagined afterlife. I have no need for invisible friends. I know I'm only talking to myself. If only I could stop.

I wonder if that machine will be able to eavesdrop on our conversation.

I stood with you at your trial, as you stood with me years before when I had no other friend in the world. I swore on your sacred book of fairy tales that you'd never touched me, not once in all those years. Were the others lying, I wonder? I don't know. Judge not, I guess.

But you were judged, and found wanting. It wasn't even newsworthy—

child-fondling priests are more cliché than criminal these days, have been for years, and no one cares what happens in some dickass town up in the Territories anyway. If they'd quietly transferred you just one more time, if you'd managed to lay low just a little longer, it might not have even come to this. They could have fixed you.

Or not, now that I think of it. The Vatican came down on SWank like it came down on cloning and the Copernican solar system before it. Mustn't fuck with the way God built you. Mustn't compromise free choice, no matter how freely you'd choose to do so.

I notice that doesn't extend to tickling the temporal lobe, though. St. Michael's just spent seven million equipping their nave for Rapture on demand.

Maybe suicide was the only option left to you; maybe all you could do was follow one sin with another. It's not as though you had anything to lose; your own scriptures damn us as much for desire as for doing. I remember asking you years ago, although I'd long since thrown away my crutches: What about the sin not made manifest? What if you've coveted thy neighbour's wife or warmed yourself with thoughts of murder, but kept it all inside? You looked at me kindly, and perhaps with far greater understanding than I ever gave you credit for, before condemning me with the words of an imaginary superhero. If you've done any of these things in your heart, you said, then you've done them in the eyes of God.

— • —

I feel a sudden brief chime between my ears. I could really use a drink about now; the woody aroma of a fine old scotch curling through my sinuses would really hit the spot. I glance around, spot the billboard that zapped me. Crown Royal. Fucking head spam. I give silent thanks for legal standards outlawing the implantation of brand names; they can stick cravings in my head, but hooking me on trademarks would cross some arbitrary threshold of *free will*. It's a meaningless gesture, a sop to the civil-rights fanatics. Like the chime that preceded it: It tells me, the courts say, that I am still autonomous. As long as I *know* I'm being hacked, I've got a sporting chance to make my own decisions.

Two spots ahead of me, an old man sobs quietly. He seemed fine just a moment ago. Sometimes it happens. The ads trigger the wrong connections. SWank can't lay down hi-def sensory panoramas without a helmet; these long-range hits don't *instil* so much as *evoke*. Smell's key, they say—primitive, lobes big enough for remote targeting, simpler to hack than the vast gigapixel arrays of the visual cortex. And so *primal*, so much closer to raw reptile. They spent millions finding the universal triggers. Honeysuckle reminds you of childhood; the scent of pine recalls Christmas. They can mood us up for Norman Rockwell or the Marquis de Sade, depending on the product. Nudge the right receptor neurons and the brain builds its *own* spam.

For some people, though, honeysuckle is what you smelled when your mother got the shit beaten out of her. For some, Christmas was when you found your sister with her wrists slashed open.

It doesn't happen often. The ads provoke mild unease in one of a thousand of us, true distress in a tenth as many. Some thought even that price was too high. Others quailed at the spectre of machines instilling not just sights and sounds but *desires*, opinions, religious beliefs. But commercials featuring cute babies or sexy women also plant desire, use sight and sound to bypass the head and go for the gut. Every debate, every argument is an attempt to literally *change someone's mind*, every poem and pamphlet a viral tool for the hacking of opinions. *I'm doing it right now*, some Mindscape™ flak argued last month on MacroNet. *I'm trying to change your neural wiring using the sounds you're hearing. You want to ban SWank just because it uses sounds you* can't?

The slope is just too slippery. Ban SWank and you might as well ban art as well as advocacy. You might as well ban free speech itself.

We both know the truth of it, Father. Even words can bring one to tears.

— • —

The line moves forward. We shuffle along with smooth, ominous efficiency, one after another disappearing briefly into the buzz box, reappearing on the far side, emerging reborn from a technological baptism that elevates us all to temporary sainthood.

Compressed ultrasound, Father. That's how they cleanse us. You probably saw the hype a few years back, even up there. You must have seen the papal bull condemning it, at least. Sony filed the original patent as a game interface, just after the turn of the century; soon, they told us, the eye-phones and electrodes of yore would give way to affordable little boxes that tracked you around your living room, bypassed eyes and ears entirely, and planted five-dimensional sensory experience directly into your brain. (We're still waiting for those, actually; the tweaks may be ultrasonic but the system keeps your brain in focus by tracking EM emissions, and not many consumers Faraday their homes.) In the meantime, hospitals and airports and theme parks keep the dream alive until the price comes down. And the spin-offs—Father, the spin-offs are everywhere. The deaf can hear. The blind can see. The post-traumatised have all their acid memories washed away, just as long as they keep paying the connection fee.

That's the rub, of course. It doesn't last: The high frequencies excite some synapses and put others to sleep, but they don't actually change any of the pre-existing circuitry. The brain eventually bounces back to normal once the signal stops. Which is not only profitable for those doling out the waves, but a lot less messy in the courts. There's that whole integrity-of-the-self thing to worry about. Having your brain rewired every time you hopped a commuter flight might raise some pretty iffy legal issues.

Still. I've got to admit it speeds things up. No more time-consuming background checks, no more invasive "random" searches, no litany of questions designed to weed out the troublemakers in our midst. A dash of transcranial magnetism; a squirt of ultrasound; *next*. A year ago, I'd have been standing in line for hours. Today, I've been here scarcely fifteen minutes and I'm already in the top ten. And it's more than mere convenience: It's security; it's safety; it's a sigh of relief after a generation of Russian Roulette. No more Edmonton Infernos, no more Rio Insurrections, no more buildings slagged to glass or cities sickening in the aftermath of some dirty nuke. There are still saboteurs and terrorists loose in the world, of course. Always will be. But when they strike at all, they strike in places unprotected by SWanky McBuzz. Anyone who flies *these* friendly skies is as harmless as—as I am.

Who can argue with results like that?

— • —

In the old days I could have wished I was a psychopath. They had it easy back then. The machines only looked for emotional responses: eye saccades, skin galvanism. Anyone without a conscience could stare them down with a wide smile and an empty heart. But SWank inspired a whole new generation. The tech looks under the surface now. Prefrontal cortex stuff, glucose metabolism. Now, fiends and perverts and would-be saboteurs all get caught in the same net.

Doesn't mean they don't let us go again, of course. It's not as if sociopathy is against the law. Hell, if they screened out everyone with a broken conscience, Executive Class would be empty.

There are children scattered throughout the line. Most are accompanied by adults. Three are not, two boys and a girl. They are nervous and beautiful, like wild animals, easily startled. They are not used to being on their own. The oldest can't be more than nine, and he has a freckle on the side of his neck.

I can't stop watching him.

Suddenly children roam free again. For months now I've been seeing them in parks and plazas, unguarded, innocent, and so *vulnerable*, as though SWank has given parents everywhere an excuse to breathe. No matter that it'll be years before it trickles out of airports and government buildings and into the places children play. Mommy and Daddy are tired of waiting, take what comfort they can in the cameras mounted on every street corner, panning and scanning for all the world as if real people stood behind them. Mommy and Daddy can't be bothered to spend five minutes on the Web, compiling their own predator's handbook on the use of laser pointers and blind spots to punch holes in the surveillance society. Mommy and Daddy would rather just take all those bromides about "civil safety" on faith.

For so many years we've lived in fear. By now, people are so desperate for any pretence of safety that they'll cling to the promise of a future that hasn't even arrived yet. Not that that's anything new; whether you're talking about a house in the suburbs or the browning of Antarctica, Mommy and Daddy have *always* lived on credit.

If something *did* happen to their kids, it would serve them right.

— • —

The line moves forward. Suddenly I'm at the front of it.

A man with Authority waves me in. I step forward as if to an execution. I do this for you, Father. I do this to pay my respects. I do this to dance on your grave. If I could have avoided this moment—if this cup could have passed from me, if I could have *walked* to the Northwest Territories rather than let this obscene technology into my head—

Someone has spray-painted two words in stencilled black over the mouth of the machine: *The Shadow*. Delaying, I glance a question at the guard.

"It knows what evil lurks in the hearts of men," he says. "Bwahaha. Let's move it along."

I have no idea what he's talking about.

The walls of the booth glimmer with a tight weave of copper wire. The helmet descends from above with a soft hydraulic hiss; it sits too lightly on my head for such a massive device. The visor slides over my eyes like a blindfold. I am in a pocket universe, alone with my thoughts and an all-seeing God. Electricity hums deep in my head.

I'm innocent of any wrongdoing. I've never broken the law. Maybe God will see that if I think it hard enough. Why does it have to see anything; why does it have to *read* the palimpsest if it's just going to scribble over it again? But brains don't work like that. Each individual *is* individual, wired up in a unique and glorious tangle that must be read before it can be edited. And motivations, intents—these are endless, multiheaded things, twining and proliferating from frontal cortex to cingulate gyrus, from hypothalamus to claustrum. There's no LED that lights up when your plans are nefarious, no Aniston Neuron for mad bombers. For the safety of everyone, they must read it all. For the safety of everyone.

I have been under this helmet for what seems like forever. Nobody else took this long.

The line is not moving forward.

"Well," Security says softly. "Will you look at that."

"I'm not," I tell him. "I've never—"

"And you're not about to. Not for the next nine hours, anyway."

"I never *acted* on it." I sound petulant, childish. "Not once."

"I can see that," he says, but I know we're talking about different things.

The humming changes subtly in pitch. I can feel magnets and mosquitoes snapping in my head. I am changed by something not yet cheap enough for the home market: An ache evaporates, a dull longing so chronic I feel it now only in absentia.

"There. Now we could put you in charge of two Day Cares and a chorus of alter boys, and you wouldn't even be tempted."

The visor rises; the helmet floats away. Authority stares back at me from a gaggle of contemptuous faces.

"This is wrong," I say quietly.

"Is it, now."

"I haven't done anything."

"We haven't either. We haven't locked down your pervert brain; we haven't changed who you are. We've protected your precious constitutional rights and your god-given identity. You're as free to diddle kiddies in the park as you ever were. You just won't *want* to for a while."

"But I haven't *done* anything." I can't stop saying it.

"Nobody does, until they do." He jerks his head toward Departure. "Get out of here. You're cleared."

— • —

I am not a criminal. I have done nothing wrong. But my name is on a list now, just the same. Word of my depravity races ahead of me, checkpoint after checkpoint, like a fission of dominoes. They'll be watching, though they have to let me pass.

That could change before long. Even now, Community Standards barely recognize the difference between what we do and what we are; nudge them just a hair further and every border on the planet might close at my approach. But this is only the dawning of the new enlightenment, and the latest rules are not yet in place. For now, I am free to stand at your unconsecrated graveside, and mourn on my own recognizance.

You always were big on the power of forgiveness, Father. Seventy times seven, the most egregious sins washed away in the sight of the Lord. All it took, you insisted, was true penitence. All you had to do was accept His love.

Of course, it sounded a lot less self-serving back then.

But even the unbelievers get a clean slate now. My redeemer is a machine, and my salvation has an expiry date—but then again, I guess yours did, too.

I wonder about the machine that programmed *you*, Father, that great glacial contraption of dogma and moving parts, clacking and iterating its way through two thousand years of bloody history. I can't help but wonder at the way it rewired *your* synapses. Did it turn you into a predator, weigh you down with lunatic strictures that no sexual being could withstand, deny your very nature until you snapped? Or were you already malfunctioning when you embraced the church, hoping for some measure of strength you couldn't find in yourself?

I knew you for years, Father. Even now, I tell myself I know you—and while you may have been twisted, you were never a coward. I refuse to believe that you opted for death because it was the easy way out. I choose to believe that in those last days, you found the strength to rewrite your own programming, to turn your back on obsolete algorithms two millennia out of date, and decide for yourself the difference between a mortal sin and an act of atonement.

You loathed yourself; you loathed the things you had done. And so, finally, you made absolutely certain you could never do them again. You *acted*.

You acted as I never could, though I'd pay so much smaller a price.

There is more than this temporary absolution, you see. We have machines now that can burn the evil right out of a man, deep-focus microwave emitters that vaporize the very pathways of depravity. No one can force them on you; not yet, anyway. Member's bills wind through Parliament, legislative proposals that would see us pre-emptively reprogrammed for good instead of evil, but for now, the procedure is strictly voluntary. It *changes* you, you see. It violates some inalienable essence of selfhood. Some call it a kind of suicide in its own right.

I kept telling the man at Security: I never *acted* on it. But he could see that for himself.

I never had it fixed. I must *like* what I am.

I wonder if that makes a difference.

I wonder which of us is more guilty. ∎

Spider Robinson (spiderrobinson.com) has won three Hugos, a Nebula, and numerous other international awards. His thirty-five books are available in ten languages, and his short work has appeared in countless magazines and anthologies.

In 2006 he was chosen by the Robert A. Heinlein estate to write *Variable Star* based on an outline by Heinlein. That year he was invited to the National Book Festival in Washington, D.C., where he dined with the President and First Lady and read aloud from *Variable Star* on the National Mall.

His op-ed column "The Crazy Years" appeared in *The Globe and Mail* from 1996 to 2001. He's written and/or recorded original music with David Crosby, Todd Butler, and Amos Garrett.

Spider's been married for thirty-four years to Jeanne Robinson, a Boston-born writer, choreographer, and retired dancer, who is now co-developing a film about zero-G dance based on her and Spider's award-winning novella "Stardance," for which she was separately invited to the 2006 National Book Festival. The Robinsons have lived for ten years on Bowen Island, British Columbia, where they raise and exhibit prize hopes.

NOVELS:

Telempath (Berkley, New York, 1976)

Mindkiller (Holt, Rinehart & Winston, New York, 1982)

Night of Power (Baen, New York, 1985)

Time Pressure (Ace, New York, 1987)

Callahan's Lady (Ace, New York, 1989)

Lady Slings the Booze (Ace, New York, 1992)

The Callahan Touch (Ace, New York, 1993)

Callahan's Legacy (Tor, New York 1996)

Lifehouse (Baen, New York, 1997)

Callahan's Key (Bantam, New York, 2000)

The Free Lunch (Tor, New York, 2001)

Callahan's Con (Tor, New York, 2003)

Very Bad Deaths (Baen, New York, 2004)

Very Hard Choices (Baen, New York, 2008)

WITH JEANNE ROBINSON:

Stardance (Dial, New York, 1978)

Starseed (Ace, New York, 1991)

Starmind (Ace, New York, 1995)

WITH ROBERT A. HEINLEIN:

Variable Star (Tor, New York, 2006)

SHORT STORY COLLECTIONS:

Callahan's Crosstime Saloon (Ace, New York, 1977)

Antinomy (Dell, New York, 1980)

Time Travelers Strictly Cash (Ace, New York, 1981)

Melancholy Elephants (Penguin Canada, Toronto, 1984)

Callahan's Secret (Ace, New York, 1986)

True Minds (Pulphouse, Eugene, Oregon, 1990)

Off the Wall at Callahan's (Tor, New York, 1994)

User Friendly (Baen, New York, 1998)

By Any Other Name (Baen, New York, 2001)

God is an Iron and Other Stories (Five Star, Waterville, Maine, 2002)

YOU DON'T KNOW MY HEART

Spider Robinson

Tried to fit, I tried to blend
I learned young to pretend
'cause if they knew, the world would end

—"You Don't Know My Heart"
Janis Ian

I was onstage at Slim's, halfway through my last set, when I saw the two hitters come in.

It wasn't hard to spot them, even in the poor light. They were both *way* too straight for Slim's Elite Café. They were pretending to be a leather couple, even holding hands, but I didn't buy it and doubted many others would. No gunfighter moustaches, no visible piercings, no jewellery, the leather was brand new, the tats were fake, and the stubble on their skulls and faces was two days old, tops. Either of them alone might have been exploring the darker corners of his sexuality on vacation, a Key West cliché; together, though, the only use they'd have for a queer was as a punching bag. They were not at all uneasy in a place where their kind was doubly outnumbered—about two dykes like me to every fag, a normal night—so I assumed they were armed. I didn't panic. I know a way to get from the stage of Slim's to *elsewhere* faster than most people can react, and since I've never had to use it, I'm pretty sure it will work. I kept playing without missing a beat—okay, I fluffed a guitar fill, but it wasn't a train wreck. An old Janis Ian song; she goes over well at Slim's and I can sing in her key.

All the broken promises
all the shattered dreams
all this aching loneliness
will finally be set free
I have waited for so long
to remember what it's like
to feel somebody's arms around my life

After a minute or so, my adrenalin level dropped back to about per-formance-normal. I couldn't decide whether they were Good Guys or Bad Guys, but either way they didn't seem to be looking for me, so the question held little urgency. It was hard to tell who they *were* after. The whole room was basically a big poorly lit box of suspicious characters, flight risks, and hopeful victims—disasters looking for the spot marked x. Or, of course, I could be mistaken: The pair could be off-duty, their real assignment else-where. Or, just possibly, they might be two men in their early thirties who'd suddenly realized they were leatherboys, and by great fortune had met out on the street five minutes ago.

They had been chatting quietly together since they'd come in, ignoring those around them and, far more unforgivably, my music. But when I fin-ished the song, the applause caused one of them, the uglier of the two, to glance up at the stage and see me. One look was all he felt he needed. *Dyke*, said his face, and he looked away, subtracting me from his landscape. No, they weren't novice leatherboys—or even postulants.

Well, when someone insults my sexuality while I'm on stage, out loud or silently, I have a stock response: I sing "You Don't Know My Heart." It's another Janis Ian song, actually—one of the best songs I know about being gay, because there isn't a drop of anger in it anywhere that I can see. Just sadness. It sums up everything I've always wanted to say to dyke-hasslers and queer-bashers and minority-abusers of all stripes, all they really deserve to know, and all they should need to know, without the rage that always makes me choke if I do try and talk to them, and keeps them from listening if I succeed.

We learn to stand in the shadows
watch the way the wind blows
thinking no one knows
we're one of a kind
Shy glances at the neighboring team
Romance is a dangerous dream
never knowing if they'll laugh or scream
Living on a fault line
Will you/won't you be mine?
Hoping it will change in time

One of the two hitters got up to go to the can, leaving his friend at the table. To get there, he had to pass in front of the stage. I caught his eye and pointedly aimed the chorus of the song at him as he approached, not quite pointing to him and singing straight at him, but almost.

And if people say we chose this way
to set ourselves apart—I say
you don't know my heart
You don't know my heart

He got the message—as much of it as would penetrate—grimaced at me and glanced away.

You don't know my heart
You don't know my heart

It was when he glanced away that he suddenly acquired his target. I saw his face change, followed his gaze, and realized they were after Dora Something-or-Other.

It seemed ridiculous. Who sends a pair of pros after a drag queen?

— • —

There are people in Key West who were born in Key West, but statistically you're unlikely to meet one unless you make an effort.

It's a place most people pass through, and others end up. The lucky ones take a moment to recover, then regroup, make a plan, and go somewhere else. Others sit for a long or a short time on the bottom, half-concealed in the ooze, until one vagrant current or another stirs them up and carries them back north into the stream of life. And some sink into the mud for keeps and begin growing barnacles and coral deposits of their own. Key West is Endsville. There's just no further to run; you have to stop, steal a boat, or start swimming.

You might think a town full of losers, runaways, fugitives, and failures would have a high crime rate, but in fact there's almost none. Everyone seems to want to keep their heads down and chill; in many cases an over-gaudy lifestyle was why they had to leave America and come here in the first place. There is zero organized crime, except for municipal government. Oh, I'm sure all the big chain hotels have their liquor, linen, and garbage needs dealt with by the right firms out of Miami. Beyond that, there simply isn't anything on The Rock to interest the mob. It's a beehive of small-time tourist hustles, hard to keep track of, and beneath their dignity to tax. Circuit hookers can't compete with the constantly changing parade of semi-pros, beginners, stupefied co-eds, and reckless secretaries on vacation. Consequently, the gangsters have always treated the place as a neutral zone.

No family claims it, and if you see somebody with bodyguards, you know he must be a civilian. In a town full of illegal immigrants and bail-jumpers, KWPD has fired more cops than it has shots.

It's a wonderful place to hide. That's why most of us are there.

Including, apparently, Dora Whatsername.

— • —

What I wanted to do was catch Dora's eye, hold it long enough to engage his attention, then gesture with my eyes and eyebrows toward the hitters. It would, of course, be good to do this *without* letting the hitters catch me at it. Now was the time, then, with one of them in the can. But the remaining one happened to be the last folk music fan left outside Key West, and was watching me perform.

I had a rush of brains to the head, and began singing "You Don't Know My Heart" directly to him, just as I had to his partner a moment ago.

> *Tried to fit, I tried to blend*
> *I learned young to pretend*
> *'cause if they knew, the world would end*
> *Frightened of my family*
> *Where is anyone like me?*
> *When will I be free?*

Sure enough, the penny dropped. He started hearing the words. He, too, grimaced in disgust—*a tragic waste of pussy*—and looked away.

Moments later I had eye contact with Dora. We didn't know each other very well, and had never shared so much as a conversation—we played in different leagues—so he wasted several long seconds being surprised and puzzled. Fortunately, disgust outlasts confusion. By the time hitter number two got over being grossed out and looked back my way, Dora was discreetly clocking the guy out of the corner of his eye.

Unless specifically asked otherwise, I usually refer to drag queens as "she." I like to think it's more from politeness than political correctness. But every so often you meet one like Dora, who's so hopeless at it that "he" is the only pronoun you can bring yourself to use. I'd never quite been able to pin down what it was he got wrong. He didn't have broad shoulders, muscular arms, thick wrists, deep voice, heavy beard or prominent Adam's apple. He didn't totter on heels or sit with his legs open. His face was kind of cute, in the right light, and he didn't overdo the makeup or the camp more than a drag queen is supposed to. Yet, somehow, the overall effect was of a female impersonator impersonator.

Which was fine with me. I have no business criticizing anybody else's act: I sing folk. We moved in different circles, was all.

At first, I think Dora thought I was pointing out the leatherboy as someone he might want to fan with his false eyelashes, and, if so, he must have thought I was nuts. Nearly at once, though, I saw him pick up on the fact that the guy was a phoney—one with hard muscles and empty eyes. He glanced my way with one eyebrow raised, nodded his thanks, and went back to discreetly studying his watcher.

Hitter number one got back to the table and rejoined his partner just as I was finishing the song. Because I was looking for it, I noticed that beneath his leather pants, his right ankle was thicker on the outside than his left. That's where a right-handed man will hide a gun. So: not hitters, but shooters.

There followed an amusing charade in which the shooters tried to discuss Dora without being caught at it, and Dora pretended not to clock the whole thing. It was a lot like the mating dances going on all around the room, except that this one, I was pretty sure, was intended to end with a *literal* bang. Dora looked unconcerned, but I didn't see how he was going to get out of it. His pursuers looked fit enough to run up the side of Martello Tower; no way was he going to outrun them, not in those heels.

So I flanged up my guitar a couple of notches, called out, "Anybody feel like *dancing*?" and launched into Jimmy Buffett's "Fins."

Everybody in Key West knows every song Jimmy Buffett ever wrote; it's one of the few requirements of residence. There are at least a dozen guaranteed to make everyone in the joint pause in their seductions long enough to sing along—but "Fins" is certain to get them on their feet, the way I play it anyway. It's about being hit on in bars—fins to the left, fins to the right, and you're the only bait in town—so the lyrics tend to strike a certain chord, in predator and prey alike.

And the guitar lick would make a preacher dance the dirty boogie. Halfway into it there was a roar of recognition and approval, and by the time I started the first verse, half the place was dancing, and the other half was trying to find room to.

I lost track of Dora in the crowd at once. But I could make out the two shooters, trying to force their way across the room to him. They were better than average at it, spreading out just enough to block his escape path as they came.

I'd just finished the first verse; as I went into my guitar solo, I stepped away from the mike and began doing a Chuck Berry Strut back and forth across the stage. Bingo: An instant line dance organized itself out there on the floor and started to conga back and forth. By the time Frick and Frack managed to work their way through *that*, Dora was long gone. They stood where they'd last seen her, blank-faced as mannequins, and each turned in place five times before they gave up.

I finished the song, got a big round of applause, and, since I had everyone on their feet, went into a slow-dance song, a ballad by Woody Smith called "Afterglow."

Tending to tension by conscious intent,
declining declension, disdaining dissent,
into the dementia dimension we're sent:
we are our content,
and we are content.

The half of the crowd that wasn't doing that well tonight sat down, and the rest went into their clinches. I saw the shooters' eyes meet, saw them both consider and reject the idea of slow-dancing together for the sake of their cover. They left together, and I finished my set feeling the warm glow of the Samaritan who has managed to get away with it.

I glowed too soon. As I stepped out the back door of Slim's Elite to walk home a little after two, I heard someone nearby drive a nail deep into hardwood with a single blow. I was turning to yank the sticky door shut behind me at the time, so I even saw the nail appear, a shiny circle in the doorjamb beside me, where no nail belonged, and no nail had been a moment before. By the time my forebrain had worked out that the nail was the ass end of a silenced bullet, I was already back inside the club, running like hell.

Ever try and run carrying a guitar case? Fortunately, I gig with one of those indestructible Yamahas; I tossed it case and all behind the bar as I went past, and kept on running.

As I burst out the front door onto the deserted, poorly lit street, Dora pulled up in front of me on a Moped. I skidded to a halt. The sight was surreal and silly enough to start me wondering if all of this might not be a bad dream I was having. "Get on," he said, gesturing urgently. "Get *on*." I stood there trying to get my breath, and wondering how Dora knew I needed a ride just then. "Pat, *come o-o-o-on—*"

An angry mosquito parted my hair. Behind me someone snapped a piece of wood with a sound like a muffled gunshot—

—no. Just backwards. That had been a muffled gunshot, no louder than a snapping yardstick. That explained why I was in mid-air, in forward motion, falling toward the back of Dora's Moped—

If a man had landed there, that hard, he'd have gelded himself. It wasn't much more fun for me, and as I drew breath to yell, Dora peeled out. Fast. Somehow his Moped had the power of a real motorcycle—without the thunder. I ended up hanging onto his fake boobs for dear life. There was one last ruler-snap behind us, without mosquito this time, and then we were too far away to sweat small-arms fire. I shifted my grip down to Dora's waist and began to relax slightly.

Someone ripped my left earring out and, behind us, someone snapped a two-by-four.

"Jesus Christ," I screamed, "rifle fire!"

Dora began to deke sharply from side to side. Since he did it randomly to surprise the shooter, he kept surprising me, too, but I managed to hang on. The sniper must have realized his chance for a headshot was gone, and went for a tire. Thanks to the weaving, he blew the heel off my left shoe instead, and for the next ten or twenty busy seconds, I thought he'd shot me in the foot. I clutched Dora hard enough for a Heimlich, and preposterously he yelled, "*Hang on*," and hung a most unexpected *sharp* right into a narrow driveway. We passed between two sparsely lit houses in a controlled skid—I told myself it was controlled—heeled so far over to our right that visually it was remarkably like part of the famous scene at the end of *2001: A Space Odyssey*, lights streaking past us above and below. Nearly at once it gave way to the end of the original *Star Wars*, a smashcut montage of pitch-dark backyard / obstacle course of crap / oncoming stone wall / broken bench reconsidered as ramp / midair, like Elliot and E.T. / narrowly missed pool / asskicker landing / many naked people in great dismay / demolished flowerbed / long narrow walkway between houses like Luke's final run at the Deathstar / chainlink fence / providentially open gate / sharp left onto a deserted street where no one seemed to be firing any rifles, with or without hellish accuracy / fade to black.

Roll credits.

— • —

Dora pulled a pair of my pants up over his own red silk G-string and said, "To be honest, I'm kind of surprised."

I snorted. *To be understated, I'm kind of mindfucked.* "What exactly was it that surprised you? The gunfire? Our surviving it? How many of the people at that orgy looked good naked?" I tossed him a balled-up pair of socks.

We were at my place. He'd wrecked his frock driving a Moped like Jackie Chan. He was way too tall—and too slim-waisted, damn him—to fit into any of my jeans, but I'd found a baggy pair of painter pants around that didn't look *too* ridiculous on him, and a maroon sweatshirt, and some one-size-fits-none sandals. Half the people in Key West were dressed worse.

He unrolled the socks and stared down at them. "I'm kind of surprised you stuck your neck out for me in the first place. That's what I meant."

I said nothing. I sat on the edge of my bed, put my left foot up on my knee and checked the heel for signs of damage. The tingling had gone away by now. It looked okay. I put on my good sandals, dropped the ruined shoes in the trash, and tried a few careful steps. The heel felt a little tender, but not enough to make me limp.

"We barely know each other, Pat. We move in different circles. We play on different teams. But you took a risk for me."

"You returned the favour," I said, and even to me my voice sounded brusque.

He nodded. "Okay. I guess it's none of my business. It's just that ... well, I know a lot of dykes don't have much use for drag queens. We must make you feel a little like black people watching some clueless, happy white guy do a Stepin Fetchit routine in blackface. We revel in the very mannerisms and attitudes you're trying to get away from."

I said some more nothing. Partly that was because he was right. I try to be polite to just about anybody, on principle, but drag queens test my principles even more than skinheads. They exaggerate the aspects of stereotypical femaleness I find most infuriatingly embarrassing—and think it's screamingly funny.

"And of course the lipstick Lezzies hate us because we're so much better than they are at makeup—"

He was simply trying to be friendly, but even if he had just saved my life, I didn't want to be his friend. "You don't know my heart," I said harshly, and heard myself sounding just like the kind of uptight judgmental dyke I've always hated.

His face went blank. It was several seconds before he spoke. "You're absolutely right," he conceded then. "I have no business making presumptions. All I know about you in the world is that you sing and play guitar very well; you hate the sight of car engines, for some reason; and tonight you—"

"*What did you say?*"

Somehow he knew which clause I meant. "Don't sweat it. As phobias go, it's pretty tame. Once I happened to see you jump a foot in the air and then cross the street when someone popped the hood of his car as you were walking past. And then another time, my friend Delilah was working on her old bomber, trying to get the timing right, and she said she asked you to just sit behind the wheel and rev it when she told you, and instead, you turned white as a ghost and turned around and ran away. If I had to guess, I'd guess one of your parents was a mechanic—but I *don't* have to guess. Like you said, I don't know your heart. And nothing says I have to."

"That's right." God, would I ever say anything again that wasn't churlish?

"I just wondered why it made you stick your neck out for a stranger. That's all."

"Look, Dora, maybe sometime my heart'll make me feel like telling you why," I said. "Okay?"

He held up his hands. "Understood." His nails clashed with his—with my—sweatshirt. "You haven't asked why those two are after me. I appreciate that."

"I don't *care* why they're after you," I said. "They're after me too, now; that's all I care about at the moment. They're crazy enough to fire guns in Key West—big guns, right out in the street—and I've pissed them off. How *you* pissed them off doesn't interest me: I have to know who they are." She was frowning. "I need to know *right now*, Dora."

She looked stubborn. "Why?"

I restrained the impulse to smack her one. "Think a minute! Dangerous men are pissed at me. Pros. If they work for Charlie Pontevecchio up in Miami—or for any other private citizen, whether or not his last name happens to end in a vowel—then there probably isn't a lot they can do to locate me until Slim's reopens at nine, giving me a whole, Jesus, six hours to disappear into thin air somehow. But if those two clowns are cops, any kind of cops at all, they're probably rousting Big Chazz out of bed right now, and tough as she is, she's got her licence to think of. They could be here in half an hour. So which—?"

I didn't have to finish the question. His expression answered for him.

"Shit. What *kind* of cops?"

Very expressive face.

"Oh my god. *Federal?*"

He nodded. "Yes, but—wait!"

I'd be hard pressed to say which was moving faster, me or my brain. I'm pretty sure it took less than a single minute before the carryon bag I always keep half full under the bed was topped off with the few bits of this life I wasn't ready to abandon, and another fifteen seconds was plenty to reach the pantry, kick aside the small rug on the floor, and pull up the concealed trap door. I felt around under the near edge for the little mag lite, found it, and damn near dropped it when I popped it out of its holder.

"What the hell are you doing?" asked Dora.

"In the military, they call it retiring to a previously prepared position." I hesitated. "You can follow if you want. There's room enough for someone your size."

He looked appalled. "Under the house? Down there with the roaches and snakes and spiders and ... not on your life, girl. Forget it."

I didn't have time to argue. I sat at the edge of the hole and let my feet and legs dangle down into the damp, dank darkness. "Fine. Walk right out my front door, whenever you feel ready to be shot. Don't bother closing it behind you. Of course, you may not make the door. Every room in this dump has a window."

He shook his head. "I'm not worried about them. And listen, you don't have to be either."

"Right," I said, and let myself down into the crawl space under the house.

Damn, I thought, *I'm going to miss that Yamaha. I just got the action right.*

— • —

Only a moron would attempt to flee Key West alone by car. There's exactly one road out of town, and a dozen spots from which it can be conveniently and discreetly monitored with binoculars or long lens camera. Or sniper scope. A clay pigeon would have a much better chance: They move way faster than traffic heading up the Keys.

So my plan was to head for The Schooner, an open-air thatched-roof blues bar right next to the Land's End Marina. Its only neighbours are boat people, and its clientele aren't all fags and dykes, so it gets to stay open a little later than Slim's Elite. I knew a Rasta pot dealer named Bad Death Johnson who would probably still be there, and would certainly be able to put me on a fast boat to West Elsewhere without troubling the harbour master.

But before I'd gotten two blocks, I became aware I was being followed—so clumsily that I knew who it was. I could have outrun him. I sighed, found a dark place, and waited for Dora to catch up. When he did, I started to step out of the shadows and call to him, but I got distracted watching him. His walk was so distinctive that even dressed in gender-neutral clothes, wearing sandals, I'd have recognized him by it, even in the poor light. You'd think a drag queen would be better at disguise, but apparently he just knew the one. He was past me by the time I finished that thought train, and I was going to step out behind him and call his name softly—but then I decided the hell with it and stayed where I was. He was just going to tell me again that I didn't have to be afraid of federal agents with clearance to kill. And tell me why he wasn't, which couldn't possibly be anything but moronic.

But since Dora was heading toward the marina, now I couldn't anymore. It took me ten aggravated seconds to come up with a Plan B, and another ten to persuade myself it had a chance of success. That was good: Even a few seconds less, and I'd have strolled blithely out there and collided with the two feds as they hurried by on cat feet.

For yet another ten seconds I *couldn't* move; then I managed to take a deep breath, and that rebooted my system. Then there was *another* ten-second interlude, of hard thought, at the end of which I went with Plan C. I slipped from my place of concealment and began tailing the two fake leatherboys as they tailed Dora.

Why? Don't ask me. I don't know my *own* heart, I guess. God knows I was scared of those two. I'd been scared of people like them forever. The kind of scared where you don't have a roommate because then you won't have to explain why you wake up sobbing with terror a few nights a week. These two weren't my particular personal nightmare, but they were, as the saying goes, close enough for folk music. Dylan once wrote, "I'll let you be in my dream if I can be in yours." They wanted to kill me for stumbling into theirs. They didn't seem to have their long guns with them this time, but I could make out two lumpy right ankles. Big sticks would have been more than I could cope with.

And there was the question of why they were after Dora. While I've never been a big fan of the government, I had to concede that it probably did not covertly pop caps on American soil without a pretty good reason. On the other hand, a "good reason" in their estimation might be something like Dora's having recognized some fellow drag queen as a senator. He wasn't swarthy enough or Irish enough to be a terrorist. What would his cause be: *Free Tammy Faye Bakker*?

In between these speculations, I kept doing the math. I'd helped Dora, then Dora had helped me. The books balanced. I owed him nothing; if anything, he owed me for clothes and sandals. I didn't have to do this—

After a while, they took the last turn. From there it was a straight one-block shot to the Schooner, with almost no cover along the way. If one of them even glanced over his shoulder, he could hardly miss me. So I hung back, waiting to make the turn until they'd had time to at least build up a little more of a lead. Finally, I judged there was enough distance between us that if they did glance back, they might not necessarily recognize me. I was dressed differently than I had been at our last encounter. At the last moment, I had a rush of brains to the head and adjusted my walk to be almost as exaggeratedly feminine as Dora's. They'd never suspect it was me. I was congratulating myself on my sagacity when I turned the corner and crashed head-on into Dora, coming the other way.

— · —

It took several confused seconds for Dora to convince me she hadn't seen the feds, and for me to convince her that one minute ago they'd been no more than a block behind her. Then we stood there together and looked up and down that street for anywhere they could reasonably have gone.

After a while, Dora shrugged and gave up. "They beamed up," he said, and dismissed the matter.

Some people can do that. I sometimes wish I were one of them. When I don't understand something, I *can't* dismiss it, any more than I can ignore a stone in my shoe. I was convinced the two shooters were concealed in some cunning blind, and any second they were going to get good and ready, and drop us both—

But what could I do about it?

The Schooner was nearly deserted, down to a couple of hardcore regulars, nursing the night's last cup of cheer. No sign of Bad Death anywhere. Inside the big old mahogany racetrack of a bar, two tired young bartenders dressed like refugees had stopped serving and were into their closing-up routines when we arrived, but Dora and I were both known there. The bandshell stage was dark and empty; so was the kitchen-and-washrooms shack adjacent to the bar. We took our beers to a table between them, and thus were mostly concealed from both the street and the marina.

"You're right," Dora said. "I don't know your heart. So I have to ask again: Why did you take a chance and follow those two?"

I'd been asking myself that same question all night, and I had a pretty fair answer, but there was no way I was going to share it with him, no way in the world. I tried to think of anyone on the planet with whom I *would* share it, and failed. I thought of a great lie and decided I didn't much want to tell it. "Look—"

"Please," he said softly.

To my astonishment, I heard myself tell him the truth.

— • —

"The only thing I hate worse than winter is cars," I told him. "And the only thing I hate worse than cars is cars in winter. I hate them all the time, but especially on cold mornings. The goddam things just never want to start when it's really cold, you know?"

He said nothing.

"So I had this old beater, a Dodge. For Detroit iron it wasn't bad. Slant six, not a lot of pickup but hard to kill, easy to work on. Only, in the winter it needed working on a *lot*. On really cold mornings, getting it to start could be a major pain in the ass that left you with grease and smelly starter fluid all over your frostbitten-barked knuckles. Sometimes it *wouldn't* start. Once in a while, you'd get desperate or clumsy from the cold and use a little too much fluid, and then there'd be a carburetor blowback that could perm your bangs and fry your eyebrows right off."

He nodded.

"This was in Boston," I went on, "where the mornings are only cold on days that end in 'y.' It was February, so by now I was thoroughly sick of coaxing that beast into life every morning. So this one morning, the goddam thing wouldn't wouldn't *wouldn't* wake up, and as I got out to wrestle with it, a big guy came walking by and asked if I needed help. It was so cold, you know? Anyway, I didn't even hesitate." I took a deep breath and a deep gulp of beer. "I stuck out my tits and batted my eyelashes and showed him all my teeth and lied. Yes, I said, I sure did need help."

"And really you just wanted it."

"I never do that kind of shit, you know?" I looked up from my hands to meet his eyes pleadingly. "Not since high school, anyway. But it was so fucking cold."

"Sure."

"I mean, I wasn't proud of doing it ... but there was at least a little bit of pride in how well I was doing it, after all that time out of practice. By sheer body language, I pretty much *forced* him to say, why don't you go back inside and stay warm and I'll take care of everything, little lady. So the only actual injury I sustained, except for the temporary blindness from the flash, was one of his teeth that came through the living room window and buried itself half an inch deep in the meat of my shoulder. It got infected real bad."

"My God," Dora said, wide-eyed.

"It was one of the bigger pieces of him they recovered, actually. Half a scapula, two lawns down, that was another one."

I went to reach for my beer but found my hands were full of Dora's.

"He was a sweet guy, who just wanted to fantasize about fucking me and was willing to pay for the privilege, and I got him turned into aerosol tomato paste."

"How?"

"I had ignored one of the basic rules of Lesbianism: Never seduce a capo's daughter."

He raised one exquisite eyebrow. "Oh dear."

"For fairly obvious reasons, Adriana hadn't gotten around to mentioning what her father did for a living, but somebody else had discreetly tipped me off—after it was too late. It excited me. I had the charming idea that as long as nobody knew about me and Adriana but Adriana, I was safe." I realized how hard I was gripping his hands and eased off, marvelling that he had betrayed no sign of pain. "So after my car was blown up, I handed Adriana in and, in exchange, I got a new name, new street, city and state address, new appearance, new history, and new occupation. I used to paint, but you can't be a fugitive painter. Thank God for folk music: A chimp could learn it, and there are customers in every hamlet."

He put my right hand on my beer bottle and let go. I took a long sip.

"Now I don't own a car. And I live in a place where nobody but tourists and fools own a car, and the bicycle is king. A place where there are never, ever any cold mornings. A place with no local mob, so cheesy and sleazy no self-respecting made guy would bring his *gumar* here on vacation. Endsville. I haven't been as far north as Key Largo in ten years, haven't left the rock in five. I'm a human black hole: so far up my own ass, daylight can't reach me. An ingrown toenail of a person."

Damn. One more sip and that beer would be gone. And the two youngsters behind the bar had just put out the last of the fake hurricane lamps and gone off home.

"So your question was, why did I hang my ass out in the breeze, to help a stranger wearing false tits? And the answer is, I guess because I know a little something about being hunted. Every once in a while, just on general principles, those cocky, remorseless sons of bitches ought to get a big unpleasant surprise." I belched and frowned. "And maybe I've been safe a little too long."

"And don't feel like you deserve to be."

"To this day, I don't know *anything* about him—not his name or address, or where he was headed that morning, or whether or not he left behind a family—zilch. Once I stopped being too terrified to give a shit, stopped running long enough to wonder, I could have found out, without drawing attention. I've never even tried. What the *hell* do you suppose could have happened to those two fetishware feds?"

"Forget it," said Dora.

I nearly did as he said. But then for no reason I can explain, an odd little thought-train went through my head—one of those brain-fission deals, where several seconds worth of thought somehow take place in a split second.

Neither of those feds could possibly have concealed a long gun under that tight leather / so? / so where did they have their rifles stashed? / in a car, obviously, parked in back where the light is poorest: the first shot came as you went out the back door / okay—so if they had wheels, how come they were both tailing Dora on foot just now? / hell, you can't tail a pedestrian in a car without being spotted / fine, but wouldn't one of them at least follow in the car, staying well back? Say they bagged Dora: were they going to carry him back through the streets to their ride? In Key West, that'd be taking a big chance, even at this hour / what's your point? / I don't think they have wheels / so what? / I don't think they have rifles either—or else why leave them behind now? / one last time: so what? / so who did shoot at us with a rifle? / oh shit / and where—

That's as far as I'd gotten when I heard the floorboard creak up on the stage. I've played on that stage, I know exactly where that goddam creaky board is, and I realized instantly that a man standing there would have a clear shot at both of us. "Dora, *run!*" I cried, and kicked my chair over backward trying to move away from him.

The shooter came into view out of the darkness, and apparently let his instincts tell him to choose the larger target first; the rifle barrel settled on Dora. Now I wanted to be going in *that* direction, to take the bullet, and it was like one of those nightmares where you're trying to do a one-eighty but can't seem to overcome inertia and get moving the right way. Time slowed drastically.

The shooter was definitely not one of the feds: way shorter than either, with hair longer than Dora's wig. A gentle breeze brought scents of lime and coral. Somewhere far above, there was a small plane. Like a million gunshot victims before him, Dora flung his hand up in front of his face in a useless instinctive attempt to catch the bullet. A distant dog barked. The shooter fired. Sound no louder than a nail-gun. Dora caught the bullet. "Don't do that again," he said to the shooter.

Then nobody said or did anything for several long seconds.

The shooter shook his head once, moved the barrel in a small circle, took careful aim, and fired again. Dora caught that slug, too. "I warned you," he said sadly.

The shooter apparently decided that if Dora declined to die, maybe I'd be more cooperative. He was right, I would. I was too terrified even to put my hand up in front of my face. I saw the barrel lock on me, saw the shooter's face past it; I could even see him let out his breath and hold it. Then he squealed, because the rifle was somehow molten, dripping like so much glowing lava from his hands. They burst into flame, and the one near his cheek set his hair on fire. He drew in a deep breath to scream, but before he could, he began to vibrate. Ever see one of those machines in a hardware store shake up a can of paint? Like that. In less than a second, he began to blur; in three, he was gone. Just ... gone. So were the hot coals on the stage. Not even a bad smell left behind.

Myself and I conferred, and decided that this would be a good time for me to fall down. To help, I became unconscious.

— • —

When I opened my eyes, I was at Mallory Square, sitting up against a trashcan, staring out across a few hundred yards of dark, slow water at Tank Island. I have absolutely no idea how I got there, or why. The breeze was from the south, salty and sultry. Clouds hid the moon.

"I called my equivalent of the Triple A a couple of years ago," Dora said softly from behind me and to my right. "My tow truck should be here in only another day or two, and then I'll be leaving this charming star system behind forever. So I feel kind of bad about the two FBI agents. Hunting me was just their job. And from your point of view, hunting me is the sensible thing to do."

Somehow I was past being astonished. I'd worked it out while I was unconscious, watched all the inexplicable little pieces assemble themselves into an inescapable pattern, and accepted it. "I've never had much success identifying with any kind of hunter at all," I said.

"And you need to identify with someone before you can empathize with them."

"Well ... yeah. At least a little," I said defensively. "I mean, I can identify with *you* ... and for all I know, you're not even carbon-based. Hell, you're my imaginary role model. The stranger in a strange land. Brilliant, being a drag queen, by the way. If anybody spots a flaw in your disguise, it just makes them condescending."

"You should do what I'm doing."

"What do you mean? Pretend to be human? Go femme? Kill hit men? Catch b—"

"Go home."

Now I was astonished. I sat up and swivelled to face him. "What the hell are you talking about? You know I—"

He sat cross-legged, staring up at the night sky. At the stars. "Okay, maybe not *home*—but get out of Key West."

I looked away. "Dora, I *can't*."

"Listen to me," he said. "Pat, will you listen?"

"I'll listen."

"I've been in America a lot more recently than you have. A lot of things have changed, the last ten or fifteen years."

"Nothing really important."

"Cars have changed since you lived there. *They all start on cold mornings, now.*"

"Bullshit!"

"I swear, it's true. Nobody recognizes anything under the hood any more—but nobody cares, because they don't *need* to."

I searched his face. "Are you serious?"

"Nobody carries *jumper cables* any more. And the capo is not going to send a second mechanic after you—not after this one just vanishes without a trace, not for a purely personal beef. You can go home any time you want to, Pat. Away from here, anyway."

My head was spinning. The concept of being able to be once again what Larry McMurtry calls "a live human being, free on the earth," was way more mind-boggling than dodging certain death, or meeting a spaceman. My mother was still alive, last I'd heard. Maybe I could find out the name of the man I'd gotten killed. Maybe he'd left family behind. Maybe there was something I could do for them. Suddenly the universe was nothing but questions.

I grabbed one out of the air. "I'm throwing your own question back at you," I said. "Why did you do this? Why did you kill two men to keep them from blowing your cover ... and then five minutes later kill another one in front of me and blow your cover?" Absurdly, I felt myself getting angry. "Why did I wake up just now? Now you've got to walk around your last few days here wondering how badly I want to be on *Geraldo*. What would you take such a risk for? How the hell can you identify with *any* human well enough to empathize ... much less a dyke?"

The clouds picked that moment to let the moonlight through. I'd seen him grimace and I'd seen him grin. This was the first time I'd seen him smile, and it was so beautiful my breath caught in my throat. I've painted it several times without every really capturing it.

"You *really* don't know my heart," he said. "It has five chambers, for one thing."

Then he was gone, like the Cheshire Cat.

I never saw him again, and now every night after I get my mother to sleep, and climb into my own bed to snuggle under the covers with my dear partner, I pray to God that Dora got home safely to his own home and loved ones.

I empathize. Like the song says: He waited so long, to remember what it's like to feel somebody's arms around his life. ■

Nalo Hopkinson (nalohopkinson.com) was born in Jamaica, and has lived in Trinidad, the U.S., Guyana, and, for the past thirty years, Canada. She is the editor of the anthologies *Whispers from the Cotton Tree Root: Caribbean Fabulist Fiction* and *Mojo: Conjure Stories*, and co-editor of *So Long Been Dreaming: Postcolonial Science Fiction* (with Uppinder Mehan) and *Tesseracts Nine* (with Geoff Ryman). Her work has received an Honourable Mention in Cuba's *Casa de las Americas* literary prize, and she's won the Warner Aspect First Novel Award, the Ontario Arts Council Foundation Award for emerging writers, the John W. Campbell Award for Best New Writer, the *Locus* Award for Best New Writer, the World Fantasy Award, the Sunburst Award for Canadian Literature of the Fantastic, the Aurora Award, and the Gaylactic Spectrum Award. Her *Brown Girl in the Ring* was one of the CBC's "Canada Reads" selections for 2008. She lives in Toronto.

NOVELS:

Brown Girl in the Ring (Warner, New York, 1998)
Midnight Robber (Warner, New York, 2000)
The Salt Roads (Warner, New York, 2003)
The New Moon's Arms (Grand Central Publishing,
    New York, 2007)

SHORT STORY COLLECTION:

Skin Folk, (Warner, New York, 2001)

A RAGGY DOG, A SHAGGY DOG

Nalo Hopkinson

Have you seen a little dog anywhere about?
A raggy dog, a shaggy dog,
Who's always looking out
For some fresh mischief which he thinks
he really ought to do ...

—"My Dog"
Emily Lewis

There you are. Right on time. Yes, climb up here where we can see eye to eye. Look, see the nice plant, up on the night table? Come on. Yeah, that's better. I'm going to get off the bed and move around, but I'll do it really slowly, okay? Okay.

You know, I don't really mind when it's this hot. The orchids like it. Particularly when I make the ceiling sprinklers come on. It's pretty easy to do. I light a candle—one of the sootless types—climb up on a chair, and heat the sprinkler up good and hot. Like this. That way it only affects the sprinkler that actually feels the heat. Whoops, here comes the rain. Oh, you like it too, huh? Isn't that nice?

Wow, that's loud. No, don't go! Come back, please. The noise won't hurt you. I won't hurt you.

Thank you.

I've gotten used to the sound of fire alarms honking. When the downpour starts, the orchids and I just sit in the apartment and enjoy it, the warmth, the artificial rain trickling down the backs of our necks. The orchids like it, so long as I let them dry out quickly afterwards; it's a bit like their natural homes would be. So when I move, I try to find buildings where the basement apartments aren't built to code; the law makes them put sprinklers in those units.

It's best to do the candle trick in the summer, like now. After the fire department has gone and the sprinkler has stopped, it's easy to dry off in summer's heat. In winter, it takes longer, and it's cold. Some day I'll have my own rooms, empty save for orchids and my bed, and I'll be able to make it rain indoors as often as I like, and I won't have to move to a new apartment after I've done it any more. My rooms will be in a big house, where I'll live with someone who doesn't think I'm weird for sleeping in the greenhouse with the orchids.

My name is Tammy. Griggs. You can probably see that I'm fat. But maybe that doesn't mean anything to you. Me, I think it's pretty cool. Lots of surface for my tattoos. This one, here on my thigh? It's a Dendrobium findlayanum. I like its pale purple colour. I have a real one, in that hanging pot up there. It looks pretty good right now. In the cooler months, it starts dropping its leaves. Not really a great orchid to have in people's offices, because when the leaves fall off, they think it's because you aren't taking care of it, and sometimes they refuse to pay you. That's what I do to earn a living; I'm the one who makes those expensive living plant arrangements you see in office buildings. I go in every week and care for them. I have a bunch of clients all over the city. I've created mini jungles all over this city, with orchids in them.

This tat here on my belly is the Catasetum integerrimum. Some people think it's ugly. Looks like clumps of little green men in shrouds. Tiny green deaths, coming for you. They're cool, though. So dignified. To me they look like monks, some kind of green order of them, going to sing matins in the morning. After their singing, maybe they work in the gardens, tending the flowers and the tomatoes.

On my bicep is the Blue Drago. They call it blue, but really, it's pale purple, too. This tat underneath it is a picture of my last boyfriend. Sam. He drew it, and he put it on me. He did all these tattoos on me, in fact. Sam was really talented. He smelled good, like guy come and cigarettes. And he would read to me. Newspaper articles, goofy stuff on the backs of cereal boxes, anything. His voice was raspy. Made me feel all melty inside. He draws all the time. He's going to be a comic artist. His own stuff, indie stuff, not the company toons. I wanted him to tattoo me all over. But he'd only done a few when he started saying that the tattoos freaked him out. He said that at night he could smell them on my skin, smell the orchids of ink flowering. Got to where he wouldn't go anywhere near the real plants. He wanted me to stop working with them, to get a different kind of job. You ever had to choose between two things you love? Sam's dating some guy named Walid now. I hang out with them sometimes. Walid says if he ever gets a tat, it'll be a simple one, like a heart or something, with Sam's name on it, right on his butt. A dead tattoo. When Walid talks about it, Sam just gazes at him, struck dumb with love. I really miss Sam.

I think the orchids, the real ones, like me fat, too, like Sam did. Sometimes at night, when I've turned off the light and I'm naked in bed—those are rubber sheets, they're waterproof—and I can see only the faint glow of the paler orchids, I swear that they all incline their blooms toward me, toward my round shoulders, breasts and belly, which also glow a little in the dark. We make echoes, they and I. I *like* to smell them, the sweet ones, even the weird ones. Did you know that there's an orchid that smells like carrion? I stick my nose right in it and inhale. It smells so bad, it's good. Like a dog sniffing another dog's butt.

Hear that? It's the fire trucks coming. Time to get ready. You going to follow me? Yes, like that. Cool. I'm just going to grab the bigger plants first.

Put all my babies into the bathtub where they'll be safe. I have to move quickly. The firemen will burst in here soon, and they aren't too careful about pots of flowers. I learned that the hard way; lost a beautiful Paph once, a spicerianum. The great lump of a fireman stepped right into the pot. He asked me out, that guy did, after he and his buddies had made sure nothing was on fire. His name was Aleksandr, Sasha for short. I don't get that, but that's what he said. He and I went out a couple of times. I even went home with him once. Sasha was nice. He liked it when I sucked on his bottom lip. But I couldn't get used to the feel of his cotton sheets, and I couldn't keep seeing him, anyway; he'd have begun to get suspicious that the fire trucks kept being called to wherever I lived. I need a handsome gentleman butch or a sweet misfit guy who doesn't care how often I move house. Someone with a delicate touch, for staking the smaller orchids and, well, for other stuff. I think the next person I pick up will be like a street punk or something who doesn't even have a home, so they won't barely notice that I have a new flop every few months.

Yeah, it's really wet in here now, isn't it? I'm just going to grab that Lycaste behind you, then put the grow light on all the plants so they'll dry out. Don't want them to get crown rot. Okay, let's go. Oh, I nearly forgot my new baby! Yeah, it's a pain to carry. The vine's probably about seven feet long now. You can't tell cause I have it all curled up. Its flowers aren't quite open yet. I need to take it with us, and a few other little things.

This way. Follow the plant.

I have a routine. Once the plants are safe, I go out into the hallway. No one ever notices. Most of the tenants are usually down in the street already, standing in their nightclothes, clutching their cats and their computers. I'm soaking wet, but if anyone asks, I just tell them that the sprinklers came on, that I don't know why. People expect a chick to be dumb about things like that. I'm careful, though. Almost no electricals in my apartment. Electricity and water don't play nicely together. I use candles a lot. The grow lights for the orchids are in the bathroom, and I don't activate the sprinkler in there.

This apartment building has a secret. It's this door here, between the garbage chute and the elevator. The lock's loose. Going through this door takes me right up the secret stairs to the roof. The firemen probably won't even look there. If they did, I'd just say that I got scared and confused, just picked a door that had no smoke behind it. Yeah, you have to come up. It's where the plant's going, see?

I'm going to miss this place, with its quiet asphalt roof. This is the second time since I've been here that I've sprinklered the plants, so it's time to move on. I don't like being such a nuisance to the neighbours. One time, in another building, I flooded someone's apartment beside mine. Ruined his record collection. Made me feel really bad.

Up here it stays warm all night, and slightly sticky. I think it's the heat of the day's sun that does it, makes the asphalt just a little bit tacky. Sometimes I lie out here naked, staring up at the stars. When I roll over, there are little rocks stuck to my back, glued there by warmed asphalt. I flex my shoulders and shake my whole body to make them fall off. I like the tickling sensation they make as they come loose.

It's pretty up here tonight. You can see so many stars.

The other night, I put two blue orchid petals right on my pillow, with a petal from one of them under my tongue for good measure. It tasted like baby powder, or babies. That's a joke. Because I've got this spiky green hair and the ring through my lip, some people can't tell when I'm joking. They think that people who make holes in their bodies must be angry all the time.

I'd found the orchid petals just lying on the ground out back of my building, by the dumpster. Didn't know who would tear orchids up that way. Lots of people keep them in their apartments, or grow them competitively. The climate here is all wrong for tropical orchids, yet I bet there are almost as many growing in this city as you'd find in any jungle.

Anyway, that night, I laid my left ear—the left side of our bodies is magic, you know—on the fleshy, cool blue of the orchid petals, closed my eyes, and waited for sleep. I sucked on the petal in my mouth. They were a weird, intense kind of blue, like you get in those flower shops where they dye their orchids. They cut the stems and put the flowers in blue ink, or food colouring. The plant sucks it up, and pretty soon, the petals go blue. You can even see veins of blue in the leaves. This orchid had that fake kind of colour.

Not sure why I did that with the petals. You know how it is when you see a dog that someone has tied up outside in the cold, and it's shivering and lifting its paws to keep them from freezing, and all you really want is to saw that chain free and hug that cold dog and give it something warm to eat? Well, actually, you may not know what that's like. You'd probably rather bite a dog than cuddle it. But I'd seen those torn orchid bits lying there, and I just wanted to hold them close to me.

So there I was, with two inky orchid petals crushed between my ear and my pillow, and one under my tongue. It looked like a vanilla orchid.

I think I nodded off. I must have, because after awhile, I saw a rat the length of my forearm crawling in the open window.

I didn't want to move. I could see the rat's pointy teeth glinting; the front ones, the ones that grow and grow, so that rats must always have something on which to gnaw, or those teeth grow through their lips, seal their mouths shut, and they starve to death. Its teeth gleamed yellow-white, like some of my orchids, like my belly where the skin isn't inked.

So I didn't move. Anyway, I was dreaming. No, stay away from the flower. I know it's almost daylight, but it's not quite ready yet. It blooms in early morning, and I think this is the morning it will open completely. I guess you can tell, and that's why you came.

Anyway, in my dream, I watched while the rat climbed around my orchid pots, investigating. Some of the plants it peered at, then ignored. It only seemed interested in the ones with flowers on them. Those it sniffed at. Maybe rats don't have too good eyesight, huh? Maybe they go more by a sense of smell? Not sure how it could tell how anything smelled, cause its own smell was pretty foul. Like rotting garbage, climbing around my room. Could smell it in my sleep.

Finally, the rat seemed to find what it wanted. It nosed at my Vanilla planifolia. I was proud of that vine; it was big and healthy, and some of its flowers had just opened a few hours before. The rat climbed up onto the vine, made its way to one of the flowers, and stuck its head inside the flower. Then it climbed back down again and made its way to my window. It stood in the window for a second, shuffling back and forth as though it didn't really want to do something. Then it leapt out the open window and was gone. And this is how I knew for certain that I was dreaming; when the rat jumped, I saw that it had wings. Gossamer wings, kind of like a dragonfly's, with traceries of veins running through. Only more flexible.

That woke me right up. I sat up in bed, feeling really weird, and all I could think was, with four legs and two wings, doesn't that make six limbs? And wouldn't that be an insect, not a rat? There was another thing, too. I couldn't be sure, because it had happened so quickly, but I thought the rat wings had had a faint bluishness to them.

I got myself a glass of water and went back to bed. Next morning, the flower of my lovely Vanilla, the one the rat had rubbed itself on, was beginning to brown. That was odd, but not too strange; Vanilla flowers close within a few hours and fall off if they're not pollinated. But it now had a faint scent about it of dumpster garbage in the summer heat. Never smelt anything like it on a planifolia. Some people would say that's gross. To me, it smelt like a living thing, calling out. Scent is a message.

Look, you can see the firemen milling around outside now. That's the super, the woman with the bright yellow bathrobe. Even in the dark at this distance, you can see that it's yellow. Matter of fact, everything she wears is yellow—everything. I've seen her doing her laundry, and yep, even her undies are yellow. Weird, huh?

She's just let the firemen in. They'll go and break into my apartment, but they won't find anything.

I think the bud's beginning to open. No, you can't rub yourself on it yet. Oh, poor little guy; you're really only about half rat any more, aren't you? You've got orchid tendrils growing up into your brain cells. Does it frighten you, I wonder? Do you have the part of your brain left that can get frightened? I don't think you wanted to jump off that ledge that night, but I think the orchid made you do it. Phew, you stink! I know it's pheromones, though, not real garbage.

Even though I'd been dreaming, I closed my window from that night on. Then a little while ago, I stopped to hang with Micheline. She hooks on my street corner on weekend nights; teaching grad school doesn't earn her enough to make ends meet. Sometimes, when business is slow for her, she'll buy me a coffee at the corner coffee shop, or I'll buy her one, depending on which one of us got paid most recently. She told me the oddest thing; how the street kids are starting to tell stories that they've been seeing angels in the city. It's getting to be the end of days, the kids say, and the angels are here to take all the street kids away to heaven. The angels are small and fuzzy, and they have sharp teeth and see-through wings.

You know, I don't know how I'll ever find someone like Sam again. You'd think I'd have plenty of chances. I go out into the world every day, I meet people, I'm friendly, I'm cute—if you like your girls big and round and freaky, and many do. I get dates all the time. Smart people, interesting people. But it's so hard to find people I click with. They just, I dunno, they just don't smell right.

The great thing about orchids is that they have a million ways of getting pollinated. They trick all kinds of small creatures into collecting their pollen and passing it off to other orchids—wasps, ants, even bats. Bee orchids produce flowers that look like sexy lady bees, and when a male bee lands on the flower, ready for action, he gets covered in pollen. A Porroglossum will actually snap shut for a few seconds on an insect that stumbles amongst its blossoms and hold the insect still; just long enough for pollen to rub off on its body. Some of the Bulbophyllum smell like carrion so they can attract flies.

Us, all us orchid nuts who bring tropical orchids into places where they don't grow naturally, and who cultivate them and interbreed them; we're creating hothouse breeds that thrive in apartments, in greenhouses, in office buildings, in flower shops—all behind doors. They need to find each other to pollinate. They need pollinators. And what small animals get everywhere in a city?

Yes, you, my ugly, furry friend. You only want me for my orchid. Actually, you want me for *your* orchid, the one that's learned how to travel to where the other orchids are. Most bizarre adaptation I've ever seen. It must have gotten seeds into your fur. Some of those seeds must have germinated, put roots down into your bloodstream. I thought it was wings I saw when you jumped from my window, but it was really the outer petals of the flower, flaring out from your chest in the wind from your jump. It's a stunning blue, for all that it stinks. True blue orchids are rare. Lots of people have tried making blue hybrids. I went and looked it up. One promising possibility right now is to make a transgenic plant by incorporating enzymes found in the livers of animals. Those enzymes can react with substances called indoles to create a bright blue colour. D'you know one of the places you can find indoles? They are the growth regulators in orchids. We even put indoles in the packing mixture we use to transport orchid plants in, to keep them healthy. Your plant passenger there has tendrils in your liver, my friend. When you eat, it gets fed. I can see that you've got a new bloom on your chest there.

Maybe the plant didn't get the knack of it the first time. Maybe when the first bright blue blossom opened, you tore it out, petal by petal, before it could mature into its garbage smell. But eventually, one of the plants put roots down into your spine, travelled up to your brain, found the right synapses to tickle, and you lost the urge to destroy it. Lost the will to go about your own business. Now you can only fetch and carry for a plant, go about the business of orchid pollination. Do you know that "orchid" means "testicle?"

Cool. My flower's opened all the way. Yes, I know you can tell; look how agitated you're getting, or at least, the orchid part of your brain is. Don't worry. I'll let you at it soon.

There's a story that some people from India tell. If you want to bond a person to you forever, you have to prepare rice for them. While it's boiling, you have to squat with your naked genitals over the pot. The steam from the cooking rice will heat you up, and you'll sweat salty crotch-sweat pheromones into the pot to flavour it. Make someone eat a meal with that sweat rice, and they're yours forever. Orchids and dogs would understand that trick. Scent is a message.

Here. Come on. Come to the flower. No, I'm not going to let it go. You have to come to me. Gotcha! Don't bite me, you little devil! There. A snootful of chloroform ought to do it.

Jeez, I hope you don't die. I think I got the dosage right; you can find anything on the Web. I just don't want this to hurt you, or you to hurt me because you're scared. Look, I even brought cotton batting to keep you warm in while I do this. Good thing Sam taught me how to do a little bit of tattooing. Just inside your ear should do it. Not much fur there, so it's likely that somebody will see it.

Oo, that ear's disgusting. Good thing I brought some alcohol swabs with me. Thank heaven for the gloves, too.

There we go. There's not even a lot of blood. Your ear membranes are too thin to have many blood vessels.

You poor thing. First a chunk of your brain gets kidnapped by a flower with a massive reproductive urge, and now a human being is having her way with you. And you smell like wet garbage in the sun. But for you, that's probably a plus. Probably gets you all kinds of rat dates. I just want a chance. Want to send out my own messages, on as many channels as I can. I mean, who knows where you go in your travels? You might end up in some kind of horticultural lab, and a cute scientist might find you and see your tattoo.

Huh. You're a she rat. Sorry, sister.

I place personal ads; I dress nicely; I chat people up. Nothing. Plants, they just send their messages out on the wind, or via pollen stuck to an insect, or if they're this puppy, they travel a ratback to wherever their mates are likely to be. Human beings only have a few options. And even pheromones only work so-so with us. Never can tell if the message will get through. So I'm doing everything I can to increase my chances.

There you go, sweetie—the date, my name, my email address, and the name of the new sub-species of orchid that's flowering there on your tummy; V. planifolia var. griggsanum, after me, who discovered it first.

Please don't go into shock. I think you should be warm enough wrapped up in the cotton. I'll keep dribbling some water on your tongue, keep you hydrated until you wake up. Lemme just have a quick look at this bloom on your chest ... God, that's creepy.

The firemen are gone now. Pretty soon I'll go in and start packing. I've already put down first and last month's rent on a little place in the market; one of those trendy new lofts they've been putting there recently. It's got the right kind of sprinkler system in all the units. It's probably already got vermin, too, being in the market, but that's okay. The more of you I can find and tattoo, the better. Rats don't live very long, and I bet you that orchid-infested rats live even shorter than that.

Oh, hey. You're awake. Good girl. No, no, it's okay. I won't hurt you. The pot's here, with the flower in it, and I'll just step away from it, okay? All the way over here, see? And I won't even move. Yes, you go ahead. Go and pollinate that baby. Though if it can be pollinated, it's no baby.

I didn't squat over a boiling pot of food; I made my room steamy hot, and squatted over an orchid plant; that one right there that you're currently rubbing your body against. Watched my sweat drip into the moss in which it's planted. My calf muscles were burning from the effort by the time I straightened up. That plant's been growing in medium impregnated with my pheromones. It's exchanging scent messages with your flower right now.

You're done? You're leaving? That's okay. Just climb down carefully this time. We're way high up. Atta girl, carry my message. Fetch! ■

Robert Charles Wilson (robertcharleswilson.com) was born in California but has lived in Canada most of his life and became a Canadian citizen in 2007. He is a three-time winner of the Aurora Award, for the novels *Darwinia* and *Blind Lake* and the short story "The Perseids." He has also won the John W. Campbell Memorial Award (for *The Chronoliths*), the Philip K. Dick Award (for *Mysterium*), and the 2006 Hugo Award (for *Spin*). Several of his novels have appeared on the annual Notable Books list in *The New York Times*.

His novels and stories have been published in French, Spanish, German, Italian, Hungarian, and other foreign editions, and his work in translation has received the Geffen Award, the Kurd Lasswitz Prize, and the Czech Academy of Science Fiction, Fantasy and Horror Award. He lives in Concord, Ontario, with his wife Sharry.

The following story, "The Cartesian Theatre," won the Theodore Sturgeon Memorial Award.

NOVELS:

A Hidden Place (Bantam, New York, 1986)

Memory Wire (Bantam, New York, 1987)

Gypsies (Bantam, New York, 1989)

The Divide (Bantam, New York, 1990)

A Bridge of Years (Bantam, New York, 1991)

The Harvest (Bantam, New York, 1992)

Mysterium (Bantam, New York, 1994)

Darwinia (Tor, New York, 1998)

Bios (Tor, New York, 1999)

The Chronoliths (Tor, New York, 2001)

Blind Lake (Tor, New York, 2003)

Spin (Tor, New York, 2005)

Axis (Tor, New York, 2007)

Julian Comstock: A Story of 22nd-Century America
    (Tor, New York, 2009)

SHORT STORY COLLECTION:

The Perseids and Other Stories (Tor, New York, 2000)

THE CARTESIAN THEATRE

Robert Charles Wilson

Grandfather was dead but still fresh enough to give useful advice. So I rode transit out to his sanctuary in the suburbs, hoping he could help me solve a problem, or at least set me on the way to solving it myself.

I didn't get out this way much. It was a desolate part of town, flat in every direction where the old residences had been razed and stripped for recycling, but there was a lot of new construction going on, mostly aibot hives. It was deceptive. You catch sight of the towers from a distance and think: *I wonder who lives there?* Then you get close enough to register the colourless concrete, the blunt iteration of simple forms, and you think: *Oh, nobody's home.*

Sure looked busy out there, though. All that hurry and industry, all that rising dust—a long way from the indolent calm of Doletown.

— • —

At the sanctuary, an aibot custodian, seven feet tall and wearing a sombre black waistcoat and matching hat, led me to a door marked PACZOVSKI— Grandfather's room, where a few of his worldly possessions were arrayed to help keep his sensorium lively and alert.

He needed all the help he could get. All that remained of him was his neuroprosthetic arrays. His mortal clay had been harvested for its biomedical utilities and buried over a year ago. His epibiotic ghost survived but was slurring into Shannon entropy, a shadow of a shade of itself.

Still, he recognized me when I knocked and entered. "Toby!" his photograph called out.

The photo in its steel frame occupied most of the far wall. It smiled reflexively. That was one of the few expressions Grandfather retained. He could also do a frown of disapproval, a frown of anxiety, a frown of unhappiness, and raised eyebrows meant to register surprise or curiosity, although those last had begun to fade in recent months.

And in a few months more there would be nothing left of him but the picture itself, as inert as a bust of Judas Caesar (or whatever—history's not my long suit).

But he recognized the bottle of Sauvignon blanc I took out of my carrypack and placed on the rutted surface of an antique table he had once loved. "That's the stuff!" he roared, and, "Use a coaster, for Christ's sake, Toby; you know better than that."

I turned down his volume and stuck a handkerchief under the sweating bottle. Grandfather had always loved vintage furniture and fine wines.

"But I can't drink it," he added, sketching a frown of lament: "I'm not allowed."

Because he had no mouth or gut. Dead people tend to forget these things. The bottle was strictly for nostalgia, and to give his object-recognition faculties a little kick. "I need some advice," I said.

His eyes flickered between me and the bottle as if he couldn't decide which was real or, if real, more interesting. "Still having trouble with that woman ...?"

"Her name is Lada."

"Your employer."

"Right."

"And wife."

"That, too," I said. "Once upon a time."

"What's she done now?"

"Long story. Basically, she made me an accessory to an act of ... let's say, a questionable legal and ethical nature."

"I don't do case law any more." Grandfather had been a trial lawyer for an uptown firm, back when his heart was still beating. "Is this problem serious?"

"I washed off the blood last night," I said.

— ◆ —

Six weeks ago Lada Joshi had called me into her office and asked me if I still had any friends in Doletown.

"Same friends I always had," I told her truthfully. There was a time when I might have lied. For much of our unsuccessful marriage, Lada had tried to wean me away from my Doletown connections. It hadn't worked. Now she wanted to start exploiting them again.

Her office was high above the city deeps. Through the window over her shoulder, I could see the spine of a sunlit heat-exchanger, and beyond that a bulbous white cargodrome where unmanned aircraft buzzed like honey-fat bees.

Lada herself was beautiful and ambitious but not quite wealthy, or at least not as wealthy as she aspired to be. Her business, Ladajoshi™, was a bottom-tier novelty-trawling enterprise, one of hundreds in the city. I had been one of her stable of Doletown stringers until she married me and tried to elevate me socially. The marriage had ended in a vending-machine divorce after six months. I was just another contract employee now, far as Lada was concerned, and I hadn't done any meaningful work for weeks. Which was maybe why she was sending me back to Doletown. I asked her what the deal was.

She smiled and tapped the desktop with her one piece of expensive jewellery, a gold prosthetic left-hand index finger with solid onyx knuckles. "I've got a client who wants some work done on his behalf."

"Doletown work?"

"Partly."

"What kind of client?" Usually it was Lada who had to seek out clients, often while fending off a shoal of competitors. But it sounded as if this one had come to her.

"The client prefers to remain anonymous."

Odd, but okay. It wasn't my business, literally or figuratively. "What kind of work?"

"First, we have to bankroll an artist named—" She double-checked her palmreader. "Named Jafar Bloom, without making it too obvious we're interested and without mentioning our client."

Whom I couldn't mention in any case, since Lada wouldn't give me any hints. "What kind of artist is Jafar Bloom?"

"He has an animal act he calls 'The Chamber of Death,' and he wants to open a show under the title 'The Cartesian Theatre.' I don't know much more than that. He's deliberately obscure and supposedly difficult to work with. Probably a borderline personality disorder. He's had some encounters with the police but he's never been charged with aberrancy. Moves around a lot. I don't have a current address—you'll have to track him down."

"And then?"

"Then you front him the money to open his show."

"You want him to sign a contract?"

She gave me a steely look. "No contract. No stipulations."

"Come on, Lada, that doesn't make sense. Anybody could hand this guy cash, if that's all there is to it. Sounds like what your client wants is a cut-out—a blind middleman."

"You keep your accounts, Toby, and I'll keep mine, all right? You didn't fret about ethics when you were fucking that Belgian contortionist."

An argument I preferred not to revisit. "And after that?"

"After what? I explained—"

"You said 'First, we bankroll Jafar Bloom.' Okay, we bankroll him. Then what?"

"We'll discuss that when the time comes."

Fine. Whatever.

We agreed on a per diem and expenses and Lada gave me some background docs. I read them on the way home, then changed into my gypsy clothes—I had never thrown them away, as much as she had begged me to—and rode a transit elevator all the way down to the bottom stop, sea level, the lowest common denominator: Doletown.

— · —

An aibot constructor roared by Grandfather's window on its way to a nearby hive, momentarily drowning out conversation. I glimpsed the machine as it rumbled past. A mustard-yellow unit, not even remotely anthropomorphic. It wasn't even wearing clothes.

But it was noisy. It carried a quarter-ton sack of concrete on its broad back, and its treads stirred up chalky plumes of dust. It was headed for a nursery hive, shaped like a twenty-story artillery shell, where aibots of various phyla were created according to instructions from the Entrepreneurial Expert System that roams the cryptosphere like a benevolent ghost.

Grandfather didn't like the noisy aibots or their factories. "When I was young," he said as soon as he could make himself heard, "human beings built things for other human beings. And they did it with a decent sense of decorum. *Dulce et decorum.* All this goddamn noise!"

I let the remark pass. It was true, but I didn't want to hear his inevitable follow-up lament: *And in those days, a man had to work for his living,* etc. As if we lived in a world where nobody worked! True, since the population crash and the Rationalization, nobody has to work in order to survive ... but most of us do work.

I cleared my throat. "As I was saying—"

"Your story. Right. Jafar Bloom. Did you find him?"

"Eventually."

"He's an artist, you said?"

"Yes."

"So what's his medium?"

"Death," I said.

— • —

In fact, it had been remarkably difficult to hook up with Jafar Bloom.

Doletown, of course, is where people live who (as grandfather would say) "don't work." They subsist instead on the dole, the universal minimum allotment of food, water, shelter, and disposable income guaranteed by law to the entire ever-shrinking population of the country.

Most nations have similar arrangements, though some are still struggling to pay vig on the World Bank loans that bought them their own Entrepreneurial Expert Systems.

Back in grandfather's day, economists used to say we couldn't afford a universal dole. What if *everybody* went on it; what if *nobody* worked? Objections that seem infantile, now that economics is a real science. If nobody worked, fewer luxury goods would be produced; our EES would sense the shift in demand and adjust factory production downward, hunting a new equilibrium. Some aibots and factories would have to remodel or recycle themselves, or else the universal stipend would be juiced to compensate. Such adjustments, upward or downward, happen every day.

Of course it's a falsehood to say "nobody works," because that's the whole point of an EES / aibot-driven economy. The machines work; human labour is elective. The economy has stopped being a market in the classic sense and become a tool, the ultimate tool—the self-knapping flint, the wheel that makes more wheels and, when there are enough wheels, reconfigures itself to make some other desirable thing.

So why were people like me (and seventy-five percent of the downsized masses) still chasing bigger incomes? Because an economy is an oligarchy, not a democracy; a rich guy can buy more stuff than a dole gypsy.

And why do we want stuff? Human nature, I guess. Grandfather was still nagging me to buy him antiques and beer, even though he was far too dead to appreciate them.

Doletown, as I was saying, is where the hardcore dole gypsies live. I once counted myself among their number. Some are indolent but most are not; they "work" as hard as the rest of us, though they can't exchange their work for money (because they don't have a saleable product or don't know how to market themselves or don't care to sully themselves with commerce).

Their work is invisible but potentially exploitable. Lots of cultural ferment happens in Doletown (and every living city has a Doletown by one name or another). Which is why two-bit media brokers like Ladajoshi™ trawl the district for nascent trends and unanticipated novelties. Fish in the right Doletown pool and you might land a juicy patent or copyright co-share.

But Jafar Bloom was a hard man to reach, reclusive even by Doletown standards. None of my old cronies knew him. So I put the word out and parked myself in a few likely joints, mostly cafés and talk shops—the Seaside Room, the infamous Happy Haunt, the nameless hostelries along the infill beaches. Even so, days passed before I met anyone who would acknowledge an acquaintance with him.

"Anyone" in this case was a young woman who strode up to my table at the Haunt and said, "People say you're curious about Jafar Bloom. But you don't look like a creep or a sadist."

"Sit down and have a drink," I said. "Then you can tell me what I am."

She sat. She wore gypsy rags bearing logo stamps from a shop run by aibot recyclers down by the docks. I used to shop there myself. I pretended to admire the tattoo in the shape of the Greek letter omega that covered her cheeks and forehead. It looked as if a dray horse had kicked her in the face. I asked her if she knew Jafar Bloom personally.

"Somewhat," she said. "We're not, um, intimate friends. He doesn't really *have* any intimate friends. He doesn't like people much. How did you hear about him?"

"Word gets around."

"Well, that's how I heard of *you*. What do you want from Bloom?"

"I just want to see the show. That's all. Can you introduce me to him?"

"Maybe."

"Maybe if?"

"Maybe if you buy me something," she said demurely.

So I took her to a mall on one of the abandoned quays where the air smelled of salt and diesel fuel. The mall's location and inventory was dictated by the commercial strategies and profit-optimizing algorithms of the EES, but it stocked some nice carriage-trade items that had never seen the inside of an aibot workshop. She admired (and I bought for her) a soapstone drug pipe inlaid with chips of turquoise—her birthstone, she claimed.

Three days later, she took me to a housing bloc built into the interstices of an elevated roadway and left me at an unmarked steel door, on which I knocked three times.

A few minutes later, a young man opened it, looking belligerent.

"I don't kill animals for fun," he said, "if that's what you're here for."

Jafar Bloom was tall, lean, pale. His blond hair was long and lank. He wore a pair of yellow culottes, no shirt. "I was told you do theatre," I said.

"That's exactly what I do. But rumours get out that I'm torturing animals. So I have the Ethical Police dropping by, or untreated ginks who want to see something get hurt."

"I just want to talk business."

"Business?"

"Strictly."

"I've got nothing to sell."

"May I come in?"

"I guess so," he said, adding a glare that said, *but you're on probation.* "I heard you were looking for me."

I stepped inside. His apartment looked like a studio, or a lab, or a kennel—or a combination of all three. Electronic items were stacked in one dim corner. Cables veined across the floor. Against another wall was a stack of cages containing animals, mostly rats but also a couple of forlorn dogs.

The skylight admitted a narrow wedge of cloudy daylight. The air was hot and still and had a kind of sour jungle odour.

"I'm completely aboveboard here," Bloom said. "I have to be. Do you know what the consequence would be if I was needlessly inflicting pain on living things?"

Same consequence as for any other demonstrable mental aberration. We don't punish cruelty, we treat it. Humanely.

"I'd be psychiatrically modified," Bloom said, "I don't want that. And I don't deserve it. So if you're here to see something *hurt*—"

"I already said I wasn't. But if you don't deal in cruelty—"

"I deal in art," he said crisply.

"The subject of which is—?"

"Death."

"Death, but not cruelty?"

"That's the point. That's *exactly* the point. How do you begin to study or examine something, Mr.—?"

"Paczovski."

"How do you study a thing unless you isolate it from its environment? You want to study methane, you distil it from crude petroleum, right? You want gold, you distil it from dross."

"That's what you do? You distil death?"

"That's exactly what I do."

I walked over to the cages and looked more closely at one of the dogs. It was a breedless mutt, the kind of animal you find nosing through empty houses out in the suburbs. It dozed with its head on its paws. It didn't look like it had been mistreated. It looked, if anything, a little overfed.

It had been fitted with a collar—not an ordinary dog collar but a metallic band bearing bulbous black extrusions and webs of wire that blurred into the animal's coat.

The dog opened one bloodshot eye and looked back at me.

"Good trick, distilling death. How do you do that, exactly?"

"I'm not sure I should answer any questions until you tell me what you want to buy."

Bloom stared at me challengingly. I knew he'd been telling the truth about the Ethical Police. Some of their reports had been included in Lada's dossier. None of these animals had been or would be harmed. Not directly.

"I don't want to buy anything," I said.

"You said this was a business deal."

"Business or charity, depending on how you look at it." I figured I might as well lay it out for him as explicitly as possible. "I don't know what you do, Mr. Bloom. I represent an anonymous investor who's willing to put money into something called 'The Cartesian Theatre.' All he wants in return is your written assurance that you'll use the money for this theatrical project rather than, say, buggering off to Djibouti with it. How's that sound?"

It sounded unconvincing, even to me. Bloom's skepticism was painfully obvious. "Nobody's giving away free money but the EES."

"Given the investor's wish for anonymity, there's no further explanation I can offer."

"I'm not signing away my intellectual property rights. I've got patents pending. And I refuse to divulge my techniques."

"Nobody's asking you to."

"Can I have *that* in writing?"

"In triplicate, if you want."

Suddenly he wasn't sure of himself. "Bullshit," he said finally. "Nobody invests money without at least a chance of profiting by it."

"Mr. Bloom, I can't answer all your questions. To be honest, you're right. It stands to reason the investor hopes to gain something by your success. But it might not be money. Maybe he's an art lover. Or maybe he's a philanthropist; it makes him feel good to drop large amounts of cash in dark places."

Or maybe he shared Bloom's fascination with death.

"How much money are we talking about?"

I told him.

He tried to be cool about it. But his eyes went a little misty.

"I'll give it some thought," he said.

— • —

Grandfather had been a trial lawyer during his life. His epibiotic ghost probably didn't remember much of that. Long-term memory was unstable in even the most expensive neuroprostheses. But there was enough of the law book left in him that his photo grew more animated when I mentioned open-ended contracts or the Ethical Police.

He said, "Exactly how much did you know about this guy going in?"

"Everything that was publicly available. Bloom was born in Cleveland and raised by his father, an accountant. Showed signs of high intellect at an early age. He studied electronic arts and designed some well-received neural interfaces before he quit the business and disappeared into Doletown. He's eccentric and probably obsessive, but nothing you could force-treat him for."

"And I assume he took the money you offered."

"Correct." Half up front, half when The Cartesian Theatre was ready to open.

"So what *was* he doing with those animals?"

One of the sanctuary aibots passed the open door of Grandfather's memorial chamber. It paused a moment, adjusting its tie and tugging at its tailed vest. It swivelled its eyestalks briefly toward us, then wheeled on down the corridor. "Nosy fucking things," Grandfather said.

"Soon as Bloom signed the contract he invited me to what he called a 'dress rehearsal.' But it wasn't any kind of formal performance. It was really just an experiment, a kind of dry run. He sold admission to a few local freaks, people he was ashamed of knowing. People who liked the idea of watching an animal die in agony."

"You said he didn't hurt or kill anything."

"Not as far as the law's concerned, anyway."

— • —

Bloom explained it all to me as he set up the night's exhibition. He seemed to welcome the opportunity to talk about his work with someone who wasn't, as he said, "quietly deranged." He hammered that idea pretty hard, as if to establish his own sanity. But how sane is a man whose overweening ambition is to make an art form of death?

He selected one of the dogs and pulled its cage from the rack. The other dogs he released into a makeshift kennel on an adjoining roof. "They get upset if they see what happens, even though they're not in any danger."

Then he put the selected animal into a transparent box the size of a shipping crate. The glass walls of the box were pierced with ventilator holes and inlaid with a mesh of ultra-fine inductors. A cable as thick as my arm snaked from the box to the rack of electronic instrumentation. "You recognize the devices on the dog's collar?"

"Neuroprostheses," I said. "The kind they attach to old people." The kind they had attached to Grandfather, back when he was merely dying, not entirely dead.

"Right," Bloom said, his face simmering with enthusiasm. "The mind, your mind, any mind—the dog's mind, in this case—is really a sort of parliament of competing neural subroutines. When people get old, some or all of those functions start to fail. So we build various kinds of prostheses to support aging mentation. Emotive functions, limbic functions, memory, the senses—we can sub for each of those things with an external device."

That was essentially what Grandfather had done for the last five years of his life: shared more and more of his essential self with a small army of artificial devices. And when he eventually died, much of him was still running in these clusters of epibiotic prostheses. But eventually, over time, without a physical body to order and replenish them, the machines would drift back to simple default states, and that would be the end of Grandfather as a coherent entity. It was a useful but ultimately imperfect technology.

"Our set-up's a little different," Bloom said. "The prostheses here aren't subbing for lost functions—the dog isn't injured or old. They're just doubling the dog's ordinary brain states. When I disconnect the prostheses, the dog won't even notice; he's fully functional without them. But the ghost in the prostheses—the dog's intellectual double—goes on without him."

"Yeah, for thirty seconds or so," I said. Such experiments had been attempted before. Imagine being able to run a perfect copy of yourself in a digital environment—to download yourself to an electronic device, like in the movies. Wouldn't that be great? Well, you *can*, sort of, and the process worked the way Bloom described it. But only briefly. The fully complex digital model succumbs to something called "Shannon entropy" in less than a minute. It's not dynamically stable.

(Postmortem arrays like Grandfather last longer—up to a couple of years—but only because they're radically simplified, more a collection of vocal tics than a real personality.)

"Thirty seconds is enough," Bloom said.

"For what?"

"You'll see."

About this time, the evening's audience began to drift in. Or maybe "audience" is too generous a word. It consisted of five furtive-looking guys in cloaks and rags, each of whom slipped Bloom a few bills and then retreated to the shadows. They spoke not at all, even to each other, and they stared at the dog in its glass chamber with strange, hungry eyes. The dog paced, understandably nervously.

Now Bloom rolled out another, nearly identical chamber. The "death chamber." It contained not a dog but a sphere of some pink, slightly sparkly substance.

"Electrosensitive facsimile gel," Bloom whispered. "Do you know what that is?"

I'd heard of it. Facsimile gel is often used for stage and movie effects.

If you want an inert duplicate of a valuable object or a bankable star, you scan the item in question and map it onto gel with EM fields. The gel expands and morphs until it's visually identical to the scanned object, right down to colour and micron-level detail, if you use the expensive stuff. Difference was, the duplicate would be rigid, hollow, and nearly massless—a useful prop, but delicate.

"You duplicate the dog?" I asked.

"I make a *dynamic* duplicate. It changes continuously, in synch with the real thing. I've got a patent application on it. Watch." He dimmed the lights and threw a few switches on his bank of homemade electronics.

The result was eerie. The lump of gel pulsed a few times, expanded as if it had taken a deep breath, grew legs, and became ... a dog.

Became, in fact, the dog in the adjacent glass cage.

The real dog looked at the fake dog with obvious distress. It whined. The fake dog made the same gesture simultaneously, but no sound came out.

Two tongues lolled. Two tails drooped.

Now the freaks in the audience were almost slavering with anticipation.

I whispered, "And this proves what?"

Bloom raised his voice so the ginks could hear—a couple of them were new and needed the explanation. "Two dogs," he said. "One real. One artificial. The living dog is fitted with an array of neuroprostheses that duplicate its brain states. The dog's brain states are modelled in the electronics, here. Got that?"

We all got it. The audience nodded in unison.

"The dog's essence, its sense of self, is distributed between its organic brain and the remote prostheses. At the moment it's controlling the gel duplicate, too. When the real dog lifts his head and sniffs the air—like that: See?—he lifts the fake dog's head simultaneously. The illusion mimics the reality. The twinned soul operates twin bodies, through the medium of the machine."

His hand approached another switch.

"But when I throw *this* switch, the living dog's link to the prosthetics is severed. The original dog becomes merely itself—it won't even notice that the connection has been cut."

He threw the switch; the audience gasped—but again, nothing obvious happened.

Both dogs continued to pace, as if disturbed by the sharp smell of sweat and ionization.

"As of now," Bloom said, "the artificial animal is dynamically controlled *solely by the neuroprostheses*. It's an illusion operated by a machine. But it moves as if it had mass; it sees as if it had eyes; it retains a capacity for pleasure or pain."

Now the behaviour of the two dogs began to fall out of synchronization, subtly at first, and then more radically. Neither dog seemed to like what was happening. They eyed each other through their respective glass walls and backed away, snarling.

"Of course," Bloom added, his voice thick with an excitement he couldn't disguise, "without a biological model, the neuroprostheses lose coherence. Shannon entropy sets in. Ten seconds have passed since I threw the final switch." He checked his watch. "Twenty."

The fake dog shook its head and emitted a silent whine.

It moved in a circle, panting.

It tried to scratch itself. But its legs tangled and bent spasmodically. It teetered a moment, then fell on its side. Its ribs pumped as if it were really breathing, and I guess it thought it *was* breathing—gasping for air it didn't really need and couldn't use.

It raised its muzzle and bared its teeth.

Its eyes rolled aimlessly. Then they turned opaque and dissolved into raw gel.

The artificial dog made more voiceless screaming gestures. Other parts of it began to fall off and dissolve. It arched its back. Its flanks cracked open and, for a moment, I could see the shadowy hollowness inside.

The agony went on for what seemed like centuries but was probably not more than a minute or two. I had to turn away.

The audience liked it, though. This was what they had come for, this simulation of death.

They held their breath until the decoherent mass of gel had stopped moving altogether; then they sighed; they applauded timidly. It was only when the lights came up that they began to look ashamed. "Now get out," Bloom told them, and when they had finished shuffling out the door, heads down, avoiding eye contact, he whispered to me, "I hate those guys. They are truly fucking demented."

I looked back at the two glass cages.

The original dog was trembling but unhurt. The duplicate was a quiescent puddle of goo. It had left a sharp tang in the air, and I imagined it was the smell of pain. The thing had clearly been in pain. "You said there was no cruelty involved."

"No cruelty *to animals*," Bloom corrected me.

"So what do you call this?"

"There's only one animal in the room, Mr. Paczovski, and it's completely safe, as you can see. What took shape in the gel box was an animation controlled by a machine. It didn't die because it was never alive."

"But it was in agony."

"By definition, no, it wasn't. A machine can only *simulate* pain. Look it up in the statutes. Machines have no legal standing in this regard."

"Yeah, but a complex-enough machine—"

"The law doesn't make that distinction. The EES is complex. Aibots are complex: They're all linked together in one big neural net. Does that make them people? Does that make it an act of sadism if you kick a vacuum cleaner or default on a loan?"

Guess not. Anyway, it was his show, not mine. I meant to ask him if the dog act was the entire substance of his proposed Cartesian Theatre ... and why he thought anyone would want to see such a thing, apart from a few unmedicated sadists.

But this wasn't about dogs, not really. It was a test run. When Bloom turned away from me, I could see a telltale cluster of bulges between his shoulder blades. He was wearing a full array of neuroprostheses. That's what he meant when he said the dogs were experiments. He was using them to refine his technique. Ultimately, he meant to do this *to himself.*

—— • ——

"Technically," Grandfather said, "he's right. About the law, I mean. What he's doing, it's ingenious and it's perfectly legal."

"Lada's lawyers told her the same thing."

"A machine, or a distributed network of machines, can be intelligent. But it can never be a person under the law. It can't even be a legal dog. Bloom wasn't shitting you. If he'd hurt the animal in any way, he would have been remanded for treatment. But the fake dog, legally, is only a *representation* of an animal, like an elaborate photograph."

"Like you," I pointed out.

He ignored this. "Tell me, did any of the ginks attending this show look rich?"

"Hardly."

"So the anonymous investor isn't one of them."

"Unless he was in disguise, no. And I doubt Bloom would have turned down a cash gift even if it came from his creepy audience—the investor wouldn't have needed me or Lada if he had a direct line to Bloom."

"So how did your investor hear about Bloom in the first place, if he isn't friendly with him or part of his audience?"

Good question.

I didn't have an answer.

—— • ——

When I told Lada what I'd seen, she frowned and ran her gold finger over her rose-pink lower lip, a signal of deep interest, the kind of gesture professional gamblers call a "tell."

I said, "I did what you asked me to. Is there a problem with that?"

"No—no problem at all. You did fine, Toby. I just wonder if we should have taken a piece for ourselves. A side agreement of some kind, in case this really does pan out."

"If *what* pans out? When you come down to it, all Bloom has to peddle is an elaborate special effect. A stage trick, and not a very appealing one. The ancillary technology might be interesting, but he says he already filed patents."

"The investor obviously feels differently. And he probably didn't get rich by backing losers."

"How well do you know this investor?"

She smiled. "All honesty? I've never met him. He's a text-mail address."

"You're sure about his gender, at least?"

"No, but, you know, *death*, *pain*—it all seems a little masculine, doesn't it?"

"So is there a next step or do we just wait for Bloom to put together his show?"

"Oh," and here she grinned in a way I didn't like, "there's *definitely* a next step."

She gave me another name. Philo Novembre.

— • —

"Rings a bell," Grandfather said. "Faintly. But then, I've forgotten so much."

— • —

Philo Novembre was easier to find than Jafar Bloom. At least, his address was easier to find—holding a conversation with him was another matter.

Philo Novembre was ten years short of a century old. He lived in an offshore retirement eden called Wintergarden Estates, connected to the mainland by a scenic causeway. I was the most conspicuously youthful visitor in the commute bus from the docks, not that the sample was representative: There were only three other passengers aboard. Aibot transports hogged the rest of the road, shuttling supplies to the Wintergarden. Their big eyes tracked the bus absently and they looked bored, even for machines.

Novembre, of course, had not invited me to visit, so the aibot staffing the reception desk asked me to wait in the garden while it paged him— warning me that Mr. Novembre didn't always answer his pages promptly. So I found a bench in the atrium and settled down.

The Wintergarden was named for its atrium. I don't know anything about flowers, but there was a gaudy assortment of them here, crowding their beds and creeping over walkways and climbing the latticed walls, pushing out crayon-coloured blooms. Old people are supposed to like this kind of thing. Maybe they do, maybe they don't; Grandfather had never demonstrated an interest in botany, and he had died at the age of a century and change. But the garden was pretty to look at and it flushed the air with complex fragrances, like a dream of an opium den. I was nearly dozing when Philo Novembre finally showed up.

He crossed the atrium like a force of nature. Elderly strollers made way for his passage; garden-tending aibots the size of cats dodged his footfalls with quick, knowing lunges. His face was lined but sharp, not sagging, and his eyes were the colour of water under ice. His left arm was unapologetically prosthetic, clad in powder-black brushed titanium. His guide, a thigh-high aibot in brown slacks and a golf shirt, pointed at me and then scuttled away.

I stood up to meet him. He was a centimetre or two taller than me. His huge grey gull-winged eyebrows contracted. He said, "I don't know you."

"No sir, you don't. My name is Toby Paczovski, and I'd be honoured if you'd let me buy you lunch."

It took some haggling, but eventually he let me lead him to one of the five restaurants in the Wintergarden complex. He ordered a robust meal, I ordered coffee, and both of us ignored the elderly customers at the adjoining tables, some so extensively doctored that their physical and mental prostheses had become their defining characteristics. One old gink sucked creamed corn through a tube that issued from his jaw like an insect tongue, while his partner glared at me through lidless ebony-black eyes. I don't plan ever to get old. It's unseemly.

"The reason I'm here," I began, but Novembre interrupted:

"No need to prolong this. You bought me a decent meal, Mr. Paczovski. I owe you a little candour, if nothing else. So let me explain something. Three or four times a year, somebody like yourself shows up here at the Wintergarden and flatters me and asks me to submit to an interview or a public appearance. This person might represent a more or less respectable agency or he might be a stringer or a media pimp, but it always comes down to the same pitch: Once-famous enemy of automated commerce survives into the golden age of the EES. What they want from me is either a gesture of defiance or a mumbled admission of defeat. They say they'll pay generously for the right note of bathos. But the real irony is that these people have come on a quest as quixotic as anything I ever undertook. Because I don't make public appearances. Period. I don't sign contracts. Period. I'm retired. In every sense of the word. Now: Do you want to spend your time more profitably elsewhere, or shall we order another round of coffee and discuss other things?"

"Uh," I said.

"And, of course, in case you're already recording, I explicitly claim all rights to any words I've spoken or will speak at this meeting or henceforth, subject to the Peking Accords and the Fifty-second Amendment."

He grinned. His teeth looked convincingly real. But most people's teeth look real these days, except the true ancients, like the guy at the next table.

— • —

"Well, he knows his intellectual property law," Grandfather said. "He's got you dead to rights on that one."

"Probably so," I said, "but it doesn't matter. I wasn't there to buy his signature on a contract."

"So what *did* you want from him? Or should I say, what did Lada want from him?"

"She wanted me to tell him about Jafar Bloom. Basically, she wanted me to invite him to opening night at The Cartesian Theatre."

"That's it?"

"That's it."

"So this client of hers was setting up a scenario in which Novembre was present for Bloom's death act."

"Basically, yeah."

"For no stated reason." Grandfather's photograph was motionless a few moments. Implying deep thought, or a voltage sag.

I said, "Do you remember Philo Novembre back when he was famous? The 'eighties, that would have been."

"The 2080s," Grandfather mused. "I don't know. I remember that I once remembered those years. I have a memory of having a memory. My memories are like bubbles, Toby. There's nothing substantial inside, and when I touch them, they tend to disappear."

— • —

Philo Novembre had been a celebrity intellectual back in the 2080s, a philosopher, a sort of Twenty-first-Century Socrates or Aristotle.

In those days—the global population having recently restabilized at two billion after the radical decline of the Plague Years—everyday conveniences were still a dream of the emerging Rationalization. Automated expert systems, neuroprostheses, resource-allocation protocols, the dole: All these things were new and contentious, and Philo Novembre was suspicious of all of them.

He had belonged to no party and supported no movement, although many claimed him. He had written a book, *The Twilight of the Human Soul*, and he had stomped for it like a backwoods evangelist, but what had made him a media celebrity was his personal style: modest at first; then fierce, scolding, bitter, moralistic.

He had claimed that ancient virtues were being lost or forgotten in the rush to a rationalized economy, that expert systems and globally distributed AI, no matter how sophisticated, could never emulate true moral sensitivity—a human sense of right and wrong.

That was the big debate of the day, simplistic as it sounds, and it ultimately ended in a sort of draw. Aibots and expert systems were granted legal status *in loco humanis* for economic purposes but were denied any broader rights, duties, privileges, or protection under the law. Machines aren't people, the courts said, and if the machines said anything in response, they said it only to each other.

And we all prospered in the aftermath, as the old, clunky, oscillating global marketplace grew increasingly supple, responsive, and bias-free. Novembre had eventually disappeared from public life as people lost interest in his jeremiads and embraced the rising prosperity.

Lada had given me a dossier of press clippings on Novembre's decline from fame. Around about the turn of the century, he was discovered in a Dade County doletown, chronically drunk. A few months later, he stumbled into the path of a street-cleaning aibot, and his left arm was crushed before the startled and penitent machine could reverse its momentum. A local hospital had replaced his arm—it was still the only prosthesis he was willing to wear—and incidentally cured his alcoholism, fitting him with a minor corticolimbic mod that damped his craving. He subsequently attempted to sue the hospital for neurological intervention without written consent, but his case was so flimsy it was thrown out of court.

After which, Novembre vanished into utter obscurity and eventually signed over his dole annuities to the Wintergarden Retirement Commune.

From which he would not budge, even for a blind date with Jafar Bloom. I told Lada so when I made it back to the mainland.

"We have not yet begun to fight," Lada said.

"Meaning—?"

"Meaning let me work it for a little while. Stay cozy with Jafar Bloom; make sure he's doing what we need him to do. Call me in a week. I'll come up with something."

She was thinking hard ... which, with Lada, was generally a sign of trouble brewing.

— • —

Unfortunately, I had begun to despise Jafar Bloom.

As much as Bloom affected to disdain the ginks and gaffers who paid to see his animal tests, he was just as twisted as his audience—more so, in his own way. Morbid narcissism wafted off him like a bad smell.

But Lada had asked me to make sure Bloom followed through on his promise. So I dutifully spent time with him during the month it took to rig his show. We rented an abandoned theatre in the old district of Doletown and I helped him fix it up, bossing a fleet of renovation aibots who painted the mildewed walls, replaced fractured seats, restored the stage, and patched the flaking proscenium. We ordered industrial quantities of reprogels and commissioned a control rig of Bloom's design from an electronics prototyper.

During one of these sessions, I asked him why he called his show "The Cartesian Theatre."

He smiled a little coyly. "You know the name Descartes?"

No. I used to know a Belgian acrobat called Giselle de Canton, but the less said about that the better.

"The philosopher Descartes," Bloom said patiently. "René Descartes, 1596-1650. *Discourse on Method. Rules for the Direction of the Mind.*"

"Sorry, no," I said.

"Well. In one of his books, Descartes imagines the self—the human sense of identity, that is—as a kind of internal gnome, a little creature hooked up to the outside world through the senses, like a gink in a one-room apartment, staring out the window and sniffing the air."

"So you believe that?"

"I believe in it as a metaphor. What I mean to do on stage is externalize my Cartesian self, or at least a copy of it. Let the gnome out for a few seconds. Modern science, of course, says there is no unitary self, that what we call a 'self' is only the collective voice of dozens of neural subsystems working competitively and collaboratively—"

"What else could it be?"

"According to the ancients, it could be a human soul."

"But your version of it dies in agony in less than a minute."

"Right. If you believed in the existence of the soul, you could construe what I do as an act of murder. Except, of course, the soul in question is dwelling in a machine at the moment of its death. And we have ruled, in all our wisdom, that machines don't *have* souls."

"Nobody believes in souls," I said.

But I guess there were a few exceptions.

Philo Novembre, for one.

— • —

Lada called me into her office the following week and handed me another dossier of historical files. "More background?"

"Leverage," she said. "Information Mr. Novembre would prefer to keep quiet."

"You're asking me to blackmail him?"

"God, Toby. Settle down. The word 'blackmail' has really awkward legal connotations. So let's not use it, shall we?"

"If I threaten him, he's liable to get violent." Novembre was old, but that titanium forearm had looked intimidating.

"I don't pay you to do the easy things."

"I'm not sure you pay me enough to do the hard things. So where'd this information come from? Looks like ancient police files."

"Our client submitted it," Lada said.

— • —

"What did you ever see in this woman?" Grandfather asked.

Good question, although he had asked it a dozen times before, in fact, whenever I visited him. I didn't bother answering anymore.

I had come to the city a dozen years ago from a ghost town in the hinterland—one of those wheat towns decimated by the population implosion and rendered obsolete by aifarming—after my parents were killed when a malfunctioning grain transport dropped out of the sky onto our old house on Nightshade Street. Grandfather had been my only living relative, and he had helped me find Doletown digs and cooked me an old-fashioned meal every Sunday.

City life had been a welcome distraction and the dole had seemed generous, at least until grief faded and ambition set in. Then I had gone looking for work, and Lada Joshi had been kind enough, as I saw it then, to hire me as one of her barely paid Doletown scouts.

Which was fine, until the connection between us got more personal. Lada saw me as a diamond-in-the-rough, begging for her lapidary attention. While I saw her as an ultimately inscrutable amalgam of love, sex, and money

It worked out about as well as you'd expect

— • —

Novembre's official biography, widely distributed back when he was famous, made him out to be the dutiful son of a Presbyterian pastor and a classical flautist, both parents lost in the last plagues of the Implosion. The truth, according to Lada's files, was a little uglier. Philo Novembre's real name was Cassius Flynn, and he had been raised by a couple of marginally sane marijuana farmers in rural Minnesota. The elder Flynns had been repeatedly arrested on drug and domestic violence charges, back in the days before the Rationalization and the Ethical Police. Their death had, in a sense, been a boon for young Cassius, who had flourished in one of the big residential schools run by the federal government for orphans of the Plague Years.

Nothing too outrageous, but it would have been prime blackmail material back in the day. But Novembre wasn't especially impressed when I showed him what we had.

"I made my name," he said, "by proclaiming a belief in the existence of metaphysical good and evil independent of social norms. I allowed a publicist to talk me into a lie about my childhood, mainly because I didn't want to be presented to the world as a psychological case study. Yes, my parents were cruel, petty, and venal human beings. Yes, that probably did contribute to the trajectory of my life and work. And yes, it still embarrasses me. But I'm far too old and obscure to be blackmailed. Isn't that obvious? Go tell the world, Mr. Paczovski. See if the world cares."

"Yeah," I said, "it did seem like kind of a long shot."

"What intrigues me is that you would go to these lengths to convince me to attend a one-shot theatrical production, for purposes you can't explain. Who hired you, Mr. Paczovski?"

He didn't mean Lada. She was only an intermediary. "Truly, I don't know."

"That sounds like an honest answer. But it begs another question. Who, frankly, imagines my presence at Mr. Bloom's performance would be in any way meaningful?" He lowered his head a moment, pondering. Then he raised it. "Do you know how my work is described in the *Encyclopaedia of Twenty-First Century American Thought*? As—and I'm quoting—'a humanistic questioning of economic automation, embodied in a quest to prove the existence of transcendent good and evil, apart from the acts encouraged or proscribed by law under the Rationalization.'"

"Transcendent," I said. "That's an interesting word." I wondered what it meant.

"Because it sounds like your Mr. Bloom has discovered just that—a profoundly evil act, for which he can't be prosecuted under existing law."

"Does that mean you're interested?"

"It means I'm curious. Not quite the same thing."

But he was hooked. I could hear it in his voice. The blackmail had had its intended effect, though not in the customary way.

— • —

"Entertainment," Grandfather said.

"What?"

"That's really the only human business anymore. Aibots do all the physical labour and the EES sorts out supply and demand. What do *we* do that *bots* can't do? Entertain each other, mostly. Lie, gossip, and dance. That, or practice law."

"Yeah, but so?"

"It's why someone wanted to put Bloom and Novembre together. For the entertainment value." His photographed stared while I blinked. "The *motive*, stupid," he said.

"Motive implies a crime."

"You mentioned blood. So I assume Novembre made the show."

"It opened last night." And closed.

"You want to tell me about it?"

Suddenly, no, I didn't. I didn't even want to think about it.

But I was in too deep to stop. Story of my life.

— • —

Doletown, of course, is a museum of lost causes and curious passions, which means there's plenty of live theatre in Doletown, most of it eccentric or execrably bad. But Bloom's production didn't rise even to that level. It lacked plot, stagecraft, publicity, or much of an audience, and none of that mattered to Jafar Bloom. As with his animal experiments, public display was only a way of raising money, never an end in itself. He didn't care who watched, or if anyone watched.

The Cartesian Theatre opened on a windy, hot night in August. The moon was full and the streets were full of bored and restless dole gypsies, but none of them wanted to come inside. I showed up early, not that I was looking forward to the show.

Bloom rolled his glassy Death Chamber onto the stage without even glancing at the seats, most of which were empty, the rest occupied by the same morbid gaffers who had attended his animal experiments. There were, in fact, more aibots than live flesh in the house. The ushers alone—wheeled units in cheap black tuxedos—outnumbered the paying customers.

Philo Novembre, dressed in grey, came late. He took an empty seat beside me, front-row-centre.

"Here I am," he whispered. "Now, who have I satisfied? Who wants me here?"

He looked around but sighted no obvious culprit. Nor did I, although it could have been someone in dole drag: The wealthy have been known to dress down and go slumming. Still, none of these ten or twelve furtive patrons of the arts looked plausibly like a high-stakes benefactor.

The theatre smelled of mildew and mothballs, despite everything we'd done to disinfect it.

"What it is," Novembre mooted to me as he watched Bloom plug in a set of cables, "is a sort of philosophical grudge match, yes? Do you see that, Mr. Paczovski? Me, the archaic humanist who believes in the soul but can't establish the existence of it, and Mr. Bloom," here he gestured contemptuously at the stage, "who generates evil as casually as an animal marking its territory with urine. A modern man, in other words."

"Yeah, I guess so," I said. In truth, all this metaphysical stuff was beyond me.

Eventually the lights dimmed, and Novembre slouched into his seat and crossed his good arm over his prosthesis.

And the show began.

Began prosaically. Bloom strolled to the front of the stage and explained what was about to happen. The walls of the Death Chamber, he said, were made of mirrored glass. The audience would be able to see inside but the occupant—or occupants—couldn't see out. The interior of the chamber was divided into two identical cubicles, each roughly two metres on a side. Each cubicle contained a chair, a small wooden table, a fluted glass, and a bottle of champagne.

Bloom would occupy one chamber. Once he was inside, his body would be scanned and a duplicate of it would take shape in the other. Both Bloom and counter-Bloom would look and act identically. Just like the dogs in his earlier experiment.

Novembre leaned toward my right ear. "*I see now what he intends,*" the old man whispered. "*The genius of it—*"

There was scattered applause as Bloom opened the chamber door and stepped inside.

"*The perverse genius,*" Novembre whispered, "*is that Bloom himself won't know—*"

And in response to his presence, hidden nozzles filled the duplicate chamber with pink electrosensitive gel, which contracted under the pressure of invisible sculpting fields into a crude replica of Bloom, a man-shaped form lacking only the finer detail.

"*He won't know which is which, or rather—*"

Another bank of electronics flickered to life, stage rear. The gel duplicate clarified in an instant, and although I knew what it was—a hollow shell of adaptive molecules—it looked as substantial, as weighty, as Bloom himself.

Bloom's neural impulses were controlling both bodies now. He lifted the champagne bottle and filled the waiting glass. His dutiful reflection did likewise, at the same time and with the same tight, demented smile. He toasted the audience he couldn't see.

"*Or rather, he won't know which is himself—each entity will believe, feel, intuit that it's the true and only Bloom, until one—*"

Now Bloom replaced the glass on the table top, cueing an aibot stage-hand in the wings. The house lights flickered off and after a moment were replaced by a pair of baby spots, one for each division of the Death Chamber.

This was the signal that Bloom had cut the link between himself and the machinery. The neuroprostheses were running on a kind of cybernetic inertia. The duplicate Bloom was on borrowed time, but didn't know it.

The two Blooms continued to stare at one another. Narcissus in Hades.

And Novembre was right, of course: The copy couldn't tell itself from the real thing, the real thing from the copy.

"*Until one begins to decohere,*" Novembre finished. "*Until the agony begins.*"

Thirty seconds.

I resisted the urge to look at my watch.

The old philosopher leaned forward in his seat.

Bloom and anti-Bloom raised glasses to each other. Both appeared to drink. Both had Bloom's memory. Both had Bloom's motivation. Each believed himself to be the authentic Bloom.

And both must have harboured doubts. Both thinking: I know I'm the real item; I can't be anything else, but what if—*what if*—?

A trickle of sweat ran down the temples of both Blooms.

Both Blooms crossed their legs and both attempted another noncha-lant sip of champagne.

But now they had begun to fall just slightly out of synchronization.

The Bloom on the right seemed to gag at the liquid.

The Bloom on the left saw the miscue and liked what he saw.

The Bloom on the right fumbled the champagne glass and dropped it. The glass shattered on the chamber floor.

The opposite Bloom widened his eyes and threw his own glass down. The right-hand Bloom stared in disbelief.

That was the worst thing: that look of dawning understanding, incipient terror.

The audience—including Novembre—leaned toward the action. "God help us," the old philosopher said.

Now Bloom's electronic neuroprostheses, divorced from their biological source, began to lose coherence more rapidly. Feedback loops in the hardware read the dissolution as physical pain. The false Bloom opened his mouth—attempting a scream, though he had no lungs to force out air. Wisps of gel rose from his skin: He looked like he was dissolving into meat-coloured smoke. His eyes turned black and slid down his cheeks. His remaining features twisted into a grimace of agony.

The real Bloom grinned in triumph. He looked like a man who had won a desperate gamble, which, in a sense, he had. He had wagered against his own death and survived his own suicide.

I didn't want to watch, but this time I couldn't turn away—it absorbed my attention so completely that I didn't realize Philo Novembre had left his seat until I saw him lunge across the stage.

I was instantly afraid for Bloom, the real Bloom. The philosopher was swinging his titanium arm like a club and his face was a mask of rage. But he aimed his first blow not at Bloom but at the subchamber where his double was noisily dying. I think he meant to end its suffering.

A single swing of his arm cracked the wall, rupturing the embedded sensors and controllers.

Aibot ushers and stagehands suddenly hustled toward the Death Chamber as if straining for a view. The dying duplicate of Bloom turned what remained of his head toward the audience, as if he had heard a distant sound. Then he collapsed with absolute finality into a puddle of amorphous foam.

Bloom forced open his own chamber door and ran for the wings. Novembre spotted him and gave chase. I tried to follow, but the crowd of aibots closed ranks and barred my way.

Lada would love this, I thought. Lada would make serious money if she could retail a recording of this event. But I wasn't logging it and nobody else seemed to be, except, of course, the aibots, who remember everything; but their memories are legally protected, shared only by other machines.

This was unrecorded history, unhappening even as it happened.

— • —

I caught up with Bloom in the alley behind The Cartesian Theatre. Too late. Novembre had caught up with him first. Bloom was on the ground, his skull opened like a ripe melon. A little grey aibot with EMS protocols sat astride Bloom's chest, stimulating his heart and blowing air into his lungs—uselessly. Bloom was dead, irretrievably dead, long before the ambulance arrived and gathered him into its motherly arms.

As for Novembre—

It looked, at first, as if he he'd escaped into the crowd. But I went back into the theatre on a hunch, and I found him there, hidden in the fractured ruin of Jafar Bloom's Death Chamber, where he had opened his own throat with a sliver of broken glass and somehow found time to write the words BUT IT EXISTS in blood on the chamber wall.

— • —

"Yup, it was a show," Grandfather said.

I gave his image an exasperated look. "Of course it was a show. 'The Cartesian Theatre' —what else could it be?"

"Not that. I mean the mutual self-destruction of Bloom and Novembre. You see it, Toby? The deliberate irony? Novembre believes in humanity and hates intellectual machines. But he takes pity on the fake Bloom as it dies, and by doing so, he tacitly admits that a machine can harbour something akin to a human soul. He found what he had been looking for all his life, a metaphysical expression of human suffering outside the laws of the Rationalization—but he found it in a rack of electronics. We have to assume that's what your client wanted and expected to happen. A philosophical tragedy, culminating in a murder-suicide."

This was Grandfather's trial-lawyer subroutine talking, but what he said made a certain amount of sense. It was as if I had played a supporting role in a drama crafted by an omniscient playwright. Except—

"Except," I said, "who saw it?"

"One of the attendees might have recorded it surreptitiously."

"No one witnessed both deaths, according to the police, and they searched the witnesses for wires."

"But the transaction was completed? Lada was paid for her services?"

I had talked to her this morning. Yes, she was paid. Generously and in full. The client had evidently received value for money.

"So you have to ask yourself," Grandfather said, "—and I no longer possess the imagination to suggest an answer—who could have known about both Bloom and Novembre? Who could have conceived this scenario? Who understood the motivation of both men intimately enough to predict a bloody outcome? To whose taste does this tragedy cater, and how was that taste satisfied if the client was not physically present?"

"Fuck, I don't know."

Grandfather nodded. He understood ignorance. His own curiosity had flickered briefly but it died like a spent match. "You came here with a problem to solve ..."

"Right," I said. "Here's the thing. Lada's happy with how this whole scenario worked. She said I outdid myself. She says the client wants to work with her again, maybe on a regular basis. She offered to hire me back full-time and even increase my salary."

"Which is what you'd been hoping for, yes?"

"But suddenly the whole idea makes me a little queasy—I don't know why. So what do you think? Should I re-up, take the money, make a success of myself? Maybe hook up with Lada again, on a personal level, I mean, if things go well? Because I could do that. It would be easy. But I keep thinking it'd be even easier to find a place by the docks and live on dole and watch the waves roll in."

Watch the aibots build more hives and nurseries. Watch the population decline.

"I'm far too dead," Grandfather said, "to offer sensible advice. Anyway, it sounds as if you've already decided."

And I realized he was right—I had.

— • —

On the way out of the sanctuary where Grandfather was stored, I passed a gaggle of utility aibots. They were lined up along the corridor in serried ranks, motionless, and their eyes scanned me as I passed.

And as I approached the exit, the chief custodial aibot—a tall, lanky unit in a black vest and felt hat—stepped into my path. He turned his face down to me and said, "Do you know Sophocles, Mr. Paczovski?"

I was almost too surprised to answer. "Sophocles who?"

"*Ajax,*" he said cryptically. "The Chorus. *When Reason's day / Sets ray-less—joyless—quenched in cold decay / Better to die, and sleep / The never-waking sleep, than linger on, / And dare to live, when the soul's life is gone.*"

And while I stared, the gathered aibots—the ones with hands, at least—began gently to applaud. ■

LIGHTNING ROUND

The world's top two scientific journals are the American *Science* and the British *Nature*. In recent years, *Nature* has been running very short science-fiction stories, each no more than eight hundred words in length, as a feature called "Futures." The initial offering was by none other than Arthur C. Clarke. Five of the authors who have longer stories in this anthology have also contributed pieces to *Nature*, which we offer here—a final lightning round of distant early warnings.

ARS LONGA, VITA BREVIS

James Alan Gardner

November 9, 2270: In a move described as "long overdue," the Astronomy department of UC Berkeley has been dissolved. Faculty and students from the defunct department will be shifted into other areas of the university, particularly sociology and fine arts. Berkeley's astronomy program was the last of its kind at any major educational institution.

"We tried to keep the place going," said former department chair Dr. Jeremy Washburn, "but with Astronomy departments folding in so many other universities, we knew it was just a matter of time. The enthusiasm just isn't there anymore.

"I confess," Dr. Washburn continued, "I understand how other people feel. Celestial mechanics really lost its charm when we learned all the weird stuff is artificial."

Dr. Washburn was referring to revelations from advanced extraterrestrial races that they are personally responsible for prominent astronomical phenomena. For example, the Vingex of Betelgeuse claim to have created all the binary and trinary solar systems in our galaxy by dragging stars closer to each other.

"It makes for more attractive visual composition," said Speaker 183-478D, cultural attaché to the Vingex embassy on Earth. "Which is more interesting: a single sun just sitting in the middle of nowhere, or a group of colour-coordinated suns that set each other off nicely against the black background? And it's even better when you add a few planets to weave in and out between the stars. The orbits aren't stable gravitationally, but you can keep them in line with a ..." [Here the Speaker's translator implant whistled several times, representing an untranslatable word—presumably the name of a Vingex device for adjusting the orbits of wayward planets.]

Later in the same interview, Speaker 183-478D repeated the Vingex's offer to procure a binary companion for Sol, Earth's own sun. While the Speaker declined to say which star might be chosen as a suitable partner for Sol, ("We want it to be a surprise"), hints were given that the star is blue-white, well-established in the main sequence, and "seldom given to solar prominences or other unattractive outbursts."

When asked to comment on the Vingex offer, Dr. Washburn of Berkeley said it was just the sort of thing that had taken the fun out of astronomy. "There was a time when we'd have been fascinated by a blue-white sun locked close to a yellow one like Sol. It would have been worth a few review letters and perhaps a Ph.D. thesis. Now it tells us more about the Vingex's aesthetic sense than it does about stellar evolution."

The Vingex are not the only race involved in large-scale cosmological manipulation. It is well known, of course, that *Homo sapiens* first made contact with alien life forms when a group of Pleonines arrived in our solar system to "freshen up" the rings around Saturn and other outer planets. According to the Pleonines, several millennia had passed since the rings last received any touch-up work; colours were badly faded, and visual appeal had suffered. During the restoration work, the Pleonines demonstrated techniques for creating new rings, as well as simulating colours through diffraction and producing complicated "braid" patterns. They also added two more giant red spots to Jupiter's atmosphere and moved Pluto four billion kilometres closer to Earth, since humans were having trouble seeing it where it was.

"We enjoy giving others the chance to view our work," the Pleonine

Queen explained. Though members of her race are primarily interested in expressing themselves through planetary rings and giant atmospheric anomalies, the queen has adorned the entire surface of Pluto with a portrait of herself, created via meteorite collisions. The portrait appears to be rendered in the style of the early Cubists; in the queen's case, however, this may actually be photo-realism.

Once the Pleonines had "broken the ice" by making contact with humankind, other aliens soon arrived to ask our opinion of their art. Notable amongst these visitors were the all-mechanical Regimoids, creators of every pulsar in the universe ("Pulsars ... are ... regular ... Pulsars ... are ... beautiful ..."), the Über-Masons who constructed the Great Wall, and the so-called Bangers responsible for supernovas.

"Oh yes," said Dr. Washburn of Berkeley, "I knew our department was in trouble when I heard about supernovas. We had all those great theories about stellar collapse ... then, suddenly, we found out novas were just the work of E.T. punks who liked blowing things up. The very next day, one of our best Astronomy professors transferred into Humanities. She still gives the same slide show she did in Astro 101, but now it's called Art History.

"That was discouraging enough," continued Dr. Washburn, "but the thing that broke my heart was those jelly people showing up to take credit for the Horsehead Nebula. I can still remember their words: 'My God, from this angle it looks *fabulous!*'" Dr. Washburn sighed. "I used to think it did, too."

Shaking his head sorrowfully, Dr. Washburn cleaned off his desk, left his office, and locked the door behind him. ■

MEN SELL NOT SUCH IN ANY TOWN

Nalo Hopkinson

"Did you hear? Rivener has created a new fruit!"

"How dull. Her last piece was a fruit, too."

"Not like this one!" Salope said. She sat me at the table, murmuring the evening benediction as she did so. She draped my long sleeves artfully against the arms of the chair. She took my hat and veil, hung them on the peg. She plucked the malachite pins from my hair, one by one. She shook the dark springing mass free, and refashioned it into a plait down my back. I endured as long as I could, then leaned back and stared up into her cool granite eyes.

"Tell me of Rivener's creation," I commanded her.

She came around to my side. She slipped her fingertips into the pockets of her white apron and composed herself for the tale. She stood quite straight, as was proper. My blood quickened.

"Rivener's previous fruit," she said, "only sang like a rain forest full of parrots; only enhanced the prescient abilities of those who ate it. This one is the pinnacle." She stopped, though she didn't need breath. I felt a single drop of sweat start its slow trickle between my breasts. The heavy silks were stifling. "Stop dawdling; tell me!"

She caught her bottom lip between gleaming teeth. She came and draped my sleeves into the shapes of mourning doves. I gritted my teeth. She continued: "It is the colour of early autumn, they say, and the scent lifting off its skin is a fine bouquet of virgin desire and dandy's sweat, with a top note of baby's breath. It fits in the palm, any palm. Its flesh is firm as a loving father's shoulder."

She stopped to dab at my face with a cutwork linen handkerchief from her pocket, and I nearly screamed. She resumed: "The fruit shucks off its own peel at a touch, revealing itself once only; to its devourer. A northern dictator burst into tears at the first taste of its pulp on his lips, and begged the forgiveness of his people."

"Poet and thrice-cursed child of a damned poet!" Her father, too, had played this game of stirring exalted cravings in me. I lifted the bodice away from my skin, fanned it to let air in. It wasn't enough.

Salope squatted in her sturdy black shoes, square at heel and toe. This exposed her strong thighs, brought her face level with my bosom. "I'm making you hungry, aren't I? Thirsty?"

"Bring me some water. No, wine."

"At once." She left the room, returned with a sleek glass pitcher and a glass on a silver tray. The golden liquid was cold, and beaded the pitcher. Salope poured for me, tilted the glass to my lips. I tasted the wine. It was dry and dusty in my mouth. I turned my head away. "What does Rivener call this wonder?" I asked.

"'The God Under the Tongue.'" Salope put the glass down on the table and took the appropriate step backwards. "There are one hundred and seventeen, limited edition, each one infused with her signature histamine."

"The one that makes the fingertips tingle?"

"The very same."

This heat! It distracted one so. "I wish to purchase one of these marvellous fruits."

"To taste it?"

"Of course, to taste it! Bring me my meal."

"Instantly." She went. Returned with a gold dish, covered with a lid of sleekest bone. Fashioned from the pelvis of a whale; I knew this. She put the dish down, uncovered it. A fine steam rose from it. "Here is your supper, Enlightened."

I picked up the golden spoon. "Contact the auction house."

Salope barely smiled. "I already have. It's too late. All one hundred and seventeen of 'The God Under the Tongue' are already spoken for."

I slammed the spoon back down onto the table. "Tell them I will pay! Command Rivener to make another! Just one more!"

Salope looked down at the ground. When she returned her gaze to mine, she was serene. "It's too late, Enlightened. The Academy has decided. Rivener has been transmigrated to Level Sublime. She is beyond your reach."

"Machine."

"There is no need for insult, Enlightened."

"Go away."

Salope bowed, returned the spoon to my hand, and dissipated into black smoke. I preferred a pale rose mist, but Salope kept stubbornly reverting to black. It had been her father's favourite colour.

Perverse poet's child; how she could arouse the senses! Her father finally pushed me too far. I'd ordered him to dissolve himself permanently from my aura. I had grieved for two voluptuous years, then sought everywhere for his like. Nothing. Eventually, in desperation, I had summoned his daughter.

I am Amaxon Corazn Junia Principia Delgado the Third, and I bent over my meal and wept luxurious tears into my green banana porridge. It was a perfect decoction, and it now would not satisfy me. Only the poet's daughter, and her father before her, ever saw me so transported.

The room spoke. "Thank you, Enlightened. I consider myself well paid for today's session. Please recommend me to your acquaintances."

I would. ■

THE ABDICATION OF POPE MARY III

Robert J. Sawyer

Darth Vader's booming voice, still the network's trademark six hundred years after its founding: "This is CNN."

And then the news anchor: "Our top story: Pope Mary III abdicated this morning. Giancarlo DiMarco, our correspondent in Vatican City, has the details. Giancarlo?"

"Thanks, Lisa. The unprecedented has indeed happened: after three hundred and twelve years of service, Pope Mary III stepped down today. Traditionally, the conclave of Roman Catholic cardinals waits eighteen days after the death of a pope before beginning deliberations to choose a successor, but Mary—who has returned to her birth name of Sharon Cheung—is alive and well, and so the members of the conclave have already been sealed inside the Vatican Palace, where they will remain until they've chosen Mary's replacement. Although no new pope has been elected for over three hundred years, the traditional voting method will be used. We are now watching the Sistine Chapel for the smoke that indicates the ballots have been burned following a round of voting. And—Lisa, Lisa, it's happening right now! There's smoke coming out, and—no, you can hear the disappointment of the crowd. It's black smoke; that means no candidate has yet received the required majority of two-thirds plus one. But we'll keep watching."

"Thank you, Giancarlo. Let's take a look at Pope Mary's press conference, given earlier today."

Tight shot on Mary, looking only a tenth of her four hundred years: "Since Vatican IV reaffirmed the principle of papal infallibility," she said, "and since I now believe that I was indeed in error two hundred and sixteen years ago when I issued a bull instructing Catholics to reject the evidence of the two Benmergui experiments, I feel compelled to step down ..."

— • —

"We're joined now in studio by Joginder Singh, professor of physics at the University of Toronto. Dr. Singh, can you explain the Benmergui experiments for our viewers?"

"Certainly, Lisa," said Singh. "The first proved that John Cramer's transactional interpretation of quantum mechanics, proposed in the late Twentieth Century, is in fact correct."

"And that means ...?"

"It means that the many-worlds interpretation is flat-out wrong: New parallel universes are not spawned each time a quantum event could go multiple ways. This is the one and only extant iteration of reality."

"And Dr. Benmergui's second experiment?"

"It proved the current cycle of creation was only the *seventh* such ever; just six other big-bang / big-crunch oscillations preceded our current universe. The combined effect of these two facts led directly to Pope Mary's crisis of faith, specifically because they proved the existence of—one might as well use the word—God."

"How? I'm sure our viewers are scratching their heads ..."

"Well, you see, the observation, dating back to the Twentieth Century, that the fundamental parameters of the universe seem fine-tuned to an almost infinite degree specifically to give rise to life, could previously be dismissed as a statistical artifact caused by the existence of many contemporaneous parallel universes or a multitude of previous ones. In all of that, every possible combination would crop up by chance, and so it wouldn't be remarkable that there was a universe like this one—one in which the force of gravity is just strong enough to allow stars and planets to coalesce but not just a little bit stronger, causing the universe to collapse long before life could have developed. Likewise, the value of the strong nuclear force, which holds atoms together, seems finely tuned, as do the thermal properties of water, and on and on."

"So our universe is a very special place?"

"Exactly. And since, as Kathryn Benmergui proved, this is the *only* current universe, and one of just a handful that have ever existed, then the life-generating properties of the very specific fundamental constants that define reality are virtually impossible to explain except as the results of deliberate design."

"But then why would Pope Mary resign? Surely if science has proven the existence of a creator ...?"

Singh smiled. "Ah, but that creator is clearly not the God of the Bible or the Torah or the Qur'an. Rather, the creator is a physicist, and we are one of his or her experiments. Science hasn't reconciled itself with religion; it has *superseded* it, and—"

"I'm sorry to interrupt, Dr. Singh, but our reporter in Vatican City has some breaking news. Giancarlo, over to you ..."

"Lisa, Lisa—the incredible is happening. At first I thought they were just tourists coming out of the Sistine Chapel, but they're not—I recognize Fontecchio and Leopardi and several of the others. But none of them are wearing robes; they're in street clothes. I haven't taken my eyes off the chapel: There's been no plume of white smoke, meaning they haven't elected a new leader of the church. But the cardinals *are* coming out. They're coming outside, heading into St. Peter's Square. The crowd is stunned, Lisa—it can only mean one thing ..." ■

REPEATING THE PAST

Peter Watts

What you did to your uncle's grave was unforgivable.

Your mother blamed herself, as always. You didn't know what you were doing, she said. I could accept that when you traded the shofar I gave you for that *eMotiv* headset of yours, perhaps, or even when you befriended those young toughs with the shaved heads and the filthy mouths. I would *never* have forgiven the swastika on your game pod, but you are my daughter's son, not mine. Maybe it *was* only adolescent rebellion. How could you know, after all? How could any child really *know*, here in 2017? Genocide is far too monstrous a thing for history books and grainy old photographs to convey. You were not there; you could never understand.

We told ourselves you were a good boy at heart, that it was ancient history to you, abstract and unreal. Both of us doctors, both all too familiar with the sad stereotype of the self-loathing Jew, we talked ourselves into treating you like some kind of *victim*. And then the police brought you back from the cemetery and you looked at us with those dull, indifferent eyes, and I stopped making excuses. It wasn't just your uncle's grave. You were spitting on six million others, and you *knew*, and it meant nothing.

Your mother cried for hours. Hadn't she shown you the old albums, the online archives, the family tree with so many branches hacked off in mid-century? Hadn't we both tried to tell you the stories? I tried to comfort her. An impossible task, I said, explaining *Never Again* to someone whose only knowledge of murder is the score he racks up playing *Zombie Hunter* all day—

And that was when I knew what to do.

I waited. A week, two, long enough to let you think I'd excused and forgiven as I always have. But I knew your weak spot. Nothing happens fast enough for you. These miraculous toys of yours—electrodes that read the emotions, take orders directly from the subconscious—they bore you now. You've seen the ads for *Improved Reality*™: sensation planted directly into the brain! Throw away the goggles and earphones and the gloves, throw away the keys! *Feel* the breezes of fantasy worlds against your skin, *smell* the smoke of battle, *taste* the blood of your toy monsters, so easily killed! Immerse all your senses in the slaughter!

You were tired of playing with cartoons, and the new model wouldn't be out for so very long. You jumped at my suggestion: *You know, your mother's working on something like that. It's medical, of course, but it works the same way. She might even have some sensory samplers loaded for testing purposes.*

Maybe, if you promise not to tell, we could sneak you in ...

Retired, yes, but I never gave up my privileges. Almost two decades since I closed my practice but I still spend time in your mother's lab, lend a hand now and then. I still marvel at her passion to know how the mind works, how it keeps *breaking*. She got that from me. *I* got it from Treblinka, when I was only half your age. I, too, grew up driven to fix broken souls— but the psychiatrist's tools were such blunt things back then. Scalpels to open flesh, words and drugs to open minds. Our techniques had all the precision of a drunkard stomping on the floor, trying to move glasses on the bar with the vibrations of his boot.

These machines your mother has, though! Transcranial superconductors, deep-focus microwave emitters, Szpindel Resonators! Specific pathways targeted, rewritten, erased completely! Their very names sound like incantations!

I cannot use them as she can. I only know the basics. I can't implant sights or sounds, can't create actual memories. Not declarative ones, anyway.

But *procedural* memory? That I can do. The right frontal lobe, the hippocampus, basic fear and anxiety responses. The reptile is easily awakened. And you didn't need the details. No need to remember my baby sister face-down like a pile of sticks in the mud. No need for the colour of the sky that day, as I stood frozen and fearful of some *real* monster's notice should I go to her. You didn't need the actual lesson.

The moral would do.

Afterwards, you sat up, confused, then disappointed, then resentful. "That was *nothing!* It didn't even *work!*" I needed no machines to see into your head then. *Senile old fart, doesn't know half as much as he thinks.* And as one day went by, and another, I began to fear you were right.

But then came the retching sounds from behind the bathroom door. All those hours hidden away in your room, your game pod abandoned on the living-room floor. And then your mother came to me, eyes brimming with worry: Never seen you like this, she said. Jumping at shadows. Not sleeping at night. This morning she found you throwing clothes into your backpack—*they're coming, they're coming, we gotta* run—and when she asked who *they* were, you couldn't tell her.

So here we are. You huddle in the corner, your eyes black begging holes that can't stop moving, that see horrors in every shadow. Your fists bleed, nails gouging the palms. I remember when I was your age. I cut myself to feel alive. Sometimes I still do. It never really stops.

Some day, your mother says, her machines will exorcise my demons. Doesn't she understand what a terrible mistake that would be? Doesn't history, once forgotten, repeat? Didn't even the worst president in history admit that memories belong to *everyone*?

I say nothing to you. We know each other, now, so much deeper than words.

I have made you wise, grandson. I have shown you the world.

Now I will help you to live with it. ■

THE GREAT GOODBYE

Robert Charles Wilson

The hardest part of the Great Goodbye, for me, was knowing I wouldn't see my grandfather again. We had developed that rare thing, a friendship that crossed the line of the post-evolutionary divide, and I loved him very much.

Humanity had become, by that autumn of 2350, two very distinct human species—if I can use that antiquated term. Oh, the Stock Humans remain a "species" in the classical evolutionary sense; while New People, of course, have forgone all that. Post-evolutionary, post-biological, budded or engineered, New People are gloriously free from all the old human restraints. What unites us all is our common source, the Divine Complexity that shaped the primordial quart plasma into stars, planets, planaria, people. Grandfather taught me that.

I had always known that one day we would be separated. But we first spoke of it, tentatively and reluctantly, when Grandfather went with me to the Museum of Devices in Brussels, a day trip. I was young and easily impressed by the full-scale model of a "steam train" in the Machine Gallery—an amazingly baroque contrivance of ancient metalwork and gas-pressure technology. Staring at it, I thought (because Grandfather had taught me some of his "religion"): *Complexity made this. This is made of stardust, by stardust.*

We walked from the Machine Gallery to the Gallery of the Planets, drawing more than a few stares from the Stock People (children, especially) we passed. It was uncommon to see a New Person fully embodied and in public. The Great Goodbye had been going on for more than a century, but New People were already scarce on Earth, and a New Person walking with a Stock Person was an even more unusual sight—risqué, even shocking. We bore the attention gamely. Grandfather held his head high and ignored the muttered insults.

The Gallery of the Planets recorded humanity's expansion into the Solar System, and I hoped the irony was obvious to everyone who sniffed at our presence there. Stock People could not have colonized any of these forbidding places (consider Ganymede in its primeval state!) without the partnership of the New. In a way, Grandfather said, this was the most appropriate place we could have come. It was a monument to the long collaboration that was rapidly reaching its end.

The stars, at last, were within our grasp. The grasp, anyhow, of the New People. Was this, I asked Grandfather, why he and I had to be so different from one another?

"Some people," he said, "some families, just happen to prefer the old ways. Soon enough Earth will belong to the Stocks once again, though I'm not sure that's entirely a good thing." He looked at me sadly. "We've learned a lot from each other. We could have learned more."

"I wish we could be together for centuries and centuries," I said.

— • —

I saw him for the last time (some years ago now) at the Shipworks, where the picturesque ruins of Detroit rise from the Michigan Waters, and the star-travelling Polises are assembled and wait like bright green baubles to lift, at last and forever, into the sky. Grandfather had arranged this final meeting—in the flesh, so to speak.

We had delayed it as long as possible. New People are patient: in a way, that's the point. Stock Humans have always dreamed of the stars, but the stars will always be beyond their reach. A Stock Human lifetime is simply too short; one or two hundred years won't take you far enough. Relativistic constraints demand that travellers between the stars must be at home between the stars. Only New People have the continuity, the patience, the flexibility to endure and prosper in the Galaxy's immense voids.

I greeted Grandfather on the high embarkation platform where the wind was brisk and cool. He lifted me up in his arms and admired me with his bright blue eyes. We talked about trivial things, for the simple pleasure of talking. Then he said, "This isn't easy, this saying goodbye. It makes me think of mortality—that old enemy."

"It's all right," I said.

"You could still change your mind, you know."

I shook my head. A New Person can transform himself into a Stock Person and vice versa, but the social taboos were strong, the obstacles (family dissension, legal entanglements) almost always insurmountable, as Grandfather knew too well. And in any case, that wasn't my choice. I was content the way I was. Or so I chose to believe.

"Well, then," he said, empty, for once, of words. He looked away. The Polis would be rising soon, beginning its eons-long exploration of our near stellar neighbours. Discovering, no doubt, great wonders.

"Goodbye, boy," he said.

I said, "Goodbye, Grandfather."

Then he rose to his full height on his many translucent legs, winked one dish-sized glacial blue eye, and walked with a slow machinely dignity to the vessel that would carry him away. And I watched, desolate, alone on the platform with the wind in my hair, as his ship rose into the arc of the high, clean noonday sky. ■

STARS

Carolyn Clink

Pinwheel down, down
into a spiral
galaxy, light blueshifting
back in time
to when stars exploded
from the pressure
within
their hearts

AWARD-WINNING
CANADIAN SCIENCE FICTION AND FANTASY

An asterisk (*) marks works that have won multiple awards
SF=Science Fiction; F=Fantasy

AURORA AWARD (NOVELS)

The Aurora is Canada's "people's choice" award. Ballots are distributed online and through Canadian SF specialty bookstores, periodicals, and conventions. Below are the English-language fiction winners; Auroras are also given to works in French.

2008: *The New Moon's Arms* (F) by **Nalo Hopkinson** of Toronto, Ontario. Warner, 2007.*

2007: *Children of Chaos* (F) by **Dave Duncan** of Vancouver, British Columbia. Tor, 2006.

2006: *Cagebird* (SF) by **Karin Lowachee** of Mississauga, Ontario. Warner, 2005.

2005: *Wolf Pack* (F) by **Edo van Belkom** of Brampton, Ontario. Tundra, 2004.

2004: *Blind Lake* (SF) by **Robert Charles Wilson** of Concord, Ontario. Tor, 2003.

2003: *Permanence* (SF) by **Karl Schroeder** of Toronto, Ontario. Tor, 2002.

2002: *In the Company of Others* (SF) by **Julie E. Czerneda** of Orillia, Ontario. DAW, 2001.

2001: *The Snow Queen* (F) by **Eileen Kernaghan** of New Westminster, British Columbia. Thistledown, 2000.

2000: *Flashforward* (SF) by **Robert J. Sawyer** then of Thornhill, Ontario. Tor, 1999.

1999: *Darwinia* (SF) by **Robert Charles Wilson** then of Toronto, Ontario. Tor, 1999.

1998: *Black Wine* (F) by **Candas Jane Dorsey** of Edmonton, Alberta. Tor, 1998.*

1997: *Starplex* (SF) by **Robert J. Sawyer** then of Thornhill, Ontario. Ace, 1996.*

1996: *The Terminal Experiment* (SF) by **Robert J. Sawyer** then of Thornhill, Ontario. HarperPrism, 1995.*

1995: *Virtual Light* (SF) by **William Gibson** of Vancouver, British Columbia. Bantam, 1993.

1994: *Nobody's Son* (F) by **Sean Stewart**, now of Davis, California. Maxwell MacMillan, 1993; Ace, 1995.

1993: *Passion Play* (SF) by **Sean Stewart** now of Davis, California. Beach Holme, 1992.*

1992: *Golden Fleece* (SF) by **Robert J. Sawyer** then of Toronto, Ontario. Warner Questar, 1990.*

1991: *Tigana* (F) by **Guy Gavriel Kay** of Toronto, Ontario. Penguin, 1990.

1990: *West of January* (F) by **Dave Duncan** then of Calgary, Alberta. Del Rey, 1989.

1989: *Mona Lisa Overdrive* (SF) by **William Gibson** of Vancouver, British Columbia. Bantam, 1988.

1988: *Jack, the Giant Killer* (F) by **Charles de Lint** of Ottawa, Ontario. Ace, 1987.

1987: *The Wandering Fire* (F) by **Guy Gavriel Kay** of Toronto, Ontario. Collins, 1986.

1985: *Songs From The Drowned Lands* (F) by **Eileen Kernaghan** of Burnaby, British Columbia. Ace, 1983.

1982: *A Judgment of Dragons* (SF) by **Phyllis Gotlieb** of Toronto, Ontario. Berkley, 1980.

AURORA AWARD (SHORT FICTION)

2008: "Like Water in the Desert" (SF) by **Hayden Trenholm** of Ottawa, Ontario. In *Challenging Destiny*, August 2007.

2007: "Biding Time" (SF) by **Robert J. Sawyer** of Mississauga, Ontario. In *Slipstreams*, John Helfers and Martin H. Greenberg, eds., DAW, 2006.

2006: "Transubstantiation" (SF) by **Derwin Mak** of Toronto, Ontario. In *Northwest Passages: A Cascadian Anthology*, Cris DiMarco, ed., CascadiaCon, 2005.

2005: "When the Morning Stars Sang Together" (SF) by **Isaac Szpindel** of Toronto, Ontario. In *ReVisions*, Julie E. Czerneda and Isaac Szpindel, eds., DAW, 2004.

2004: "Scream Angel" (SF) by **Douglas Smith** of Aurora, Ontario. In *Low Port*, Sharon Lee and Steve Miller, eds., Meisha Merlin, 2003.

2003: "Ineluctable" (SF) by **Robert J. Sawyer** of Mississauga, Ontario. In *Analog*, November 2002.

2002: "Left Foot on a Blind Man" (SF) by **Julie E. Czerneda** of Orillia, Ontario. In *Silicon Dreams*, Martin H. Greenberg and Larry Segriff, eds., DAW, 2001.

2000: "Stream of Consciousness" (SF) by **Robert J. Sawyer** of Mississauga, Ontario. In *Packing Fraction*, Julie E. Czerneda, ed., Trifolium, 1999.

1999: "Hockey's Night in Canada" (SF) by **Edo van Belkom** of Brampton, Ontario. In *Arrowdreams: An Anthology of Alternate Canadas*, Mark Shainblum and John Dupuis, eds., Editions NuAge, 1998.

1998: "Three Hearings on the Existence of Snakes in the Human Bloodstream" (F) by **James Alan Gardner** of Waterloo, Ontario. In *Asimov's Science Fiction Magazine*, February 1997.

1997: "Peking Man" (F) by **Robert J. Sawyer** then of Thornhill, Ontario. In *Dark Destiny III*, Edward E. Kramer, ed., White Wolf, 1996.

1996: "The Perseids" (F) by **Robert Charles Wilson** then of Toronto, Ontario. In *Northern Frights 3*, Don Hutchison, ed., Mosaic, 1995.

1995: "The Fragrance of Orchids" (SF) by **Sally McBride** now of Toronto, Ontario. In *Asimov's Science Fiction Magazine*, May 1994.

1994: "Just Like Old Times" (SF) by **Robert J. Sawyer** then of Thornhill, Ontario. In *On Spec*, Summer 1993, and *Dinosaur Fantastic*, Mike Resnick, ed., DAW, 1993.*

1993: "The Toy Mill" (F) by **David Nickle** and **Karl Schroeder**, both of Toronto, Ontario. In *Tesseracts 4*, 1992.

1992: "A Niche" (SF) by **Peter Watts** then of Vancouver, British Columbia, and **"Breaking Ball"** (SF) by **Michael Skeet** of Toronto, Ontario [tie]. Both in *Tesseracts 3*, 1990.

1991: "Muffin Explains Teleology to the World at Large" (F) by **James Alan Gardner** of Waterloo, Ontario. In *On Spec*, Spring 1990, and *Tesseracts 3*.

1990: "Carpe Diem" (SF) by **Eileen Kernaghan** of New Westminster, British Columbia. In *On Spec*, Fall 1989.

1989: "Sleeping in a Box" (SF) by **Candas Jane Dorsey** of Edmonton, Alberta. In her *Machine Sex and Other Stories*, Beach Holme, 1988.

ANALYTICAL LABORATORY AWARD

Voted on annually by the readers of Analog Science Fiction and Fact, the world's best-selling English-language science-fiction magazine, for the best material published by the magazine.

2005: "Shed Skin" (SF) by **Robert J. Sawyer** of Mississauga, Ontario. Short Story, January / February 2004.

2003: "In Spirit" (SF) by **Paddy Forde** of Waterloo, Ontario. Novella, September 2002.

1988: "The Gift" (SF) by **Paddy Forde** of Waterloo, Ontario. Novella / Novelette, December 1987.

1983: "Melancholy Elephants" (SF) by **Spider Robinson** then of Halifax, Nova Scotia. Short Story, June 1982.[x]

1979: "Stardance II" (SF) by **Spider & Jeanne Robinson** then of Halifax, Nova Scotia. Serial, September, October, November 1978.

BRITISH SCIENCE FICTION AWARD

Given annually by the British Science Fiction Association.

1977: *Brontomek!* (SF) by **Michael Coney** of Sidney, British Columbia. Gollancz, 1976.

JOHN W. CAMPBELL MEMORIAL AWARD

The top juried award in the SF field, given annually since 1973 for best SF novel of the year.

2006: *Mindscan* (SF) by **Robert J. Sawyer** of Mississauga, Ontario. Tor, 2005.

2002: *The Chronoliths* (SF) by **Robert Charles Wilson** of Concord, Ontario. Tor, 2001.

1990: *The Child Garden* (SF) by **Geoff Ryman** now of Manchester, U.K. Unwin, 1989.

ARTHUR C. CLARKE AWARD

A juried award for the best SF novel published in Great Britain.

1987: *The Handmaid's Tale* (SF) by **Margaret Atwood** of Toronto, Ontario. Canadian edition: McClelland & Stewart, 1985.

WILLIAM L. CRAWFORD FANTASY AWARD

A juried award for the best book-length debut of the year in the fantasy field, presented by the International Association for the Fantastic in the Arts.

1997: *Black Wine* (F) by **Candas Jane Dorsey** of Edmonton, Alberta. Tor, 1997.*

1984: *The Riddle of the Wren* (F) and *Moonheart* (F), both by **Charles de Lint** of Ottawa, Ontario. Both Ace, 1984.

COMPTON CROOK MEMORIAL AWARD

The Baltimore SF Society's juried award for the best first novel of the year.

1983: *Courtship Rite* (SF) by **Donald Kingsbury** of Montreal, Quebec. Simon & Schuster, 1982.

PHILIP K. DICK AWARD

An American juried award for the best SF novel first published in paperback.

1999: *The Print Remix* (SF) by **Geoff Ryman** now of Manchester, U.K. St. Martin's, 1998.

1994: *Mysterium* (SF) by **Robert Charles Wilson** then of Toronto, Ontario. Bantam, 1994.

1984: *Neuromancer* (SF) by **William Gibson** of Vancouver, British Columbia. Ace, 1984.*

ARTHUR ELLIS AWARD

A juried award presented annually since 1983 by the Crime Writers of Canada, which has twice gone to SF / mystery crossover works.

1993 Short Story: "Just Like Old Times" (SF) by **Robert J. Sawyer** then of Thornhill, Ontario.*

1992 First Novel: *Passion Play* (SF) by **Sean Stewart** now of Davis, California. Beach Holme, 1992.*

GEFFEN AWARD

Israel's top science-fiction and fantasy award.

2006 Science Fiction Novel: *Spin* (SF) by **Robert Charles Wilson** of Concord, Ontario. Graff Publishing, 2006.*

2004 Science Fiction Novel: *Warchild* (SF) by **Karin Lowachee** of Mississauga, Ontario. Opus Press, 2004.*

HOMER AWARD

Voted on by the 30,000 online members of CompuServe's Science Fiction and Fantasy Literature Forum; presented annually to works published from 1990 to 2000.

2000 Novel: *Calculating God* (SF) by **Robert J. Sawyer** then of Thornhill, Ontario. Tor, 2000.

1998 Short Story: "Face of God" (F) by **Barbara Galler-Smith** of Edmonton, Alberta. In *On Spec*, Winter 1998.

1997 Novel: *Broken Blade* (F) by **Ann Marston** of Edmonton, Alberta. HarperCollins, 1997.

1996 Novel: *Starplex* (SF) by **Robert J. Sawyer** then of Thornhill, Ontario. Ace, 1996.

1995 Novel: *The Terminal Experiment* (SF) by **Robert J. Sawyer** then of Thornhill, Ontario. HarperPrism, 1995.*

1994 Novel: *End of an Era* (SF) by **Robert J. Sawyer** then of Thornhill, Ontario. Ace, 1994.*

1993 Novel: *Fossil Hunter* (SF) by **Robert J. Sawyer** then of Thornhill, Ontario. Ace, 1993.

1992 Novel: *Far-Seer* (SF) by **Robert J. Sawyer** of Toronto, Ontario. Ace, 1992.

1996 Short Story: "Above It All" (F) by **Robert J. Sawyer** then of Thornhill, Ontario. In *Dante's Disciples*, Peter Crowther and Edward E. Kramer, eds., White Wolf, 1996.

1995 Short Story: "You See But You Do Not Observe" (SF) by **Robert J. Sawyer** then of Thornhill, Otario.*

1992 Short Story: "Black Ice" (F) by **Barbara Delaplace** now of Gainesville, Florida. In *Aladdin: Master of the Lamp*, Mike Resnick, ed., DAW, 1992.

1991 Fantasy Novel: *The Little Country* (F) by **Charles de Lint** of Ottawa, Ontario. Morrow, 1991.

1990 First Novel: *Golden Fleece* (SF) by **Robert J. Sawyer** then of Toronto, Ontario. Warner Questar, 1990.*

HUGO AWARD

The world's top science-fiction award, voted on by the members of the annual World Science Fiction Convention.

2006 Novel: *Spin* (SF) by **Robert Charles Wilson** of Concord, Ontario. Tor, 2005.*

2003 Novel: *Hominids* (SF) by **Robert J. Sawyer** of Mississauga, Ontario. Tor, 2002.

1985 Novel: *Neuromancer* (SF) by **William Gibson** of Vancouver, British Columbia. Ace, 1984.*

1983 Short Story: "Melancholy Elephants" (SF) by **Spider Robinson** then of Halifax, Nova Scotia. In his *Melancholy Elephants*. Penguin, 1984.*

1978 Novella: "Stardance" (SF) by **Spider** and **Jeanne Robinson** then of Halifax, Nova Scotia. Part of *Stardance*. Dial, 1979 [reprinted by Tor, 1986].*

1977 Novella: "By Any Other Name" (SF) by **Spider Robinson** then of Halifax, Nova Scotia. Part of *Telempath*. Berkley, 1976 [reprinted by Tor, 1988].

LE GRAND PRIX DE L'IMAGINAIRE

France's top SF award.

2007 Foreign Novel: *Spin* (SF) by **Robert Charles Wilson** of Concord, Ontario. Denoël, 2007.*

1996 Foreign Short Story: "You See But You Do Not Observe" (SF) by **Robert J. Sawyer** then of Thornhill, Ontario. In *Sherlock Holmes in Orbit*, Mike Resnick and Martin H. Greenberg, eds., DAW, 1995.*

1993 Foreign Novel: *Dark Matter* (SF) by **Garfield Reeves-Stevens** then of Thornhill, Ontario. Pocket, 1993.

KURD LASSWITZ PREIS

Germany's top science-fiction award.

2007 Foreign Novel: *Spin* (SF) by **Robert Charles Wilson** of Concord, Ontario. Heyne, 2006.*

NEBULA AWARD

The "Academy Award of SF," voted on by the members of the Science Fiction and Fantasy Writers of America.

1995 Novel: *The Terminal Experiment* (SF) by **Robert J. Sawyer** then of Thornhill, Ontario. HarperPrism, 1995.*

1984 Novel: *Neuromancer* (SF) by **William Gibson** of Vancouver, British Columbia. Ace, 1984.*

1977 Novella: "Stardance" (SF) by **Spider** and **Jeanne Robinson** then of Halifax, Nova Scotia.*

SCIENCE FICTION CHRONICLE READER AWARD

Given annually since 1981 by the readers of Science Fiction Chronicle: The Science Fiction & Fantasy Newsmagazine, *the trade journal of the SF field published in New York.*

1997 Short Story: "The Hand You're Dealt" by **Robert J. Sawyer** then of Thornhill, Ontario. In *Free Space*, Brad Linaweaver and Edward E. Kramer, eds., Tor, 1997.

1984 Novel: *Neuromancer* by **William Gibson** of Vancouver, British Columbia. Ace, 1984.*

SEIUN AWARD

Japan's top honour in Science Fiction, voted on by the attendees of the Japanese National Science Fiction Convention.

2003: *Illegal Alien* (SF) by **Robert J. Sawyer** then of Thornhill, Ontario. Hayakawa, 2002.

2001: *Frameshift* (SF) by **Robert J. Sawyer** then of Thornhill, Ontaro. Hayakawa, 2000.*

1997: *End of an Era* (SF) by **Robert J. Sawyer** then of Thornhill, Ontario. Hayakawa, 1996.*

1987: *Neuromancer* (SF) by **William Gibson** of Vancouver, British Columbia. Hayakawa, 1986.*

BRAM STOKER AWARD

The "Academy Award" of the dark-fantasy field, presented annually by the Horror Writers Association.

1997 Short Story: "Rat Food" (F) by **Edo van Belkom** of Brampton, Ontario, and **David Nickle** of Toronto, Ontario. In *On Spec,* Spring 1997.

THEODORE STURGEON MEMORIAL AWARD

A juried award given annually since 1987, by the Center for the Study of Science Fiction in conjunction with Sturgeon's heirs.

2007 Short Story: "The Cartesian Theatre" by **Robert Charles Wilson** of Concord, Ontario. In *Futureshocks*, Lou Anders, ed., Roc, 2006.

SUNBURST AWARD

A juried award for broadly defined "Canadian fantastic literature" given annually since 2001, named for Phyllis Gotlieb's first novel.

2008: *The New Moon's Arms* (F) by **Nalo Hopkinson** of Toronto, Ontario. Warner, 2007.*

2007: *Fabrizio's Return* (F) by **Mark Frutkin** of Ottawa, Ontario. Alfred A. Knopf Canada, 2006.

2006: *In the Palace of Repose* (F) by **Holly Phillips** of Trail, British Columbia. Prime, 2005.

2005: *Air* (SF) by **Geoff Ryman** of Manchester, U.K. St. Martin's, 2004.

2004: *A Place So Foreign: and 8 more* (SF) by **Cory Doctorow** of London, U.K. Four Walls Eight Windows Press, 2003.

2003: *Skin Folk* (F) by **Nalo Hopkinson** of Toronto, Ontario. Warner, 2001.*

2002: *When Alice Lay Down with Peter* (F) by **Margaret Sweatman** of Winnipeg, Manitoba. Alfred A. Knopf Canada, 2001.

2001: *Galveston* (F) by **Sean Stewart** of Davis, California. Ace, 2000.

SUNBURST AWARD FOR YOUNG ADULT FICTION

A companion to the above: a juried award given annually since 2008 for Canadian fantastic works aimed at teenagers.

2008: *Anthem of a Reluctant Prophet* (F) by **Joanne Proulx** of Ottawa, Ontario. Viking Canada, 2007.

PREMIO UPC DE CIENCIA FICCIÓN

A juried prize—and the world's largest cash award for science fiction—presented annually by the Universitat Politècnica de Catalunya in Spain.

2004: "Identity Theft" (SF) by **Robert J. Sawyer** of Mississauga, Ontario. Science Fiction Book Club.

1998: *Flashforward* (SF) by **Robert J. Sawyer** then of Thornhill, Ontario. Tor, 1999.

1997: *Factoring Humanity* (SF) by **Robert J. Sawyer** then of Thornhill, Ontario. Tor, 1998.

WARNER ASPECT FIRST NOVEL COMPETITION

A juried contest sponsored by Warner Books to find the best novel by a previously unpublished novelist.

2001: *Warchild* (SF) by **Karin Lowachee** of Mississauga, Ontario. Warner Aspect, 2001.*

1998: *Brown Girl in the Ring* (F) by **Nalo Hopkinson** of Toronto, Ontario. Warner Aspect, 1998.

WORLD FANTASY AWARD

The world's top award for fantasy fiction; a juried award presented at the annual World Fantasy Convention.

2008 Best Novel: *Ysabel* (F) by **Guy Gavriel Kay** of Toronto, Ontario. Penguin Viking, 2007.

2002 Best Collection: *Skin Folk* (F) by **Nalo Hopkinson** of Toronto, Ontario. Warner, 2001.*

2000 Best Collection: *Moonlight and Vines* (F) by **Charles de Lint** of Ottawa, Ontario. Tor, 1999.

1984 Best Collection: *High Spirits* (F) by **Robertson Davies** of Toronto, Ontario. McClelland & Stewart, 1983.

WRITERS OF THE FUTURE AWARD

L. Ron Hubbard's Writers of the Future, an international contest carrying a $5,000 grand prize for new SF writers, with big-name SF writers as jurors.

2007 Grand Prize: "Saturn in G Minor" (SF) by **Stephen Kotowych** of Toronto, Ontario. In *Writers of the Future 23*, Galaxy, 2007.

1993 Grand Prize: "Schrödinger's Mousetrap" (SF) by **Alan Barclay** of Vancouver, British Columbia. In *Writers of the Future 10*, Bridge, 1993.

1990 Grand Prize: "The Children of Crèche" (SF) by **James Alan Gardner**. In *Writers of the Future 4*, Bridge, 1990.

Online Resources

For more information about Canadian science fiction, please see:

The Canadian SF Works Database, a wiki with comprehensive listings of Canadian science fiction and fantasy in both English and French:
www.canadiansf.com

Robert J. Sawyer's **Canadian Science Fiction Index**, including articles about Canadian SF and interviews with Canadian writers:
www.sfwriter.com/caindex.htm

Made in Canada, Don Bassie's Aurora Award-winning site devoted to Canadian science fiction:
www.geocities.com/canadian_sf

SF Canada, a national bilingual organization of SF, fantasy, and horror writers:
www.sfcanada.ca

Prix Aurora Awards, the official site of Canada's national science fiction and fantasy awards; any Canadian may nominate and vote for the Auroras:
www.*prix-aurora-awards.ca*

From Robert J. Sawyer Books

Letters from the Flesh by Marcos Donnelly

Getting Near the End by Andrew Weiner

Rogue Harvest by Danita Maslan

The Engine of Recall by Karl Schroeder

A Small and Remarkable Life by Nick DiChario

Sailing Time's Ocean by Terence M. Green

Birthstones by Phyllis Gotlieb

The Commons by Matthew Hughes

Valley of Day-Glo by Nick DiChario

The Savage Humanists edited by Fiona Kelleghan

Distant Early Warnings edited by Robert J. Sawyer

From Red Deer Press

Iterations and Other Stories by Robert J. Sawyer

Identity Theft and Other Stories by Robert J. Sawyer

www.robertjsawyerbooks.com

www.reddeerpress.com